HITLER'S SECRET

RORY CLEMENTS

ZAFFRE

First published in Great Britain in 2020 by
ZAFFRE
80–81 Wimpole St, London W1G 9RE

A CIP catalogue record for this book is
available from the British Library.

Hardback ISBN: 978–1–83877–027–3
Export ISBN: 978–1–83877–028–0

Also available as an ebook

1 3 5 7 9 10 8 6 4 2

Typeset by IDSUK (Data Connection) Ltd
Printed and bound in Great Britain by Clays Ltd, Elcograf S.p.A.

Zaffre is an imprint of Bonnier Books UK
www.bonnierbooks.co.uk

'Rory Clements's timely spy thriller set in the 1930s evokes a period of political polarisation, mistrust and simmering violence'

THE TIMES

'Clements creates lively, fast-moving plots'

SUNDAY TIMES

'Beautifully done . . . alive and tremendously engrossing'

DAILY TELEGRAPH

'Enjoyable, bloody and brutish'

GUARDIAN

'This clever novel, rich in deceptions and intrigue . . . a standout historical novel and spy thriller by an author who can turn his hand to any historical period he chooses'

DAILY EXPRESS

'A masterpiece of spies, intrigue and political shenanigans'

SUNDAY EXPRESS

'Faster moving than C. J. Sansom'

BBC RADIO 4

Rory Clements was born on the edge of England in Dover. After a career in national newspapers, he now writes full time in a quiet corner of Norfolk, where he lives with his wife, the artist Naomi Clements Wright, and their family. He won the CWA Ellis Peters Historical Award in 2010 for his second novel, *Revenger*, and the CWA Historical Dagger in 2018 for *Nucleus*. Three of his other novels – *Martyr*, *Prince* and *The Heretics* – have been shortlisted for awards.

To receive exclusive news about Rory's writing, join his Readers' Club at www.bit.ly/RoryClementsClub and to find out more go to www.roryclements.co.uk.

Also by Rory Clements

Martyr

Revenger

Prince

Traitor

The Heretics

The Queen's Man

Holy Spy

The Man in the Snow (ebook novella)

Corpus

Nucleus

Nemesis

For Sarah, with love

CHAPTER 1

The telephone had been ringing in Bormann's office all morning. Many prominent names of the greater German Reich wished to speak to the Führer and all calls had to go through Bormann. Hitler was back in Munich from the Wolfsschanze, his eastern headquarters, and it was a rare opportunity for his ministers to secure a private interview with him. The war against the Soviet Union was almost won and there was much to be discussed.

Each time the phone sounded, the efficient Bormann picked up the handset on the second ring. He spoke with exaggerated deference to the caller. *Of course, Herr Reichsmarschall Göring. Indeed, Herr General. I am at your service, Herr Doktor. Heil Hitler!* The only person with whom he was at all familiar was Himmler, the man he teasingly referred to as Uncle Heinrich.

The office stank of sweat, smoke and cologne. On the desk an ashtray overflowed with the detritus of a constant stream of cigarettes. Later, he would kick his secretary's pretty arse and tell her to clean the place up. She liked having her arse kicked. And fondled.

Sometimes he might put a caller or two through to the Führer. But not this morning. Himmler, Rommel, Goebbels, Ley, Rosenberg, Streicher . . . they could all go whistle. It made no difference to Martin Bormann how important they considered themselves; he told them all the same thing: the Führer was engaged with his chiefs of staff and could not be disturbed.

His chiefs of staff! Bormann laughed out loud at the thought, his shiny, round face stretched tight with amusement. Hitler was engaged in the far more important business of playing with the adorable German Shepherd puppy that Bormann had given him. Settling back in his leather chair, Bormann lit another cigarette. But his good humour soon vanished and his brow darkened. He looked at his watch. He had something else on his mind, something that had to be resolved without delay. Smoke drifted from the cigarette dangling from his yellow fingers. The only time he didn't smoke was when he was asleep or in the presence of the Führer.

There was a knock. Heidi's face appeared around the heavy oak door.

'You have a visitor, Herr Bormann.'

'Otto Kalt?'

'Yes, sir.'

'No reply yet from Charlie Jung?'

'His butler told me he was in Switzerland, skiing or mountain-eering.'

Charlie Jung. As elusive as smoke in fog.

'Well, find out the name of his hotel and get a message to him. I want him to call me as soon as possible.'

'Yes, sir.'

'And don't take no for an answer.' He lit another cigarette from the butt of the old one. 'Now give me two minutes, then send Kalt in. We are not to be disturbed.'

'Yes, sir. Would you like coffee?'

'No, Heidi. That is all.'

'Heil Hitler, Herr Bormann.'

Bormann opened the desk drawer and pulled out a photographic copy of a clear but slightly faded sheet of paper. It was titled *Taufschein und Geburtszeugnis* – Certificate of Baptism and Birth. He read it through carefully once more, memorising every last detail.

There was a knock at the door again.

'Enter.'

Otto Kalt was a small man with metal-rimmed spectacles and dark hair. He stood to attention, raised himself to his full height – no more than five and a half feet – and clicked his heels.

'Heil Hitler!' He shot his arm out in the fascist salute.

From behind his desk, Bormann waved at Kalt to approach. Kalt took two steps forward. No one could have looked less like the Nazis' idealised Nordic Aryan than Otto Kalt. Not even Himmler was such a poor specimen.

Bormann was not much taller, but he was broad and powerful, with the build and demeanour of a hog and the cunning of a cur. He ran his hand through his thinning, slicked-back hair and nodded to Kalt.

He had known and used Otto Kalt, who was of a similar age – early forties – half his life. They had been together since the heady days of the early 1920s. Kalt came from a rural peasant family, but he had been a Party member since the very beginning and had risen to some wealth. He was useful to Bormann, for he was obedient and had the slyness and callous brutality of his breed; he would shed blood with no more flicker of emotion than if he were killing a pig, as he had shown in the forest outside Parchim when he had slit the throat of the treacherous Walther Kadow on Bormann's orders. Kalt had always submitted to Bormann, obeying every command. Just as Bormann, in his turn, submitted to every desire of *his* master, the Führer.

Some said that Bormann was like a son to Hitler. Perhaps it was true. If so, then it was even more true that he was like a father to Otto Kalt.

Bormann's loyalty to Hitler had been repaid with immense power and he was now Head of the Party Chancellery. Kalt in his turn had been repaid for *his* loyalty – with the means to purchase a large and splendid farm a little way east of Hamburg.

Pausing for effect, Bormann stubbed out his cigarette and pulled yet another from the box on his desk, picked up the gold, swastika-embossed lighter Himmler had given him for his fortieth the previous year, flicked the wheel and lit it. As an afterthought, he offered Kalt the packet.

'American,' he said.

'Thank you, Herr Reichsleiter,' Kalt said, taking one of the Luckies.

'Otto,' Bormann said, handing him the certificate. 'I have a small task for you. Read that carefully. Note every detail and then return it to me. It is the birth and baptism record of a ten-year-old girl. I want you to find her and dispose of her – and anyone who has ever been associated with her. It is best if the world never knows she existed. Leave no trace.'

'Yes, Herr Reichsleiter.'

'I cannot stress how important this task is. You have done many favours for me over the years and I have rewarded you well. But nothing – *nothing* – has been as crucial as this one thing. Succeed and I will double your land holding.'

'I will not fail you, Herr Reichsleiter.' Kalt bowed his head.

'Good.'

Because if you do fail me, thought Bormann, *I am done for.*

In the hour before first light, Father Peter Huber pulled back the duvet and gazed at the woman's sleep-warm body. She was on her back, her hair tangled across the pillow. Her eyes drifted open and she smiled at him hazily, as though not sure whether this was still part of her dream.

'Come back to bed, Peter.' Her voice was husky, soft and full of sleep.

'You know I can't.'

He knelt at the side of the bed as though about to pray, but instead he bent forward and kissed her pubic hair lightly, breathing in the intoxicating fumes. She rolled towards him and, as he stood up, she reached out and tried to fumble beneath his priest's robes.

'Let me kiss you there, too.'

'Trudchen, you are bad.'

'But that's why you love me, Peter. And later, I will confess to the priest and will be forgiven my transgressions.'

'I *am* the priest!'

'And will you deal with me very harshly, Father? Will you make me say twelve Hail Marys?'

He laughed. 'I have made you coffee. It's in the kitchen.'

It was still dark and snowing gently when Father Huber opened the door. Trudchen's house was a little way from the village of Braundorf, a fact which made these nightly visits possible. It was a pleasant, modest chalet, high up on the *Alm*, backed by the mountains, and from there he had a pleasant stroll through the meadow back home. In the short nights of summertime, he had to leave her far earlier than this, but with the long nights of late November, they had more time together. A small but welcome blessing.

The snow had come early this year, however, which could sometimes be a problem. His tracks would be all too visible to the village gossips. And so he had to listen to the forecasts carefully. Today, it was said, the snow would fall steadily, all through the night and late into the day, and so it was proving. That meant his footprints would be erased almost as soon as they appeared.

Unfortunately for him, that also meant that Father Huber did not see two other pairs of footprints in the snow.

The church of St Mary Magdalene was almost four hundred years old. With its onion dome and its ornate, gilt interior, full of statuary and images from the Gospels, it was typical of the older churches in this part of Austria, or the province of Ostmark as the country had been designated since the Anschluss three years earlier.

The first thing you came to, by the door, beneath a colourful wooden wall carving of the Virgin, was an old octagonal baptismal font, deep enough to immerse a sizeable child. Then, ranged along the nave, came the rows of wooden pews, until, at last, you approached the high altar. For all its quaint charm, it was a small, simple church, perfectly fitting the needs of this little country community.

Father Huber entered, stamping the snow from his boots and removing his woollen hat, before lighting candles by the door and switching off his flashlight. The church had not yet been electrified so the only light came through windows or from candle flames. In the soft warm glow, he made his way down the nave and halted before the crucifix, made the sign of the cross and knelt down to say a silent prayer, confessing his sins of the night, though in his heart he could not really believe his liaison with Trudchen was wrong. Yes, the Roman Church demanded chastity of its clergy. But that was a law made by men. How could love be a sin in the sight of God?

He heard a cough. His shoulders tensed; surely Frau Giesler the cleaner could not be here so early? He knew from the way she sometimes looked at him that she had her suspicions. He rose to his feet and turned around, his hands clasped to the cross he wore around his neck. No, it wasn't Frau Giesler, but a man – someone he did not recognise. Someone small and – he hated himself for even thinking it – rather insignificant looking. A traveller, perhaps.

'*Grüss Gott.* Can I help you, sir?'

'Father Huber?'

'Yes, that's me.'

'My name is Herr Kalt, sir. Otto Kalt. I am a lawyer. Please forgive the ungodly hour of my arrival – but I have been travelling many hours from Bremen and decided to push on rather than stopping the night at a hotel.'

The priest did not like this one bit. The man might seem to be of no consequence, but appearances could be horribly deceptive. Peter

Huber forced himself to adopt a welcoming smile and extended a hand.

'And why, pray, would a lawyer wish to talk to a humble parish priest?'

Kalt took the hand and held it a few seconds without quite shaking it. His fingers were cold and limp.

'Well, first of all, I can tell you it involves a great deal of money.' He shivered. 'Is there, perhaps, somewhere a little warmer we could talk?'

'Of course. My house is next door. Let us go and have some coffee.'

'Ah, thank you, Father. A cup of coffee would certainly go down very well.'

Even though Huber had spent the night with Trudchen, his kitchen was still warm from the previous day, for the blue-tiled *Kachelofen* wood-burning stove retained its heat long after the fire had died down. The priest sat in the corner seat and poured the coffee. Were his hands shaking? He was a slender man of average height, but in these parts where the men were strong from mountain herding and harvesting, he had the appearance of a weakling. Too much time with his head in books.

'Now then, Herr Kalt, perhaps you would tell me what this is all about.'

'Real coffee, Father? What luxury. I am honoured.'

'I had it from before the war and keep it for special occasions.'

'A little sugar, too, perhaps?' He laughed although he had said nothing funny. 'If you have such a thing.'

Sugar was not as rare as coffee, but it was still a precious commodity these days. Huber smiled and gave his visitor one spoonful and left the spoon in his cup for stirring.

'Thank you. Now, Father, I am the bearer of great tidings for a young girl named Klara Wolf, who I am certain is known to you. A large bequest is due to her from a man of considerable wealth and importance, who died not long ago in Hamburg. Killed in a British air raid – can you believe that? And to think Reichsmarschall Göring said we could call him Mayer if ever a British airplane intruded on our territory! Anyway, little Klara is now a very rich girl.'

'Klara? Klara Wolf? I am trying hard to think if I know this girl. The name does not seem familiar, Herr Kalt.'

'Surely a good priest never forgets those he has baptised? Anyway, the name will come to you soon enough. The point is, you see, I require her present whereabouts – and you were the obvious man to come to.'

The hairs at the nape of Huber's neck prickled. He shook his head slowly.

'No, I am afraid not. Forgive me, sir, I fear your long journey has been wasted. Perhaps you should have called ahead.'

Kalt narrowed his small, beady eyes and smiled.

'You baptised her here in this very village, ten years ago – 1931. Her mother, Angelica Wolf – a healthy, pretty young girl of peasant stock – was present, but I believe her father was absent on military duty.'

Huber shook his head again, this time more briskly, as though he had a nervous tic.

'No, truly, I do not recall the name.'

He studied Kalt. This small man did not look like a lawyer, even with his round spectacles. But what exactly did a lawyer look like? Well-to-do, perhaps? Well fed? This man Kalt had no meat on his body, let alone fat, and his hands were rough and thick like a son of the land. In Huber's eyes, he looked like a Gestapo officer, not that he had ever seen one of that hated breed, to the best of his knowledge.

The visitor said nothing, merely stirred his coffee and kept his eyes fixed on the priest, waiting like a hyena.

'What can I say, sir?' Huber realised he was babbling, but he could not work out whether it was better to be silent or garrulous. 'If there was such a person baptised here, she is not here now. I know every boy and girl in the village, you see. No, no one of that name. Never to my knowledge. Really, your time has been wasted, Herr Kalt.'

'Oh, my time is nothing. I have all the time in the world. My instructions are to find her at all costs, given the importance of my mission. So I will be staying in the village for the foreseeable future, talking to everyone. Perhaps you would continue to rack your brains, Father. I am sure it will all come back to you in due course, for I have seen the baptism certificate and it is clear that you carried out the ceremony.'

Huber could feel his heart pumping, his lungs and throat constricting.

'No, I am sure I would remember.'

'Check the register. You'll see I'm right. Ten years is not so long ago that you can have completely forgotten.' He drank his coffee, rose from the table and held up his hand in farewell. 'My thanks for your hospitality. The coffee was excellent. I will see you again soon, I am sure.'

And then he was gone.

For a full minute, Peter Huber was transfixed with terror and indecision. These past ten years he had feared this day would come, and now it had. What to do? Men like Kalt did not simply accept a denial, shrug their shoulders and go away empty-handed.

He could not deal with this alone. His hand trembled as he picked up the telephone and asked the operator for a number in Berlin – a number he had not called for years and had intended never to call again.

The phone seemed to ring for an age. He was about to hang up when it was answered.

'Hello?' A sleepy voice. Not yet dawn.

'Frau Dietrich?'

'Who is this, please? Do you know what time it is?'

'Father Huber. You know, from Braundorf . . . Peter Huber.'

Silence.

'Frau Dietrich, are you there?'

'Peter, did you really give the operator this number?' The woman's voice was wide awake now, and incredulous. 'And you just said my name!'

'I didn't know what to do. There is a man here, asking after Klara. He says he is a lawyer with a bequest for her. But I think he is Gestapo. I thought you needed to know.'

'God in Heaven, Peter, how could you do such a thing – call me like this?' He heard a deep groan. 'Oh, Peter, it's closing in now. You have to get out of there – fast. Don't call me again.'

The line went dead.

Get out fast? How could he get out at all? It would be hard enough to leave the church and the village – but to abandon Trudchen was unthinkable and he could not ask her to go on the run with him; she knew nothing of this.

There was only one thing to be done: he had to pray.

Not even bothering to remove his slippers and put on his snow boots, he ran from his house to the church. As he opened the great doors, he knew he had made a terrible error. Two men were waiting for him, standing by the ancient font. One of the men was Kalt. The other man, a great deal larger and bulkier, also looked like Gestapo; he had the coarseness of a bull and a face that appeared as though it had never once smiled. Even as Huber shrank back into the doorway, his eyes couldn't help straying to the font. Why was it full of water? He hadn't left it like that. There hadn't been a baptism for weeks, not since September when the little Lang boy had been brought here.

'Ah, Father Huber,' Kalt said. 'This is my colleague, Herr Brunner.'

Huber clasped his hands together and bowed his head, trying to maintain his habitual humility.

'*Grüss Gott, Herr Brunner.*'

The new man, Brunner, said nothing. Without a word, he manoeuvred himself behind the priest. Huber's neck swivelled from one man to another. He realised he was shaking uncontrollably.

'Herr Brunner is my assistant.'

'It is a pleasure to meet you both, but as I have already said, I cannot help you gentlemen.'

'We have a question for you,' Kalt continued. 'Could you please tell us the full name and address of the woman you called in Berlin not five minutes ago? We will have her details soon enough, but you could save us precious time.'

'Please, Herr Kalt, I know nothing of the girl you seek. Or any woman in Berlin.'

Hans Brunner grasped him by the nape of the neck and pushed his face down into the font. The water was deep enough to accommodate a man's head, and cold. Huber's arms flailed helplessly. Kalt grabbed his wrists and restrained them. Huber was struggling to hold in his breath, to keep his lungs from filling with water, but Brunner and Kalt were too strong for him. Together they held him there, mouth and nose submerged, for a full minute, before wrenching him out again, as water sprayed across the ancient stone floor. Huber gasped for air. Brunner turned his nose up and his broad pig's nostrils flared.

'He stinks. I think the holy bastard's shat himself.'

Otto Kalt laughed. 'This is just wasting time. Finish him off. We'll find the woman in Berlin soon enough.'

Just under four minutes later, Father Peter Huber's body slid to the floor. He was dead, drowned in his own font. Brunner looked at the corpse dispassionately.

'Do you think we should search his house, too?'

Kalt looked at his partner with the forbearance of a kind and tolerant parent to an idiot son of whom little was expected.

'Yes, Hans, that would make a lot of sense. And we should search his woman's house, too, I think.'

'And what should we do with the woman?'

'Dispose of her, Hans. Turn her to ash.'

CHAPTER 2

The three engines droned. Thousands of feet below the Junkers tri-motor transport plane, the rocky plains and hills of Spain were yellow and parched. The man in the third row gazed from the small porthole and tried to imagine what was to come in Berlin. His instructions had been brief: he was to go to Germany and collect a package. The order had come from on high, via a man named Bodie Cashbone.

A package. What sort of package?

'I have no further details to give you at this stage.' Bodie Cashbone had sat back and folded his meaty arms. 'You'll find out when you get there.' He'd leant forward. 'All I know is that it's straightforward, but . . .' He'd tailed off and shrugged.

Straightforward? How, in the late autumn of 1941 with Europe at war, could any secret mission to Germany be *straightforward*?

'Why me?' he had demanded. 'I've never been to the country before. I speak the language well enough – but no one would take me for a German.'

'You're not meant to be a German. You are Mr Tomas Esser, an American citizen of German heritage, a sympathetic businessman. That should get you in to Germany, but it won't help you if you're caught. This is off the books. Washington will not own you.'

'But they'll know I've come from England. They'll suspect me immediately.'

'No, they'll think you've travelled from America. It's all been arranged.'

'And how will I get out?'

'You'll have assistance. Failing that, I'm told you have a very big brain,' Cashbone had said. 'You'll find a way.'

*

Ten days earlier Tom Wilde – the man now posing as Tomas Esser – had been in his rooms preparing a lecture on the Elizabethan world view for the handful of history undergraduates remaining in Cambridge. In the real world, history was happening – even Cambridge had been bombed – so what, he wondered, was the point in teaching it?

He pushed the papers away, stretched his arms and leant back. Rubbing his tired eyes, he got up and pulled back the blackouts. Outside it was daylight and he realised he'd lost track of time. From his window he looked out on the bleak and chilly scene of the old court, disfigured by a shed full of armaments at one end and a massive air-raid shelter dug into the other. The only bright spot was the family of ducks that had taken up residence in the unsightly water tank that occupied much of the lawn in the centre of the court.

Yawning, Professor Wilde packed up his things, descended the staircase and came out into the crisp autumn air. As he crossed into the new court, he nodded to the master, who was emerging from the lodge with a couple of pinstriped men who looked as though they belonged to one of the ministries that had been evacuated here from London. And then he saw Scobie, the head porter, coming towards him.

'Morning, Scobie.'

'I was on my way to fetch you, Professor Wilde. Tried calling through, but the lines are down.'

'Something up?'

'Couple of visitors to see you, sir. Mr Eaton and an American gentleman named Cashbone. I've shown them through to the combination room.'

Eaton? He knew Philip Eaton well. He also knew that his arrival was never accompanied by good news. The urbane Mr Eaton was a senior MI6 officer. He never made social calls, which meant he wanted something.

The name Cashbone, however, rang no bells.

'Thank you, Scobie. Perhaps you'd organise some coffee?'

'Of course, professor.'

Wilde changed direction. The combination room was next to the Hall. What in God's name, he wondered, did Eaton want with him this time?

As he opened the solid oak door he saw that the ancient panelled room had only two occupants. They were standing by the central table near some upturned sherry glasses and were inspecting the contents of the betting book with evident amusement. Both men turned his way as he entered. Eaton smiled.

'Wilde.'

'Hello, Eaton.'

He looked a great deal healthier than the last time they'd met, when Eaton was battling to recover from a dreadful incident in which he was hit by a speeding van, losing his left arm and badly injuring his left leg. A lot of the colour had come back to his cheeks. But as he moved towards Wilde his lameness was still painfully obvious.

'Let me introduce Bodie Cashbone, a compatriot of yours,' Eaton said. 'New military attaché at the US embassy. Attached to the COI. I don't believe you've met.'

No, Wilde, thought, looking Cashbone over. Standing a head above Eaton and with the girth of a shire horse, he was not the sort of man you could easily forget. Clearly, the American visitor liked his T-bones big, but despite a double chin, he was curiously handsome for such a large man. His thick hair was well cut and he had warm brown eyes. Wilde guessed his age at mid-thirties, but it was hard to tell. And here in Cambridge, England, in the chilly month of November, his glowing tan told the world he was newly arrived from warmer climes.

The newcomer's meaty paw shot out.

'Professor Wilde, it's my pleasure, sir.'

They shook hands. 'Likewise, Mr Cashbone.'

'I believe we have a friend in common – Jim Vanderberg. We spent some time together in the State Department before his London posting.'

'Ah, Jim? How is he? He said he'd write but the mail doesn't seem to be getting through these days.'

Jim Vanderberg was his oldest and closest friend but, since late 1939, he had been working at the depleted United States embassy in Berlin. The ambassador had been called home three years earlier in protest at the Jewish pogrom that had come to be known as *Kristallnacht* – the night of broken glass. Since then, a chargé d'affaires had been left in control and Vanderberg was one of the few senior men left there.

'He's fine. But, you know, they're under a lot of pressure. The peace between Germany and the US is hanging by a thread.'

He smiled, and that was all the small talk done with.

'Right then,' Wilde said. 'I'm pretty sure this isn't a courtesy call, so tell me – what can I do for you gentlemen?' His gaze shifted between the two visitors.

Eaton nodded. 'I'll leave this to Cashbone. I'm only here to make the introductions. You see, the Office of the COI has been working closely with us.'

'You know about the COI, I take it, Wilde?' Cashbone asked.

'The Co-ordinator of Information – Bill Donovan's intelligence outfit?'

'Yup, that's right. We collate information from the various agencies and report directly to the President. Well, a new COI office is being set up in London, under the command of William Dwight Whitney. I'm part of the small team he's brought over with him.' He inclined his head. 'I'll cut to the chase – I'm here to recruit you, too, Wilde.'

Wilde found himself smiling. This all came as no surprise; in some ways he'd probably been waiting for it all his life. It was, after all, the reason he had been studying German so assiduously for the last two years. But he still wanted to be courted and convinced; he had learned that those who worked in intelligence were not always entirely trustworthy.

'Is this all above board, Eaton? Do they know I'm but a humble history professor?'

'They do. And you fit the bill. In America, Donovan's busy raiding Harvard and Princeton for their finest minds. Intellectuals are the order of the day.'

'And the British are OK with a foreign agency working here alongside them?'

'Astute as ever, Wilde,' Eaton said. 'Yes, some noses have been put out of joint, but Churchill's given the go-ahead, so that's the way it's going to be. We will co-operate. So what do you say?'

'Depends what's wanted of me. Also depends what Lydia has to say. I'm a father now, you know.'

'How are they?'

'Come along for lunch and find out for yourselves. Both of you.'

Eaton and Cashbone exchanged glances.

'We'd love to,' the American said.

Wilde managed four hours' sleep before Lydia woke him at noon with a cup of coffee.

'Your friends will be here soon, darling.'

'My friends? I never thought of Eaton as a friend.'

Lydia laughed. 'I think you love him and loathe him in equal measure. Get yourself shaved and dressed. You're about to have a job interview.'

'Not exactly. They've already offered me the job. I'll be interviewing them. Sorry, *we'll* be interviewing them – you and me.'

'If you insist.'

'Well, it's true.'

'Tom, darling, you have been gearing up for this for two years now. Do you think I didn't realise why you were putting so much bloody effort into your language training? What will you be doing – code-breaking?'

Wilde said nothing. What was there to say? She was only telling the truth.

'Where's Johnny?' he demanded.

'Morning nap. Just like you. In fact, he's becoming more like you every day. Head in the clouds, hair too long, does nothing around the house, loves a fight . . .'

Wilde laughed out loud. 'Who's he been fighting? He's nineteen months old!'

'Ripped poor teddy's ear off last night, and his eye is hanging by a thread. Come on – drink your coffee.'

Wilde swung his legs from the bed and rose to his full six feet. Lydia, dressed for warmth in a woollen skirt and an old fisherman's pullover, put her arms around him, her head against his bare chest, soaking up his warmth.

'Lydia? Are you crying?'

'You can't go, Tom. I can't bear you to go away. We need you, Johnny and I. Your undergraduates need you.'

'Oh, Lydia . . .'

'I know, Tom. You have to go.' She sniffed. 'That's why I can't keep these bloody tears in. God, I hate crying.'

'You had better explain exactly what you want from me,' Wilde said at last, when the meal of lamb chops and sautéed potatoes was finished and the plates had been cleared away.

Lydia picked up Johnny, who'd already closed his eyes, to put him to bed.

'I'll let you boys get on with your secret talk,' she said. 'Don't want the little woman hearing, do you? I might let slip a secret at the WI.'

'Now hold on, Miss Morris,' Eaton said. 'You know it's not like that. We need to hear exactly where you stand on all this.'

Wilde was grinning. 'She's having you on, Eaton. She doesn't even belong to the bloody WI.'

Lydia blew them a kiss. 'Don't worry. I don't really want to know what you're planning. Whatever it is, you have my blessing. Just get my husband home safe.'

'Husband? Have you two lovebirds finally tied the knot?'

Lydia looked to Wilde for guidance. He shrugged.

'Not exactly . . . not in the legal sense,' he said. 'But it makes it easier to use those terms – husband, wife. English sensibilities, Eaton. You know about those.'

'So, a common-law marriage?'

'A magistrates' court might put it like that, I suppose.'

'Well, whatever you call it, you both look very happy – and your little boy is adorable.'

Wilde grinned. 'I rather wanted to call him Horace – but Lydia had a veto on that. To tell the truth, I'm rather glad she did – the boy's a Johnny through and through. Johnny Wilde . . . has a certain ring to it, I think.'

Cashbone nodded his approval. 'He's a swell kid, whatever his name.'

'Thank you,' Lydia said. 'But I repeat, keep Tom alive. His son needs a father.'

So now there were just the three of them. Eaton rose stiffly from the table and went to the window, looking out over the space where Wilde's house had once stood. Wilde and Lydia had been neighbours before they became lovers. And then his house had burned down. Now it was a vegetable patch.

'You didn't think of rebuilding it after the fire, then?'

'There was no point, Eaton. I already spent most of my time here in Lydia's house. Why rebuild when I had no intention of moving back next door?'

'So you just knocked it down, cleared away the rubble and turned it over to cabbages.'

'And carrots and potatoes – oh, and an Anderson shelter. But let's get back to my question, shall we? Mr Cashbone – you do the talking. Tell me what you want from me, and tell it straight.'

The flight seemed to go on for ever. They had already refuelled in Madrid. Next stop Barcelona, then Lyon, and finally Berlin, weather permitting. Stuttgart was a possible alternative, the pilot had announced. In which case, they would have to wait for another flight there or continue the last leg of their journey by train.

A blonde hostess in a Deutsche Lufthansa uniform with a swastika armband arrived at his side.

'Would you care for a drink, Herr Esser?'

'I don't suppose you have Scotch whisky?' Wilde said hopefully.

He couldn't help admiring the woman's figure and her fresh-faced good looks. For some reason he found himself thinking of newspaper pictures he'd seen of Magda Goebbels, but this woman was younger and a great deal friendlier than he imagined the propaganda minister's wife would be.

'I'm sorry, no whisky – but we do have a fine cognac.'

'I'll have a shot of that, then. By the way, you speak good English, Fräulein.'

She had already switched languages for his benefit. In truth Wilde was a little put out. He had done a great deal of hard work getting his German up to a good standard. Initially, the tuition had come from a modern-languages professor at Peterhouse, before he was called off to some intelligence outpost to do war work; after that, the professor's wife, who'd been born in Germany, had taken over, and in the last few days, Mrs Kemp had taken over from her. Wilde was rather pleased with the result; this air hostess seemed less impressed.

'Thank you, sir. It was required before the war, when I flew on the London route. It is good to practise it. You are American, are you not, Herr Esser?'

'Indeed I am, with German forebears.'

'From which part, sir?'

'My grandfather was an engineer in Krefeld. He moved to New York in 1895. He didn't intend the move to be permanent, but he met my grandmother, whose family was also of German stock – from Cologne. And then my father came along – and they stayed. I wish I had paid more attention to my German lessons at school.'

'Oh, don't worry about that, sir. You speak the language extremely well. Anyway, you'll be made very welcome in the new Germany.' She bowed her head – almost a curtsy – and gave him a warm smile. 'I will fetch your drink.'

When he had embarked, the hostess, her colleague and the pilots had all given the Heil Hitler salute, which he had forced himself to return with feigned enthusiasm. But thankfully that had all stopped for the duration of the flight, and he was almost able to imagine himself on a peacetime plane journey.

The reality, however, was very different: he was flying in a Nazi-controlled airplane over fascist Spain towards occupied France, and then into the very heart of Hitler's Reich. His preparation for the mission had been crunched into ten exhausting days. Ten days of getting the cover story right, of getting used to the name Esser, of ensuring there were no British labels or laundry marks on any item of clothing, that his United States papers were in order. And what seemed like a hundred other tiny details which could catch him out.

Ten days in which he had grown a moustache and become accustomed to wearing spectacles all the time.

Cashbone didn't have the expertise to train him in tradecraft, so Eaton had brought in Britain's SOE to help. And if the training had been short, it had been correspondingly intensive. He'd felt as if he was on a dizzying roller coaster.

Going down to London after that lunch with Lydia, he had fondly imagined he would be taking control of an office, helping to build up the new COI organisation as Roosevelt and Bill Donovan desired. It had not occurred to him that he would be thrust straight into the field, on a mission involving extreme danger.

When he had expressed his reservations, Cashbone had been apologetic.

'Something's come up, I'm afraid. We have no one else to call on. The package is vital – it's a mission that could have a profound bearing on the course of the war. For the present I can't tell you any more than that.'

What could he do? He had always believed that one had to fight for peace and freedom, however contradictory that sounded. He had missed the first war; he couldn't miss this one – and so he had said yes, without having any real idea of what he was letting himself in for. And then, for ten days solid, from before break-fast until late at night, he had worked on transforming himself into Tomas Esser, American businessman, opportunist and Nazi sympathiser.

From London, he had been driven back northwards to a safe house not far from Cambridge, where he had remained under the tutelage of a stern, matronly woman named Rosamund Kemp, who was employed by the SOE to teach agents the German language and German customs. She was in her forties, he guessed, tidy, with a keen, clever eye.

They had talked German all day every day; she had prepared German food for each meal. And she had called him by his new name. In the beginning he had found her rather forbidding, but he had quickly grown to respect and even like her.

'I'm not trying to make you seem German, Herr Esser. That would be impossible. But I want you to be at ease among Germans, so that you get the drift of what they are saying, especially when they think you won't.'

When he left she did not wish him good luck. She merely said, 'Hopefully, if all goes to plan, I will see you again in a week or two.'

He liked that.

Now that he was aboard the flight, he knew he would not have long to wait until he put Mrs Kemp's tuition to the test.

The cognac arrived. Wilde inhaled its heady fumes, took a sip then knocked the rest back in one. He held the glass out for another, but then thought better of it and put his hand over the top. He would need a clear head. Death only required a single misstep.

His journey thus far had been circuitous. In America, he had been told, the real Tomas Esser had not been entirely co-operative at first. It wasn't true that he was a Nazi sympathiser, but nor was he inclined to do anything to harm Germany or his company's potential for dealing with the regime.

In the end, under pressure from Roosevelt, via his close aide Bill Donovan, he had acceded to the COI's entreaties and handed over his passport. It was clear to the few people in the know about this mission that it would be better to use genuine papers rather than forgeries. The fact that Esser bore a passing resemblance to Wilde made this feasible.

One of the obvious differences was that Esser wore spectacles in his passport photograph, while Wilde wore them only for reading. In New York, a pair had been made up in Esser's frames with the lenses Wilde used in his research studies. He would wear them halfway down his nose so that he could peer over the top. Esser also had a thin moustache, so Wilde had had to grow one. Put side by side, the real Tomas Esser and the fake one would be easy to distinguish, but against a battered passport photo, Wilde was confident he could pass muster.

The real Tomas Esser, meanwhile, had been taken to a safe house in Vermont – again, unwillingly. There were too many Nazi spies in America for him to be allowed to roam free. All his secretary would be able to say was that her boss had left the office for a few days; and no, she was unable to say where he had gone or when he'd be back.

While the hapless Esser enjoyed an enforced furlough of fishing and long walks in New England, the copy of his spectacles, along with his actual passport, had been shipped to Horta in the Azores aboard the Clipper flying boat service. Wilde, meanwhile, had been taken to the islands by a fast Royal Navy corvette. It would have been preferable, perhaps, for him to travel to America and start his journey as Tomas Esser there, but time was of the essence – and picking the flight up in the Azores instead had been a risk worth taking. The chances that Nazi agents were monitoring the passenger lists in Port Washington, New York, were surely minimal.

From the Azores, Wilde and his new accoutrements – glasses, papers, American clothes, a battered old suitcase belonging to Esser, toiletries from Saks Fifth Avenue and a new, shorter haircut – had joined the Pan Am craft for the last leg of the journey to the seaplane base on the Tagus river, close to the Portuguese capital, Lisbon.

For three days, he had stayed at the elegant Avenida Palace hotel, aware that he was being watched all the while by the German agents who crowded into its restaurant and bar. It was curious listening to – and mostly understanding – the stentorian babel of German voices. Even the laughter sounded Germanic. English and American voices were evident in other parts of the city, along with French, Spanish, and guttural sounds from Eastern Europe – tongues he could not identify. And Portuguese, too, of course. Their city, neutral territory in a Europe aflame, might have become occupied by half the world, seeking sanctuary, but it still belonged to them.

It was strangely unnerving to find himself in a country at peace.

Where Cambridge was grey, damp and rationed, Portugal was full of bright colours, delicious cooking smells and fine weather. And then a German diplomat named Anton Offenbach came to his hotel room, introduced himself and asked him about his plans to visit Berlin.

'You know about me, then?' Wilde instantly took the man to be a spy.

'Of course, Herr Esser. You were expected – I saw your seaplane arrive at the Cabo Ruivo. How could we not know of you? Your visit is eagerly anticipated in Berlin. And on that subject, I have been asked to convey to my superiors exactly what it is that you are offering. While of great interest, the various messages that have been passed to us from your office in New York have not been altogether clear, I believe.'

'I'm afraid that will have to wait until I'm there, Herr Offenbach. These are complex matters – not the sort of information to be transmitted down wires or by regular mail.'

'Not even the diplomatic bag from our Lisbon embassy? I assure you it is quite secure.'

'No, Herr Offenbach, not even that. And with all due respect, I don't even know for sure who you are. You could be an English or American spy for all I know. You certainly speak remarkably good English, and I'm told this town is full of secret agents.'

Offenbach smiled reassuringly. 'I studied modern languages at Oxford University, hence the English. Of course it did not harm my prospects of a position in the *Auswärtiges Amt*.'

Of course it didn't. Junker class. Same story everywhere in the world – upper-middle-class scions fast-tracked into important and safe roles in foreign ministries. Same story at the State Department in Washington and the FO in London. Seamless rise to the top and a long way from the front line. But Wilde had no intention of letting him off the hook.

'I only have your word for that.'

'I understand entirely. But what of you, Herr Esser – are *you* a spy?'

'Do I look like one?'

The man who called himself Offenbach laughed.

'If you must know, you look like one of my old professors at University College, though rather more muscular in build. Appearances clearly mean nothing. So be it. Your flight to Berlin leaves in the morning. Nine sharp.'

He did not mention that he would be on the same flight, a fact which rather threw Wilde the next morning when he boarded the plane and saw him a couple of rows in front. Offenbach turned, and they exchanged perfunctory salutes.

And that was all it had taken. How easy it seemed, entering the lion's cage.

CHAPTER 3

The passport control officer at Tempelhof aerodrome spent an age studying his photograph.

'Your face is fuller in the picture, Herr Esser,' he said at last.

'I've lost some weight.'

'It seems from the stamps that you have travelled extensively – particularly South America: Rio, Montevideo, Santiago, Buenos Aires . . .'

'My company has business interests in those countries, among others.'

'What of England, Herr Esser? Have you ever been there?'

'No.' He spoke the lie with a straight face. 'We don't trade with Britain.'

'And you have not been to Germany before?'

'Once, in childhood, that's all. My parents took me home to meet long-lost relatives, mostly in Krefeld.'

'But you speak German?'

'After a fashion. My father insisted I was taught.'

'You are not related to the Führer's old comrade Hermann Esser?'

'Not to my knowledge. I'm afraid I have not heard of the man.'

'And do you know where your German relatives are now, sir?'

'No. We lost touch before the last war.'

'I would like their names, if I may.'

'Well, I'll tell you what I remember. But you know, I was six years old. I have little recollection of that time. Now let's see . . . There were two uncles – Sebastian and Johann, both engineers like my father, I believe. And some cousins, whose names escape me. No, hang on, I remember one little girl about my age – Petra, that was her name. Petra Esser. They were all Essers.'

'Very well. Do you have non-Aryan blood in your lineage?'

'You mean Jewish? No, we're not Jews.'

'Or Slav, or Gypsy?'

'German. Pure-bred German. Just like the Führer himself.'

The official stiffened visibly. 'Please, Herr Esser, do not compare yourself to the Führer.'

He inclined his head. 'Forgive me.'

The official signalled to a man in a suit standing in a doorway to the right of the passport hall. As he stepped forward, Wilde saw that it was Anton Offenbach.

'Everything fine?' he asked.

'*Jawohl, Herr Offenbach*. He is all yours now.'

Wilde gave the passport officer a farewell nod and turned towards Offenbach.

From behind him, a last rejoinder from the passport man.

'And may I wish you a happy birthday, sir.'

Wilde turned back. 'Oh that was last month.'

You don't catch me that easily.

'Indeed, Herr Esser. I hope you had a party and nice gifts.'

'I'm far too old for all that sort of stuff.'

Wilde turned his attention to Offenbach. After meeting him in Lisbon, he had not expected to see him again. Now he studied him intently and saw the sort of clean, well-groomed young man he had often met in diplomatic circles, both in America and London. Brushed-back hair, smooth shave with a light tan from the Portuguese sun, bright eyes and a ready smile that didn't need to be genuine in his line of work, but managed to charm nonetheless. He might have been a spy, but he looked exactly what he claimed to be – a young attaché in his country's foreign service.

'I am to be your guide and interpreter, Herr Esser.'

'That sounds like menial work for someone of your seniority, Herr Offenbach.'

'Not at all – you are a very important person. I must see that your every need is catered for.'

'I guess I should be flattered.'

'Of course, we would not wish to hinder you in any way, but I must do my duty. You come from the peaceful streets and fields of America; here we are engaged in the greatest war in history. Which means precautions are needed. I am sorry to say that relations between your country and mine are not as good as they might be. Also, the British are making air raids. We wish to take care of you. We would not want anything to happen to our esteemed American visitor . . .'

Was that some kind of threat? If so, Offenbach managed to conceal it with a warm smile and the briefest touch of his delicate fingers on Wilde's shoulder. Wilde decided that Anton Offenbach was either an artist or a pianist in his spare time. He also found himself wondering about the man's time at Oxford; it brought up all sorts of unpleasant possibilities. What if Wilde were to run into someone who had studied at Cambridge recently? The thought didn't bear thinking about.

'And I can tell you, sir,' Offenbach continued, 'that Reichsminister Todt himself is very much looking forward to meeting you tomorrow morning. He spends much time with the Führer at the Wolfsschanze, but by good fortune he is in Berlin for a day or two and you are at the top of his appointments list.'

Wilde felt his stomach churning. God, how could he – a history professor – talk technical detail with a man of such renown as Fritz Todt? This was the man who'd built the autobahns and now had total control over Germany's war machine. He affected a dubious expression.

'To be honest, Offenbach, I'm more interested in meeting your industrialists – they're the ones who will understand what I can offer. As I'm sure you're aware, I am a great admirer of Herr Hitler and the National Socialist ideology, but this mission of mine is pure business. Money, not politics.'

'Please, do not underestimate Herr Doktor Todt. He is a highly qualified engineer and will understand you perfectly, however intricate your explanations. And, of course, as armaments and munitions minister he holds the purse strings and is answerable only to the Führer himself.'

'But I'll be able to meet the industry men, too?'

'Of course.'

'OK, but before meeting Herr Doktor Todt I intend to visit the US embassy.'

Offenbach was clearly shocked. 'Why would you wish to do that, Herr Esser?'

'To pay my respects. I am not here illegally, and just because I wish to trade with Germany, that does not make me a traitor to America, even if I have to bypass certain embargoes. My company . . . we are not politicians or crusaders. Profit is paramount.'

'I will have to take advice on this.'

'Take all the advice you want, buddy. The fact is I hate Roosevelt's guts, as do all decent right-thinking Americans. He's gone way too far down the wrong road with his Lend-Lease Bill. But still, I am a patriot and it is a custom of mine to make my presence known to the local mission or consulate wherever I travel. More than that, I have an old friend in what remains of the embassy – James Vanderberg. Used to go sailing together on Lake Michigan. I don't want him thinking I came here in any sort of undercover capacity.'

Offenbach seemed at a loss, clearly discomfited.

Wilde put an overfamiliar arm around his shoulders.

'Cheer up, Offenbach. I've only just arrived – but with my ancestry, I'm one of you and I'll shout *Sieg Heil* with the best. In the meantime, I could do with a long bath, a hot meal and a couple of drinks.'

He thought back to the words of Philip Eaton, the evening before he boarded the corvette for the Azores.

'Whatever you do, Wilde – don't overdo it. Yes, you're supposed to be a Nazi sympathiser, but don't make yourself a fanatic. A good intelligence officer – and the Germans have those – will spot you a mile off if you're too zealous.'

Wilde took note.

At last the German relaxed.

'Well, Herr Esser, your personal comfort is easily arranged. A car is waiting – and you have a suite booked at the Adlon. Everything has been laid on at our expense. But first, you must pass through customs.' He picked up Wilde's suitcase and steered him towards a doorway. 'They will wish to inspect your luggage. A mere formality, of course.'

Wilde was impressed by his hotel suite. It had every comfort, including a fine shower and separate study and dining room. Bottles of Henkell Sekt and Margaux were waiting for him, along with a box of Swiss chocolates and a bowl of fresh fruit which, he guessed, must be like gold dust in 1941 Berlin, especially this late in the year.

Offenbach had invited him to join him for dinner in the Adlon's restaurant, but Wilde had declined, saying he was tired and would take some food in his room. They would meet instead at breakfast.

Now he was alone. Glass of red wine in hand, he took his time examining the undersides of the tables and the wall sconces, trying to find the microphones. He couldn't find any, but he was certain they must be there – perhaps buried in the walls or behind the skirting. One way or another, the Gestapo would be listening to him. Perhaps he should snore, just to keep them awake. At the airport, they had certainly gone through his bag with scrupulous care, taking note of the labels, asking him searching questions about the provenance of certain items, such as his razor and notebook.

Offenbach had noted the lack of any technical papers. Wilde had laughed at his surprise.

'I'm not giving this away, Herr Offenbach. It's all in my head. If you want it, then you must pay.'

The more he thought about it – and he had thought about this insane mission a great deal – the more he realised that his only hope of survival lay in the overconfidence of the all-conquering Third Reich. They could surely afford to give him the benefit of the doubt. They occupied most of Western Europe and were busy crushing the Reds in the east. Why, as undisputed masters of a rapidly growing empire, wouldn't they trust a German-American bearing the promise of a great gift for their war effort? Their country was already overrun by guest workers who threatened to outnumber the locals. What could one Yankee with scholarly glasses and an academic air do to hurt them? Why not just let him go about his business and hope he gave them what they wanted? And if they treated him graciously, he would return to America with a fat contract and would speak highly of the new Germany, and denounce the interventionists and the lend-leasers.

Wilde pulled back the curtain an inch and saw only pitch-dark night. The blackout was in force here, too. Just like England.

Romy Dietrich knew she would die soon. She was sure that poor, foolish Father Huber had already been killed and that the men who did it would find her too. They would torture her – and when she broke and revealed Klara's whereabouts, they would kill her. And then they would kill Klara.

She knew this as certainly as she knew her face in the mirror. An attractive, well-preserved Aryan face, wide-eyed, intelligent and afraid. Too old to call herself young; too young to die.

She was scared of dying, but even more than that she feared pain; she knew she would never withstand it. If – *when* – she was tortured, she would do or say anything required to put an end to it.

Romy wanted to warn Klara and her guardians. But she could not go to them in case she was already being watched. She could not write because everyone's post was monitored; likewise the telephone exchange, which had surely already been the downfall of Father Huber.

This stinking guest house in the northern part of Charlottenburg in Berlin, close to the Plötzensee prison, would not protect her for long. The landlady was already suspicious of her. Most of those who roomed here were factory workers from France, the Netherlands and Bohemia, employed at the Siemens plants around Spandau. Why, the good Frau wanted to know, would a respectable middle-aged woman with a rural dialect that clearly marked her down as Austrian be seeking shelter here? From what was she hiding? Was she, perhaps, Jewish?

Romy denied it scornfully.

'Look at my colouring, dear lady, do I *look* like a Jew?'

'Many Jews do not look like Jews. Berlin is full of these dirty U-boats.'

'Well, I am not one of them.'

The landlady, Frau Schlegel, looked with disdain upon her guest.

'Others will decide that, not you. Perhaps you are Roman Catholic, which is as bad in my book. Who knows? It is the religion in

Ostmark, is it not? We shall see in due course, Frau Dietrich – if that is your real name.'

Of course it was her real name. She had fled her flat in a leafy but unremarkable street in Kreuzberg within an hour of the call from Father Huber. Nor had she been back to the Friedrichshain municipal hospital where she worked as a midwife. With such haste, she had had no way of securing false papers.

She knew what the damned Schlegel woman would do next: denounce her to the district council leader, the winter relief collector or a local SA member, any one of whom would then pass on the information to the Gestapo. These were dangerous days for anyone suspected of having unsound politics or, worse, of being a Jew. Since September, they had been forced to wear the yellow star, and everyone was aware of the dawn raids around the city as increasing numbers were deported eastwards. No one intervened, of course; they were just grateful if they had been left alone.

What was less certain was who exactly was after her. Was the Gestapo even involved, or was this a private operation by men reporting to Bormann? She had no proof, of course. No evidence even that she was being trailed. She just knew. Intuition based on ten long years of waiting for this to happen.

She needed to move again, and move fast. But where could she go? She feared she could be traced anywhere in Germany. If only she could stay hidden with friends or family, but she could not put that burden on them; it would be a death sentence.

One more night, then. She would stay in this filthy hovel just one more night, and then she would move on and never set eyes on the contemptible Schlegel woman again. Her only plan was to catch a train into the heartland of Germany and see where it stopped. Take a chance on some small town, spend a few days there and then move on again. Thank God she had some money.

Later that night, when Kalt and Brunner took her, she cursed herself for not leaving earlier. What she did not know was that they had found her several days ago, that they had been watching her and waiting, all the time hoping to lull her into a belief that she was safe, so that they could follow her if she went to the girl. The option of escape was never open to her.

Kalt had decided he could wait no longer. His last phone call with Bormann had been bad. It was as if the Reichsleiter's spittle and venom could travel along the wires into his ear, so that he had to hold the phone away from his head. And so the days of waiting for Romy Dietrich to lead him to the girl were over. They would extract the information from her by less subtle means.

She woke at midnight to light flooding in through the open door to her attic room. Two men she had never seen before stood there, standing either side of Frau Schlegel. One of the men was huge, the other small and bespectacled.

'That's her,' the landlady said. 'She owes me money.'

'Send your bill to Prinz-Albrecht-Strasse,' Kalt said dismissively. 'Now leave us.'

'What is she, then – a filthy Jew? I did my duty and informed the authorities that she was trying to hide out here. The least I deserve is the money I'm owed.'

Kalt hustled the woman away without bothering to answer and the two men stepped into the room. Romy was in her nightgown, sitting up against the pillows, fully awake now, clutching the thin blankets to her chest. Brunner grabbed her by the hair and dragged her from the bed. She hit the floor hard.

'Get up!' Kalt barked.

'Who are you? What do you want? I'm not Jewish,' she managed to say through teeth chattering with fear.

'We know who you are and what you are. You are Romy Dietrich and you are a midwife. You are coming with us. Get dressed. Don't bother to struggle or to argue. It will only make it more painful for you.'

At the bottom of the narrow staircase, they encountered Frau Schlegel again. Brunner was bundling Romy towards the door. Kalt gestured to the landlady to approach.

'Tell me what you know of this woman.'

The woman's shoulders stiffened proudly, like a soldier on parade.

'I knew she was hiding from something, sir.' She glared at Romy. 'I was right, sir, wasn't I? Is she a Jew?'

'You spoke with her?'

'Yes, sir. I wanted to discover the truth.'

'And she gave her name as what?'

'Frau Dietrich. Romy Dietrich.'

Leave no trace. Those were the Reichsleiter's words. Maybe Frau Schlegel knew nothing about the girl – but what if Dietrich had let slip some information? Unlikely, perhaps, but still . . .

Kalt nodded to Brunner and shifted his grey eyes sideways to indicate the landlady. Brunner immediately released his grip on Romy and turned his attention to Frau Schlegel. He was twice her size and it was easy for him to grasp her neck in his powerful hands and snap it. Like a farmer despatching a chicken.

CHAPTER 4

At first Wilde didn't understand what he was hearing. His confusion lasted all of five seconds, then he jumped out of bed. It was an air-raid siren.

The concierge had explained the procedure in great deal. Guests were to proceed without delay to the cellars, where they were to wait until the all-clear. Wilde had feigned bemusement.

'Surely Berlin is not being bombed?'

He knew, of course, that it was, that there had been a British raid that very month. He had seen some minor damage on the way in to the city centre from Tempelhof.

'It is nothing, sir,' the concierge had assured him. 'A token gesture by the British before they capitulate. Really, you have nothing to fear.'

Wilde had shrugged. 'I'll have to take your word for it.'

He wasn't worried, though. London had been wounded badly by the Blitz; from what he had seen this was but a pinprick in comparison.

Now he was in the cellar, waiting for the explosions to start. The extensive rooms were full of guests and staff. He took time to study the faces of those forced into this unlikely congregation. He had half-expected Offenbach to be there. But, of course, this was the night shift. Someone else would have been keeping watch on his suite. The bellboy, perhaps, or the room service guy. Or someone posing as a guest.

And then he saw a face he recognised.

It was his old friend Jim Vanderberg: the man who was supposed to present him with the package. He seemed to be looking straight through him, as though they were strangers. But then he winked, very subtly, so that only Wilde would have noticed.

The morning was grey and damp. From his window, Wilde looked out across the dreary thoroughfare of Unter den Linden and the Brandenburg Gate. Through the light drizzle, the only colour was provided by the slashes of red in the great swastika pennants that hung limply from the buildings. At breakfast, Offenbach reassured Wilde that the forecast was for better weather; this afternoon the sun would shine and he would see the Third Reich in all its glory.

'It's all the same by me,' Wilde said. 'My favourite time of year.'

'Your meeting with Herr Doktor Todt is scheduled for ten. I trust that is convenient.'

He had been hoping to call in on the US embassy first, make proper contact with Jim. But that would have to wait. What had he been doing in the Adlon cellar? Was it mere coincidence – he'd happened to be there after a night's drinking – or had he gone there deliberately to see if Wilde had arrived safely? Hopefully, he'd discover soon enough.

'Sure, ten is fine,' he replied to Offenbach.

'Good. I will walk with you to the ministry and act as your interpreter.'

'I think I'll do well enough speaking German, but thank you.'

The waiter poured coffee. Wilde took a sip and almost spat it out. 'What is this stuff?'

'Ah, I am afraid it is ersatz – probably acorns or chicory. We have trouble importing the real thing. But if you care to wait a short while, Herr Esser, I am sure proper coffee will be available when you are with the Reichsminister.'

Wilde put his cup down.

'Yes, I think I'll wait.'

They ate rye bread and cheese with thin slices of sausage, and Wilde drank fresh milk. Offenbach, who seemed happy enough with the acorn coffee, pressed him again on his motives for coming all this way, into the centre of a war zone.

'As I told you, profit,' Wilde said. 'Just like the merchant venturers of old. The further you travel, the greater the danger, the more handsome the profit. It was ever thus, Herr Offenbach.' He cast his eyes around the hotel restaurant. The tables were served by liveried waiters and waitresses; the settings were white linen and bone china. 'Anyway, this doesn't seem dangerous. This feels like travelling to the heart of a great empire. And the war? That'll be over soon, won't it?'

'Of course. Stalin has already been crushed. Our forces are merely engaged in mopping-up operations. Moscow and St Petersburg will be in our hands by Christmas.'

'Good timing on my part, then. But tell me – you say you are my guide and interpreter, so why does it feel like you're my prison escort?'

The coffee cup stopped halfway to Offenbach's lips.

'You are not in prison, Herr Esser.'

'No? I'm very pleased to hear that.'

The ministry was frantically busy. Everywhere, Wilde's ears were assailed by the clatter of typewriters, operated by an army of female secretaries. Civil servants, some in military uniform, seemed to occupy every spare metre of space, working on papers, maps, and banks of telephones, or rushing about carrying messages, the clump of boots echoing down the corridors. This, he could see, was the engine room of the German war machine and, appropriately, it generated something approaching the din of a battle tank at full throttle.

Once Wilde had entered Reichsminster Fritz Todt's inner sanctum, however, and the heavy door was closed behind him, the noise all but vanished, to be replaced by an eerie calm. Todt looked up from some papers, leant forward in his chair and met Wilde's eyes. He did not perform the Hitler salute, but offered his hand. Wilde reached across and shook it. Todt's grip was strong, his skin rough.

'Good day, Herr Esser,' Todt said.

'Reichsminister, it is an honour to meet you.'

Todt grunted. 'Let's get straight to business. First of all, tell me exactly who you are.'

'I am a motorcycle manufacturer. We are called Esser Trautmann.'

'And do you have politics? Are you a member of the German American Bund?'

'I stay clear of politics, but it is true I have great admiration for the achievements of the National Socialists. You have done great things in Germany.'

Todt ignored the flattery. 'Let me be frank, Herr Esser. I am suspicious as to why you are here. You have arrived in Germany at a time when your country is supplying materiel to our enemies.'

Wilde nodded. 'That's exactly why I have come, sir. I believe my government is making a grave error in helping Britain – and I wish to redress the balance a little, if I can.'

The German minister stared at Wilde for two or three seconds, sizing him up. Finally he smiled.

'Then I must welcome you. And let me say first that I have ridden one of your motorcycles – before the war. The Brooklyn 650.'

'Well, well, that really is something. What did you think?'

Talk more slowly, Wilde. You've been through this a dozen times in training; you know all this back to front. Calm down. The sweat is cold on your back, on your neck. Don't let him see that.

'A good, solid machine. Yes, I liked it. Fine construction. Given the size of the engine, I recall that it might have lacked a little power, but that would be my one complaint.'

'That's a fair criticism. I ride one myself, but then I'm not looking to race it. We sold a few in Germany. Not enough, I'm afraid. And since November 1938 it has been nigh on impossible to trade here.'

Todt was a handsome man. He wore a military uniform which Wilde couldn't identify; it looked lived in, worn and a little shabby, rather than purely ceremonial. Todt was clearly not afraid to get his hands dirty. He had the look of a hard-driving foreman rather than a company chairman.

Wilde, by contrast, wore a tailored New York suit, made of fine wool. And a silk tie. He didn't look scholarly today; he looked businesslike, and he didn't feel entirely comfortable playing the part.

'A shame,' the Reichsminister said. 'It is a machine of some quality. That's why I was interested when you said you believed you might have something to offer us. By the way, who is Trautmann?'

'Oh, he's long deceased. He was my father's partner. It's fully Esser-owned now. No sense in changing the name, though.'

'But you are not a big company?'

Wilde shook his head. 'Not big enough. We have good products but not enough cash to expand as fast as we'd like.'

Todt's office was an unpleasant room, full of heavy, dark furniture which did not match the practical air of the man who sat behind the dreadnought-like desk. Behind him – all-seeing perhaps? – was a painting of the Führer astride a horse, in the full armour of a knight of legend, complete with lance. Did Todt actually *like* the picture? Difficult to imagine of a man with such achievements, both civilian and military, to his name.

At Todt's side, just at his shoulder, stood Offenbach, mostly silent but interpreting when necessary.

'Now then,' Todt said. 'to business. What do you have to offer me – and how much do you want for it?'

Wilde sipped the coffee. This was the real deal. Strong, black and fresh-roasted. Just what he needed on this grim, grey morning.

'I'm offering you fuel – gasoline.'

'And you can ship that to Germany?'

'No, I can't do that. But there are many different ways of looking at a problem. Correct me if I'm wrong, Herr Doktor Todt, but you could do with a great deal more gasoline than you have. You may be winning the war in Russia, but your men and machines have to travel enormous distances.'

Todt frowned. 'We have enough oil.'

'OK, but you could always do with more. Word from the Russians is that your advance is stalling.'

'Of course they would say that. You should not listen to such things.'

'But if it was true, then what? They have an endless supply of men. They are building planes and tanks faster than you. So are the British. They both have greater fuel reserves than you, do they not? The longer this war goes on, the more you're going to be stretched.'

'Where do you hear this nonsense?'

'Tell me I'm wrong, Herr Doktor.'

Todt was silent.

Wilde continued. All this information had been drummed into him during an intensive two-day course at an Edwardian manor house in the home counties north of London, following his week with Mrs Kemp in Cambridgeshire.

'And if I'm right? Well, at a guess, you must understand the implications better than anyone in the Third Reich.'

'You have come halfway around the world to spout propaganda at me, have you, Herr Esser? I thought you had something to sell.

If you are not going to send tankers across the Atlantic, perhaps you have a new method of producing synthetic fuel, something we haven't already devised for ourselves? Surely not wood-gas generators – we have that old technology.'

Todt must have known that wasn't what he was offering; he was a details man, after all, and the wires from New York to Berlin had been specific in what was on offer, if not the actual science.

'Synthetic fuel is a fine idea,' Wilde said. 'But surely you know the true reason for my visit.'

Todt smiled affably. 'I receive few Americans. In fact, I believe you must be the first since ... what, 1938 or 1939. Messages get lost in transmission. Yes, we both know what you are offering – improved fuel consumption. But you must also know that this is something we are already working on.'

Wilde knew, from his briefings, that oil – or lack of it – was the great problem facing the Nazi regime. Their reserves amounted to no more than a million tons, a tenth of that held by the British. And, stretched to the limit in the supply line through Russia, the German situation would soon become desperate if total victory was not achieved imminently. Germany needed a knockout blow, or a swift infusion of raw materials, the most pressing of which was oil.

It was hard to imagine warming to a Nazi, but on the surface, at least, Todt seemed genial and engaging. But who knew what lay beneath? He was no doubt efficient and single-minded. You had to be those things to have achieved what he had. But did that make him ruthless? Wilde really didn't want to find out.

'So you're working on it. In which case, why did you agree to my visit?' Wilde asked.

'I am a man with an open mind. All innovations interest me. But you have to prove to me that you are worth dealing with.'

'That is not easy. I am not just going to give you my technology. We need to meet on neutral territory where I can demonstrate what I am offering without revealing the method until a deal is struck and money – gold – paid up front, deposited in a neutral country.'

'You do not trust me?'

'I am a businessman and you're engaged in a war. A gentleman's handshake will not suffice in such circumstances. Look, what do your motorcycles average – maybe forty-five to fifty-five miles to the gallon in clear conditions on open roads? A lot less on difficult terrain and in poor weather. Well I can improve that dramatically – ninety miles to the gallon. And that's a conservative estimate.'

'Do you have machines in production that can achieve such consumption?'

'No, but I have a prototype.'

'And you have tested it exhaustively, yes?'

'Of course.'

'Ninety miles per US gallon?'

'Ninety-two, to be precise.'

'Which in metric . . . that's thirty-nine, almost forty, kilometres per litre.' It took him all of two seconds to work it out. 'Impressive, Herr Esser. Are you sure of this? Do you have a photograph of this motorcycle?'

Wilde laughed. 'I have a photograph of my wife and children – but not the bike. And no, before you ask, I have not brought diagrams. What I can tell you is that the prototype has the body of the Brooklyn, so nothing special to look at, really. The change is all internal – I'm not talking aerodynamics here. I promise you this, though – it works. My problem is that America isn't interested. They want speed and power. Gasoline is dirt cheap and plentiful. No one gives a goddamn how much fuel their cars and motorcycles use so long as they can burn up the highway. I can't compete with

Harley, so if we're going to expand I need to sell to someone who does care about fuel economy. Someone to whom it means a great deal right now. That's why I thought of Germany.' He pursed his lips and appeared to hesitate. 'Look, I'll come clean with you. My firm is in trouble – a deal with you could save it.'

Todt was silent, thinking.

Wilde read his thoughts. 'And if my method works for motorcycles – which I assure you it does – then there is no reason why it shouldn't work for tanks and armoured vehicles, too.'

The Reichsminister glanced at the wall clock, then picked up the phone and dialled a single number.

'Come in here, please.'

A junior officer entered the office.

'Yes, sir?'

'Get me Porsche, if you would.'

'I believe he's in Stuttgart, Herr Reichsminister.'

'Call him – find out his movements. Tell him to make his way to Berlin as soon as he can. If not today, then tomorrow.'

'Right away, Herr Reichsminister.'

The officer nodded and left the room.

'You have heard of Ferdinand Porsche, Herr Esser?'

'Of course.'

'If we are to continue this conversation, we need him here.' Todt began to rise from his chair. 'Forgive me, sir, I have an important meeting I must attend. But believe me, I am extremely interested in your innovation. Come here again tomorrow. If all goes well, Herr Porsche will be here too. Then we can try to make progress to everyone's satisfaction.'

Wilde stood, picking up his grey American hat from the floor at the side of the chair.

'Thank you for your time, Herr Doktor Todt.'

Todt shook hands. 'In the meantime, enjoy Berlin. It is a fine city, though not at its very best at this time of year. I'm sure you will find much to interest and amuse you, however. The museums, the Tiergarten, the bustle of city life. Herr Offenbach will advise you. Just make sure not to speak English too loudly – I'm afraid some Americans have found themselves at the wrong end of a fist for speaking the language of our enemies.' And then he reached out and touched the scarred groove in the side of Wilde's head. 'That looks like a bullet wound. Hunting accident – or war?'

'Lacrosse stick.'

'Isn't that for girls?'

'You obviously haven't played it, Herr Doktor Todt.'

The Reichsminister laughed. 'You Americans and your games! When will you stop playing and join the real world?'

Wilde realised he had gone into the meeting as good as naked. The truth was he had nothing to offer Todt except the vague promise of a good idea. The figures were invented, the proposal insubstantial – and it was an indication of Germany's fuel shortage that Todt was willing to listen. If there was anything at all in the idea, even if the figures were over-egged, it would be transformative for the Third Reich.

For Wilde, the longer the meeting had gone on, the more he had sweated. As for the head wound, it had been caused by a bullet, an attempt on his life five years earlier. But that was not something he could tell Todt, for his very own regime had been behind the attack. Wilde took a deep breath. God, he was glad to be out in the fresh air.

Yes, he knew just about all there was to know about Tomas Esser. He had worked damned hard on every detail of the man. But that didn't mean he couldn't get caught out. Given Esser's German background, it was also a horrifying possibility that Wilde might run into someone in this city who knew him. Or that Todt might know a mutual acquaintance.

Yes, he also knew about motorbikes. He could maintain one and strip it down if need be. He had even ridden an Esser Trautmann Brooklyn 650 for a couple of days in Massachusetts during his last visit to the States in 1939. He hadn't liked it much. Todt was right – it was underpowered.

But the very idea of having to discuss complex technologies with Ferdinand Porsche was too much. Which meant Wilde had to move fast – get the package and somehow get out of this hellhole of a country.

CHAPTER 5

Romy Dietrich was carried in the back of a black delivery van deep into the farmlands and forests of northern Germany. She was bound, but not gagged. Otto Kalt sat on a bench seat watching her the whole time, while Brunner drove.

'Frau Dietrich,' Kalt said. 'You know very well what I am looking for – *who* I am looking for. If you tell me now, it will save me time and you considerable pain.'

Romy swallowed. Deep down, she knew there was no hope, but she had to keep trying.

'I think you have the wrong person.'

'You are Romy Dietrich?'

'But maybe there are others with the same name?'

'Romy Dietrich, midwife at Friedrichshain hospital, home address in Kreuzberg, originally from Upper Austria.'

'Yes, I am a midwife.'

'Father Peter Huber called you from Braundorf on the day he died.'

Romy shuddered. Tears began to fall.

'You seem upset, Frau Dietrich.'

'Of course I am upset – I have been abducted.'

'So it is not the death of Father Huber that distresses you?'

'I know no such man – and I have received no phone call from him. And where is Braundorf?'

'This is pointless. Soon you will be telling me the truth – and begging me to believe you.'

Romy felt her limbs begin to shake uncontrollably.

'Won't you let me go, sir? Please. I will do anything for you. I am told I am still an attractive woman . . .'

'That's true.'

She fell from the bench seat on to her knees.

'I beg you. I am innocent of any crime.'

'I don't doubt it,' Kalt replied.

They hung her by her wrists from a wall in the barn where the sows suckled. The acrid reek of the animals' excrement was overpowering. Kalt's wife, Johanna, twice the size of her husband in girth, glanced at the proceedings, blank-eyed. She wore a blood- and mud-spattered housecoat that might never have been washed.

Johanna Kalt spat on the ground, then carried on her work shovelling up pig shit from the enclosures as though nothing was amiss, as though a terrified woman, her clothes coated in mud and other filth, was not hanging like the Christ from the old brick wall. Johanna Kalt was a farmwife; one creature's distress was the same as another's, and no concern of hers as long as the pigs got to market.

Kalt and Brunner went about their business with grim efficiency, suggesting this might be something they had done before. After binding Romy Dietrich's wrists and attaching them to old iron hooks high up in the wall so that her stockinged feet were suspended inches from the ground, Kalt asked her again.

'Now then, Frau Dietrich, where is the girl? Klara Wolf – where is she?'

Romy shook her head. Her throat was constricted and she was gasping for breath.

Kalt shrugged and put his arm around Brunner's shoulders.

'Let us have a bottle of beer, Hans. We'll come back in half an hour . . .' He spoke the words loud enough that she was sure to hear. '. . . with the tools.'

*

It was a short walk from Todt's office on Wilhelmstrasse to the US Embassy in the old Blücher Palace at the Brandenburg Gate. The consular section gave out on to Hermann Göring Strasse, but it was the embassy on Pariser Platz which Wilde and Offenbach now approached, for this was where the remnants of the American diplomatic mission were presently housed. The light drizzle had stopped and the day was a great deal brighter. Todt had been right – it promised to be a fine afternoon.

The mass of humanity passed him by, heads bowed against the cold. They all looked so shabbily dressed and down at heel. This was the people that had conquered most of Europe and was now marching halfway across Asia in its push to the east – its *Drang nach Osten* – but they hardly looked like victors. How different was the reality of this drab, grey city from the sharply choreographed propaganda films, full of smartly attired citizens, put out by Doktor Goebbels.

One policeman stood guard outside the front of the building, also keeping watch on Goebbels's propaganda ministry next door. He made no attempt to stop Wilde from entering the embassy. Nor did the doorman. Wilde turned to shake hands with Offenbach.

'I will see you at lunch perhaps, Herr Esser,' the German said.

Wilde had loosened his tie. He was enjoying the cool autumnal air on his neck. He smiled at his escort. Could this confident official of the Nazi regime really be as confused and deflated as he seemed, as if he didn't know quite what to make of the American visitor? Wilde gave him a questioning look.

'Why don't you come in with me?' he said, as certain as he could be that Offenbach would decline the invitation. 'I'm sure you'd be very welcome – you're not at war with us, you know.'

'No, I will wait for you at the Adlon.'

'Could be hours. I may have lunch here. We'll see.' Wilde took pity on the man. 'Look, buddy, I know this isn't easy for you. But the Reichsminister said I should enjoy your fine city, and I intend to do so. This is just my first stop – I don't need my hand held.'

Offenbach stared at him, unsmiling, for several seconds, then clicked his heels together, stiffened his spine and threw out his right arm.

'Heil Hitler!' he said.

Wilde told reception that he was an American citizen, Tomas Esser, and that he wished to speak with Mr James Vanderberg. After a brief internal phone call, an ancient and tortoise-slow porter showed him upstairs and along a corridor to a large office. As the door opened, Jim immediately got up from behind his desk, thanked the porter and bustled him out, closing the door after him.

'Tomas Esser, old buddy, it's wonderful to see you. What in God's name are you doing in Berlin?'

He immediately put a finger to his lips, and indicated various points in the room which Wilde took to be the locations of concealed microphones, then embraced his old friend.

'Oh, you know, I like to turn up in curious places. Never liked bandwagons – if everyone else is going one way, I go the other. Sorry if I gave you a shock.'

'Shock's only the half of it. Don't get a lot of visitors here these days. Well, I'm damned, it's been years.'

'Too many, Jim.'

'I'll say. How's the motorbike business? Come on, spill the beans – what exactly are you doing here, Tom? You didn't come for your health, old man – bombs have been falling hereabouts.'

'I'm on holiday.'

'That won't wash, Tom. I know you too well.'

'Nothing illegal – beyond that I'd rather not say.'

Vanderberg sighed audibly. 'Have it your own way. I'll let it ride for the moment, but you know our top men here might inquire a little more deeply. Until then, it's just damned good to see you. Coffee?'

'Is it real?'

'Oh yes, buddy. This is American territory. No ersatz acorn stuff in here. Come and sit yourself down.'

He indicated a leather sofa close to the window, then picked up a pen and notepad from his desk. In small letters he wrote, '*Keep talking domestic stuff, OK.*'

'Then yes, coffee for me. What a swell office, Jim. I guess you live the high life here.'

'You'd be amazed. More diplomatic parties than you could imagine. Of course some missions are missing, but that means more wine and eats for the rest of us.'

As he spoke, he had handed Wilde a couple of sheets of foolscap paper with dense writing in black ink.

'Sounds like a good time.'

'Tell you what, Tom, I'll just leave you for a couple of minutes while I seek out that coffee. You sit here and read *The New Yorker* – we get it shipped in with the pouch.'

There was no magazine, not that Wilde could see anyway, just the two sheets covered in Vanderberg's neat handwriting. It was a hand that Wilde had known as well as his own since their days rooming together at Chicago half a lifetime ago.

Vanderberg left the room with exaggerated footsteps and a firm closing of the door. Wilde began to read.

Tom, we can't talk. We are pretty sure they hear everything we say since we moved here a couple of years back, so be on your guard not to mention Britain or Lydia or Cambridge. You have to remain Tomas Esser, American motorbike manufacturer. This paper you're reading has only just been written by me and no one else has seen it, nor will they. I will burn it as soon as you have read it, so memorise everything. OK, this is what it's about: you will have been told to collect a package. Well, buddy, I have to tell you that the package is, in fact, a ten-year-old girl born Klara Wolf, now known as Klara Rieger. No one outside Germany except FDR and Bill Donovan know of her existence. Not even the COI guys in London — which is why you could not be told the whole truth about your mission.

Klara Wolf is an important young lady, although she almost certainly doesn't know it. She is presently living in a village near Berlin and, unknown to her or her adoptive parents, is in grave and imminent danger. The reason for this goes back ten years to her birth in a village named Braundorf in Upper Austria, not far from the German border. According to her birth and baptism certificate — and I have a copy of this in the safe — her mother's name was Angelica Wolf. This was not true: her mother's true name was Angela or Angelica Raubal. Her father was not named, merely marked down as 'soldier, absent'.

Angelica Raubal was always known by a shortened version of her name, Geli. She was a niece of Adolf Hitler, the daughter of his half-sister, who is still alive and is also called Angela. Geli was much favoured by Hitler for several years in the late 1920s and early thirties, to the extent that she went to live with him in his Munich apartment, with a room of her own. They spent a lot of time together — picnics, opera, the whole thing. Almost certainly bed, too.

In September 1931, however, she died of a gunshot wound in his apartment. The weapon used was Hitler's own pistol, though Hitler was apparently not present at the time and the death was recorded as suicide, though those who knew her said she was the happiest, least suicidal person they had ever met. The death was not completely hushed up, but it was played down. The would-be Führer was grief-stricken by her death, but could not be blamed; he was away on a campaigning trip at the time of death. This much is known. But there is something else that not even Hitler knows: Geli had a baby a few months before she died.

The words brought Wilde up with a jolt. The implication was obvious and astonishing. He continued reading.

There is much else that was never told and the world never knew, including the true circumstances surrounding Geli's death and the reason she died. These facts, if they were to come out, would have seismic repercussions for the Nazi hierarchy and Germany as a whole.

Later, when we are out of the range of microphones, I will tell you more of what is known — their days out when he'd watch her swimming naked in pools and lakes, his jealousy when he thought there might be other men in her life — particularly his driver Emil Maurice and a music teacher in Austria.

At times it all became too much for the girl. She got claustrophobic because Uncle Alf — that's what she called him — didn't let her out much. But late in 1930, early 1931, she managed to get away to Austria for three or four months. However, that absence had less to do with claustrophobia and more to do with the pregnancy she was desperate to keep secret from him and everyone else. The only person in Germany who knew the truth was her mother, who kept house for Hitler at his other home, a modest mountain chalet named Haus Wachenfeld before it was expanded and renamed the Berghof.

Geli's mother warned her that Uncle Alf could not be distracted from his political work by family matters. He was on the brink of power and nothing must stand in his way. Whether or not he was the father, she must have an abortion. Otherwise, there would be gossip and his standing would suffer because he portrayed himself as a man married to his country. Even if Geli denied he was the father, the fact that she lived with him at 16 Prinzregentenplatz in Munich would set tongues wagging. In Catholic Bavaria, the idea that a 42-year-old man had fathered a child by his 22-year-old niece out of wedlock would have caused massive damage to his electoral chances. He has sold himself — or been sold by Goebbels — as a man who has sacrificed his own domestic happiness for the good of the nation, forgoing the love of a wife and family for his love of Germany. And his image of self-sacrifice has worked — the fact is, Hitler is beloved by women more even than by men. That love would have turned sour in a heartbeat if whispers of an illegitimate child leaked out.

Wilde hadn't quite finished reading, but the door opened and Vanderberg backed in carrying a tray with cups, coffee pot, milk and sugar.

'Coffee, Tom. Just like they make it in the States. Sorry to keep you so long, but you know, I wasn't expecting such an esteemed visitor this morning.'

They chatted aimlessly for a few minutes and drank their coffee. In the gaps, Wilde finished his reading.

Geli gave birth to Klara in the village of Braundorf in March 1931. She was taken into the care of a couple whose names I know but have not met. They knew the child's history and the danger of revealing the truth, and so they removed themselves to Germany, because the Hitlers and Raubals were too well known in that part of Austria. And for ten years they have been bringing up the child as their own. I'm pretty sure she has no idea of her true parentage.

Two weeks ago everything changed. No, I have to go back a bit first. September 1931 is when it changed – the time of Geli's death. You may not have heard of a man called Martin Bormann, but you will. Some believe him to be the most dangerous man in Germany other than Hitler himself. It's said he wields more power than Göring, Himmler, Goebbels or Heydrich because he is Hitler's gatekeeper. No one can get to the Führer without Bormann's say-so. He signs all the edicts, controls the finances, translates the Führer's decisions into actions. He is violently loathed by all and sundry, high and low. Everyone save Hitler, in fact – Hitler depends upon him utterly. He tells Bormann to do something, it gets done. They call him the Brown Eminence. But that's now.

Back then in 1931, Bormann was a nobody. But he was an ambitious, ruthless nobody. In the summer of that year he discovered the truth about Geli Raubal's absence the previous winter. Did her mother reveal it in drink? I don't know the answer to that. But he certainly found out – and he wanted to discover more. He realised the power he could wield with such knowledge. When Hitler departed on his campaigning tour, it is believed Bormann went to see Geli at the Munich apartment and demanded the truth. Where was the baby? My source speculates that he threatened her and when she refused to talk and, indeed, threatened him back, he shot her in blind panic, then made it look like suicide. He's been terrified ever since that the truth would come out – that his meteoric rise would end in disgrace and the guillotine. Because whatever Hitler might have thought about Geli being pregnant, there is no doubt he loved her. Whether sexually or platonically can be debated, but love her, he did. Her room *hasn't been touched since the day she died. It's like a shrine. Every day his housekeeper brings fresh flowers. She was the only woman Hitler has ever loved.*

Which brings us to 1941. It seems Martin Bormann has discovered the trail. And he's closing in on little Klara. There may already have been deaths. That's where you come in, Tom. You've got to get her out of the country to safety. But that has been arranged – and you will have assistance.

Wilde looked at Vanderberg open-mouthed. So this was 'the package'.

'Finished, Tom? Good coffee, huh?'

'Extraordinary.'

Vanderberg gathered up the papers, struck a match and burnt them over a metal wastepaper bin, until they were nothing but blackened ashes. He opened a desk drawer and pulled out a small photograph of a girl. He turned it around so that Wilde could read the name Geli Raubal on the back, then handed the picture to Wilde to study.

The girl in the picture had a warm, friendly face with a little mischief in her smiling eyes. She didn't have movie star good looks, but there was a sexual magnetism there, a sense that here was a girl who liked a good time, and all that that entailed. Jim Vanderberg took the picture back and replaced it in the drawer.

'What are you doing for the rest of the day, Tom?'

'Well, to be honest I've got time to kill, so I was going to do the tourist thing.'

'I've got a better idea. George Kennan, our administrative officer, has offered me the use of his sailboat which he keeps out on the Havel at Wannsee – that's Potsdam way. It's going to be a fine afternoon. Want to come out with me, like the old days? Probably my last chance before winter sets in. We can chat some more. Shoot the breeze properly.'

'You're mad, Jim. Sailing in December?'

'Where's your sense of adventure? We can drive out there by way of my apartment. I've got spare waterproofs. I seem to remember we wear the same size shoes. You'll be fine.'

'And we can do this in the middle of a war?'

'Why not, Tom? Life goes on.'

CHAPTER 6

Wilde wandered back to the Adlon, hands in pockets, as casually as though he were strolling through the streets of Cambridge. He checked in with Offenbach and told him he was going sightseeing in the afternoon.

'I would very much like to accompany you, sir. I could show you the best that Berlin has to offer.'

'I'm sure you could, but I have other plans.'

Offenbach gave a stiff nod of the head. 'As you wish, Herr Esser. Won't you at least join me for lunch first?'

Was it wise to alarm this man any more than necessary? Probably not.

'OK,' Wilde said. 'But just something light. An omelette, perhaps.'

Offenbach's shoulders relaxed. His relief was evident.

'I'm sure the Adlon chef could manage that. Now tell me, did you meet your old friend in the embassy?'

'I sure did.'

'He must have been surprised to see you.'

'That's an understatement.'

'And a little suspicious, perhaps?'

'If he was, he was too much the gentleman to show it. To tell the truth, Herr Offenbach, I don't care – I'll deal with all that when I get home. Or who knows, I might decide to stay here for the duration if my negotiations go well – and if you'll have me. Get my wife and kids shipped over. Germany is increasingly looking like the safest place in the world. Do you think the Reich would allow me to stay?'

'That would not be for me to decide.'

'Of course not. Just thinking aloud, friend.' He paused. 'But enough about *me* – tell me about yourself, Herr Offenbach. Are you a good National Socialist?'

If the German hesitated, it was barely discernible.

'Of course,' he said.

Wilde allowed himself a smile. 'And your name – are you related to the composer?'

'No, I am related to the city – Offenbach am Main.' He smiled. 'Forgive me, that is my idea of a joke.'

Lunch lasted an hour and Offenbach was crestfallen when, despite his entreaties that no one knew Berlin better than he did, Wilde insisted on going his own way. He met up with Vanderberg in the embassy courtyard, where his Packard was parked, complete with diplomatic plates, then they drove across to his apartment on the far side of the Tiergarten.

Vanderberg found some old slacks, a heavy pullover and oilskins for Wilde, then handed him his razor.

'Cut it off, Tom – the moustache. And ditch the glasses.'

It took Wilde mere moments to shave his upper lip and then he stood against a plain wall while his old friend took his photograph with a large camera.

'We have an excellent forger resident at the embassy. I'll have your new papers with you this evening. Keep the Esser papers for the moment, but try to avoid the Gestapo until then.'

'You know, Jim, if this weren't so serious I might actually be amused by your attempts at humour.'

Jim grinned. 'Come on, let's go sailing while there's still some light.'

They drove westwards. Berlin was an eerie place. The anti-aircraft guns were silhouetted against a bright blue sky; occasionally a line of tanks or troop carriers trundled by, all seeming to be heading east. In places there was minor bomb damage, piles of rubble pushed to the side of the road, but mostly the city appeared much as it must have done in peacetime, with tree-lined residential streets untouched by the horrors of war. Men and women caught buses and trams and crowded around shops; children laughed and played in large squares bedecked with swastika pennants. Street signs and plaques all used the elaborate Gothic script – a type that had always made Wilde intensely uncomfortable. All told, though, this looked pretty much like a city at peace with itself.

'Sorry about the secret stuff back there,' Vanderberg said as they cruised along an open road. 'We've swept all the offices, but we think mikes are almost certainly buried within the walls. The Nazis would have had easy access during the restoration and refurbishment work.'

'It suits you, Jim – all the spy stuff.'

Vanderberg laughed out loud. They were heading through Dahlem, south of the skeletal woodlands of Grunewald, towards the western extremities of Berlin. The residential suburbs seemed to be giving way to acres of barracks, closely guarded by heavily armed sentries and watchtowers.

'War,' Vanderberg said dismissively. 'This area used to be a lot prettier.' He changed the subject. 'What did you think of Todt? Good name, huh? Sounds like *Tod* – death.'

'I didn't want to, but I warmed to him. He's hard working. The sort of man who built America.'

'I know what you mean, but don't go too easy on him. He's effectively using slave labour these days – hundreds of thousands of men from the occupied territories. Fritz Todt is as hard as they come. The fact that he's hard on himself too doesn't change that. Perhaps you didn't notice the death's head ring he wears.'

Wilde hadn't. 'Well, with luck I won't have to see him again.'

Vanderberg was driving. The car was open-topped with white-wall tyres and running boards – and the engine noise was loud.

'Don't look around, Tom, but we're being followed.'

'What a surprise.'

'But we can talk. There's no way of bugging us here.'

'Good. Then answer me this, Jim – are you really saying this Klara Wolf is Adolf's daughter?'

'On the balance of probabilities, I'd say yes – but who knows? And why not? He has a mistress, you know. A woman named Eva Braun, though no one outside his close circle knows it. She lives in the Berghof – and they have adjoining bedrooms.'

'God, Jim, I always thought he was asexual. You know – no interest.'

'That's what you're supposed to think. But for a man whose relationships with women are supposed to be purely platonic, he sure seems to stir some dark and deadly passions. Geli, dead, shot with Hitler's own pistol. Unity Mitford – who was desperate to marry him – shot herself in the head at the start of the war. Two years before that, the actress Renate Müller threw herself to her death from a window after their relationship ended. I've heard a rumour that Eva Braun also took an overdose of sleeping pills but survived. Maybe Herr Hitler is just unlucky – but Tom, there's a pattern there.'

Wilde said nothing; this was all new to him. Why didn't these details make the press?

'Oh, and there's more,' Vanderberg said. 'His own mother's name was Klara and he has often liked to go by the name Wolf.'

'Compelling evidence – but not conclusive.'

'As you say. But Freudians might also note that there is another pattern here. The age gap between Hitler and Geli – twenty years – is very similar to the age gap between Hitler's father and mother. Apparently there are some pictures somewhere – intimate drawings Hitler made of Geli. Not in the manner of a life class, but of the boudoir, if you get my meaning.'

'Jim, how do you know all this?'

'I've got most of it direct from the midwife who delivered Geli's baby. She came to the embassy with this tale just over two weeks ago, and she was desperate. I believed her instantly. She laid it all out to me while we walked in the Tiergarten and down by the canal. She said the whole thing had been discovered and she was desperate to escape – and get the little girl to safety. She believed Bormann's men would be on to her within hours.'

'Do you think Hitler would have his own daughter killed?'

'Good God no. But Bormann would kill her. He has to cover his tracks. He knows his days would be numbered if Hitler ever discovered the truth about Geli's pregnancy and death. Bormann will be desperate to keep everything under wraps – silence anyone who might know too much.'

'Including the midwife?'

'Particularly the midwife, Romy Dietrich. She feared that her phone might already be tapped – and that prevented her getting a warning through to Klara's adoptive parents. She wanted to use our phones, but I had to tell her that they, too, are compromised. Romy was the only link between Braundorf and little Klara's new family, you see, so she's an obvious target. Romy came to me because she had nowhere else to go. Pointless going to the police in a police state. She hoped we might be able to do something to protect the child.'

'You keep mentioning this guy Bormann, but I've got to be honest, Jim, I've never heard of the fellow.'

'Nor have most people in Germany. If they had, they'd be making jokes about him instead of Goebbels. But he's real enough. I heard about him – and about Eva Braun – through diplomatic gossip. Our endless cocktail parties do serve some purpose, you know. He's as oily as a snake in slime. Goebbels, who loathes him, hit the nail on the head when he described him to a friend as "a glorified butler". A butler, maybe – but no butler ever exercised more power. He has made himself very rich, has numerous mistresses, and he'll do anything – including murder – to please his master. I believed the midwife's story about him straight away. How would she have made up such a thing?'

'And how did *she* find out about his role?'

'Through Geli herself. Romy wasn't just the midwife, she was the girl's friend and confidante. She was also close to Geli's mother, Hitler's half-sister. Romy Dietrich says Frau Raubal had her suspicions about Bormann as soon as Geli was killed. She had felt uneasy ever since she foolishly dripped word of the baby into his ear. Apparently it never made sense to Frau Raubal that her daughter had shot herself. She guessed straight away that it was Bormann – but she couldn't say a word to her brother.'

'Hitler, you mean?'

Vanderberg nodded. 'She's terrified of him.'

'Where is Geli's mother now?'

'Well, she was a widow back in 1931, but five years ago she remarried – a professor – and went to live with him in Dresden.'

'And Romy, where is *she* now?'

Vanderberg turned and gave his friend a look of such pain that Wilde shuddered.

'You don't think Bormann's found her?'

'I have my fears. God, I wish I could have done more for her. But there was no way of getting her out of the country. I didn't know what to say to the poor woman. All I could do was tell her to keep in touch and that I would see if there was any way of helping her. She told me she had moved out from her home in Kreuzberg and wouldn't be going back to work, and gave me her new, temporary address. After I saw you in the Adlon air raid cellar and knew you were safely arrived, I went to see Romy first thing this morning – but a cop car was there. And a neighbour said there had been a murder. A woman had had her neck snapped. He thought it was probably the landlady, but I rather think it was probably poor Romy.'

'In which case . . .'

'. . . we have to pray that she didn't talk first. Because if she did, then we're too late.'

Wilde had deep forebodings about the way this operation might go. It was already looking deeply flawed. Why, he wondered, had he been sent here in the first place? Why not send in a highly trained fighting force – go in by parachute, get out by submarine? He knew the answer, of course: this was an American operation – a marker for the coming war. And the US did not have the bases or necessary men to carry out such a mission. As things stood, sending him in openly by semi-legal means was the only option, even though his death or incarceration were the most likely outcomes.

'Where is Klara?'

'Village a little way north of Berlin. She's living with a couple named Rieger – Matthias and Maria Rieger – and has taken their name. He's a schoolteacher and she's a Hausfrau. They lived in Braundorf before and were known to the priest as good Christians who would take the baby in and give her a home. The village where they now live is called Kossertheim. They have a former farmhouse called Der Steinhof at the northern end of the village, near the river. I'm told their property is just outside the settlement, which should be to your advantage.'

'And what am I supposed to do?'

'According to Romy, the Riegers will understand the danger instantly – and will help you get the girl away. They will tell her she is being taken off to boarding school. They have known all along that this might happen one day.'

'Any ideas how to get her out of Germany?'

'You'll be told by your contact soon enough.'

'Contact?'

'I'll explain all when we're afloat.' He applied the footbrake. 'Here we are – our boat awaits.'

They had emerged from woodland along a rough but well-used track. The broad sweep of Lake Havel – a bulge in the river – lay before them. Ahead of them a single sailing boat was tied up against a long wooden jetty. Surprisingly, its sail was up, flapping in the breeze. The area was deserted. Who the hell would come out here to go sailing on a chilly day in early December, in wartime?

'What do you think?'

'I think you're mad, Jim.'

'There's method in my madness. Don't look back, but our pursuers are parked a little way behind us, in the woods. They'll find it impossible to follow us downriver. This is how you get lost, Tom. Come on, let's get the tarp off and set sail before someone decides to stop us.'

The boat was a single-master with a small cabin. Wilde looked her over with admiration. The wood was richly grained and beautifully polished; she was well looked after.

'What is she, twenty foot?' Wilde asked as they jumped aboard, pulled the tarpaulin off the stern and took positions rehearsed in many hours afloat together.

'Twenty-one, locally built. George Kennan spends a lot of time out here. In fact he was out here this morning preparing the boat for us. Come on, let's push off.' He raised his chin towards land. 'Look over there.'

Wilde had already seen the four men behind them on the track at the edge of the woods. They were making no attempt to conceal themselves now. One of them had a pistol dangling from his right hand.

And then they were as ready as they were going to be. Vanderberg untied, and they were off and under sail. A good breeze was up; the sail filled and carried them north, aided by the current.

'Where now?'

'Not far, you'll see.' Vanderberg laughed, his eyes still to landward. 'Now look at them.'

The four pursuers were standing on the jetty. Their movements suggested panic. Two of them ran back to their car, presumably to try to follow the boat downstream along riverside trails.

'They don't stand a chance,' Vanderberg said.

'What about when you bring the boat back without me – what will they do then?'

'What can they do? I'll tell them I'm a diplomat and have immunity from questioning – but of course they already know that. If they persist, I will tell them that you wanted to go exploring, that you said you'd make your own way back – and that you were a free man so what you chose to do was none of my business. I've seen them before – they're regulation Gestapo, not Bormann's men. Now let's get back to the details of what you're going to do when I drop you off.'

'Drop me off? Alone in bloody Germany with the Gestapo and SS hunting me? Good grief, Jim, this is crazy. Fantasy land. I have no transport, no papers – and I don't really know where I'm going. Tell me – did *you* suggest me for this assignment? I thought we were friends.'

'No, Tom. I believe Roosevelt suggested you. Remember you met him a couple of years back? Seems you made an impression.'

'Why don't I feel flattered?' The boat lurched to starboard and the boom almost hit his head as he ducked. 'Damn it, Jim, why exactly am I putting my life at risk to rescue one girl when thousands of others are dying unaided on the Eastern Front?'

'Because she's a ten-year-old child and she's being hunted by murderers.'

'But there's some politics here, too.'

'Inevitably, yes. This girl is important on many levels. If this works, there is potential to undermine the power base in the Nazi hierarchy. You must be able to see that.'

Wilde sighed. 'Nothing more to be said, then.'

'There is one other thing. Your contact is a woman named Sigrun Somerfeld, who has done some work for me these past two years. She has good connections and is pretty fearless. She will meet you when I leave you downriver. As soon as you go missing, you will be a wanted man. You will dress down and become an *Aüslander* – a foreign worker. She'll pick up your papers, which are being prepared even as we speak. We have a dead letter drop, from where she will retrieve them.'

'And Sigrun Somerfeld – what's her background?'

'Actually, everyone calls her Sunny – she picked the name up in America. She's German-American, you see, but she only has German citizenship. Father is a successful Berlin entrepreneur – in the oil business, I believe. Mother comes from Lexington, Kentucky. She spent her childhood flitting back and forth between Berlin and America, so got to know both cultures pretty well, but has a preference for Germany. What she can't stand is the Nazis, because they are destroying her country. She's not alone in that among certain sections of polite Berlin society. Anyway, look over there.' He pointed at the dense woodland on the far side of the river. They were more than a mile downriver from their starting point, and had gone through two bends, so were completely invisible from their pursuers. 'You'll go ashore there and get under cover of the woods as soon as you can. Sunny will be watching for you.'

Wilde didn't know what to say; this was really happening. Within moments he would be an outlaw in a country where fugitives could be thrown into the cellars of the Gestapo or the torture chambers of the SS, without access to legal protection.

Until now, Vanderberg's attitude had been jaunty. Suddenly he was serious.

'Before we part, please, do tell me about Lydia and the baby. Very little has been getting through. It must have been one heck of a wrench for them when you embarked on this mission.'

'Oh, Lydia's the same old Lydia. Hated me going, didn't try to stop me. Gave me a kiss and said it would have to do as a battle flag. As for little Johnny – well, he's not exactly a baby any more. Walking. Almost talking, I think. Could have sworn he said "Dada" the other day. What about Juliet and the boys – do you hear from them?'

'Of course. Their letters come through with the pouch. Henry and William are at school in Chicago, and Juliet's doing charity work for the Red Cross. You know how strong she is, but, well, it's not easy for either of us being apart. I'm praying I'll see them soon, though. I've already been recalled by Washington and I have my exit visa. Should be off in the next couple of days. But let's not think about that now. Say hello to Sunny. I believe with all my heart that she's trustworthy.'

Wilde nodded.

'She'll talk you through everything, but I can tell you you're going to be . . . a foreign worker from France. The Gestapo are not all the brightest, but they are hot on detail, so pay attention to everything she tells you. If you are approached, let her do all the talking or just say a few words in French. And by the way, your new name is Sable – Thomas Sable – and you are from Toulouse – a place that I know you are familiar with.'

Wilde shook his head, trying to take it all in.

'I have a hundred other questions to ask you, Jim.'

Vanderberg smiled. 'But no time. This is your stop.'

The little sailing boat moved alongside a small jetty of rotting wood. Vanderberg reached out and held the vessel steady, but didn't tie up.

'Here we are. Careful of these planks – just walk into the woods.' His smile turned to a deeply etched frown, then he leant across and touched his friend's arm. 'God go with you.'

There was a path into the woods. Wilde walked slowly. After less than a minute, a woman appeared in front of him.

'*Monsieur Sable?*'

'*Oui.*'

She immediately reverted to English, her voice soft.

'I'm Sunny, but you must always call me Frau Somerfeld. Talk quietly. I have two bicycles – we are riding to Potsdam. You will follow me. You know how to ride a bike, I take it?'

'Yes.'

'But first, remove your oilskin and put these on.'

She held up a dark blue jacket of heavy wool, the sort a working man might wear in winter, along with a knitted grey scarf and a beret. Then she handed him a pair of bicycle clips, and he fixed them around the bottom of his trousers.

Wilde obeyed her. She took the oilskin from him, then covered it in small branches and a blanket of leaves, a little way off the path.

'Now let's move. Ride slowly – for the moment, you're a workman going home from Jonas Ferret company at Charlottenburg. They use a lot of foreign labour, and you are a cook in the canteen.'

CHAPTER 7

The ride was eight miles and took just over an hour on the old black bicycles. Most of the time, Sunny Somerfeld led the way along forested paths and roads, but at other times she slowed down so that he could ride alongside her. He had a chance to study her. Her manner was that of a European aristocrat, yet her physical vitality suggested a Midwestern farm girl. It was a curious mixture, and not unattractive. He guessed she was in her late twenties – perhaps a year or two younger than Lydia. Her eyes were intelligent and constantly scanning her surroundings.

The worst moment came as they entered Potsdam. A car that Wilde was convinced was the Mercedes driven by Jim Vanderberg's pursuers was parked at the kerb. Two men leant against it, hands on pistols, studying the passing traffic and pedestrians. They glanced at Wilde and Sunny, but then their gaze drifted away.

The ride continued westwards until they came to the gateway to a large park. Sunny stopped.

'That's Sanssouci. You've heard of it?'

'Of course. Frederick the Great's summer palace.'

'My neighbour. And so it means we're almost home. I will ride fifty metres ahead. You will see me entering the house, then ride on past. In five minutes you will return. If no one is about, you will enter by way of the main gate and go down the passage to the left of the house. Prop the bike against the wall. The side door – tradesman's entrance as the English say – will be open. Act quite naturally, look like a working man come to fix the boiler or some such. What matters is that you do not raise suspicions among my neighbours, for there are some who would happily denounce me.'

Wilde half-expected a stately home but, in one of the narrower streets of this imperial town, they came to something rather more prosaic – a large three-storey house with a gated entrance. A house fit for a bourgeois businessman or lawyer, perhaps, but certainly not a palace. Sunny dismounted and he rode on as instructed. When he returned a few minutes later, the street was clear and a grey darkness was beginning to descend. Soon he was indoors, in a large reception room, standing in front of a log fire which had just been lit. The windows were blacked out and again he had that uneasy feeling of being enclosed in a sarcophagus.

Sunny was removing her coat and her woollen cap. Her hair was short, not at all conforming to the German image of beauty dictated by Hitler and Himmler. She wore a knee-length woollen skirt, grey woollen stockings and a red blouse. Not a million miles from the sort of thing Lydia wore.

'Who else is in this house?' Wilde asked.

'No one. The female servants have gone to munitions work or nursing, the men have been called up for the army. I have no help, so you will find dust everywhere. We had two maids, a butler, a chauffeur and two gardeners – and I'm afraid this house really doesn't run on its own. As you can see, I've even had to learn how to light a fire! Now first of all – do you still have your papers and passport in the name of Tomas Esser?'

'Yes.'

'Give them to me.' She held her hand out impatiently.

Wilde fished the documents from his pockets and handed them over. She glanced at them, then tossed them in the fire.

'That name is gone for ever. You are now Thomas Sable. So tell me, Monsieur Sable, what languages do you speak?'

'English, of course, and German well enough to follow a conversation. I've been working hard at it for quite some time, but I can be slow to frame an adequate response. Lack of confidence, I guess.'

Sunny nodded. 'All you need to know is *Ich bin Aüslander*. Or better, *Je suis Français*. Even the dimmest Gestapo officer should be able to work out what that means. There are plenty of free workers around, particularly French – so no one will be surprised by your presence.'

'I think I can manage *Je suis Français*.'

'This is important, you know. How good is your French?'

'It's not good.'

'You must have learnt French at school?'

Wilde looked doubtful. 'Up to a point.'

'Really? You don't speak French?' She laughed despairingly. 'Gott in bloody Himmel, why have you been sent here?'

'I've been wondering the same thing. Perhaps there was no one else?'

She shook her head in disbelief, then she gave a scornful shrug.

'Oh well, perhaps you have other skills. At least we know that you are brave . . . or stupid.'

She did not sound convinced that it was the former.

'I'm sorry, I'm just trying to help.'

'Help do what? Get us both killed? But seriously, you have *some* French, yes?'

'Schoolboy French. My German is a great deal better.'

'You do realise you're to be a foreign worker from Nantes, employed by me?'

'I heard it was Toulouse.'

'Good. At least you are paying attention. And you can drive, I take it?'

'Yes, I can drive.'

'That is important because you are to be my chauffeur.'

Wilde was surprised. He had been told in his brief training sessions that fuel was so tightly rationed in Germany that few civilians were allowed to drive. The only reason Vanderberg had been able to use a car was his diplomatic status. Wilde made the point now to Sunny Somerfeld.

'I have a special dispensation,' she said. 'As the widow of a highly decorated officer of the Luftwaffe such things are permissible.'

'God, I'm sorry – I didn't know.'

'That I had a husband and he is dead? Would you like to see the letter of condolence from Adolf? There is much you and I don't know about each other, Monsieur Sable, and perhaps it is better kept that way. But I tell you this – I am no traitor to my country. I will *never* work against Germany. I will do everything in my power to harm Hitler and the Nazis, for they are greater enemies of this country than even Winston Churchill, but nothing would ever induce me to work against my homeland. Hitler and Himmler, Heydrich and Goebbels – *they* are the traitors.'

'Your husband . . .'

She shrugged. 'His plane blew up in mid-air three months ago, while flying from Berlin to Paris. It wasn't even the English that shot him down. Officially, it was engine failure – but everyone knows there was a bomb on board. My husband had more enemies in Germany than abroad. He was a fine man, my husband, the youngest general in the Luftwaffe – Spanish Cross in Gold with Swords and Diamonds, Knight's Cross of the Iron Cross with Oak Leaves, Swords and Diamonds. Yes, Generalmajor Werner Somerfeld was a true hero with seventeen confirmed kills to his name.' She shrugged. 'But I think I would rather have my husband.'

'Of course.'

'Ah, I am crazy telling you these things. But I have always spoken my mind – why should I shut my mouth just because the criminals are in charge? It has always been my way. Of course they do not like women to have voices. We are here to breed children, wear dirndls and milk cows. That is our purpose in life.'

'Perhaps you spent too much time in America. You've grown used to free speech.'

'That must be it.'

'And your husband? This is none of my business, but you said he had enemies . . .'

'He felt the same way about the Nazis as I do. So did many among his comrades in the Luftwaffe, and many in the army. You look around you and you see cruelty and brutality, but we are better than this. Now, though, with these victories in the west and the great advances in the east, the true heroes are silenced.'

Her eyes told Wilde that she considered him a poor substitute for her heroic husband, and he wasn't about to argue.

'Look, Frau Somerfeld,' he said. 'I understand that I may not be what you were hoping for – but I had no idea what I was letting myself in for either. I was sent here to collect a package. Nothing more. Now I'm told the package is a little girl.'

She waved away his protestations as if they were of no interest and returned to the subject of his cover story.

'What you are is a free worker – and that is what your ID papers will say. So dredge up as much French as you can. When I have to speak to you in front of others, I will use very simple language to you. Look for my head movements – if I'm expecting a "*Oui, madame*" response, I will make an almost imperceptible nod of the head. Likewise, a shake for a "*Non*". And we must hope we come across no francophone members of the Gestapo.' She met his eyes. 'Now then, *voulez-vous quelque chose à boire, Monsieur Sable?*'

'*Oui, s'il vous plait.*'

'Well, that's something at least. Try to exaggerate the accent – you sound too American. God, it will be a miracle if either of us gets out of this alive.'

'What about that drink?'

She raised an eyebrow and half a smile.

'Jim Vanderberg tells me you like whisky.'

'Really? You have whisky? Nothing would suit me better.'

She fetched a bottle and two tumblers from a sideboard and poured two drinks, then clinked glasses.

'Cheers. *Prost.*'

'*Salut.*'

She downed the drink in one swallow.

'Now I must leave you and go to fetch your papers. It is safer you stay here – every trip out without them is a risk. Don't touch the blackouts – I can do without a twenty-mark fine.'

'OK. I understand.'

'When I come back, we will eat, then a few hours' sleep. In the night we will drive to Kossertheim – about an hour from here – and pick up our package. Like the Gestapo, we shall arrive just before dawn. The German school day begins at eight o'clock, so we must be there before seven-thirty at the very latest.'

'Wait a minute – can we talk a bit more? We need to think what we do when – if – we manage to remove the package? How do we look after her? More importantly, how do we get her to safety?'

'By sea, but I will give you the details later. We will talk over some supper and more whisky. Don't worry, though – I have made arrangements. In the meantime, I will find the uniform of my old chauffeur for you. He was about your height, but a little wider around the waist. A couple of stitches should fix it. It will help you, because we Germans always respect a uniform.'

'Even a chauffeur's uniform?'

'Even that.'

'Where is he now, your chauffeur?'

'Out east, I imagine, killing Slavs and Jews. He was a ghastly Brownshirt, a March martyr. He used to spy on us, but we were wise to him. It was a fine day when he was called up. You will make a wonderful replacement.'

Romy Dietrich was lying on the shit-slick floor of the pigsty. Her legs were bound, the mutilated fingers of her left hand were dripping blood. The side of her blood-streaked face and lank hair were lit by the hot white light of a hurricane lamp which stood on the ground a foot from her head. Pieces of straw were scattered in the dirt.

Otto Kalt descended to his haunches and spoke to her quietly.

'The time has come, Frau Dietrich. Now is the time to talk – to end this. An address will do – that's all I need – half a dozen little words. My friend Herr Brunner will carry this on for hours if necessary. Let us put an end to his great pleasure, shall we?'

Brunner was standing behind him, his arms folded.

Romy's eyes were closed. Tears ran in rivulets into the blood on her cheeks. Her breathing came in fast sobs.

Kalt stroked her cheek with the back of his hand.

'Thus far, I have gone easy with you, dear lady, for I know you to be a good and innocent woman. But I cannot wait for ever. Next come your other fingers, then your bones. My friend Brunner will break them one by one, big bones and small bones. He will break them slowly to increase the pain. And if you still do not talk, he will turn his attention to your fleshy parts – he likes to slice off nipples and, if allowed, the whole of each breast, like a butcher with a slaughtered pig. Except you will still be alive.'

Please, just shoot me. Had she said those words, or just imagined them?

'Not yet. You know I can't do that. Not until you tell us where we can find Klara Wolf.'

Romy had always known she would talk. She had prayed she would be able to withstand torture, but she couldn't. No one could, not this. She had had no idea such pain existed in the world. The things they had already done to her: the pain, the fear, the indignity of her own loss of bladder control. Indignity . . . why in such circumstances should anyone care that they had pissed themselves? And yet she did. Just as she cared that she had vomited on her dress in front of these men.

Her eyes opened and met his grey eyes.

'Will you kill me then? If I tell you?'

'No, of course not. I will take you back to your home in Berlin and ensure you have medical attention.'

She knew he was lying, knew he was jesting at her expense. She wanted to say the words. She *so* wanted to tell them the name of the village, but the words still stuck in her throat. What was the point in waiting longer, when she knew what the end would be: that she *would* talk, and she would die. Why should she suffer more agony so that another human being lived a few minutes longer? What did she owe the girl anyway? She had brought Klara into the world and had helped her disappear – was that not enough? Surely she did not have to do more for her.

'Can I have a sip of water, please? If I had water, I could talk.'

Kalt nodded to Brunner, who turned and trudged off without question.

'Brunner will fetch you water and you shall have a sip for every word of the address that you speak to me. Now, let me have the first one – the city where she lives. Is it Berlin? Munich? Essen? Stuttgart, perhaps?'

'Kossertheim.'

She had said the name so quietly that Kalt did not hear it properly, but he realised she had said something.

'What was that?'

'Kossertheim,' she said again.

Brunner had returned with a beaker of water. Kalt took it from him and fed a few drops to Romy with his fingers.

'Does that help? Now speak more clearly. Spell the name, because I cannot understand what you are saying.'

She said the name of the village again.

'Did you say Kossertheim?' he asked

'Yes.'

'I don't think I have heard of it.'

'Village,' she said. What was the point in stopping now? They would find Kossertheim eventually. 'Not far from Berlin.'

'That wasn't so difficult, was it? Now tell me where I will find her within this village – and what name she goes by now.'

'More water. Please, at least untie me.'

'As you wish.' He turned to the other man. 'Herr Brunner, if you would be so good.'

The bigger man grabbed her by the arm and pulled her up. She screamed with pain as her other hand, with the nails missing, scraped across the filthy stone floor. She had no strength in her arms since being hung from the wall. The cramp had been excruciating.

Kalt pulled up a three-legged stool and Brunner sat her down on it. They helped her to drink the rest of the water. Kalt's fat wife had shuffled up behind the two men and was watching them with cold eyes.

'Now,' Kalt said. 'I have done more for you than I promised. So it is time for you to keep your side of the bargain, Frau Dietrich.'

'Her name is Klara Rieger. She lives with adopted parents, Matthias and Maria Rieger. The old farm on Schorfheidestrasse. But she knows nothing of her birth – just kill me. That's all you need do.'

'I fear that's out of my hands, Frau Dietrich.'

'I beg you, sir, do not hurt the child. Do not cause her pain.'

Kalt smiled. 'Do you take us for brutes, Frau Dietrich? Of course we would not do such a thing to a child. But tell me – your name, Dietrich. Are you by any chance related to Sepp Dietrich? SS-Oberst-Gruppenführer Dietrich?'

'Yes, he is my cousin. My father was his father's first cousin. We lived close to him in Bavaria. We always called him Uncle Sepp – but he was a cousin, not an uncle.'

The words spilled out, but none of it was true – it was just something that they had joked about when first they heard of Hitler's highly esteemed bodyguard. Dietrich was a common enough name, of course, and the part of Austria where she was born and raised was but a few kilometres from Sepp Dietrich's homeland, so who knew? Perhaps, just perhaps, it might help. What harm could it do? She was already as good as dead.

'Interesting,' Kalt said. 'Most interesting.'

Brunner looked at his master expectantly. A look that Kalt knew well. Kalt shook his head.

'Not yet. Not until we know she is telling the truth.' He turned to his wife. 'Take care of this woman, Johanna, give her a little cabbage soup. This is Oberst-Gruppenführer Dietrich's cousin. A little cabbage soup and perhaps some straw to lie on until we return.' He turned his head towards Romy. 'And you, I hope you have told me the truth, for if you have not, I shall make an early Christmas gift of you to my friend Brunner here, to enjoy at his leisure.'

CHAPTER 8

The knock at the door was heavy. There was a pause and then it came again, even more forcefully. Wilde was in the large room, in front of the fire, trying to read a French book that Sunny had given him. The blackouts were firmly in place, so surely no light was getting out – nothing to disturb the air-raid people on their evening rounds, nor let any police or other officials know that someone was at home.

Wilde kept utterly still. He didn't even put the book down, imagining even the rustle of a page could be heard. The fire was lower now, but still he thought he could hear it crackling, along with the soughing of the wind down the chimney. Someone must know he was in here.

She had been gone more than three hours, so surely she should be back by now? But that couldn't be her at the door; she would simply let herself in. Silently, Wilde placed the book on a side table, then bent down and undid his laces before slipping his feet out of his shoes. He padded from the room into the large and gloomily lit entrance hallway and approached the front door. The floor was stone so there was no creaking of boards. From outside, the hammering had become more insistent. He put his ear to the door. He could hear an angry voice – a woman's voice. He did not catch most of the words, but he heard the name Somerfeld, he was sure. Someone believed Sunny was here and was demanding she open the door.

He heard another voice and relief washed over him: it was Sunny. But her voice was raised. So was the other woman's in reply. There was some kind of trouble. Caught between wanting to help Sunny and the impossibility of making his presence known, he stayed behind the door.

He heard the dull clatter of a key entering the lock and began to back away. But it all happened too fast. Even as he scuttled back towards the big room, the front door began to open.

Wilde turned at the last moment. Sunny was there, but so was another woman of a similar age, clutching the hand of a small fair-haired boy of six or seven with one hand and, in the other, holding a bright red tin. His eyes met hers. He nodded and flashed a nervous smile, then vanished into the room and shut the door behind him.

From behind the door he heard a heated argument in German – too fast and muffled for him to understand – then footsteps, another few sharp words and the sound of the front door slamming shut.

Sunny Somerfeld came through into the reception room and glared at Wilde.

'You let the bitch see you.'

'Who was she?'

'That was Hedwig Drexler. Collecting for the *Winterhilfswerk*. Winter aid for the German people. We all have to pay or have our windows smashed. German people! Most of the money goes straight to the Brown House in Munich to fill the Party's coffers. But that's not the point, Monsieur Sable – you let Frau Drexler see you.'

'I'm sorry – I didn't know what was happening.'

'Well, we are done for – or I am.'

'What did you say?'

'I told her you were an old family friend and of course she wanted to be introduced to you. I just told her she couldn't. What else was I to say? Then I just told her I was tired and didn't have time for any of this and pushed her out. Gott in bloody Himmel, she won't let it rest. Her husband Friedrich is SA – and he will know about you within the hour.'

'Maybe we should leave straight away?'

'No, I have to carry on living here. When Friedrich Drexler comes around – as most certainly he will, and probably with a band of his bully-boy friends – I shall tell him you have left to catch the train for Berlin. It still won't wash with him, but twenty Reichsmarks might help. And to think I already gave the bitch ten Reichsmarks as I was getting rid of her!'

'I'm sorry.'

'The problem is, you see, I was already a marked woman because I don't wear the Winter Aid badge or the Party badge, but this will go even further to convince them I am not one of them. It is a bad thing to be an outsider in today's Germany. There will be an inquiry. And now they've got me where they want me.'

'What will you do?'

'I suppose I'll have to retreat to the country for a few months. The thing is, I can't explain you away now. They'll want full details of who you are, your address and why you were here. And they will follow it through. You can never argue with these people. They are right and I am wrong. No trial, straight off to Ravensbrück.'

'But you must have friends in high places?'

'In the Wehrmacht, yes. Not in the Party. The Nazis revere my dead husband's name under sufferance, for fear of upsetting his Luftwaffe allies. Ach, come, let's get you fed and hidden. Bread, cheese and pickles is your lot.'

'Fine by me. And then we have to talk details.'

'It is very simple, but very dangerous too. We pick up the girl, then we will drive to the Baltic coast, where you will be taken in by a friend, the owner of a trawler. When the time is right – when mist covers the sea – he will convey you to Sweden. That is all there is to it.'

God willing, thought Wilde. But if it was so simple, why was this woman so on edge – and why did he feel such trepidation? This sensation of utter vulnerability, that events were out of his control, was new to him. He had been in difficult – even deadly – spots before, but never had he felt so unsure of himself. For a confident man not lacking in courage, it was a discomfiting experience. He was at the mercy of this woman's decisions – and, frankly, he wasn't even totally sure who she was or whether he trusted her.

She hid him in the attic. Some time later, from the depths of the dark and dusty space – full of trunks and obsolete furnishings – Wilde heard the muffled and distant sound of the front door opening. A minute later, he heard it close, and then Sunny Somerfeld appeared at the hatch and shone a torch in his direction.

'You can come out now, Monsieur Sable. We'll have no more trouble from the Drexlers.'

What had changed? As they returned to the whisky bottle and cheese sandwiches, Sunny was grinning.

'I had a sudden idea,' she said. 'I told him in a confidential whisper that you were an important person and that it would be unwise to ask too many questions. That unsettled him. Then I went further. I told him very quietly that they must tell no one, but you were, in fact, Hans Frank.'

'I think I've heard that name.'

'He is governor-general of occupied Poland and an old Party stalwart, right back to the Munich putsch. One of the filthiest and most terrifying of them all.'

'And he looks like me, does he?'

Sunny studied him, as though sizing him up, then laughed.

'No, he is nothing like you, monsieur. About the same age, perhaps, but that is all. He is much more handsome and dashing!'

'Thank you.'

'Seriously, the thing is, I told Drexler he was back on leave from Poland – and I intimated that we had a liaison and that his wife might not approve. I begged him not to tell any of the other neighbours or his SA friends, because if word got out that he was gossiping about a senior-ranking member of the Party, it would not be good for him or anyone else. That shut him up straight away. He couldn't get away from my door fast enough. If there's one thing a Brownshirt fears, it's anyone in authority over them. It is what makes the whole regime so sclerotic – everything is duplicated, everyone is scared of being denounced, so much gets left undone.'

'Why him – why Hans Frank?'

'His name just happened to be the first that came to mind. I have met him in the past at a drinks party we held here, when my husband was alive. It is just possible Frau Drexler saw him then arriving among other guests. But she could not have got a clear view of him then, nor of you this evening.'

'And this might help you in the longer term, do you think?'

'Oh, very much so. I doubt I will be pestered for any more *Winterhilfswerk* contributions for a while. *Beziehungen* – friends in high places – that is the watchword in Germany these days. It's who you know, you see. If you want service at the grocer's or you want to stop a cop beating you up, you must mention your *Beziehungen* – and the higher up they are in the Party, the better. Without *Beziehungen* you are nothing in Hitler's Germany.' She dug into her handbag and pulled out an envelope. 'This is for you,' she said. 'Inside, you will find your *Ausweis* – identity card – and your *Aufenthaltserlaubnis* or

residency permit. Also ration card, which you won't use – but you will
need to show.'

'And are they genuine?

'They are very good forgeries. Your embassy knows how to do
these things. There is one eventuality which they can't help with,
however. If anything were to happen, if we were to become separated, you would need a travel permit to use public transport – a
Polizeiliche Erlaubnis. But you would need to apply for it. So I can't
help you with that – and nor can Jim Vanderberg. Let us make sure
this all works first time, as planned.'

Romy Dietrich was bound to a chair in the large, dark room
that served as the Kalts' kitchen. A stench of cooking grease and
boiled meat hung in the air. Kalt's wife was feeding her soup
from a bowl.

Her hands were tied behind her back and the fingers on her left
hand were pulsing with agony where her nails had been drawn out
slowly, one by one. Johanna Kalt had not bothered to bathe her
wounds, nor bandage her. Nor did she utter a word as she fed her;
she was merely following her husband's orders to the letter – feeding his prisoner cabbage soup.

'Do you think I might wash a little, Frau Kalt?' Romy pleaded.
'You could bring me a bowl of water to the table and leave my feet
bound. I couldn't possibly escape. My wounds, you see . . .'

The large farmwife looked at her with indifference and continued to hold another spoonful in front of her face, waiting for Romy
to stop talking and open her mouth.

'At least give me a little bread. Surely you could spare me a little
bread – one human being to another. You are a woman like me –
perhaps you are a mother, dear lady. I promise I will not say a word
to your husband.'

Johanna Kalt thrust the spoon forward as soon as Romy had finished speaking. The metal banged against her teeth and she quickly opened her mouth to accept the soup. It was not the worst food Romy had tasted in wartime Germany, but she didn't really want it. A cup of water and bread with its wholesome solidity would have been far more welcome.

The farmwife shrugged and took away the remains of the soup, to go with a pile of other dishes and bowls at the side of a large ceramic sink. She wiped the soup from her hands on her grubby housecoat and set about untying Romy's feet from the legs of the chair, and then retying them, ankle to ankle. Frau Kalt stood back for a moment, perhaps wondering how to do this. Even in her pain and distress, Romy could not help noticing the smell of the woman, as though she had not washed for months.

Johanna Kalt made up her mind. She pushed the chair over sideways with her captive still sitting on it. Romy was flung to the floor and grunted with pain as her shoulder hit the sawdust-strewn linoleum. Without ceremony, Frau Kalt knelt behind her and loosened her hands, effectively releasing her from the chair. A second later, she pulled her wrists together.

Romy tried to fight against her hands being bound, but the woman was used to controlling powerful farm animals and was far too strong. She bound her wrists together tightly, then untied her feet again and pushed her, stumbling, from the room, towards a small pantry.

Sunny Somerfeld's car was a large grey Horch cabriolet with the soft top pulled up for the colder months. An expensive car, fit for a Luftwaffe Generalmajor and now for his widow, even though she was living in somewhat reduced circumstances, with no servants and little status.

The car was kept at the side of the house and had a coating of mud and oil which failed to detract from its handsome appearance. This was a fine car, even if the lack of a chauffeur had led to its being neglected. Wilde took the wheel, a peaked cap on his head and epaulettes on the shoulders of his chauffeur's uniform. The outfit wasn't such a bad fit. The trousers would have stayed up even without braces, and the jacket was not too loose. The cap was a little large, but nothing that a strip of newspaper tucked inside could not rectify.

'*Allons-y, monsieur.*'

'*Oui, madame.*'

The night was dark and quiet, the streets of Potsdam unlit, and no bombers or searchlights in the sky. Wilde drove north and they were soon out of town, skirting the Havel lakes, through the broad-leafed woodlands of Brandenburg, now stripped down to their winter nakedness. Wilde took the roads at a steady speed; nothing to disturb local police. The one thing that concerned them above all was the likelihood of meeting checkpoints. They had a story ready – Frau Somerfeld had been to a party at a great house in Potsdam and was returning to her country estate near Neustrelitz. A simple tale, and immediately plausible, so long as her questioners did not dig any deeper. And she had a pass from the president of the Berlin police allowing her to use the car and acquire petrol, in recognition of her husband's outstanding service to the Reich.

They gave a wide berth to the Krampnitz armoured division headquarters, at Fahrland just north of Potsdam, but they did meet roadblocks: one near another military installation, two at large river bridges and at a major guard post close to the Heinkel aircraft works at Oranienburg. In each case, the road was obstructed by movable barriers of barbed wire set between steel struts. The soldier demanded the same thing each time: '*Halt! Ausweis!*' Their papers were perused thoroughly but politely and found to be in order. Sunny did the talking and her explanation that Wilde was a free worker from France was accepted unquestioningly. Perhaps the story was helped by slipping in the fact that she was the widow of a Wehrmacht general, a hero of the Third Reich. How could such a woman and her chauffeur be anything but what they seemed? The blockade was moved aside and they were waved on, with good wishes for a safe journey.

In the meantime, Sunny directed proceedings from the rear seat, dictating the route in the autocratic manner of a great lady which, Wilde conceded, she was. Certainly she had been a woman of influence at other times in her life, even if the present regime kept her on the sidelines and watched her with a wary eye.

In one village, near the town of Oranienburg, they came across a sign – stretched on cord right across the street – saying: '*Juden sind hier unerwünscht!*' Wilde had enough German to know that it translated as 'Jews are not wanted here'.

Sunny leant forward. 'You understand that?'

'Yes.'

'You'll see plenty more of those.'

Although the roads were mostly deserted – save when they met columns of army vehicles trundling eastwards – the journey took a lot longer than Sunny had anticipated. She had suggested it was an hour's drive, but by the time they entered the village of Kossertheim, they had been on the road for more than two and it was already after 7 a.m.

'Now where?' Wilde demanded.

The drive here, with the constant threat of being exposed, would have shredded the nerves of most people. But Wilde had been surprised to find that he was becoming increasingly alert and ready for whatever lay ahead. He reasoned that it was the fighter in him.

Once the training was over, once you were in the ring, gloved up, your primal instincts took over and you were at your strongest, fastest and sharpest. There was no longer any room in your head for fear.

'The house is supposed to be at the north end of the village,' she said. 'Slow right down – be prepared to go straight on if all is not well.'

Much of the country they had travelled through was forested, gradually giving way to flat, open farmland, much like the fens and fields of Cambridgeshire. Now the countryside was beginning to change again.

'We are close to the Schorfheide forest here,' she said. 'A hunting ground.'

This village, like many they had passed through, was mostly made up of dull farmworkers' cottages, and had very little charm. Wilde supposed there must be some better properties away from the main road, but they were not visible.

Then they were through the village, the headlamps illuminating a tree-lined avenue that stretched straight ahead for a mile or more before disappearing into another area of woodland. The sky was still dark, but the horizon to the east was beginning to glow with the first inklings of sunrise.

'We must have passed it,' Wilde said.

'No, carry on. I was told it was well beyond the village. There should be a rough track on the left. The farm is called Der Steinhof, but there's no sign by the road, only a pair of white boulders on either side of the track.'

Wilde slowed down even further, the engine growling smoothly. He didn't want to miss the track, but his mind was also racing ahead. What if it was the wrong house? They couldn't afford that at any price.

'Here,' Sunny said, her voice rising a notch. 'I think that's it – look, two large stones.'

Wilde stopped. 'I'm not going to drive in. We should park the car and approach on foot, check out the lay of the land. They're not expecting visitors.'

Sunny Somerfeld was silent for a few moments, then shrugged. 'I don't know . . .'

'Trust me on this,' he said.

CHAPTER 9

Wilde parked the car off the road, a hundred yards down from the two white boulders that proclaimed the entrance to the farm track.

There was enough light from the approaching dawn for them to walk without a flashlight.

He was acutely aware that neither of them knew for sure what they were walking into.

'So you have never spoken to the Riegers?'

'Everything I know comes from Jim Vanderberg. He knows me too well – he knew that I couldn't refuse to help this child.'

Wilde increased his pace.

A delivery van and a car were parked in the driveway. The black-outs were still up at the windows, but they were not well secured, and Wilde could see chinks of yellow light showing at the edges.

The farm track had taken them far from the road – at least half a mile. They had walked to the edge of the field, then into a wood. Now they stood at the edge of a clearing, watching the house.

'Why do they have a van?' Wilde said.

'Why not? It is a useful thing. Perhaps they use it to take produce to market.'

'But Matthias Rieger is a schoolteacher.'

'Ach, in the countryside, everyone has a few animals or grows things to sell.'

'Well, from the lights, I guess they're all up, probably having breakfast. You go and knock at the door, Frau Somerfeld. Better a woman alone than a strange man who doesn't speak good German. I'll wait back here until you signal me to come.'

Sunny Somerfeld crossed the forecourt of the farm. The building looked at least two hundred years old but had been renovated quite recently. It was three storeys high and a great deal more attractive than the houses Wilde had seen in the villages on the way there. Not a manor house by any means, but the property of a reasonably well-to-do farmer at some point in its history.

Her knock was tentative, and there was no answer. She knocked again, a little louder. Still nothing. Finally, she rapped hard. When there was no reply, she turned to Wilde and shrugged. He made a motion with his hand as though twisting a doorknob. She nodded, and the door opened.

Light flooded out. She turned back to Wilde.

'Call out to them,' he said, his voice little more than a whisper.

She stepped inside the house.

'Frau Rieger . . . Herr Rieger.' Her voice was friendly and unthreatening. 'Hallo?'

And then she was staggering backwards out of the door, her hand to her mouth, moaning as if overcome by some unspoken horror.

Matthias Rieger had prayed that this day would never come. He and Maria were devout Christians and each night they had knelt together by their bed and communed with the Lord, entreating Him to protect their adopted daughter and keep her safe. She had, after all, been a gift from God, long after they had resigned themselves to childlessness.

Now, it seemed, their prayers had not been enough. The barking of the dog in the middle of the night had seen to that. God giveth, man taketh away.

But, of course, it hadn't been God who delivered the baby to their welcoming arms. It had been dear Father Huber and the likeable but rather earnest midwife, Romy Dietrich.

They knew the truth about the baby's birth and had passed it on to Matthias and Maria, swearing them to secrecy. Even before the man with the toothbrush moustache became Chancellor, they knew it was a secret that would have to be kept for ever, for he was surrounded by dangerous and desperate people. But secrets have a habit of eventually emerging into daylight. And then ... And then ...

Matthias Rieger had been considering retirement for several years now. He was sixty and his poor, ailing wife was sixty-two, and she required more of his time to care for her, especially with the needs of a ten-year-old to be considered. But it was not just these matters that made him want to leave the teaching profession. He was also increasingly uncomfortable with the National Socialist curriculum. Why did the boys and girls have to wear the uniforms of the Hitler Youth and the League of Girls in the classroom? Why did the school principal insist that every teacher should give lectures on race at least twice a week, even if their subject had no possible connection? The children they taught knew nothing of these people from other countries and so, in their trusting way, they soaked all this poison up and rejoiced in the knowledge that they, as good Nordic Aryan Germans, were superior to all.

One day Klara came home with a song that she and her classmates had been taught. She sang it to Matthias and Maria at the dinner table: *Adolf Hitler is our saviour . . . for Hitler we live, for Hitler we die . . . Hitler is our Lord, who rules a bold new world . . .*

Matthias almost found himself almost hating the girl. Whatever else he thought of Hitler, he knew that Jesus Christ alone was his Lord and Saviour. In other circumstances, he would have stormed into the principal's office to demand the song be banned. But he couldn't do that; he could never draw attention to himself in any way, for that route would lead to disaster.

Another thing he had had to do was to give up the Roman Catholicism of his birth and baptism in favour of worshipping in the local Lutheran church. There were no Catholics in this village, so it was safer that way. The only thing they held on to was the crucifix above their bed.

Nor could he give up teaching. With so many young men disappearing from the profession to join the Wehrmacht or the SS, the principal had made it quite clear that retirement was out of the question until the war in the east had ended. And he had the backing of the local SA leader in this. Again, Matthias Rieger had to accept his lot, and it had kept them safe.

Now, tonight, there was the barking of the dog.

Bismarck was a good dog, a rottweiler. A true and faithful guard dog with a loud and aggressive bark that reverberated around the house if any vehicle or person came within a hundred metres of the property. Rieger woke instantly. It wasn't just the dog, there was the sound of a vehicle engine and the crunch of wheels on the track. He was out of bed within seconds. He tried to alert Maria, but she was ill and could not easily be woken. There was simply no time to shake her awake and warn her.

So he went straight through to Klara's room and pulled her from the bed.

'Pappi?'

'Come on, Klara, it's time. You know what to do.'

'But, Pappi, it's dark. I'm tired.'

He carried her downstairs in his arms. There wasn't even time for her to get dressed and so she was still in her pretty new nightgown. In the corridor leading to the back door, he grabbed her coat and buckled shoes – the shoes she had put out for St Nicholas the previous day. Now he helped her push her feet into them and wrapped the coat over her shoulders. Then he urged her out of the door and told her to go, as fast as she could.

'Run, Klara. Go to the place.'

'Come with me, Pappi.' Her eyes were wide and afraid. 'I don't want to go alone . . .'

'I can't – I'm too slow. Go, Klara. You must go.'

He pushed her across the little lawn into the night. And all the time, Bismarck barked from his post in the hallway at the front of the house.

Klara disappeared into the darkness of the woods just as he heard the sound of the front door being forced open. A shot rang out and the barking ceased.

And then there came the rough voices of men, and the clang of metallic heels on stone.

Wilde ran towards the house. Sunny Somerfeld was on her knees, shaking. He pushed past her into the light of the hallway. He saw that the door was damaged, but at first sight he could not understand what she had seen that had so terrified her. He looked to the left and immediately understood. Blood seemed to be everywhere. It streaked the floor and spattered the wallpaper. The corpse of a large brown and black dog was splayed across the floor, half in and half out of the little side room. Its head had been reduced to a bloody pulp.

His stomach was churning, not so much at the sight of the dead dog, but at the prospect of what else he might find.

He carried on into the house. A woman's body lay lifeless at the bottom of a staircase, a mass of grey, untamed hair covering her face. Wilde put fingers to her neck but felt no pulse. Carefully, he stepped over her and crept upstairs. There was no sound, but that did not mean that there was no one up there waiting for him.

The landing was large with three doors opening on to it – and a staircase leading to the top floor.

He went through the rooms one by one. Each had its wardrobe doors thrown open, every laundry chest had been rifled, beds had been turned upside down. The little girl's room was the most poignant of all. Her dolls were scattered across the floor, her clothes flung about, the sheet and duvet ripped from the bed. The only thing untouched was a framed portrait of the Führer, gazing down balefully on the scene of chaos and destruction from above the bed.

Where were they? If the dead woman was Maria Rieger, then where was her husband and where was Klara?

More than that, what about the people who had come here? Was that their van outside? If so, then that meant they were still somewhere in the vicinity, and, judging from the state of the dog, armed with heavy-duty weapons, while Wilde didn't even have a knife to defend himself.

He went quickly upstairs to the top floor and found the same situation: the rooms had been ransacked. Wilde hurried downstairs.

Sunny was at the foot of the stairs, staring with dismay at the woman's body.

'Come on,' he said. 'We need to get out of here.'

'We were too slow.'

He clutched her arm. 'Outside.'

At the front of the house, he went up to the van and put his hand on the bonnet. It was warm but not hot. This was the vehicle that had brought the killers, but it might have been some while ago. One thing was certain; they were still around here somewhere.

And then he heard a gunshot. In the echoing stillness of dawn, it seemed close by, but Wilde's instinct told him it came from deep in the woods at the back of the property. Sunny clutched at him in terror. He put an arm around her and quickly guided her towards the woods where they could conceal themselves. Hopefully their presence here had not been noticed. Thank God they had left the car on the main road. What now?

'Go back to the car,' Wilde whispered. 'You'll be safer there.'

'No, please,' Sunny begged. 'I don't want to be on my own. I . . . I wasn't expecting anything like this.'

'OK, then we work our way through the woods towards the back of the house. But we mustn't make a sound. Do you understand?'

She nodded.

'I'll go ahead – ten metres ahead. If I'm discovered, if there's a shot or voices, then you stop where you are, stay in the undergrowth and remain very, very still. No reason for us both to get killed.'

The first glimmerings of sunrise had lit the bare trunks and branches. They could see where they were going through the gaunt mass of trees, but it also meant that they could be seen. The ground was covered with a thick layer of dried leaves, which made moving silently almost impossible. But after several agonising minutes, Wilde reached the back of the house. He waited for Sunny to catch him up. The back door of the house was open and light was streaming out. It looked as if someone had left in a hurry.

Suddenly he gasped, feeling a hand on his shoulder.

CHAPTER 10

'*Sshh, schweigen Sie,*' a voice said, low and insistent. '*Bleib ruhig.*'

Keep quiet . . . Stay calm.

Wilde turned in an instant, his hand reaching for the man's throat, before stopping himself. Barefoot and wearing woollen pyjamas, the man he saw in front of him was old and grey.

'*Die Bewaffneten sind dort drüben.*' He was pointing to the right – to the west. *The gunmen are over there.*

'Herr Rieger?'

He nodded and put a finger to his lips. 'Sshh.' Then he sank into a crouch, urging Wilde and Sunny to do likewise with the flat of his hand. 'Who are you?' he asked in German.

'Friends. We came to warn you,' Sunny said. 'But too late, it seems.'

'I can see you are not with the gunmen. But I ask again, who *are* you?'

'I am Frau Somerfeld, this is Monsieur Sable. But we are all in grave danger, Herr Rieger.'

'We are safe for the moment – they are four hundred metres away.'

He turned to Wilde and began talking in rapid French. Wilde's blank expression gave him away immediately.

'You are not French,' Rieger said. 'I am a languages teacher – I know the look on a boy's face when he cannot understand me.'

There was no use pretending.

'He's American,' Sunny said. 'We discovered there was a threat to Klara. We are here to help you get her to safety.'

Rieger nodded. He gripped Wilde's arm.

'Please, can I ask you . . . you have been in the house. Did you see Maria, my wife? I had to leave her to save the child.'

For Wilde's benefit, he had switched languages to perfect, though accented, English.

He didn't want to distress the old man, but Wilde had no option.

'I'm sorry,' he said. 'She is dead. It looks as though she fell down the stairs.'

Rieger nodded slowly. 'More likely thrown. Those filthy bastards.' His Adam's apple was moving, as though he were struggling to contain his emotions. 'I heard nothing, so I feared . . . the worst.' The tears in his eyes were bright in the dawn light. Then he seemed to steel himself. 'That is for later. Now we must move. Follow me – I hear and see them. I think they have heard us for they are starting to come this way – two armed men.'

'Where are we going?'

'I am drawing them away from Klara. Over the years I have made it my business to know every centimetre of these woods – and so I deliberately snap a small branch or make some other small sound, and they follow me instead of her. Come.'

Matthias Rieger moved eastwards, towards the rising light. He was bent forward, like an animal. He might not have been young, but he moved smoothly and it was clear to Wilde that he was telling no more than the truth when he said he knew these woods well. Now and then he stopped and urged them forward.

'Look back – over there. They are lost, but we must carry on.'

'What of Klara? Where is she?'

'All in good time, when it is safe. She knows what she is doing. We have rehearsed this on many occasions.'

'Does she know *why* she has to hide?'

'No. Only that there are dangerous men in the world. She believes every child is given this secret escape route by her parents, for that is what I have told her. Now then, you must have come by car – where is it?'

Romy Dietrich lay quietly in a pitch-dark room, her hands still tightly bound and her ankles retied so harshly that they were beginning to feel numb. But she was still alive, which surprised her. Did they really think she might be related to Sepp Dietrich? Was there a slight chance she might be spared because of it? Logic told her not – that the opposite was probably true, that they wouldn't dare keep her alive if they thought for a moment that she could denounce them to one of Hitler's most senior men. The only reason she was alive was that Otto Kalt wasn't certain she had told him the truth about Klara's whereabouts. If they didn't find her, they would return and torture her more; if they did get to Klara, then they would come back to finish her off.

Frau Kalt was an obedient wife. She had fed the prisoner cabbage soup as ordered and had then thrown straw onto the floor as a bed for her prisoner. Obedient to a fault, perhaps, but not the cleverest. Yes, she had bound her captive hand and foot – her husband's final instruction, received in bovine silence like every other communication – but she had not tied her prisoner *to* anything. After a while, lying in agony in the dark, the realisation hit Romy like a sudden shaft of light. She tried moving and discovered that, with great difficulty and constant pain, she could propel herself forward by bending her knees and extending her elbows.

She could hear Frau Kalt moving about elsewhere in the house. There was some clattering as though a metal pan had been dropped, then light as the farmwife opened the door and looked in on her captive. Satisfied that all was well, she went out again and the next thing Romy heard was the sound of an outside door opening and closing.

Whether Frau Kalt had gone back to her work in the piggery or had found some other chore, Romy had no idea. But if she was to have any chance of escape, she had to take it now. She summoned all her remaining strength and edged herself towards the door. It was pushed closed, but there was no latch so she was not locked in.

Suppressing the instinct to cry out in pain every time her bloody, throbbing fingers scraped the floor, she turned on her side and managed to ease the door open. Perhaps there was a God after all, something she had come to doubt these past hours.

It was only two metres to the large farmhouse kitchen where she had been fed the soup. Still flat on the ground, she raised her head to get her bearings. There were kitchen tools, knives and other implements, but they were all out of reach. There had to be something. Dear God, any sharp-edged instrument might work. But where could she find such a thing?

Outside, perhaps? Scythes, sickles, shears? But could she even get there? More importantly, could she get outside without being noticed by Frau Kalt. The barn used as a piggery was fifty metres across a slurry-strewn courtyard, but closer to the house she had noted several smaller buildings – most likely workshops, a tack room or stores.

She had nothing to lose by trying it. Perhaps the dim light was on her side. But her first problem was how to get up – and get outside. She had heard the back door shut. She couldn't reach the handle, could she?

If only there was some way of standing up. Was that possible? So far, it hadn't seemed so, but then she thought of where she was: the interior kitchen doorway. The pain in her spine, her wrists, her ankles and fingers was getting worse, but she managed to wedge herself sidelong between the jambs so that her back was against one side and her bound feet against the other, giving her leverage. Centimetre by centimetre, fighting against the agony and the ebbing of her strength, she managed to raise herself to her feet. She was breathing heavily, her whole body was screaming in pain, but at last here she was, standing up on bound feet. Now she could hop like a rabbit.

She scanned the kitchen for tools. The best one was a bloodsmeared carving knife left on a butcher's block near the window. No curtains or blackout here in the middle of the countryside, which meant that if she was in front of the window and if the woman came across the yard, she would be seen instantly.

She would have to risk it. She hopped to the block and, using her nose, knocked the knife to the floor. Now she had to get herself down again, which was easy enough. She gritted her teeth and grasped the handle of the knife in her undamaged hand, then bent her knees and pushed her hands as low as they would go to saw at the cords that bound her feet.

The knife was sharp and within two or three minutes – each second of which felt like an hour – her ankles were free and she was able to stand up. Unfortunately there was no way of dealing with the wrist knots. She wanted to keep the knife though, so she twisted her arms around and tucked it behind her in the waistband of her skirt.

She opened the back door, looked around as well as she could in the darkness. Light came from the barn, but she saw no sign of Frau Kalt. To her left was the road along which she was pretty sure she had been brought here in the back of the van. So that had to be the way to go.

Romy Dietrich began to run.

*

Wilde and Sunny followed Matthias Rieger through the trees towards the main road until they could see a strange glowing light a hundred metres ahead of them. Wilde had a sinking feeling that he knew what this meant but before he could urge them to stop the whole forest suddenly lit up – trees silhouetted against dazzling yellow and white – and then, a second later, they heard the roar of an explosion ripping through the morning air as the fuel tank on the Horch went up. The gunmen had got there first.

'So,' Matthias Rieger said. 'No car. And now they know I am not alone.'

They crouched in the undergrowth, the smell of rotting leaves and damp earth obliterated by the stench of burning gasoline. Wilde was feeling increasingly naked without a weapon. A slender five-foot branch lay at his feet. He picked it up and swung it back and forth. It had a pleasing heft.

'Are you sure there are only two gunmen?' Wilde asked.

'No, I am not sure. Come, I think I have played their game long enough. It is not so easy with three of us, so we must split up. I will take you to safety and then you two must go your own way.'

He changed direction, turning from east to north, and signalled Wilde and Sunny to crouch lower, and to take care with every step. For fifteen minutes they moved like this, slowly zigzagging in a northerly direction. Every few seconds they heard a speculative gunshot. The crack of a rifle, then for the first time a burst of sub-machine gun fire. Every shot sounded like a cannon, the blast echoing off the trees.

'MP 40,' Rieger said, listening to the rattle of the machine pistol. His lined face became yet more drawn and his brow creased in thought. Finally he looked up. He had made a decision. 'You must go to Klara. These men will not give up, so I will lead them away westwards while you turn east. They may be killers, but they are not huntsmen. It is our fortune that they do not know how to stalk prey. But you must get away before full daylight. Then it will be easier for them.'

'Where is Klara?' Wilde asked.

'All being well, she should be four kilometres from here, to the north-east, by a lake. There is a jetty there. She is near there, close to a very large oak, in a cave beneath a concealed trapdoor. I learned about digging trenches and hides on the Western Front. Were you there, Monsieur Sable?'

Wilde hadn't been. He had been in America, safe, while his English public school friends were being called up and marched off to the murderous battlefields. He sometimes thought his shame would never be absolved. Perhaps now was his chance.

'Where shall we meet you?'

'You won't. They don't know who you are. But me? They can find out everything about me from the village. People talk – they are scared not to. I do not know who you are, but I have no choice but to trust you and so I must pray that Klara will be in good hands with you. I have taught her languages. Her English is good. When you have her in a place of real safety, perhaps you will find some way to let me know.'

His words hung in the cool morning air. Would he still be alive to receive such news?

'No, come with us. She will be waiting for you.'

The elderly schoolteacher smiled and shook his head sadly.

'I must stay with Maria.'

Wilde took Herr Rieger's hands between his own. He was a man he would like to have known better, to have talked with over a few glasses of whisky or schnapps.

'I'm sorry, Herr Rieger. Truly. If only we had arrived earlier . . .'

'Oh, you know, it really would have made no difference.' Rieger managed a sad smile and squeezed Wilde's hands back. 'Maria was too ill to run.'

Sunny had been hanging back. Now she crept forward. Rieger took her hands as Wilde had taken his.

'And you, dear lady, my heartfelt thanks go with you for what you are trying to do.'

'We will need precise instructions if we are to find your daughter, Herr Rieger,' she said.

Her voice, so confident back in Potsdam, was tremulous now. Perhaps unsurprising, given the events in the house and this deadly cat-and-mouse game in the woods.

'You must get to the road and go still further northwards – a thousand five hundred metres further, all the while staying in the trees for cover in case of passing traffic. You will see a woodland path on your right. It is unsigned, but there is a cross – a small wooden cross nailed to a tree to mark the way. Take the path and stay on it until you come to a lake. On the southern bank, two hundred metres from the western extremity, there is the jetty I mentioned. It is old and ruined. Look directly south and you will see the oak tree. It is much larger than anything else in the area, a little way into the woods from the lakeside, and it is marked with another cross, this time carved into the bark, at a height of two metres. The hide is on the far side of the tree at a distance of three metres. The top of the trapdoor has a camouflage of leaves and other woodland detritus. If you were not looking for it, you would not see it. But you *will* be looking for it.'

'Thank you.'

'She is a brave girl, but like all children she has her own ideas and is no saint. She will be cold and scared, for she has only her nightgown and coat and a pair of shoes. But say to her these words:

Bismarck loves carrots. That is our code. Bismarck is – was – our beautiful dog, and he did eat carrots when we cooked them. Once you have spoken those words, she will know to trust you.'

Wilde nodded.

Rieger's eyes bored into Wilde. It was a look of infinite sadness but there was hope in it, too. The eyes were entreating him: don't let me down.

'God go with you both,' he said. 'You are here at great risk to yourselves, Monsieur Sable, and you, dear lady, for which I thank you. I pray with all my heart that you can get Klara to safety. She is an innocent in all this – a pawn in the game of a powerful man who fears her more than anything or anyone else in the world.'

'Martin Bormann?'

He nodded. 'I wanted to leave Germany, but Maria would not have it. I never told her how great was the threat we faced. I knew, you see, that if he ever found us, he would not stop until he had killed her. She is living evidence of his own murderous crimes. I could not share this with Maria. She has never been a healthy woman – her nerves would not have taken it.'

'You can trust us to do all we can,' Wilde said. 'That's all I can promise. God go with you, too, Herr Rieger.'

'Just one more thing – do not carry on walking towards the east along the line of the lake or you will almost certainly come across a great number of soldiers. There is an army training camp there. And the Luftwaffe has a fighter base nearby.'

From somewhere to the south they heard another burst of machine-gun fire. It seemed random, but vaguely in their direction, for bullets smacked into the trees nearby. Wilde instinctively dropped to the ground, as did Matthias and Sunny. The volley had been close. Too close.

In the dim morning light, he looked to his side, to Matthias Rieger, and felt sick to the stomach. A bullet had hit Rieger. His head and face were a mass of blood. He had been hit with some sort of exploding bullet, the same as the one that had torn his guard dog apart.

Wilde urgently grabbed Sunny's hand.

'Move.'

CHAPTER 11

A pair of jackdaws rose lazily into the air, replete from a feast of carrion. The sun was up now, shimmering across the waters of the lake. The sounds of shooting had grown more and more distant and then ceased.

Wilde had walked ahead by a couple of hundred metres; now he was sure they had reached their destination, so he turned and waited for Sunny to catch up with him. As she approached, he reappraised her. The upper-class flying ace's widow no longer cut the domineering figure that she had in Potsdam a few hours earlier. Her skirt and wool stockings were torn, her hair was a tangled mess and her hands and face had cuts and scratches from pushing her way through the undergrowth. On meeting her, he had thought her rather attractive in a no-nonsense American sort of way. Not pretty, but oozing self-assurance. Now she appeared to have lost her confidence.

'I think this is it,' he said, pointing to the woods across a narrow clearing that edged the lake. One oak tree stood out. 'Can you see the cross cut in the oak?'

She nodded.

'Come on, then. Let's find the poor girl.'

'First, Monsieur Sable – Tom – I must apologise to you. I fell apart back there. I was no use to you or Herr Rieger.'

He understood. Having himself been in the heat of the action before, he knew how the stoutest of hearts could falter. He put an arm around her shoulder, comforting her like a comrade, not as a man comforts a woman.

'It was like a battleground. You saw terrible things.'

'So what are we going to do? We have no car, and we're halfway between Berlin and the Baltic coast. I think we need to know what we are going to do before we introduce ourselves to her. We must look confident if she is to trust us – and I tell you, I no longer feel sure about anything.'

Wilde was thinking much the same. Until now they had been pre-occupied with evading the enemy. But with the guns gone silent, he allowed himself to hope that the men were no longer on their trail. And so he was racking his brain for the next move. One thing seemed obvious: they needed another car or some other form of transport. They couldn't simply walk to the coast, could they? Not with a ten-year-old girl in tow. But to steal a car would be a huge risk.

From what Sunny had said about the need for travel papers, a train was impossible too.

First though, there was the question of whether the girl would even accept her rescuers. She might very well refuse to go with them and there would be nothing they could do to force her. Had he been in her position when he was a child, he could not imagine agreeing to go away with a pair of strangers. But there was no other option for her now; there was no going home for Klara Rieger, née Wolf – real name Raubal. Death waited for her there. So, one way or another, she had to be persuaded that it was in her best interests to accompany them.

'We need a car,' he said. 'But if we steal one we'll unleash every police officer in northern Germany. Maybe the army, too. Can cars be hired?'

'No.'

'Perhaps we could buy one. Surely a town would have cars for sale?'

'Very few people even have permission to drive. Anyway there would be great suspicion and the Gestapo would be on to us soon enough.'

'This is getting us nowhere. How well do you know this area, Frau Somerfeld?'

'Well enough. I have friends with country houses around here. One place in particular where my husband and I used to spend weekends.'

'Would they help you?'

'Gott in bloody Himmel, Tom – we can't just call on my friends!'

'All we want to do is borrow a car. You could return it within a day. Anyway, do you have a better idea?'

'I'm really not sure. I don't like it.'

'What are their politics?'

She was frowning. 'Well, they are not part of any underground resistance. Like many people, they just keep their heads down and look forward to the day this is all over and the criminals are all dead or in prison rather than running the country. They would certainly not help us if they knew the truth about us and what we are doing. And as for you, Tom – well, they are educated people who speak French. They'd see through you in an instant.'

'How far are these friends from here?'

'Ten to twelve kilometres, I think. Two, three hours walk.'

'We have to do it. We'll work out a story on the way.'

Wilde tapped the ground with his stick. The trapdoor was well hidden under a covering of brush and leaves and it was ten minutes before they found it. When they prised it open, Wilde saw movement in the darkness of a small underground chamber, as the occupant shrank back into a corner.

Sunny knelt at the edge of the pit.

'Fräulein Rieger – Klara – we are your friends.' Her voice was warm and encouraging, like a nurse or a nanny. 'Your father has sent us.' She was speaking softly, in German.

The chamber was at least eight feet deep and six feet long by four feet wide, with a couple of steps leading down into the darkness. Like a front-line bunker, it had supporting beams, walls fortified with planking and duckboards at the base. It was reasonably dry but the smell was musty and it was cold and unfriendly. No place for a child.

Wilde wondered how long the hide had been there. At what age did Matthias Rieger first bring her here and instruct her in its use? He must have trained her well over the years to seek out this sanctuary without question when danger threatened. But how long would she have stayed here if they had not come and found her?

Right now she was terrified. Like a cornered animal.

The girl did not say a word, but her eyes were wide. Wilde was sure he could hear her teeth chattering. Poor child, she must have been cowering in the darkness for an hour, perhaps two. She must be freezing. Of course, he could step down into the cave and lift her out, but much better if she were to emerge of her own volition; it would not be a good start to use physical coercion of any kind on the girl. If this was to work, if they were to preserve the 'package', she would have to learn to trust them in very short order.

Sunny had a box of matches and lit one beneath her own face, so that the girl could see her, and smiled kindly. She lit two more.

'Won't you come out, dear Klara? We are here to help you. And I know I must say to you that Bismarck loves carrots.'

Wilde heard a gasp of recognition from the girl.

'Come on, *liebling*, come out. My name is Sunny, and this is my friend Tom. Your father, Matthias, sent us. Bad men came to your house, but now you will be safe with us. I promise you this with all my heart.'

Slowly, the girl's head rose from the gloom. She had long wavy fair hair, though now it was caked in mud and dust. And then came her face, wide-eyed and full, much like the picture of her true mother Geli Raubal – the one Wilde had been shown by Jim Vanderberg in the American embassy.

She climbed the steps that her father had built, looked nervously in all directions, then stepped out into the light of day. She was wearing a coat over her nightgown, and school shoes without socks and she was shivering.

Sunny smiled and held out her hand.

Klara looked at the woman's hand, then gave a stiff little bow of her head, but instead of taking the hand, she threw out her right arm in a salute.

'Heil Hitler,' she said.

Sunny seemed taken aback, but quickly responded in kind.

'Heil Hitler.'

Wilde did the same. He had seen the picture of the Führer in the girl's bedroom, and he knew that the children of Germany were taught in school to believe that Adolf Hitler was the father of the nation. This was not the time to try to disabuse Klara of all she had been told.

'Will you come with us, Klara?'

The girl nodded. Her shoulders were back now, her fear controlled.

'We have a long walk.'

They made their way to the far side of the lake, then strode out northwards through woods and back into open farmland. If they saw a road, they avoided it. The flat fields, rivers and woodlands of Germany stretched out endlessly; one could almost imagine that the sea must be just beyond the horizon. But that was wishful thinking.

The countryside was coming alive in a rush. Teams of workers marched along the roads and farm tracks. Fields were soon full of men and women bringing in winter crops. Ploughmen were out with their horses, preparing the soil. Wilde tried to skirt these fields and keep them out of sight. He stopped his two companions at the edge of a field. Dozens of men and women were out among the furrows, harvesting a root crop.

'*Zwangsarbeiter*,' Sunny said. 'Forced labourers from the east. Look at the letters on their jackets – OST. They are from the eastern Baltic beyond Poland.'

'Will there be guards?'

'Of course.'

'Then we have to go another way. We can't easily explain ourselves.'

'But this is the right direction. The guards will not care about us.'

'I disagree,' Wilde said. 'We have to avoid anyone in uniform – even if it means going the long way round.'

The ten-year-old girl had barely spoken. Suddenly she turned to Wilde.

'You are speaking funny! You are not German – you are the enemy.'

'No, truly, I'm your friend.'

Sunny was agitated. 'Tom is French, Klara. A guest worker in Germany.'

'I speak some French, too.'

'But I am *not* so good with French,' Sunny said. 'So let us all speak the same language for the moment, please? German it is.'

Klara was computing this information. At last she nodded.

'As you wish,' she said. 'But you haven't told me yet – what has happened at home?'

Wilde had been dreading this. He had been trying to work out what he knew about ten-year-olds; it had always seemed to him that children first became aware of adult concepts at the age of eight, so by ten they must be well aware of certain realities. And the truth about what had happened at Der Steinhof could not be held back for long. But the reality was so horrible and stark that he could not find the words.

'Sunny?' he said.

'Your family is dead, Klara.' Her voice was soothing but nothing could conceal the brutality of the message. 'Men came in the night with guns. That is why your father sent you to safety. That is also why he asked Tom and me to help you, to bring you to a safe place. You cannot go home.'

No tears came. The girl's shoulders did not slump as she received the dread news.

'What of Bismarck?'

Sunny nodded sadly. 'Bismarck, too. He is dead.'

For the first time, the girl's lip seemed to quiver, but still she did not break down; the full enormity of the news had not entered her consciousness yet. Or perhaps she did not yet understand the finality of death.

Sunny put her arm around Klara, enveloping her like a mother.

'They are dirty beasts,' the girl said. 'I want to kill them back.'

Wilde looked at the woman and the nightgown-clad girl, and then down at his own curious chauffeur's outfit and wondered what anyone they encountered would make of them. They would have a lot of difficult explaining to do. The reality was that their chances did not look at all good.

'Come, child, let us move on,' Sunny said. 'We must find you some food and clothes.'

Klara shook herself free from Sunny's comforting arm.

'I am ten years old,' she said. 'I am not a baby. What we must do now is find the Führer. He will look after us and deal with the bad men.'

Johanna Kalt looked at the telephone as it rang and rang. She did not like the device, did not trust it. She could not understand how voices came through it when there was no one there in the room with her. It was a witches' device, a thing of darkness. She wished that Otto had never had it brought here.

But today it was especially disagreeable to hear its incessant ringing, because she knew that Otto would be on the other end – and she really did not want to have to tell him what had happened. At last, it was too much and so she picked it up and held it to her ear. She said nothing, just waited.

'Johanna, is that you?'

'Yes.'

'Kill the woman. We have no more use for her. Cut her up and feed her to the pigs.'

Johanna Kalt said nothing. What could she say?

'Johanna, did you hear me?'

'Yes, I heard you.'

'And you will do that?'

She was silent again.

'Johanna, has something happened there?'

'The woman has gone.' There, she had said it.

'What do you mean, she has gone?'

'I don't know. But she is not where I put her.'

'And she was tied up?'

'Yes.'

'Shit, you stupid bitch, how did this happen?'

'I went to her – she was gone.'

'And the rope you tied her with?'

'One length was there, not the other.'

'Then her hands are still bound, but not her feet. She can't have got far like that. Johanna, you had better find her.'

'I can't. I've looked.'

'Then keep looking – and take my rifle. And I tell you this – if you don't find her and do for her, I will butcher *you* and feed *you* to the pigs.'

Otto Kalt slammed the phone down, then picked it up again. He had another call to make, one that was necessary but was likely to be even more difficult than the one to his wife. Bormann's secretary put him straight through.

'Otto, where are you?'

'Brandenburg – north-west of Eberswalde.'

'OK, now be circumspect, Otto.'

'I understand.'

Bormann did not know whether his phone was tapped. Everyone else in government circles was listened to, so one could never be sure.

'You found what you were looking for?'

'Almost.'

Bormann's voice sharpened. 'Almost? What do you mean? I do not like the sound of that.'

'A slight hitch. We'll find it soon. There are others involved.'

'Others?' One word, but a whole world of menace.

'While we were there a car turned up, an expensive Horch. We did not get sight of the occupants but I felt there were two people in it. Perhaps a man and a woman, for there was a smell of perfume.'

'Kalt . . .'

'Yes, Herr Reichsleiter.'

'I trusted you with this. What is happening there? Who are these others?'

'I have the car number plate. Perhaps your contacts might help, Herr Reichsleiter.'

'Give me the number. Where is the car?'

'The car is no more. Burnt out.'

'What? Why?'

'We couldn't stay with it – and we couldn't leave it for them.'

'Damn your incompetence, Kalt. I ask you to do one simple thing and you let me down! All I have done for you these past years. Give me the number.'

Kalt took out sheets of printed paper torn from a copy of *Mein Kampf* and, using a code they had used before, he gave his master the number plate details. Page eighteen, line one, seventh letter; page three, last line, eighth letter . . . and so on. No one would be able to break the code unless they knew the book he was using.

'Call me again in half an hour, Kalt. And don't tell me you have *almost* found what we are looking for. I want to know that it has been found and despatched. Do you understand?'

'Yes, Herr Reichsleiter.'

This time Kalt put the phone down more gently. The call had not been as bad as he feared, but there would be a great deal worse to come if the task was not completed with great haste. And he hadn't even dared mention that the midwife was missing. To think that the night had started so promisingly. How had it ended like this?

Martin Bormann paced the room, a lit cigarette in either hand. They had left Bavaria and were back in East Prussia at the Wolfsschanze. He liked it here, away from the filthy Munich cabal. Here he held sway. No Eva Braun here to whisper against him in the dead of night.

The internal phone rang. The Führer wanted him. For a few moments, Bormann drew on first one cigarette, then the other, trying to work out what to do about the events in northern Germany. His administrator's brain was ranging through various possibilities and their potential drawbacks.

He was livid – murderously so. What the hell were Kalt and that illiterate sidekick of his doing? If they had taken the midwife and she had led them to the correct place, how had they let the child evade them?

But he really couldn't think about this now. The master would not wait, and nor did he want him to. Hitler had to believe that he could not manage his great responsibilities without the aid of his loyal servant. He stubbed out both cigarettes and waved helplessly at the air around him, as though somehow he could rid himself of the smell the Führer so disliked.

In any other circumstances, he would have called straight through to Himmler to get the whole of the local Gestapo and SS involved. But of course he couldn't do that. No one, not even Uncle Heinrich, could ever be allowed to know about the events of September 1931. Nor could he himself leave the Führer's headquarters, not even for half a day. Perhaps there was some other assistance to be had.

Jung. It had to be Charlie Jung.

There was something else on his mind, too. Something that might seem of little consequence – something for Heydrich and the SD to deal with under normal circumstances. An American had arrived, legally, and had then disappeared after visiting the American embassy. This might have meant nothing to Bormann, but Kalt had discovered something while torturing the midwife;

she revealed that in the hours between Braundorf and Berlin, she had gone to the American diplomatic mission and had met a man named Vanderberg and had begged him for help. That was all, but it was enough to jangle the nerves. Who exactly was Vanderberg? And who was this new American visitor who had disappeared? Things were spiralling out of control.

As he strode across the concrete walkway to the reception room where the Führer awaited him, Bormann was on edge. He still hadn't heard back from that bastard Jung. Skiing in Switzerland? Mountaineering? *Scheisse*, why wasn't he in the Wehrmacht or the SS? Didn't he know there was a bloody war to be fought? Damned playboy. Money could buy exemption from anything. But if Kalt was failing, then Jung was his only hope. Kalt might be ruthless and brutal, but so was Jung. And he was a great deal more clever.

CHAPTER 12

Wilde left Sunny and Klara in the trees by a railway track and made his way stealthily towards the back garden of the isolated cottage that they had been studying for the last fifteen minutes. A line of clothes fluttered in the breeze. Sheets and shirts and, most importantly, a dark skirt and white blouse that looked from a distance as though it might belong to a girl of Klara's age or thereabouts.

'That's like my JM uniform,' Klara had said.

'*Jungmädelbund*,' Sunny whispered to Wilde. 'Young Girls' League, you'd call it. Junior section of the BDM – the female version of the Hitler Youth.'

'But what are you going to do?' Klara asked.

'I'll get the clothes and bring them to you,' Wilde said.

'You cannot just steal clothes!'

'But you have to have something to wear, Klara.'

'Then at least leave money to pay for them. We are not Jews.'

Wilde brought out his wallet and removed a twenty Reichsmark note.

'Is that enough?'

'That is plenty.'

'Stupid to put washing out on such a day anyway,' Sunny said. 'Who puts out washing on the line in December? They deserve to lose it.'

No one had entered or left the cottage in the past quarter of an hour. Hopefully that meant everyone was out; it was a chance Wilde had to take, but he was still worried about dogs.

With only one outhouse, the property did not have the look of a farm. The main building was small and modest, the bricks rendered with a dull grey wash. Wilde wondered whether it might be a railway worker's home, given the proximity of the line. Up the track there was a signal box. Perhaps that was where the householder worked. With luck he would be there now, the children would be at school and the wife off queuing at the shops. Although the house had no immediate neighbours, Wilde could see a church steeple not more than half a mile away, behind trees, so there must be a village or town there. An unmade road led in that direction from the front of the house. If the woman of the house came back with her shopping, they should see her in time.

Wilde opened the garden gate. He was very exposed here. Beyond the fence there were fields with labourers, but none close enough to see what was going on. Within seconds he had unpegged the skirt and blouse, both already dry. He put the twenty Reichsmark note on a flat stone close to the washing line, and secured it with two smaller stones so that it was easily visible and would not blow away.

He stood for a few moments looking about him, half-expecting to be discovered. But there was no one there. He looked across to Sunny and Klara, standing at the edge of the leafless woodland. The child looked strong, but she must be getting hungry and thirsty. They had already trekked some distance and there was likely to be a great deal further to go. Wilde walked a few paces to the kitchen window. Crouching down, he slowly rose until he had a view inside. No one was there. Surely they must have some food. He could leave a little more money.

The door was open. For a second he wondered whether he should call out, but thought better of it, and slipped straight into the little kitchen. A side of bacon was hanging from a ceiling hook. By the range he saw a selection of knives. He took a carver and cut a good half-pound slice off the bacon and thrust it in his pocket. He also cut a doorstop from a black loaf, which just about fitted in his other jacket pocket, then looked about for some bottle or flask in which to carry some water, but there was nothing but cups and glasses. He took another five Reichsmarks from his wallet and placed the money by the knife. He was about to leave when he had a rethink, and picked up the knife, too.

At the back door, something made him stop and he decided to look further into the house, not sure what he was hoping to find – a firearm, perhaps, or a flask. He peered around the door to the front parlour and instantly cursed himself for his idiocy. Someone was there – an old man. No, an *ancient* man, sitting in a stiff-backed chair by the fireplace.

Wilde froze.

The old man looked at him through watery eyes.

Wilde found himself putting up a hand in an inane greeting.

'*Guten tag,*' he said.

The old man nodded, then closed his eyes.

'Shit,' Wilde said to himself under his breath. Hopefully the old man would dismiss the encounter as a dream.

Outside, Wilde breathed again. Damn it, that was close. He gazed across to Sunny. She was gesticulating to him frantically as though saying 'Hurry up, for God's sake.' He waved back at her and made clear he was coming now. But she was beating the air, as though he should drop down or take cover.

It was as he emerged from the gate that he realised what she had been warning him about. A troop of a dozen or so Hitler Youth was marching across the meadow, all in their warm winter uniforms of dark, belted woollen blousons and trousers, with caps similar to the army's, and the ubiquitous swastika armbands.

They were approaching him. The boys were all about fifteen or sixteen years old. It was possible he might be able to outrun them, but where would he go? And running was a bad idea because only fugitives ran – and he couldn't afford to look like a fugitive. He tried to hide the skirt and blouse behind his back.

The troop came to a halt in front of him. As one, they stood to attention, clicked their heels and threw out their arms with a crisp 'Heil Hitler', Wilde fervently returned the salute while with his other arm he desperately tried to thrust the stolen clothes in the waistband of his trousers under his jacket.

One of the youths, with epaulettes of rank, stepped forward.

'Who are you?' He spoke in German.

Wilde understood the question readily enough.

'*Je suis Francais. Je m'appelle Monsieur Sable.*'

'What is wrong with your left arm? What are you hiding?'

The German had continued to talk in his own language. Wilde breathed out; if the boy had replied in French, he would have been lost. The skirt and blouse were tucked away now and he brought his left arm to the front and held up his hand to show it contained nothing.

'*Entschuldigung, aber ich nicht verstehen Sie. Ich bin Gastarbeiter.*'

I'm sorry, I don't understand you – I am a guest worker.

He made a motion with his hands as though holding a steering wheel.

'*Ich bin Chauffeur.*'

'*Franzose*, huh?'

'*Oui, je suis Français.*'

'And what were you doing in Frau Spitzweg's house?'

'*Ich wollte Milch kaufen.*' *I wanted to buy milk.*

The boy, who had the correct Aryan attributes of a fair complexion and strong, lean body, turned to his equally healthy looking friends and laughed. He made an obscene gesture, ringing the thumb and forefinger of his left hand and thrusting his right forefinger in and out of the hole.

'Milk! He wanted milk from Frau Spitzweg!' The troop fell about laughing. He turned back to Wilde. 'And Katharina, too – do you ask *her* for milk?'

Once again, the boys laughed loudly. Wilde laughed with them. Clearly the disreputable Spitzweg mother and daughter were a source of local amusement. He gave the young men a lingering, conspiratorial smile, then touched the peak of his chauffeur's cap and edged sideways to take his leave.

'*Papiere*,' the troop leader said, stepping in front of Wilde to block his way. 'Show me your papers.'

'*Ah, natürlich*,' Wilde said.

He dug into his inside pocket and produced his identity card and ration card.

The youth looked at them, and studied the photo against Wilde's face. He nodded in approval and handed them back. Wilde thanked him, gave a Hitler salute and tried once more to take his leave.

'You forgot your residency permit,' the youth said.

Wilde had deliberately avoided handing it over, as it gave an address in Potsdam. He would need to explain why he was out here in Brandenburg, many miles from home. Things were becoming complicated. He noted that the rest of the troop was grinning and sniggering. It was a big joke for them – let's play at tormenting the Frenchman.

The residency permit came out. Once more, the Hitler Youth took an age studying it.

'This says you are resident in Potsdam,' he said at last.

'I was driving my mistress. *Auto kaput*.'

He was struggling for German now. He couldn't keep this up much longer.

'Then we will accompany you,' the youth said.

'*Nein danke*,' Wilde said, vigorously shaking his head.

'Yes, it is no problem for us. Where is the car. Perhaps we can fix it. And where is your mistress?'

Wilde could not allow this to happen. He also had to get away from there before any occupant of the house appeared. The day was not warm, but sweat was dripping down the back of his neck and he feared his uneasiness must be visible on his face.

For a few moments, he wondered about taking them on. He was a fully grown man, an amateur boxer and, if all else failed, he had a kitchen carving knife. But there were twelve of these boys, and some of them were over six feet tall. And they had sheathed daggers at their belts. Wilde might get a few punches in, but the end result was inevitable.

'She is with the car,' he said.

The Hitler Youth leader was no longer looking at him. Wilde followed his eyes.

In the sky, to the west, an airplane was approaching. It was coming in low, not more than a few hundred feet off the ground, and its markings did not look German. Some sort of twin-engined bomber, with a star on the fuselage and tail fin. One engine was spluttering, and a thin trail of black smoke and oil drifted in its wake. How the hell had a Soviet plane got this far from the front? And why?

It was a mile or two away, losing height. And then something else appeared in the sky. Something dark, falling behind the plane. Of course, a parachute. One of the crew bailing out.

The troop leader looked at his comrades, then grinned at Wilde.

'*Auf wiedersehen, Franzose.* Good luck with the car.'

He tossed the residency permit to Wilde and then they all broke into a run. They had found a better game to play: hunt the parachutist.

'Gott in bloody Himmel, Tom – how did you get out of that?'

'Luck. Pure bloody luck, Sunny. I thought I was done for.' He handed the clothes to her. 'I'll explain all as we walk. First, you two had better slip behind a tree and get the young lady dressed. Then the faster we move on, the better. The good news is, I've got a bit of food.'

His relief was tempered with shock. That had been a great deal too close; he had acted recklessly. One more mistake like that and they would all be done for.

Romy had no idea where she was or where to go. Her whole body was racked with pain. Soon after getting away from the farmhouse, she had run full on into a tree and had fallen, unconscious, into a bed of leaves. When she came to, her forehead throbbing, she did not know how long she had been there, and she had lost all sense of direction.

She thought of her impending death. She had loved every day of her old life, bringing children into the world. It was always her tragedy that she had been unable to have children of her own, a failing that had brought her marriage to an end. Franzchen was a weak man and he had wanted children more than he had wanted her.

Rising to her feet, she flexed her shoulders and neck, then ran again until she fell again, exhausted, in the lee of a hedge close to a village which had no name post. Not that knowing the name of the village would have helped her. She didn't even know whether she had travelled east, west, north or south. If only she could find some way of cutting her wrists free of the cords that seemed to bite deeper into her flesh with each passing minute.

Bound like this, she couldn't even get on to a bus or train without arousing instant suspicion. The police would be called – and what would they do with her then?

Here, beneath the hedge, she slept fitfully. The pain in her head and neck only exceeded by the nightmare of her fingers where the nails had been drawn out one by one.

As morning grew lighter, she got up again.

Would anyone help her – or would they hand her back to the farmwife and her husband? She had no idea who these people were or what sway they held in this district. If they worked for Martin Bormann, then they must have influence. She had the knife, but no way of applying it to the bindings. Several times, she buried the handle in the earth and sat with her back to it, pressing the knot between her wrists against the blade, but the knife just fell away. She tried the same thing with the blade against the trunk of a tree, but she couldn't hold the blade steady enough to saw at the knotted cords.

'Good day, Fräulein.'

The words made her legs go weak. She turned to face the man behind the voice. As she did so, a shot rang out.

CHAPTER 13

Charlie Jung was wearing his Chinese-silk dressing gown, eating a leisurely late breakfast of pork escalopes and fried potatoes in his splendid dining room overlooking an endless vista of lake and forest. Occasionally, he caught his young mistress's eye and smiled at her. He was already tiring of the slut. His reverie was disturbed by the arrival of his butler.

'The telephone, Herr Jung.'

'I haven't finished my breakfast.'

'The call is from Führer headquarters, Herr Jung. Reichsleiter Bormann wishes to speak with you.'

Bormann. That was a name to spoil a man's otherwise perfect morning. His butler had told him Bormann had been trying to get hold of him, but Jung had studiously avoided returning the calls. Their business together finished years ago. He was hoping their paths would never cross again.

'What does he want?'

'He didn't say, sir. But he says if you don't come to the phone, he will have you in Sachsenhausen by nightfall.'

Very funny.

'Well, then, I'd better take the call, I suppose. Keep my food hot.'

Jung rose from the white-linen table, bowed to the full-breasted and underdressed Astrid, and said, 'Forgive me, my dear, I'm sure this will only take a few moments.'

In his office, he paused, then steeled himself and picked up the phone.

'Hello, Martin? Long time—'

'Charlie, where the fuck have you been?'

'Oh, here and there, Martin – or perhaps I should call you Herr Reichsleiter now that you have risen to Valhalla with the gods of war.'

'Enough bullshit. Martin will do. We are old friends, after all.'

'Then I feel very honoured.'

Jung felt nothing of the kind. Nor were they old friends. Bormann didn't have friends.

'Good . . . good. All is well with you, Charlie? What are you doing for the war effort these days? Skiing? Making love to beautiful women? Drinking fine wine?'

'All those and more.'

'Charlie, you just lounge around your ancient *Schloss* doing nothing. Well, I'm about to disturb your peace and quiet, I'm afraid. I have a matter of utmost urgency and secrecy.'

'Then you had better tell me what it is.'

'Not on the phone. A Heinkel transport will be arriving at your airstrip within the hour – and you will be flown straight here.'

'Which is where exactly? One never knows where Führer headquarters is based these days.'

Bormann ignored the question. 'We will meet, and you will be flown straight back. Understood?'

'Of course. Do I at least have time to finish my breakfast and fuck my new mistress?'

'Is she remarkably beautiful?'

'Of course, blue-eyed Danish. As sinuous as an adder in spring. A month ago she came here a chambermaid. Now she is my mistress and ski partner. Next week she will be fired and on her way back to Copenhagen.'

'Good man. Well, perhaps don't fire her – just pass her on to me when you've done with her. In the meantime, you are about to repay me the favour you owe me.'

'I thought you had already had your share.'

'Really? Did you think that? Oh, Charlie, I can't believe a man of your great intelligence ever thought such a thing.'

Three and a half hours later, Jung was closeted with Bormann in his private residence at the Wolfsschanze – the Führer's headquarters deep in the heart of the Masurian forest in East Prussia. The building was a short walk from Hitler's much larger bunker in the northern sector of the base, where the Führer directed the war.

The whole complex of buildings – massively reinforced concrete or brick and designed as a defensive fortification – was like a small town with its own roads, railway and airstrip. It was crawling with at least two thousand SS troops, senior Wehrmacht officers and guards. Everyone but the chiefs of staff and government officials carried sidearms and sub-machine guns. This was the control centre for the greatest invasion the world had ever known.

The base covered over fifteen hundred acres and was surrounded by a secure perimeter heavily fortified with wire and mines, and armed watchtowers, giving way to a dense forest of firs, with all roads in and out patrolled and protected by staff cars and Panzers. It was known as the 'wolf's lair' in honour of the Führer, who had often enjoyed going by the sobriquet Wolf, particularly in the early days of his political career.

Artillery and anti-aircraft deployments were strategically positioned among the dozens of buildings. Amid these were the personal residences of the Wehrmacht high command and government members, conference rooms, map rooms and, further out, large barrack blocks. All had flat roofs camouflaged with bushes and undergrowth to meld in with the forest and prevent them being seen from the air.

One thing above all others was noted by all who came here: this place was built by men for men, with few women, and then only in the role of stenographers or nurses. But it was a paradox, for as well as the officers' messes, there was a cinema here, cafés, even a Turkish bath. A swimming pool was under construction. The Wolfsschanze was designed for the long haul.

A rail track cut through the middle, dividing the north and south of the camp. On the short drive from the Rastenburg airfield, Jung had spotted Hitler's private train, complete with its own flak battery, in a siding close to the camp's private station. It was guarded by SS men.

'Coffee, Charlie?'

'With brandy. Judging by the landing we somehow survived, I think your pilot must have driven tractors before the war.'

Bormann ordered his secretary, Heidi, to bring the drinks, then closed the door and sat close to Jung, keeping his voice low.

'I am going to get straight to the point, without euphemisms. I had entrusted a task to Kalt, but all is not going as well as planned. You remember Otto Kalt, don't you, Charlie?'

'How could I forget him?'

Kalt was the man who had killed Miriam and her parents back in January '37.

'Well, he's fouling up.' Bormann stubbed out one American cigarette and lit another. 'He was supposed to have liquidated a girl named Klara Rieger, but she gave them the slip. Her adoptive parents have been taken care of, but I fear someone else is involved in her escape.'

'Who is this girl? Why do you want her dead?'

'Keep your damned voice down, Charlie. Anyway, those are things you don't need to know. In fact it is *safer* for you that you don't know. All you need to do is find her and despatch her, just as Kalt did with your wife and her parents.'

'Now, Martin, I owe you nothing for that. You were paid hand-somely, more than we even agreed.'

Bormann stood up and paced around, drawing deeply on his cigarette all the while. Then he pulled his Luger from its holster and pushed the muzzle into Jung's face.

'Don't ever think you owe me nothing, Charlie. I could have you sent to a concentration camp or worse with a click of my fin-gers. How about a punishment battalion on the Eastern Front? You might even survive half a day.'

Jung remained calm. 'You don't need to threaten me, Martin.'

'Don't I? Good. But just to be clear, do you think I did not keep evidence – *proof* – of your part in the murders of your wife and her family? You owe me everything – your wealth, your women, your very life – and I could just as easily take them away.'

Jung raised a hand, the palm pressed against the end of the cold black gun barrel.

'I'm sorry. I understand, of course.'

'Do you, Charlie?'

'Yes, I'm sorry. You're right – I have become too comfortable.'

'Well, there is a war on, so now is the time to snap out of it.' Bormann studied him from head to toe, then flicked his tie with a sneer. 'What is this, silk? Look at you – you are dressed like an English fucking gentleman.'

'That's because I am an English fucking gentleman, Martin.' Apart from the female secretaries, he was the only person at this redoubt in the east of the former Poland, not in uniform, but wearing an expensive suit and handmade shoes.

'Well, for pity's sake, don't let the Führer see you or he'll think you're a homosexual and have you shot. Charlie, you know I am beginning to think a few months in Dachau would do you the world of good after all. Toughen you up.'

Jung tried to smile, but it was becoming difficult to maintain his cool demeanour.

'Your message has got through to me, Martin.'

'Herr Reichsleiter. You call me Herr Reichsleiter.'

'Forgive me, Herr Reichsleiter, I promise I will do my very best on your behalf. For you are right, I owe you my whole world.'

'Then here it is. Klara Rieger is ten years old. When you have done with her you will dispose of her corpse in a way that ensures it will never be found. By fire, in the depths of the sea or acid – I don't care – so long as the body is gone for ever. And you will kill anyone associated with her.'

Charlie Jung nodded. He was feeling a little sick.

'She lives at a house named Der Steinhof in the village of Kossertheim, north of Berlin to the west of the Schorfheide. Her adoptive father Matthias was a schoolmaster and is now dead, as is the mother. But Klara Rieger vanished and is still missing. Kalt and his man Brunner found a car nearby, the engine warm. They burnt it out but gave me the number. It belonged to Generalmajor Werner Somerfeld of the Luftwaffe. You have heard of him?'

'Of course, but he is dead, isn't he? I thought his plane blew up a few months ago. It made the wireless broadcasts and news-papers.'

'Which means the car belonged to his wife. Somerfeld was never trusted by the Party, nor was his wife. They are of that class . . . well, you know the sort. They think themselves Junkers, a cut above us, Charlie. But they will all get their deserts when the war is over and they're no longer needed.'

'So you think Frau Somerfeld is somehow involved in this girl's disappearance?'

'I think it's clear-cut, don't you.'

'So find the woman and I find the girl.'

'There's something else. Kalt found out the whereabouts of the girl from a midwife named Romy Dietrich. She is of no importance and will have been despatched by now, but there was something curious about her movements in the days before Kalt got to her. It seems she entered the American embassy and there met one of the senior men, James Vanderberg.'

'Is he involved?'

Bormann shrugged. 'I don't know. Indirectly, perhaps. The way things are between us and the Americans, they are in no position to undermine us from within. But that's not the end of the story. Two days ago, another American arrived in Berlin, a businessman with some idea for alleviating our oil shortfall. I'm told he was asking for a great deal of money in return for some unspecified technology. He, too, went to the embassy – and later went sailing with Vanderberg at Havel or Wannsee. He disappeared. Just stepped off the boat on the western bank and vanished. Not a sign of him since. The Gestapo have drawn a blank.'

Jung chewed his lip. 'Where does Frau Somerfeld live?'

'Now you're thinking along the right lines. I knew I was right to engage you, Charlie. Potsdam. She has a large villa in Potsdam. Very convenient for Wannsee.'

'What was the name of this American businessman?'

'On his passport, Tomas Esser. But now? Who knows?'

'Was someone assigned to him – one of the Gestapo boys?'

'Anton Offenbach of the foreign office. I think he might also be attached to the Abwehr, but that is for you to discover. He met Esser in Portugal and accompanied him on the flight to Berlin. By the way, Esser did have a meeting with Todt to discuss his idea.'

'Then I think I need to speak to Herr Offenbach – and see if I can find Frau Somerfeld. Todt might be a bit more difficult to access.'

'Well, he's back here at the Wolfsschanze, not more than fifty metres away. Go and see him, use your charm. Perhaps it would be best if you don't mention me, for we are not the best of friends.'

'I'll do my best.'

'And when you fly home, use your contacts at Prinz-Albrecht-Strasse. But remember this – you will never mention why you are asking for assistance or for whom you are working. Nor will you allow the Gestapo to raise a general alert on your behalf – for that would instantly become known to others. This is just between you and me, Charlie. No Gestapo, no SS, no SD. And be careful regarding the American. The Führer does not want to provoke America into war. Not yet. Not until the decisive blow has done for Stalin.'

'I understand, truly I do.'

'Good, I'm glad of it. For I would hate to have to let the world know you had your wife and her parents slaughtered in their beds for the Höffle millions while you were sticking your grubby little prick in the whores of Paris.'

'The Höffles were Jews, Herr Reichsleiter. I was under pressure from the Party to divorce the woman anyway. Quicker and simpler the way I chose.'

They had been butchered by Kalt and Brunner at the beginning of 1937, in his wife's parents' beautiful home in Dahlem. Brunner had gone with his knife to the parents' room while Kalt dealt with Frau Miriam Jung himself. It had been a bloody business, but the police had not been particularly interested. No one inquired too deeply into the deaths of Jews in case the Party had a hand in it. The Berlin newspapers made a page lead out of it, but then dropped the story. The law shrugged and looked away.

Jung had met Miriam Höffle in 1921, a year after arriving in Hamburg from Tilbury docks. Her father hired Jung, even though he was just eighteen years old, because he wanted a well-bred English-speaker in the auction room. Jung's smoothness worked well and old man Höffle liked him, which was all that mattered. Miriam was a plain and obedient girl. It did not take Charlie Jung long to realise his suit would be well received by both father and daughter. Only the mother had doubts. She told him once that he was a chameleon, and it had been meant as an insult. Jung took it as a compliment.

And Höffle was prospering. The early 1920s was the time of the great inflation and he was making use of it, buying up great art-works dirt cheap from families desperately fighting to save their businesses and estates by selling off their heirlooms at a fraction of their true value. The worse the inflation, the richer Höffle became, selling the works abroad; but Höffle was also storing up trouble, because with wealth came envy and hatred from all those who had come to grief. With the arrival of the Nazis, prosperous families such as the Höffles had no hiding place. And few tears were shed when the family was murdered.

In the remnants of his soul, Jung cringed at Bormann's choice of language. The coarseness of Martin Bormann never ceased to appal him. Some years ago, Bormann had served a purpose and had been paid well for it; why did the ghastly man still have this hold over him?

There was a knock at the door.

'Enter.'

'Your coffee and brandy, Herr Bormann.'

'Good girl, Heidi. Turn around if you would for Herr Jung, show him your arse.'

The young secretary did as she was bidden.

'Well, Charlie – how does your pretty Dane compare to that?'

'I'd have to see them together to be sure.'

'Let's see if we can't arrange that, then. Now drink your coffee and brandy. You have no time to lose – and my master needs me, as always. After you have seen Todt, come back here. Heidi will give you a code. It will be very basic, but there may be times when you find it safer to use a transmitter than a telephone to communicate with me. Get to it, Charlie.'

It was not Jung's charm that secured the interview with Todt, but the mention – through the minister's secretary – of the missing Tomas Esser.

Todt did not rise from his desk, nor did he salute or invite the visitor to sit down. He looked up from the table covered with plans with cold eyes.

'You mentioned Esser to my secretary – have you heard something about the American, Herr Jung? Is that why you're here?'

'No, sir, I am looking for him.'

'I know you, don't I? You inherited the Höffle Galleries.'

'Indeed, it is now the Jung Galleries. But that is not why I am here. I leave all that to my managers while I do my bit for the war.'

'Doing what exactly?'

'Providing taxes, Herr Todt. And much else which modesty precludes me from mentioning. The fact that I am wealthy should not be held against me. I just happened to marry Herr Höffle's daughter and when the tragedy befell them, I found myself in control of their great company. But it was clear to me that my expertise lay elsewhere, for I was educated in diplomacy and foreign affairs.'

'Well, you look like a greasy lawyer to me.'

'Very well then, I will tell you, sir. I am working on behalf of the foreign ministry.'

He managed a reassuring smile. Lying came easy to Charlie Jung; it always had. As a boy he had been sent home from India to a third-rate prep school where beatings and cross-country runs and bitterly cold dormitories had been designed to toughen up small boys for the rigours of service life.

Jung – Charles Young as he then was – had learned fast. A boy had to lie and cheat and use every means at his disposal to survive the hellhole to which he had been despatched by uncaring parents.

From there he had been shunted to a minor public school, the sort of place which churned out colonial administrators by the shipload: civil servants, prison governors, district officers. Charlie was never going to accept that sort of life. He had no intention of emulating his parents with their false life of luxury in the empire: servants by the dozen and then, for those who survived and came 'home', impoverished retirement in the Weald of Kent when they discovered that they were excluded and sneered at by those who mattered in Britain. The old families still owned the land and they still ruled the country.

He despised all his teachers and all the other pupils, with their second-rate ambitions: church, army, colonial service or, for the slightly brighter ones, law or medicine. He learned to steal, to dissimulate, to use sex as a means of control – of both men and women.

At seventeen, he ran away, with a plan. Although he had never been to Germany or Austria, he was fascinated by what he had read of their culture and had always been good at languages. That was where the future lay. He took a train to London, bought a set of working man's clothes and made his way to the docks at Tilbury, where he picked up work on a freighter bound for Hamburg.

He arrived in 1920, when things were looking very bad for Germany. He enjoyed the irony; the British Empire was at its zenith, Germany was in the depths. When things are at rock bottom, he reasoned, the only way is up.

'Who is your superior?' Todt demanded.

'Ultimately, Ribbentrop. Beyond that I cannot say, for I am in internal security. What I can tell you is that when Esser's disappearance came to our attention, there was considerable alarm. We now believe it likely that Herr Esser is an agent of an enemy power.'

'I think I had worked out that one for myself, Jung. What do you want from me – and why isn't the Gestapo dealing with this?'

'The Gestapo are cattle-brained. Good for dawn raids and stopping traffic, but this will take a little more thought. It is no task for them. Relations with America are at a most delicate stage, so we don't want Himmler's thugs blundering in. The longer we can keep Roosevelt out of the war the better. I'm sure you are aware that the Führer does not wish to open a second front in the west until the east is dealt with.'

'Yes, yes, I don't need a damned lecture, Jung. Just tell me what you need to know about the American.'

'A description of Tomas Esser would be a good start, Herr Todt.'

'Tall. Perhaps six feet. Spectacles, thin moustache. I don't know how much German he understands. We had an interpreter with us, Herr Offenbach. As to his character, he seemed confident, at his ease. He loved motorcycles – I recall that well enough. There was one other thing. He had a scar on the side of his head, half hidden by hair, but I noted it for I wondered if it was caused by bullet or shrapnel in the last war. But he said it was a sports injury.'

'Thank you, sir. And where was he lodging?'

'The Adlon, I believe. You can easily check with them. You must know that he went sailing with someone from the American embassy, and disappeared.'

'When you met him, did you have suspicions – or did he seem genuine?'

Todt thought for a moment. 'That is a good question. Did he seem genuine? Well, yes, he did. You know he was quite plausible.

He suggested he had a fuel-saving technology for the internal combustion engine. That is inherently feasible – and it would undoubtedly be useful.'

'How did he come here from America, Herr Reichsminister. How was contact made?'

'That, too, is a good question, Herr Jung. As I recall, the first I heard of him was a memorandum from the *Auswärtiges Amt* – your lot.'

'The memorandum must have been signed, sir.'

'Indeed, indeed . . .'

Jung watched him and waited. During the short walk to the south of the complex from Bormann's residence, he had begun his own thinking process. One thing was abundantly clear: someone at the very heart of the regime was involved in this. How else would this American have managed to get to Berlin, gain access to Todt – and then disappear? He had to have had assistance at a high level. And common sense suggested that if it was in any way linked to Frau Somerfeld and the missing girl, then that assistance must have come from an enemy of Martin Bormann.

But who was Bormann's enemy? That was a senseless question. The list was as long as the road back to Berlin. Everyone save Hitler detested and feared Bormann. It was the one thing the senior men had in common.

'I would have to get my Berlin secretary to fish out the paper. As I recall it was *per procurationem* Ribbentrop, but he certainly didn't sign it himself. Nor did he mention it to me in person. But as I saw it there was no security issue – the American was said to be a businessman with links to the German-American Bund. He wasn't asking me for information – just wanted me to listen, which I did.'

'I would be grateful if you could place a call to your office, sir. The sooner I have the name of the *pp*, the sooner I can interview him.'

Todt picked up the phone and barked an order to his secretary. A few moments later he was through to Berlin. He demanded details of the original of the memorandum, then put down the phone.

'Well, Jung, they will look in the archives. It may take a little while. Where can I find you.'

'I am to fly back west within the hour.'

'Call me when you arrive. I should have the name for you by then. And check with your own people at the foreign ministry. Someone there must know who sent the memorandum – you can talk to them directly, get the provenance of this whole disturbing affair. When you find the American, inform me. I wish to know exactly what is behind this. Good day.'

He dismissed him with a wave of the hand.

CHAPTER 14

The shot missed Romy Dietrich but cut a deep gash in the birch tree a metre to her left, making her knees buckle. Her eyes darted everywhere, and through a haze of confusion, she saw the blank face of Frau Kalt. She was crouching at a gap in the hedge ten metres away, a rifle at her shoulder. And then, even as Romy tried to dodge the second shot, she caught a glimpse of the man who had spoken, looming above her. Who was he? Why was he here?

Then something else was happening. The man who had spoken – who had said an amiable 'Good day, Fräulein' in a curious accent – was turning in the direction of Johanna Kalt, who was now beginning to turn the long, slender rifle on *him*.

He was much too quick and decisive for the farmwife. Even as the sights of her rifle were swivelling towards him, he was upon her, grabbing the barrel as she squeezed the trigger, the bullet burying itself harmlessly in the earth in front of her feet before the gun was wrenched roughly from her grasp.

Frau Kalt looked bemused as she struggled to get the rifle back from the stranger, baring her black and yellow teeth like a dog at bay. But the man was much too powerful, fending her off with one hand while he held the weapon out of her reach. Realising she could not regain the rifle, Frau Kalt pulled a short paring knife from the front pocket of her grubby blue housecoat. She lunged past the man and turned her attention back to Romy. But again she was too slow; the man brought the butt of the rifle down smartly on to the back of her head and sent her sprawling into the meadow grass.

Romy was retreating, scrabbling away in a panic, trying to make sense of what she was witnessing. Would the man turn on *her* now?

'What is this?' he said, stepping over the unconscious farmwife towards Romy. 'Why are you bound – and why was that woman trying to kill you?'

His German was a long way from perfect and heavily accented, and then she noticed the identifying brassard on his arm, like a swastika band but with a large yellow 'P' rather than the Nazi emblem. It meant he was Polish, a forced worker. He was tall and thin – probably underfed – but his eyes were bright and kind.

'Well?'

'Please,' she said, 'won't you cut me free?'

'Of course . . . Of course . . .' He picked up the farmwife's knife. 'Turn around, Fräulein.'

Romy still felt uncertain; if this man wore the armband of a Polish slave worker, he might have escaped – and might be desperate. The thought of turning her back on him suddenly alarmed her.

The man strove to reassure her. 'Lady, I will not hurt you, I promise. I think I may have just saved your life.'

'Of course.' She began to turn around so that he could see the knot binding her. 'I'm sorry – I have been so scared.'

'Keep still.' The paring knife was not strong enough for the job. He saw the carving knife and tried that instead. Within a minute, he had cut through the cords. 'There. That is better, yes. But what has happened to your fingers? They are covered in blood. And your head is bruised.'

She clasped her hands lightly against her chest.

'That woman . . . Her husband was torturing me. I escaped.'

The Pole looked anxious. 'Is he still around?'

'He went away – but he may be back. I don't know.'

'I think we had better get you away from here, Fräulein . . . What is your name?'

'Dietrich. Romy Dietrich.'

'I am Slavo Olkowski. Everyone calls me Slavo the slave.' He laughed out loud. 'Come, we will get you to safety. We need to find bandages for your fingers. Do you know this area? Could you find a doctor to help you?'

'If we can find clean water and a clean cloth I can deal with it myself. I am a nurse and midwife by training. But I am worried about you, Herr Olkowski. If you are a forced worker, you will be in danger by leaving your post.'

'Oh, please do not concern yourself on my behalf. I worked on a farm thirty kilometres from here. But I have had enough of this country. I am walking home to Warsaw. If I'm shot on the way, well, so what? Better than being worked to death like a horse at the wheel.'

Romy tensed again. 'Shouldn't you take the armband off?'

He shook his head. 'Nobody takes any notice of the foreign workers. But if someone says hello thinking I am a German and I reply with a Polish accent, then I will have trouble.'

She put her uninjured hand on his arm. 'Thank you for helping me.'

He nodded towards the unconscious Frau Kalt and grinned.

'That one looks like a witch. Now tell me, dear lady, where is safe for you – where do you want to go? You want to come to Warsaw with me?'

'Berlin. I have to get to Berlin.'

She said it without thinking. Back to Berlin? Was that really the best idea? Switzerland or Sweden would be safe – but, of course, she had no way of getting there. And in Berlin . . . well, a woman could lose herself there. The irony of the idea did not instantly occur to her; that she had tried to lose herself in Berlin very recently, and had ended up having her fingernails drawn out millimetre by agonising millimetre.

'Then I get you on a train. I know where the track is – and we follow that. Perhaps you jump a ride on a freight train. You will be OK. And on the way to the track you can tell me all about this terrible event.' He picked up the gun, weighed it appreciatively in his hands, then squinted down the sight. 'It's an old Mannlicher-Schönauer,' he said. 'Good hunting weapon. I had one at home.' For a few moments, he seemed lost in a reverie of a faraway place and time, probably gone for ever. 'The question is, should I take it? I could kill some rabbits to eat.'

'Dangerous to be seen with it, though.'

'I think I take it all the same. But tell me, *why* was the witch hunting you, Fräulein? You still haven't told me.'

'It's a long story.'

'Well, tell me on the way.'

He turned and saw that the farmwife was regaining consciousness. Casually, he spat in her direction.

Raising herself to her elbows, Frau Johanna Kalt clutched her head where she had been hit. She realised there was nothing left for her to do but go home, tend to the livestock and await another savage beating from her husband. Perhaps this would be the last one. Perhaps this time he really *would* feed her to the pigs, as he had threatened to do so many times before.

'I knew this would happen one day. Pappi told me it would happen. I think the men who killed him must have been Jews or Slavs.'

'That is nonsense, Klara,' Sunny said. 'You must not say such things.'

'But it's true. The whole world is against our dear Führer – and the Jews and Slavs are the very worst of our enemies.'

'Your head is full of bees, Klara. Jews and Slavs are just people like the rest of us. Some good, some not so good.'

Klara stopped, then she stamped a foot. 'No, that is not the case. There is a notice board in class and I have learnt it thoroughly. We are at the top – Nordic Aryan Germans – followed by Scandinavians, then the Dutch and English, the Scots, the Flemings and the Irish, though even some of those are our enemies now. Behind them come the French, Italians, Greeks, Poles, Czechs and other eastern and southern Europeans. There are others further down and then, right at the bottom, the Gypsies, the American Indians, the Jews, the Africans, the Arabs, the Aborigines, the Pacific islanders and Eskimos. Are you saying my teachers were all wrong – and that the poster was wrong?'

Sunny raised her hand and, for a moment, Wilde feared she was about to slap the girl. He could not help but share her dismay at the poison spilling from the mouth of a ten-year-old, but he reached out and gently moved the hand back down, shaking his head in warning.

'Leave it, Sunny. All being well, there should be time enough to talk about such things with her later.'

The girl had backed away, her nose in the air.

'She is a little bitch,' Sunny said quietly. 'A Narzisse.'

'What does that mean?'

'It's what we call the fanatical female Nazis. A Narzisse in English is a narcissus or daffodil – a pretty spring flower. But in German slang it has a double-edged meaning. Magda Goebbels – she is a Narzisse.'

'Well, don't say it to Klara's face. The poor girl has suffered enough as it is – and it's not her fault if she's been fed the ghastly Nazi poison.' He looked around him; they were following a stream through woodland. 'How far now? We've been walking for hours.'

'We're almost there – between the two lakes up ahead. Another kilometre, that's all.'

'You go on ahead. I'll wait with the girl until we get the all-clear from you that your friends are OK about us.'

'Tom, I haven't been quite honest with you. This estate – it's called Carinhall. Have you heard of it, perhaps?'

'No, I don't believe I have – why?'

'It's the hunting lodge of Reichsmarschall Hermann Göring.'

The blood drained from Wilde's face. For a moment, he simply stared at her, unable to quite take in what she had just said. Then he exploded.

'Good God! Why have you brought us here?'

'Because they are my friends, particularly his wife, Emmy. Göring was a great admirer of my husband and gave him rapid promotion in the Luftwaffe. We have spent many happy weekends here.'

Wilde was aghast. 'You're crazy, Sunny, we can't possibly go there. It would be putting our heads on the block.'

'Please, listen to me. Emmy may be a little grand, but she would do anything to help a friend. She helps many people – including her old Jewish friends. She wouldn't hurt a fly. All we need is a car to the coast, nothing more. I am sure she will provide us with one.'

'This place must be guarded. SS probably. Dozens of them.'

'I'll go on ahead, as you suggested. They know me – the guys in the gatehouse, the domestic staff, they all know me. It will be fine. When I come back and get you, you will act dumb, and I will talk for you.' She went over to Klara and told her much the same. 'In the house, you will be quieter than you have ever been before. The people here are friends of our beloved Führer, but we must not involve them any more than necessary in our troubles. Do you understand?'

'I'm not stupid, you know.' The girl looked sullen, still angry at being contradicted.

'Klara? This is very, very important. You will say you are my niece, that we were travelling to the coast with our French chauffeur, Monsieur Sable, when our car caught fire. We need help. That is all. You do not need to say any more than that. If you are offered food, you say yes, please and you say thank you. The same with drink. Tell me you understand all this – repeat it to me.'

'I am your niece. Tom – Monsieur Sable – is our driver. The car broke down and caught fire. And yes, I would very much like a glass of lemon cordial.'

'No.' Wilde had a very bad feeling. 'No, Sunny, I forbid this. This is insanity.'

'But, Tom, all we need is some sort of transport. Emmy would do anything for me, I promise you. We were friends even before her marriage to fat Hermann. I know Emmy will help me, so long as I don't compromise her by telling her what we are doing.'

'Her husband will have other ideas.'

'Just stay here and wait. I will go to her and make a judgement. If I am not back in an hour something bad has happened and I will have to leave you to your own devices.'

Wilde's instinct, as well as his common sense, told him they should run away from this place as fast as they could. But Sunny was right – they needed help. And sometimes the safest place to be was in the eye of the storm.

CHAPTER 15

Wilde and Klara sat down beneath a tree close to one of the hundreds of small lakes that dotted that part of northern Germany. He took the last quarter pound of bacon from his pocket, cut a slice and offered it to her. She took it and said 'Thank you.' In English.

Well, thought Wilde, that's a start. At least she has been taught some manners. Not for the first time he wondered about her true parentage. Was this really the daughter of Adolf Hitler? He studied her young face, trying to see something of the dictator in her brow, her eyes, the curve of her mouth. She clearly looked like her mother, Geli – but the question of the father was inconclusive. There could, of course, be a family resemblance to Hitler whether or not he was her father. He was, after all, Geli's uncle. As it was, Wilde couldn't see past the moustache and lick of hair across the brow when thinking about Adolf Hitler. Anyway, that was a question for another time. All that mattered that she was a child, and she was in mortal danger.

Almost as if she were reading his thoughts, she said, 'Pappi and Mutti were not my true father and mother, you know, Tom. I was adopted.'

He nodded. 'Yes, I had heard that.'

Pointless to dissemble. What little he knew about children of Klara's age made him think they were rather likely to see straight through a lie.

'I do not know who my real mother and father were, but Pappi told me they were dead. All I have of them is this.'

She pulled out a silver locket which was hanging around her neck.

'Is there a picture of them?'

'No, small locks of their hair, braided and twined together. Would you like to see?'

'If you don't mind.'

She prised the locket open with a fingernail. A curl of twined and braided hair sat behind glass in one half of the open case. To look at, it was unremarkable; the strands of hair could be anyone's.

'Do you know your birth name, Klara?'

'I do, but I am never to tell anyone, which is a shame, because I prefer it to Rieger.'

'I'm sorry. It is very sad to lose your parents. Sunny Somerfeld and I will do our very best to find you a place of safety and happiness.'

'You are not married, you and Sunny?'

'No, we are merely working together on your behalf.'

'So I will not be living with you both?'

'I promise, you will have a loving home. I hope you trust me.'

Her eyes met his, then she smiled. 'And I would like a puppy. Not to replace Bismarck, you understand – because he could never be replaced. But all the same, a puppy would make me happy.'

'I'm sure that will be possible.'

She nodded slowly, as though dreaming of the puppy that would one day be hers. They sat together in companionable silence, eating small pieces of bacon and rye bread. Wilde looked at his watch. Sunny had only been gone five minutes, but it already felt like an hour.

'Oh, it's so cold,' Klara said, shivering and crossing her arms.

Wilde took off his jacket. 'Put this around your shoulders.'

'Then you will be cold.'

'That doesn't matter.'

She took the jacket and wrapped herself in it.

'Thank you.'

'You're welcome.'

Klara looked thoughtful. 'Why did you come for me, Tom?'

The hair prickled on the back of his neck. 'What do you mean?'

'I mean, why *you*? Did Pappi call you? I don't understand who you and Sunny really are, you see. Only that Pappi's code tells me I should trust you. I heard shooting, but that wasn't you, was it?'

'No.'

'Then why were you there at my home?'

Despite not wanting to lie to her, he knew he couldn't tell her the truth.

'Sunny and I were friends of your father from a long time ago. He called us because he knew you were in danger.'

She nodded slowly once again, but something told Wilde that she didn't believe this version of events. As she said, she wasn't stupid, whatever the absurd notions with which she had been indoctrinated.

Otto Kalt was not a man to panic, but the disappearance of the girl was deeply worrying. He had never failed in a task given him by Bormann. The problem was that with only Brunner to assist him and hundreds of square kilometres of forest, it felt like a hopeless task.

Every farmhand or forestry worker they encountered was interrogated and sometimes they were fortunate. Yes, they had seen a girl, with a woman and a man – a man with a peaked cap.

And so a picture of his quarry was beginning to emerge. Also the direction of travel. Now they met a Hitler Youth troop, on the road near the site of an air crash, the wreckage still smouldering.

Kalt stopped them with a Hitler salute, his MP 40 slung from his left arm. At his side, and a step behind, the ever-present bulk of Hans Brunner, like an oversized shadow.

'Boys,' Kalt said, 'I need your help. Have you seen a girl with a man and a woman this morning?'

The troop leader shook his head. He was eyeing up the weapons carried by Kalt and his menacing sidekick.

'Not us. Why, who are they?'

'Criminals. Enemies of the state. They were last seen heading in this direction.'

'What did they look like, sir?'

'The girl is ten, the man has a peaked cap and some sort of uniform. As to the woman, I do not have a good description.'

The boy looked uneasy. 'Can I ask you, sir, who are you? You do not wear uniforms yet you carry military weapons – are you perhaps Gemeine Staatspolizei?'

Kalt did not bother to lie.

'No, sonny-boy, we are not Gestapo. But we are working in an official capacity, so you would be well advised to assist us if you can.' His voice was soft, but the threat was implicit.

The boy stiffened; he had been brought up to respect and obey authority, but everyone was aware that enemy spies were operating in Germany and it was his duty to at least demand to see papers. This man's sub-machine gun was very persuasive, however.

'Speak, sonny-boy. Tell me what you have seen.'

'Well, there was the man with the peaked cap at Frau Spitzweg's house. He was a Frenchie – a chauffeur, said he was trying to buy milk.' The troop leader frowned at the memory. 'And then he said his car was broken down. You know, I hadn't thought about it before – why did he want milk if his car was *kaput*? Surely he would have wanted the assistance of a mechanic, not a glass of milk.'

'But he was alone? No girl or woman?'

'No, he was definitely alone. His papers were in order – his name was Sable. Thomas Sable. I remember being a little surprised that his residence card gave an address in Potsdam. He said his mistress was waiting with the car. We offered to go with him and see if we could help him fix it – but then we saw the plane coming down and the parachutist baling out and so we rushed to make the arrest, as is our duty. The parachutist was already dead. We reported the burning plane to the nearby village. We helped the fire brigade, of course.'

Having started, he was now gabbling, talking too much, his eyes fixed on the firearm.

One of his comrades stepped out of the ranks.

'There *were* others – two women, I think. One of them small.'

The leader turned on him.

'What do you mean, Hamer? There was just the Frenchman, that's all.'

Hamer was standing to attention. 'No, forgive me for contradicting you, but I looked back after we had crossed the field. I saw the Frenchman joining the women at the edge of the wood on the other side of the railway line.'

Kalt took a photograph of Klara from his pocket. He had found it in the Riegers' front room and had removed it from its silver frame. He held it in front of the boy's eyes.

'Was this one of them?'

'It's possible. They were some distance away, but it could be so.'

Kalt put the picture back in his pocket, then lifted the muzzle of the MP 40 and pointed it at Hamer.

'Take me to Frau Spitzweg's house. All of you. Now!'

Frau Spitzweg was beside herself with anger.

'We have been robbed, sir. My daughter's JM skirt and blouse and some of our precious bacon. Bread, too!'

'And you didn't see the man?'

'No, but my husband's old fool of a father saw the thief. He did nothing. I think he was too scared. God help the Fatherland if our men at the front are so fearful.'

'And where is your husband?'

'He has been called up to guard a PoW camp in Silesia, so I am left with his senile dolt of a father who does nothing but sleep and eat, piss and fart.'

'And you have a daughter?'

'Yes, Katharina.'

Frau Spitzweg was a desirable woman. She stood before him with an inviting expression, her arms crossed over her ample bosom, her hips tilted invitingly. At another time, Otto Kalt would have made it his business to get her into bed. With her husband away, she would be fair game, and looked worth the effort. Perhaps he would come back here one day soon and become acquainted properly. But not today.

'Did he leave any clues? Did he say anything to your father-in-law?'

'No. But he did something strange – he left money for the food and clothes. What sort of thief does that? Not that it makes any better – for who can get hold of new clothes these days? And as for the bacon, we had been saving that to see us through to spring. Now we have hardly enough to last until Christmas.'

'Were there footprints?'

'Dust and dirt on the kitchen floor, that's all. The swine didn't even take his shoes off when he came indoors. Do you think he was a deviant? Why else would he take a girl's skirt and blouse?'

Kalt looked around the yard and found no distinctive footprints. He looked, too, at the Reichsmark notes the man had left. Again there was nothing unusual about them. Finally he tried to get some sense out of the old man rocking beside the fire, but to no avail.

'Thank you, Frau Spitzweg. I may be back.'

'You would be most welcome, Herr . . .'

'Kalt. Otto Kalt.'

'Well, I hope you catch the man. And when you do, I want him strung up. I would like to be there to see that.'

'So would I, Frau Spitzweg.'

Damn, thought Kalt. This meant the girl, with a proper outfit, would be less conspicuous. And they had food. But all was not lost, for it was clear they were still on foot and continuing in the same direction, north towards the Schorfheide – and the Hitler Youth boys had given him a much fuller description of the Frenchman in a chauffeur's uniform.

Wilde saw movement in the woods, to the east, along the path that Sunny had taken. At last she was returning; she had taken long enough – at least half an hour.

No, that wasn't her. There were two of them – shadowy figures, both much larger than Sunny Somerfeld.

He rose and grabbed Klara's hand.

'Quick. Two men are coming this way.'

Klara wrenched herself free of his grip.

'No, it's all right. They are SS men.'

CHAPTER 16

Wilde's hand went to his pocket, to the carving knife he had stolen from the house. Two young SS guards were emerging into full view. They were tall, straight-backed, with holstered pistols at their belts. Wilde's grip tightened on the hilt of the blade.

Then he saw Sunny. A head shorter than the men, and walking a little behind them, she had been almost invisible, but now he saw her talking amiably with them.

Wilde's eyes met hers and she smiled. She touched the arm of the officer nearest to her.

'Ah, here they are, Herr Major,' Sunny said in quick German. 'My driver, Sable, and my niece Klara.'

The officer ignored Wilde but bowed towards Klara and held out his gloved hand to her.

'Fräulein, it is a pleasure to meet you.'

She took his hand and smiled at him, then took a step back and gave a smart straight-arm salute. He laughed out loud and he and his companion saluted her back. At last the senior man seemed to notice Wilde.

'*Herr Sable – Monsieur Sable – vos papiers, s'il vous plaît.*'

Wilde's heart sank; the officer spoke French. He would be found out in an instant. Wilde glanced at Sunny, whose eyes were wide with apprehension but whose mouth was smiling. He looked back at the officer and gave a sharp, submissive bow of the head, loosening his grip on the knife and removing his hand from his pocket. He brought out his papers and handed them over for inspection. The officer studied them carefully, then handed them to his junior officer, who took an age comparing the picture with Wilde's face. At last he nodded and passed them back.

'You understand we have to be sure of these things,' the officer said, reverting to German. 'I believe Frau Somerfeld has told you whose estate you are entering?'

'Yes,' Wilde said, happier at the language switch and the realisation that the two men were not SS after all, but Luftwaffe officers – air force. The winged insignia on their uniforms made that clear. Still frightening, yes, but the Luftwaffe was not renowned for employing the callous cruelty of the SS.

'And you speak a little German? Good, good. Come, let us get you to the house. You all look as though you need food and rest. Frau Göring has said you are to be looked after.'

Was this really happening? Were they being escorted into the centre of Hermann Göring's country estate by two amiable air-force officers? Wilde began to wonder if he had fallen down a rabbit hole and entered a particularly alarming dreamworld. The walk was only ten minutes, but in that time, he spotted a sniper in a camouflaged tree house, covering the small group with a high-powered rifle, and saw a small herd of bison that looked as though they would have been more at home on the Great Plains of North America than the forests of northern Germany.

Sentries were on guard at the entrance, stationed inside two massive gatehouses, both twenty feet high and decorated with a coat of arms comprising crossed hunting horns, befitting Göring's title as Reich Master of the Hunt, one his many honorifics. The sentries saluted the two officers, took a perfunctory look at their papers, a slightly longer look at Wilde's and Sunny's – and then waved them all through. Another ten-minute walk followed. Neither officer tried to engage Wilde in conversation, much to his relief. Foreign workers were like furniture; they were there, because they were needed, but they did not merit attention. And as for a Frenchman, from one of the conquered territories, such a man was to be tolerated, but nothing more. Sunny also ignored him, as though she, too, considered him nothing more than a worthless flunkey, fit only for driving and carrying out her orders. Instead, she walked with Klara, holding her hand, laughing and joking with her Luftwaffe friends.

That suited Wilde fine.

Now they were at the broad-fronted house, perfectly situated on a narrow strip of land between two beautiful lakes. As someone who thought of a hunting lodge as some sort of wood hut in the forest, Wilde was astonished by the grandeur of Carinhall. A woman with a small girl at her side was standing outside the house as though waiting to greet them as guests.

Good God, that must be Emmy Göring, First Lady of the Third Reich. The nightmare was getting more bizarre by the moment.

In the trees, Otto Kalt slammed his fist on the ground. For a brief moment, he had had the girl in his sights – but then she had jumped up, and been whisked away by two Luftwaffe officers.

He thought of trying to take them all out with one sweep of his MP 40 machine pistol, but he couldn't be sure how Bormann would react to news that two senior German officers had been killed. One girl killed and buried and no one would know; they would just shrug their shoulders and get on with the war. But five people – including two members of the bloody Luftwaffe – that would raise questions. And who could tell whether there weren't other men close by. The officers' presence suggested they must be close to an airfield.

He could have killed the girl with a single shot, but then what? He could not have disposed of the body, and Bormann had been clear about that – no trace must be left that she ever existed. Otherwise questions would be asked. Awkward questions.

These computations had taken little more than a couple of seconds, but the hesitation had been enough. Now all he could do was follow them.

It was not easy. He and Brunner had to stay well back from the party of five, and Hans was not light on his feet.

Very soon, he realised that they were not alone in this forest. The place was crawling with soldiers and armed guards and it was a miracle that he and Brunner had not yet been spotted.

What the hell was this place? He had to talk with Bormann again, get new instructions.

Wilde sat at a table in the kitchen quenching his thirst with a large stein of cold, frothy beer. The cook and a couple of maids bustled around, smiling at him when he caught their eye. They brought him a plate of two large pork chops with a delicious gravy and fresh bread to mop it up. Wilde ate it with relish; he very much doubted whether the rest of the populace were able to consume such fare on a daily basis.

But what now? What were Sunny and Klara doing elsewhere in this palatial building, with its vast halls replete with tapestries, paintings and ancient statuary? All he could do was wait here and hope that Sunny somehow persuaded her hostess to provide them with a car.

'Herr Sable?'

He looked up. The cook was standing by him with another plate, this time of small cakes.

'*Danke schön.*'

'*Bitte schön,*' she replied and put down the plate in front of him.

The cook nodded and gestured to him to eat. She held up the empty stein inquiringly.

'*Noch ein bier?*'

'*Nein, danke. Das war sehr gut.*'

'*Ah, sprechen Sie Deutsch?*'

'*Ein bisschen.*'

The cook looked the part. She was about thirty, well-built and sweaty. Her hearty smile said she was one of those people who considered it their God-given purpose in life to fill people's bellies with good food. Having no idea how long it would be until his next meal, Wilde was more than happy to satisfy her desire and eat.

Sunny arrived at the door and the cook backed away. Sunny spoke in slow German.

'Frau Göring has asked us to stay the night, Sable. You will be given the use of the quarters of Herr Göring's valet, as they are both away in East Prussia. We will leave first thing in the morning.'

Sunny nodded briskly to Wilde and to the cook, and then was gone.

So, that was that. No discussion. Whatever lay behind the decision, it could not be talked of here in front of this cook and the maids. Wilde assumed that they had been invited to stay the night because Emmy Göring simply wished to spend time with her old friend Sunny.

Nothing to worry about, then. So why did he get the horrible feeling that his initial instinct had been correct? That this was a trap.

And then a large man who looked like a gardener – with untamed hair and trousers tied with string – sauntered into the kitchen and demanded, '*Òu est le français?*'

Bormann did not like to be called here at the Wolfsschanze, but there was no alternative. He picked up the phone, his voice was cold.

'Yes?'

'I found them, Herr Reichsleiter . . .'

'*But*, Kalt? You are about to say "*but*", are you not?'

'Two Luftwaffe officers arrived and took them away.'

'Luftwaffe? What has this to do with the Luftwaffe? Where are you?'

'The Schorfheide.'

'Where exactly? That is a sizeable forest.'

'Towards the west. Beyond that it is difficult to say.'

'South of Templin?'

'I would say so. I suppose there must be an air base nearby, for why else would they have chanced upon Luftwaffe officers? And I believe I saw other guards in various positions in the woods. I would say it has to be a military camp or a KZ.'

'Idiot! Do you not realise where you are? You have stumbled upon Carinhall – Fat Hermann's country estate. Thousands of hectares, all patrolled by marksmen and foresters who will slaughter you like game. Do nothing. Just find a guest house and call me with the telephone number. Do you understand, Kalt?'

'Yes, sir.'

Bormann slammed down the phone. This was spinning out of control. Kalt and Brunner were out of their depth. And the name of Göring did nothing to dispel his unease.

'*Òu est le français?*' The words, clearly spoken by a native Frenchman, sent a chill down Wilde's spine.

There was only one thing for it. Speak German; refuse to speak French.

'*Ja,*' he said, remaining seated in front of his food. '*Ich bin ein Franzose. Thomas Sable.*'

Using very basic German, he told the man he would continue to speak in German as it would be rude to exclude their hosts from the conversation by speaking French.

Pulling up a chair, the Frenchman sat down opposite Wilde and signalled to one of the maids for beer. He gave Wilde a searching look, then laughed and switched to German.

'And I am Guillaume – but maybe you should call me Wilhelm.' He reached over and shook hands. 'Guest worker, yes?'

'Yes. I'm a driver.'

'And I am one of the foresters. Where are you from?'

'Toulouse.'

'Lyon.' He patted his belly. 'The city of food. Look, perhaps we could speak a little French if we went outside. Good idea, huh? I don't get much chance, you see.'

'No. It's warm in here.'

After finishing his beer, the Frenchman tired of Wilde's refusal to engage in conversation and wandered off towards the door, kissing each of the maids on the cheek, which they did not seem to enjoy, then squeezing the cook's buttocks. She gave him a look of loathing and hit him on the offending hand with a spatula, hard. He shrugged, and then he was gone.

Wilde breathed again. But what now? Was he just supposed to stay here in these kitchens? He supposed that's what chauffeurs did when they took their masters and mistresses to great houses – either polished the car or sat in the kitchens being fed and watered. Not a bad job, perhaps, but a lot of waiting around. For a while he tried to converse with the German staff, but it was stilted and unproductive.

Outside it was getting dark. On December days the light was barely there before it had gone. He stood up, thanked the cook for her hospitality and stepped outside. He could feel the chill off the lakes and felt certain it would rain before the evening was out. He had visions of Sunny sipping expensive wine with Frau Göring in one of her enormous reception rooms. Perhaps Klara was playing with Emmy Göring's little daughter. The child was only three or four, a great deal too young to be a proper playmate for Klara, but perhaps she might enjoy teaching her new games.

At least Hermann wasn't there. Off in East Prussia with the Führer, directing the war in the east.

He felt a touch on the shoulder. Guillaume the forester and gamekeeper was standing with his hands in his pockets.

'*Vous n'êtes pas français.*' He spoke with a snort of derision.

Wilde said nothing.

The gamekeeper was silent for a few moments.

'English, perhaps? You look English – or American. What are you?'

Wilde was considering his options. The gamekeeper was now speaking heavily accented English himself. What were his intentions? Where did his sympathies lie? Some Frenchmen had welcomed the Nazis with open arms and might have been more than happy to travel here to work.

A knife to the throat? That wouldn't solve anything; he was still caught fast in this trap. Even if he abandoned Sunny and Klara, he would be utterly lost in Germany alone. His only hope would be to get back to Berlin somehow and find his way to the American embassy. But the chances of succeeding in that were vanishingly slim.

'Do you have American cigarettes?'

'*Zigaretten? Ich rauche nicht.*'

'Oh, give it a rest, Mr Sable. We both know you're not French or German.'

No, Wilde, don't fall for it, he told himself. *Keep up the pretence, even if it seems hopeless.* He simply shrugged and said, in German, that he didn't understand him.

'*Ich nicht verstehe Sie.*'

Then he turned away towards the edge of the more northerly of the two lakes.

But before he had taken more than a few steps, Guillaume's hand was on his shoulder again, this time gripping hard.

'Don't turn your back on me – I can help you or I can destroy you, mister.'

The grand door at the front of the house was opening. Sunny, Emmy Göring and the two children were emerging into the cool, late afternoon air. One of the Luftwaffe officers was with them and, a couple of steps behind them, another man, whose face was in shadow.

Wilde looked more closely and the blood drained from his face. The other man was Anton Offenbach.

What in God's name was Anton Offenbach doing here?

The only blessing was that it was getting dark and he had not yet been spotted by the little group. Wilde turned away hurriedly, moving deeper into the shadows. He affected a smile for the benefit of Guillaume. There was no time for games now, so he spoke in clear American English.

'OK, buddy, you got me. Your choice – whose side are you on?'

Guillaume grinned back. 'That depends, Monsieur Sable. That very much depends on what you can offer me.'

'I've got no cigarettes, but I've got money. Is that what you want?'

'Well, it's a start.'

'But first, we need to avoid those people – if any of them finds out I am English I truly am done for.'

Gillaume took his arm. 'Come with me.'

Jim Vanderberg was distracted as he walked through the Tiergarten back to his apartment. Two significant events had happened in the past few hours. The first of these affected him personally; his exit visa had come through and he'd be on the train to Basel in a day or two. His heart leapt at the prospect of going home to America and seeing Juliet and the boys again, but he also felt reluctant to leave his friends and colleagues – and Berlin itself – at such a critical time, both for the diplomatic mission itself, and for the history of the world.

Word had come through of an attack on the US fleet in Pearl Harbor, Hawaii, and on Americans in Manila. Many ships had been destroyed and the United States was now at war – though not yet declared – with Japan. What that would mean for US–German relations was, so far, unclear. But the implications were obvious.

With his thoughts fixed firmly on the uncertainties ahead, he did not notice the figure following him. It had become so commonplace to be tailed by the Gestapo – men in raincoats with hats dipped over their brows – that he no longer paid any attention to them. On this day, however, his shadow was not a member of the Gestapo.

It was late, well after midnight, and raining. The wires had been red-hot with rumours. Everyone in the mission had stayed at their posts, even the typists. The attack on Pearl Harbor had started about five hours earlier and at first the news coming through had been sketchy and confused. Now, though, it was all becoming clear. Roosevelt would be declaring war on Japan within the next twenty-four hours, unless Hirohito got there first.

Under the Berlin Pact, Germany was supposed to take Japan's side in any war with America. Would Hitler keep his promise? If so, then the world would explode.

The few people out at this time of night moved like ghosts through the steady rainfall. There were no street lights and the waning moon was obscured by cloud. Someone had, however, marked some of the pavement edges with luminous paint, the sort used on watch faces. And that helped him find his way.

Vanderberg was exhausted and soaking when he arrived home. As he put the key in the lock, he was still on edge. He was turning the handle when he heard a voice. As he pushed open the door, a little yellow light streamed out from a single low-wattage bulb, just enough for him to see a pitiful figure emerge from the dark. It was the woman who had come to him before, the midwife Romy Dietrich. But it couldn't be Frau Dietrich, could it? She had been murdered in her block of flats.

'My God,' he said. 'I thought you were dead.'

He pulled her inside the front hall and quickly shut the door after them. She was bent and shaking, one hand in the pocket of a grey, outsized coat that was so stained and worn, it looked as though it had been stripped from a dead soldier. Her fair hair was lank, wet and thin. Her face was drawn, her forehead had an angry bruise and her eyes were flickering and fearful.

'I am so sorry.' she said. 'I followed you from the embassy . . . I did not know what else to do. I have nowhere else to turn.'

'Hush, let me take you up to my rooms.'

He helped her up the staircase and was relieved that the landlady did not poke her nose around her door to see who he was bringing home; she must be asleep, he thought.

'Come in, Frau Dietrich,' Vanderberg said. 'Sit down. I'll get you some coffee – perhaps with a little rum.'

'Thank you.'

'I'm just relieved to find you alive. I went to your apartment and was told there had been a murder. I feared the worst.'

'They killed my landlady, Frau Schlegel. They broke her neck in front of my eyes – and then they forced me into a van.'

Slowly and painfully she removed her left hand from her coat pocket. The bandage, a strip of cotton rag, was streaked with dried blood.

He sucked in a breath. 'What did they do to you?'

'They wanted to find Klara. They ripped out my fingernails one by one to make me reveal her whereabouts. They would have killed me, but I . . . escaped.'

She couldn't continue. She was thinking of the wall in the pig-gery, of the pliers, of the blank-eyed farmwife. She started weeping, her chest heaving.

He knelt at her side. 'Take your time, Frau Dietrich.'

She took a deep breath, wiping her eyes with her good hand.

'Oh, Herr Vanderberg, I am so ashamed – I told them. I told them everything. I even told them I had come to you in the embassy. I couldn't take the pain.'

Vanderberg put an arm around her. 'Come on, let's get you that rum.' He went to the sideboard and returned with the bottle and two glasses. He poured them each a shot. 'Drink up,' he said.

She took a sip, then downed the rest in one.

'Is that better?' he asked in his most reassuring voice.

Inside he was wondering what this meant for Tom Wilde and Sunny Somerfeld? He needed to discover a great deal more from Frau Romy Dietrich. The timing of her revelation to whoever had tortured her was crucial to Wilde's chances. He desperately hoped Tom and Sunny were already on the boat to Sweden and freedom with the girl; perhaps they had already arrived.

But perhaps they had been too late.

Here in Berlin, though, he had Romy Dietrich to worry about. Perhaps himself, too, if Bormann decided US diplomats were now fair game. But that wasn't for Frau Dietrich's ears.

'You're safe with me,' he said.

Was she, though? There was a very good chance that a Gestapo agent – or Bormann's assassins – would have seen her entering the block.

CHAPTER 17

Wilde was tired but he couldn't sleep. He had to get out of this place now. Tonight. The Frenchman Guillaume could betray him at any moment. Wilde had given him all the money he had, but the wretched gamekeeper knew he had him by the throat and was determined to wring every last pfennig out of him.

'That's everything,' Wilde had said inside the gamekeeper's cabin as he counted out his Reichsmark banknotes and handed them over.

'It's not enough,' Guillaume said, stuffing the cash into his own pockets.

'What do you want, then?'

'Your watch – I like the look of it.'

'No, you're not having that.'

It had been a birthday present from Lydia. He'd fight to the death to keep it.

Gillaume scowled. 'I need enough money to get me out of this place and back to France. As it is I am taking a big risk not turning you in. If you are caught my head will be on the block for not telling them you're English right away.'

'I'm not English, I'm American.'

Gillaume shrugged, as if they were the same thing. 'Your mistress knows who you are, so get the money from her. Maybe she has jewels – get them. Tell her if she doesn't give me what I want, I'll do for her, too.'

After the confrontation, Wilde had returned to the kitchen and simply waited. Other than stealing a car and making a dash for it, he could see no alternative; he'd never get past the guard post and nor could he leave without the child.

Eventually, some other servants and estate workers arrived in the kitchen and they were all served a supper of soup and dumplings. He managed a few words of German with them and they accepted him at face value as a migrant worker.

Then Guillaume came back in and made it his business to sit beside Wilde. He spoke very deliberate German to him with a smirk that said 'I know your secret'. The other workers seemed to stay as far away as possible from the Frenchman and Wilde deduced he was not popular. He was not surprised.

Later, Wilde had been shown to a room with a comfortable bed on the first floor of the main house, and was told that it was a great honour to be sleeping in the room belonging to Göring's valet while he was away with his master. It was at the personal insistence of Frau Göring.

Now here he was, lying fully dressed on this comfortable bed, in this comfortable room, but feeling anything but comfortable, knowing he was in such close proximity to the rooms of Frau Göring and various officers and guards of the Third Reich, any one of whom could effect his immediate arrest. What if Anton Offenbach were to see him? The game would most certainly be up then. And what was bloody Offenbach doing here anyway?

But his most immediate concern was Guillaume. If he hadn't satisfied his demands by morning, the worst he could imagine would shortly follow.

From somewhere in the depths of the enormous building he heard the distant strains of a song he recognised, 'Der Wind hat mir ein Lied erzählt.' Zarah Leander, what a voice. He imagined Sunny in the ballroom with Emmy Göring and others, perhaps dancing to the gramophone and drinking champagne. He felt empty, isolated and helpless, sensations he was not used to.

Half an hour later there was a soft knock at the door. Wilde opened it and breathed deeply with relief. Sunny was standing there.

'Thank God you're here. Come in, we need to talk.'

'Everything's fine,' she said, stepping into his room.

'Where's Klara?'

'In bed. She's in Edda's room. They are getting on famously. Klara may be a Narzisse, but she will make a very good mother.'

'Edda's the Görings' daughter?'

'Yes.'

'This is bad,' Wilde said quietly. 'Very bad.'

'Calm down, Tom. I was told you had nerves of steel. You have this pleasant room and I have a fine room across the corridor where Werner and I used to stay. This is better than a hotel – and we all need a good night's rest. I'm exhausted.'

'This is insane!' he hissed.

'On the contrary,' she said, her former composure fully restored. 'This is the perfect solution. Emmy has kindly offered the use of a car from her husband's fine collection – a Buick, I believe. We will leave after breakfast.'

'You're not listening, Sunny. We have very little chance of getting anywhere near the car.'

In hushed tones, he quickly explained the problem with the Frenchman. Sunny listened intently, then shook her head.

'I know the man you mean – and he wouldn't be stupid enough to say anything. Don't worry – nothing will come of it.'

'No, he's got us cornered.'

'So what do you suggest?'

'I think we should go – now.'

'That's not possible. This place has watertight security. No one can get in or out unseen or unchallenged.'

'We have to try. It's not safe to stay here.'

'Gott in bloody Himmel, Tom, these people are my friends. They will take my side against some blackmailing French bastard. Please, just trust me on this. One night, a good sleep – and in the morning we will have a clear run to the coast.'

Wilde shook his head in frustration. 'There's worse. When I saw you earlier on, there was a man with you – a man called Anton Offenbach. He was my keeper and watcher. How in the name of God has he ended up here?'

'Anton? You know Anton?'

'He brought me from Portugal!' He fought to keep his voice under control.

'Tom, I didn't know that. But of course I am acquainted with him – we move in the same circles. This is just a class thing, the same way everyone from all the great houses in England know each other. Anton's a Junker – a nobleman or gentry, the British would say – like my Werner. These are my *Beziehungen* – my connections. Without them I would be at the mercy of the Himmlers and Heydrichs – the men behind my husband's death.'

'So Offenbach is not a Nazi?'

'There are Nazis and Nazis, Tom. Let's just say he is a patriot. Like me.'

'Is he helping us? Does he know what you're doing?'

She waved her hand in the air. 'I'm going to my room now. Get some sleep. Klara is also exhausted – she is a child and she has had the worst, most tiring day of her life. But this time tomorrow you and she will be aboard a fishing boat on your way to Sweden – then back to your beautiful wife and child and safety. Don't you want that, Tom? If so, then trust me.'

Trust me. It was the second time in two minutes that she had said these words. So why did it ring so accursedly hollow?

*

Wilde wasn't sure whether he slept or not, but he sank onto the pillow and the next thing he knew was the sound of a car pulling up outside and voices. He switched on the bedside lamp, looked at his watch and saw it was two in the morning. He turned off the light and pulled the curtain back a fraction.

A dark car stood on the roadway, its engine running and its headlights blazing. A man sat at the wheel. Two other men in uniform were dragging someone – hands bound and struggling – towards the vehicle.

One of the rear doors was open and they pushed him inside. At the last moment, Wilde caught sight of his face in the moonlight, mouth open. Half a shout emerged before the butt of a pistol smashed into the man's face. He fell backwards onto the rear seat.

It was Guillaume.

One of the uniformed men slid in beside him and the door was slammed shut. The last man went around to the other side and got into the rear seat, trapping the Frenchman in the middle. The driver put the car in gear and the car growled away into the night.

Trust me, she had said.

Wilde was still fully dressed, except for his shoes and chauffeur's cap. He padded to the door of his room and looked out along the carpeted corridor, which was lit by a single wall sconce further along, close to the grand staircase. The head and broad antlers of a deer, attached to the wall, cast strange shadows along the narrow runner. All seemed clear. He crept along the corridor and down the stairs, thinking himself insane even as he did so. What was he looking for? What could he possibly gain from this? But curiosity and frustration at his sense of powerlessness drove him on. As he approached the door a hand grasped his arm and the muzzle of a pistol caressed his cheek.

'Monsieur Sable, what exactly are you doing?'

It was the Luftwaffe major. He was speaking German.

'I . . . I needed some air.'

'And do you think it wise to go prowling at night?'

'Forgive me. I didn't think.'

'Indeed not. It is not safe outside at night, monsieur. Wolves hunt in these woods. People get hurt.'

'I'm sorry, Herr Major. Please forgive me.'

The major gave him a searching look.

'Go back to bed.'

Sunny's door was on the other side of the corridor from Wilde's, ten yards to the right, next to the children's room. He had to talk to her.

He approached the door and raised his hand to knock lightly, then stopped himself. He could hear movement inside, so she was definitely awake. But after his confrontation with the Luftwaffe officer he couldn't afford to alert anyone in this house. Instead he lowered his hand and tried turning the door handle. It was unlocked and the door opened a few inches on well-oiled hinges.

Her bedside light was on and he looked towards the bed, about to call out her name, but then pulled back without actually closing the door, and hoping to God he hadn't been seen.

Sunny was in bed with Anton Offenbach. They were both naked. She was straddling him, moaning gently, lowering herself on to him. His eyes were closed in ecstasy.

He had only glimpsed them for a moment before retreating, but it had been more than enough.

He returned to his room, quietly closed the door and sat on the bed, thinking hard. He needed to make sense of it, but nothing added up. Or, rather, the only thing that made any sense was that he had been set up.

But how? And why?

One thing seemed clear: this tryst here with her lover, Offen-bach, must have been planned. Their arrival here at the same time could not have been mere chance. That must mean that she had always been planning to bring Wilde and Klara here, one way or another.

Another thing seemed clear: not only were Sunny Somerfeld and Anton Offenbach lovers, they must also be working together.

But he *couldn't* believe that everything had been planned. Not last night, for instance. In the woods, hunted by gunmen, Sunny Somerfeld had been faint with fear, and that was not acting.

So what now? Wilde wanted to get away from her, but at the moment she still seemed like his best option of getting out of Germany. His *only* option.

Whoever had signed the foreign office memorandum requesting an interview for Tomas Esser with Herr Todt had covered their tracks well. Since arriving in Berlin, Charlie Jung had got precisely nowhere in his search. There was nothing in the foreign office archive and no one had any recollection of any such paper being signed on behalf of Ribbentrop.

Nor did Jung make any progress finding Anton Offenbach. He was not at his home in Wilmersdorf, and Jung's contact at the Abwehr offices had no information on him or his whereabouts, though he said he would look into it. An hour later he called back, having drawn a blank.

'He seems to be out of town, Charlie. No one seems to know where he has been since yesterday. Why do you want him?'

'I owe him a drink, and I was in town.'

'If I see him I'll tell him you called.'

'Don't bother. It's not important.'

Offenbach's disappearance raised a question: might he have forged the foreign office memorandum himself? It would have been an easy task for a halfway efficient officer of the Abwehr or, indeed, the foreign ministry itself. Perhaps everything started and finished with Anton Offenbach. This was all beginning to stink like an open sewer.

Jung had placed a phone call to the guest house down in the region of the Schorfheide and had made contact with Otto Kalt. It was hard to make himself understood, because Kalt spoke in riddles, as though afraid he was being eavesdropped. But there wasn't time to worry about such niceties; they had to move – and move fast. And if the Gestapo wanted to listen in, well, that was fine, too, because with Bormann's involvement this was clearly a great deal bigger than anything some junior Gestapo officers could disrupt. At last, the message got through, and Kalt said he would carry out Jung's instructions to the letter.

Jung had his doubts. There was panic in Kalt's voice. His only other leads were Frau Somerfeld's house in Potsdam and the apartment of the American diplomat James Vanderberg.

Entering the Potsdam villa was a simple matter. There was no one at home and, with the blackouts secured, he spent two hours searching every room and every drawer, but he wasn't at all sure what he was looking for.

He looked at his watch; the time was 11.30 p.m. Time to leave. He was in the front living room, which smelt of wood ash from an open fire. One last look around, and then he laughed. He had seen exactly what he was looking for, after all. How the hell had he missed it? For the first time, he felt a surge of optimism. Charlie Jung was going to land on his feet again.

*

A short time later he was standing in the teeming rain outside the apartment of James Vanderberg, to the north of the Tiergarten, and was deciding on his next move. He had never seen Vanderberg before, but he assumed that the man who turned up after midnight was the man he sought.

Who, though, he wondered, was the bedraggled woman who accosted the American, begging admittance to the house? Not Frau Somerfeld, that was certain, for he had seen her photographs in her grand Potsdam villa. Nor was this woman a prostitute; you'd have to be desperate as hell to pay fifty pfennigs for this appalling drab.

He turned to walk away. He didn't have time for this; he'd let others investigate the woman. One phone call should take care of it.

CHAPTER 18

Somehow, Wilde managed a couple of hours' sleep. In the morning, after a bath and shave, he took breakfast in the kitchens with the estate workers. No one mentioned the Frenchman. He had been conveniently removed. That was the way things happened in totalitarian police states and it gave him no comfort; the same thing could just as easily happen to him.

He met Sunny on the forecourt at 8.30. If she knew that he had seen her in bed with Anton Offenbach, it did not register on her face.

'The car is being brought around, Monsieur Sable,' she said.

'Where's Klara?'

'Frau Göring will bring her out. Be careful to salute her properly and with deference. You can manage that, can't you?'

He rather thought she was mocking him, but he let it pass.

'In the night I saw them taking the French blackmailer away,' he said.

'Yes, I heard he had been arrested. Apparently he was listening to a foreign wireless station – the BBC, I believe. That's a serious offence.'

'So he'll end up in Sachsenhausen?'

'I believe not. It seems he begged to stop because he was desperate to relieve himself when they were driving through a dense part of the woods. Being gentlemen, the officers agreed to his request – but then he tried to make a run for it. I'm afraid he was shot dead. Very sad, don't you think?'

Wilde paled. 'You mean they murdered him?'

'He would have done the same to you,' she said with a shrug. Here . . .' She opened her bag, took out a purse, and removed a bundle of banknotes. 'These were found on him. I believe they're yours. Now do you trust me?'

Emmy Göring walked out of the front door with a child clutching each hand and a lion cub padding along at her side. A liveried servant accompanied her, holding a large umbrella over their heads. Emmy had a grand position to maintain as First Lady and always had to look her best, even in the light rain now falling. Wilde knew she had been a famous actress in the past, but her glamour days were gone and despite the best efforts of her tailor and coiffeuse to maintain her reputation as the best-dressed woman in Germany, she had the look of a frumpy Hausfrau who thought she was the lady of the manor, and the mixture didn't quite work.

Wilde bowed to her with great deference, wondering whether she also required the Hitler salute. As she did not proffer one, he decided he wouldn't either.

'Herr Sable,' she said.

He wasn't certain how to respond. Frau Reichsmarschall? Frau Göring? Meine Dame? Instead, he simply bowed again.

She spoke in quick German. 'Now drive carefully, Herr Sable, for the Reichsmarschall may not be in a forgiving mood should you damage his beloved Buick motor car. But more importantly, take care of dear little Klara and my lovely friend Sunny.'

Sunny translated into slow French, even though he had already understood the German.

'And be sure to return the car before the end of the week. We will then get you to the railway station at Eberswalde so that you can return to Potsdam.'

'*Danke sehr, Frau Göring,*' he said, touching his cap, and was rewarded with a warm smile.

Klara stroked the lion cub as though it were a kitten, then hugged Emmy Göring and climbed into the back of the Buick.

The car was large and square, a hard-top with whitewall tyres and a swanky running board; a car fit for a movie star – or a vainglorious Reichsmarschall. Wilde drove steadily with Sunny at his side and Klara bouncing about in the roomy rear seat.

They passed through two Carinhall guard posts, including the main gatehouses, and were waved through with straight-arm salutes; their exit had been cleared in advance and they had been given official headed papers, signed by the Luftwaffe major, authorising the use of the vehicle. Once out on the open road, on a lakeside route in the depths of the Schorfheide, Sunny delved into her bag and, out of sight of Klara, handed Wilde a pistol.

'A Walther. You know how to use it?'

'Oh yes.' He grinned.

'Just in case. At Carinhall we were protected. Now we are at the mercy of our enemies.'

'What is Frau Göring's role in all this?'

'I told you, she's my friend. It's in her nature to help people.'

'And her husband, the big man himself? He's one of the first and worst Nazis. The whole world knows that.'

'This is war, Tom. We can't pick and choose. Just as Churchill now cosies up to Stalin, a man with whom he has nothing in common but a common enemy.'

'But Göring—'

'Forget about him. You ask too many questions. All you need to know is one thing – I have the best interests of Klara at heart. Now, just drive. Keep it steady, there's only one road out for the moment.'

Wilde was glad to see the back of Carinhall. Whatever Sunny said, it had never felt safe to him – more like a pit of vipers.

'You won't have heard the news,' Sunny said. 'Japan has attacked the American Fleet in Hawaii.'

'Are you serious?'

'I guess it now really will be a world war.'

He gripped the steering wheel tightly. 'Hell.'

A good distance ahead of them, just before the first crossroads, he saw a checkpoint and began to slow down. Two soldiers in field-grey greatcoats with sub-machine guns stepped into the road. One of them, much smaller than his comrade and wearing spectacles, raised his right hand, palm forward.

'What do you think, Sunny?'

'I don't know.'

'Well, I don't like it.' He pulled the Walther from the glovebox where he had stowed it. 'I take it this thing's loaded?'

'What are you going to do?'

Wilde stopped the Buick a hundred yards back from the checkpoint. And waited.

'What's happening? What's happening?' Klara's voice came from the back seat.

'Hush, Klara. We don't know yet. Lie flat on the seat and keep your head down. Get ready to get out and run if we say so. OK?'

Wilde narrowed his eyes, squinting through the drizzle. There was a dark-coloured vehicle parked close to the two soldiers. At first he had thought it must be some sort of armoured car or troop carrier, but now he wasn't so sure.

'You see that black vehicle, Sunny? Just hidden in the trees . . . that's not military. Looks very like the van we saw at Der Steinhof.'

'God, you're right.'

With the pistol on his lap, Wilde wrenched the gearstick into reverse, but it was stiff and he stalled the engine.

'God damn it.'

He turned the ignition key to 'off' and tried to restart the car, but the engine wouldn't catch. The two men in field-grey army greatcoats and steel helmets were advancing down the centre of the narrow road, MP 40s at their chests. Suddenly the smaller of the two men stopped, took quick aim, and a burst of gunfire followed. Bullets peppered the Buick's bonnet. Wilde desperately tried the ignition again. This time it roared into life. He hit reverse once more and let out the clutch. The wheels spun as he accelerated back down the road, trying to hold a line and not veer off into the trees.

The checkpoint sentries broke into a trot.

Wilde was desperate to turn the car round so he could build up some speed, but the road was a narrow single track and the steering circle of the Buick was made for the open highway. Then over his shoulder he saw another car approaching from the rear. Now they were trapped. He pushed down hard on the horn, hoping the other car would take evasive action and drive off the road.

Instead, the other car ground to a halt, almost at the Buick's rear bumper, closing off all retreat. Wilde grabbed the Walther, threw open the car door and rolled out, firing towards the checkpoint sentries. Three shots in quick succession, with barely time to aim. The two men stopped in their tracks, ranged their weapons towards him and fired again. Wilde rose into a crouch, partially shielded by the wheel arch, and took proper aim. Did the Walther have six bullets? Eight? He didn't know, but he had to make every bullet count. Once the chamber was empty, he had no more.

He loosed off two shots at the larger of the two men, who made a bigger target. The man took a step backwards and his machine pistol jerked into the air, letting rip with a stream of bullets.

Before he could range his sight on the second man, Wilde caught some movement in his peripheral vision. Three men were jumping out of the car behind them. He swivelled to see that they were fanning out and he was now hopelessly outgunned from front and rear. He felt death closing in, but at least he'd take one of the bastards with him. He levelled the Walther at the uniformed man to his left, his finger on the trigger, then dropped his arm as realisation dawned.

They weren't going to attack him; their weapons were aimed at the checkpoint guards.

He turned towards Sunny, still in the front passenger seat of the Buick. Her eyes were wide, almost exultant, as she looked towards the guards. The larger one was doubled up, clutching his throat; even from this distance Wilde could see the blood pulsing through the man's fingers as he crumpled to the ground.

Turning back to the three men from the car behind, Wilde realised they were familiar – the two Luftwaffe officers and Anton Offenbach. They had taken up positions now, with weapons raised and were firing on the other checkpoint soldier, who was already backing away towards the woods, firing from the hip as he went.

Wilde moved away from the car and followed the fugitive. He reached the figure of the man he had hit, lying in the road, a puddle of dark red blood around his head. His helmet lay on the road a few yards away. Wilde could see he was close to death. He wrenched the MP 40 from his feeble grip and hurried after the man's fleeing comrade into the thin, leafless trees, but he had vanished into the darkness. Reluctantly, he turned back. The van was still there, and he saw that it was, indeed, the vehicle they had seen at the Riegers' house in the village of Kossertheim.

He looked at the limp body of the dead guard again and noted that under the army greatcoat he was wearing rough civilian clothes. His instinct had been correct; this had not been an official roadblock. For a few moments he looked down into the man's face. The lips were peeled back, revealing broken and blackened teeth. Wilde couldn't help thinking he looked like a beached shark. He reached into the dead man's pockets and found an identity card and other papers with the name Hans Brunner. Also an address in a town which meant nothing to him. He took the papers and walked back towards the Buick. Sunny was a few metres from the car, kneeling on the roadway with the two Luftwaffe officers close by. There was no sign of Klara or Offenbach. Wilde quickened his pace. He looked in the car and was relieved to see Klara still there, crouching in the back seat and very much alive. He smiled at her.

'Stay there.'

Klara was shaking. 'What's happening, Tom?'

'The bad men – but we're all right now. Hush. Just wait a moment for me.'

He smiled again and closed the car door.

Ten yards to the rear, Sunny was still on her knees and he could tell that she was weeping. Then Wilde saw why. Before her lay the motionless figure of Anton Offenbach.

The Luftwaffe major bent down and gently took hold of Sunny's arm.

'Frau Somerfeld, you have to go. Anyone could come at any time.'

'I can't leave him.'

'Dear lady, Herr Offenbach is dead. Please leave this to us now. You must go, straight away, or we will not be able to help you.'

She was kissing Offenbach's deathly white cheeks. Her tears were falling into his hair, merging with the rain.

The major pulled her to her feet while his junior officer attended to Offenbach's body.

'Go, dear lady, or you will put us all in danger.'

Wilde understood the urgency. He took hold of her other arm and together they dragged her back towards the Buick. She emitted a wail of animal grief, but did nothing to stop them pushing her into her seat and closing the door after her.

'Get out of here, Sable,' the major said. 'As fast as you can. And say nothing.'

'What will you do?'

'Don't worry. As far as the world is concerned, we just walked into this.'

CHAPTER 19

Jim Vanderberg and Romy Dietrich stayed up long into the night, discussing what to do next. The chances were that the Gestapo must know she was here, but that did not mean they would act on the information. His apartment was always watched but he was hopeful that the secret police would not storm into the home of an American diplomat – at least not while some sort of tenuous peace persisted between their countries.

He ran her a bath and then bandaged her injured fingers as best he could, giving her his own pyjamas and dressing gown.

Finally they broached the subject that had brought them together – Geli Raubal.

'I knew her from her childhood days in Vienna. I suppose I was almost like an aunt to her at first, but then we became close friends. We lived in the same apartment block, you see. Her mother, who was widowed by then, was out all the time cooking in the Jewish Hostel. I was a few years older than Geli, training to be a midwife while she was at high school. We always got on well. She was so full of life. A charming, happy girl. If I had had a hard day, she made me smile. In the summer we went on cycle rides into the countryside around Vienna, and in winter we went ice skating together. She always attracted attention from boys – and if they said anything indecent, she inevitably gave them a sharp and amusing riposte.'

'Was Hitler part of her life in those days?'

'Oh, certainly not. He had had nothing to do with his half-sister since a month or two after Geli was born, which would have been before the Great War – 1908, I think. But, you know, Frau Raubal always admired her brother, even from a distance.

No, it was more than that – she *worshipped* him. She cut out any newspaper stories and told Geli and the other children – Friedl and Leo – all about their clever and talented uncle. She told everyone about his exquisite piano playing, the wonderful pictures he painted and his brilliant mind. He became a mythical, almost mystical, figure to Geli.'

'How did they meet?'

'I remember it well – it was when Hitler was in the Landsberg prison after the Munich Putsch. Hitler's friend Putzi Hanfstaengl had fled to Austria and he looked up Frau Raubal, who was so ashamed of the way they lived that she wouldn't let him in to her apartment. Anyway, he insisted on taking her and the children to a cafe and paying for a slap-up meal. I think that was when he suggested they should visit Hitler in prison. I believe Hanfstaengl provided the funds for their journey, because it must be five hundred kilometres from Vienna to Landsberg and Frau Raubal was in dire straits. She couldn't afford new shoes for her children, let alone such an expensive journey.'

'The prison meeting – that must have been interesting.'

Romy laughed. 'Indeed! Geli told me they found him holding court in a cell that was like an upper-class hotel room – certainly a great deal more comfortable than their own shabby apartment in Vienna. It was a hot June afternoon and Uncle Alf – that's what she called him – was wearing his leather shorts, which he always loved in those days. He was surrounded by men who treated him like a king. Even the jailers saluted him – can you imagine? He was charm itself with his long lost sister – and formed an instant rapport with Geli, who was fifteen or sixteen. She made him laugh and clap his hands with delight. She could always make herself attractive to men – and her uncle was as smitten as the rest.'

'And she told you all about it?'

'Everything. She always told me everything apart from the most intimate details of her life. And if she was away she wrote me letters or telephoned, right up until her death. Anyway, back then, I think she was immediately besotted by Hitler, even though he was twenty years older than her. Her mother had built him up so much in her mind, you see.

'A few months later she went to Munich on a school trip and was desperate to see Uncle Alf again. He greeted her, of course, but couldn't spend any time with her and got one of his men to show her the sights. She was very disappointed and told me that she had been wrong, that her uncle wasn't interested in her after all. She was miserable for weeks.

'But everything changed in March 1927. I remember, because that was when I became fully qualified as a midwife. Hitler rented a house in the Bavarian Alps – at a village called Obersalzberg – and asked Frau Raubal to be his housekeeper. She jumped at the chance – it would be a far more comfortable job than cooking kosher food for a load of students for a pittance. Geli couldn't go with her straight away, however – she had to stay on in Vienna until she had finished her school certificate. During those months we spent a lot of time together. I helped her with her studies and made sure she was eating properly.'

'And then she joined her mother?'

'In fact Uncle Alf came and collected her in his chauffeur-driven supercharged Mercedes. They did the journey back at breakneck speed, for Hitler always liked to be driven fast. What a way to travel for a humble girl from the back streets of Vienna! If she was besotted with her uncle before, she was in love with him after that. That summer was idyllic for them. Geli wrote me long letters and telephoned when she could. She told me all about their picnics at Chiemsee. She would go swimming naked while he lay in a deckchair reading the newspaper, or he would stand at the edge of the lake skimming stones like a little boy. She always made sure that he got a good look at her body when she was dripping wet from a swim. They ate wonderful food and sang songs around a fire or listened to one of Hitler's aides playing guitar.'

Vanderberg shook his head, bemused. This did not sound like the monster who was enslaving half the world.

'She was a very earthy girl, you know. And she looked much younger than her real age. And do you know what he called her?' She smiled at the thought. 'Princess. Can you imagine the Führer calling anyone Princess?'

'I confess I can't.

'Well, he did.'

'When did she move into his apartment?'

'I'll come to that in due course. First, that autumn, he found her a tiny apartment of her own in Munich and encouraged her to enrol as a medical student at the university, something totally unsuited to her. She wasn't stupid, don't get me wrong, for she had passed her school certificate, but she had a very light outlook on life and didn't really want to do anything as serious as medicine.

'She just wanted to have fun. Hitler took her to the cinema, the theatre, the opera and all his favourite restaurants. He loved showing her off – and she loved all the attention. The trouble started when other men took an interest in her. How could they not when she flirted so much? She was the sort of girl any man would fall for.'

'So there were other men in her life?'

Romy yawned and shook her head. 'Herr Vanderberg, I will tell you more tomorrow. For now, I think I really have to sleep.'

'Of course.'

*

Wilde drove, but he had little idea where he was going. In the rain, with no sun, he couldn't tell north from south or east from west, and so he had to have Sunny's assistance. But she was curled up in her seat, still weeping, and in no state to help. After two miles, he pulled over in a lay-by at the side of a broad, fast-flowing river.

Gently he touched her shoulder. 'Sunny, you have to help me. I can't do this without you.'

'He was everything to me.'

'I understand, Sunny, truly I do. I liked the guy. And you'll have time to grieve for him properly. But now you have to save our lives – and only you can tell me the way to go. Only you can get us through roadblocks. As it is, I'm terrified this car is about to give out on us – it must have been damaged when the bullets hit the radiator grille.'

'He stood up to them, Tom. Someone has to stand up to these filthy murderers and bullies – and he stood up to them. You didn't see the real Anton.'

Perhaps that was the case, but she still hadn't explained what exactly he was doing, or what his true role was. Those, however, had to be questions for another time. Right now, they had more pressing issues to deal with – namely getting a ten-year-old child to the coast and from there, God willing, across the Baltic to the safety of Sweden.

'Sunny, please, which way do we go?'

She choked back her tears and wiped her eyes and cheeks with her sleeve.

'There's a village ahead. I'll show you the way from there. Pray to God we don't meet any checkpoints. I'm in no fit state . . .'

'We're bound to – but we got through them before on the way to Kossertheim and the papers seem sound. I'm more worried about the fuel gauge right now. What if we sprung a leak from one of those damned bullets?'

'If we have to, we can stop for fuel. Emmy ensured we had a requisition form. But I'd rather not – too many questions.'

So they would just have to make a run for it and hope for the best. Wilde put the car in gear and eased away from the kerb. He would keep to a steady pace, no more than seventy kph, both to conserve fuel and to avoid unwanted attention.

From the back seat, they heard a voice. Klara had been silent until now, hadn't said a word since the events back on the road outside Carinhall. Matthias Rieger had trained her well for all eventualities. But now she spoke up.

'What happened back there? You still haven't told me.'

Sunny turned and reached out a hand to stroke her hair.

'Those were the men who killed your pappi and mutti. We won't have any more trouble from them.'

'Did you kill them?'

'One of them.'

'I wish you had killed them both. I hate them.'

Charlie Jung looked up at the rather splendid little house. It was close to the beach, in the centre of the small coastal town of Schalhagen, next door to a boatyard. The thatched roof needed a bit of work, but other than that, it was a fine seaside holiday home befitting a bourgeois Berliner. He held up the photographs he had ripped from the album he had found in the Somerfeld house in Potsdam. Conveniently, it had a few words in black ink on the back. '*Home from home! Schalhagen, July 1937. Sunshine, soft sand and fine wine. Our perfect summer.*' No doubt about it; this was the holiday home of the air ace Werner Somerfeld and his wife.

He walked through a side gate, and made his way to the rear of the house. The windows were all shuttered. There was a terrace and a pair of closed and locked French windows. Jung took in his surroundings. The house was separated from the boatyard by a two-metre-high wooden fence and did not seem to be overlooked.

Gazing out to the north, the Baltic was cold and dark. A pair of small grey warships were patrolling, cruising the 100-kilometre stretch of coastline between Stralsund and Swinemünde, protecting the Fatherland. These were not easy waters to get through, either into or out of Germany.

And yet they would come here, the unholy trinity of the child, the woman and the man; he was certain of it. If Kalt missed them, then they would make their way here, because this was their best hope of departing the country, the mighty Kriegsmarine notwithstanding; either Sunny Somerfeld had a boat of her own, or she knew someone who would take them. Most likely destination? Sweden, of course – along the smugglers' route that brought illicit food and American cigarettes back to Germany for the black market. Jung had taken advantage of it himself these past two years. Man could not survive on ration coupons alone. Not when he had mistresses to feed.

Charlie Jung strolled back to the little inn. The landlady, Frau Winkler, a woman of thirty with five children ranging in age from infancy to eight to keep her busy, had been reluctant to open up for him.

'My husband is away and our restaurant is closed for the winter, sir. We only do breakfasts and suppers for the naval men lodged here.'

Of course they weren't fully open; no one came to Schalhagen on holiday in December, especially not when there was a war on and the beach was decorated with tank traps. But Jung had pulled out his wallet and discovered that money talked, as always. Then he had shown her the picture of the thatched house and had been directed three hundred metres down the street.

'Just the other side of the boatyard.'

'Thank you. It belongs to old friends.'

'You know the Somerfelds, Herr Jung?'

'Indeed, they have long been my dearest friends. Do *you* know the family, Frau Winkler?'

'Of course, sir. Oh dear, such a sad thing. Herr Generalmajor Somerfeld was much loved in these parts. Such a terrible way to go. Frau Somerfeld has not been here since . . . well, you know the story, sir . . . a terrible tragedy.'

'He was a brave man, fighting for his country. Well, I thought I would go and look at the house as I was passing. Perhaps you would make me something to eat in the meantime?'

'Of course, sir.' She lowered her voice. 'We even have a little meat and some potatoes.'

'You are most kind.'

'Will you require a room, sir?'

'Is anyone else here?'

'Two junior naval officers, sir.'

'I probably have to get on with my journey, but we shall see.'

He could tell that she was eyeing up his expensive clothes, thinking there must be more money to come from this man. A natural enough thought when a woman has five small children to feed.

Now he was back, sitting in Frau Winkler's kitchen as she fried up a thin beefsteak with potatoes and an egg. The children – all boys, it seemed – were crowded around the range, looking at the meal hungrily.

'I suppose someone in the village keeps the key and looks after the place for Frau Somerfeld,' he said casually.

'I believe there is a key at the boatyard.'

'The boatyard? Who would I speak to there?'

'Herr Schmidt. Friedrich Schmidt. He is the proprietor. A very old friend of the Somerfelds. Like yourself, sir.'

'Of course. I believe they may have mentioned him. He has some large seagoing boats, yes?'

She nodded, stiffly, and Jung realised he had asked one question too many. Coastal people were all in it together when it came to smuggling. There might well have been more to her sudden clamming up, however – for a little way east of Schalhagen, he had come across military installations. That would explain the presence of the naval men. The locals would have had the dangers of potential spies drummed into them. Time to change the subject.

'Do you have any brandy, Frau Winkler?'

'A little rum, sir.'

'That would be a fine thing. It's getting colder.' He brought out his wallet and handed her thirty Reichsmarks. 'For your excellent hospitality, dear lady. Perhaps you will find some sweets to buy for your fine boys. For St Nicholas Day.'

'Oh, sir, that is too much,' she said, stuffing the notes into her apron pocket. 'Nicholas Day has gone now, but I will see if I can find them something for Christmas. They will be so pleased.'

'And while I am here at the coast, I would like to buy some fresh fish to take home. Would anyone local be able to supply me? Herr Schmidt, perhaps? You know what, I think I must go and talk with him when I have eaten the excellent meal you are preparing. But first, I need to use your telephone again . . .'

He had tried to make a call to Kalt already that morning, but the guest house where they had lodged said he and Herr Brunner had gone out but had not yet returned. They had said they did not know when they would return. Now Jung called the guest house again.

The proprietor sounded wary; perhaps it was the click on the line.

'Yes, sir, Herr Kalt is back here, but not Herr Brunner.'

'Then fetch him.'

Otto Kalt was not a man given to fear, but he was uncertain how to proceed. He had lost Brunner and he had lost their transport. More than that, he had lost his civilian clothes and was now stuck in the field grey of a Feldwebel, a sergeant in the army – a uniform which had been hard come by, involving a visit to a bar near a barracks fifteen miles west of the dump he was now in. Brunner had found nothing to fit him except a greatcoat.

'Herr Jung?' Kalt said cautiously.

'Are you alone? Has the proprietor gone?'

'Yes, I'm alone. But this line—'

'Damn the phone line, Kalt. What's happened to Brunner?'

'Dead. The man and the woman seemed ready for our checkpoint ambush. And then, I don't know how, they were reinforced by two Luftwaffe officers and another man. I lost the van. Fortunately, I quickly got a lift back here.'

Fortunately? There was nothing at all fortunate about Kalt's position. A man could only fail Martin Bormann so many times and survive.

'Stay there, Kalt, and await my orders.'

Jung replaced the phone and went back to the kitchen. Without another word, he wolfed down the meal, then nodded briskly to Frau Winkler and strode off to the boatyard. This whole area was crawling with military personnel. Something was definitely going on: would Somerfeld, Esser and the girl really risk coming here? Jung was beginning to have severe doubts.

The boatyard was bleak and windswept. The only person in evidence was an old man who was varnishing the wooden deck of an expensive yacht, his knuckles white with cold. He stopped for a moment, looked up at the newcomer, nodded in acknowledgment and carried on working.

'Are you Schmidt?'

The old man stopped his work again.

'Yes, why?'

'The people who own the house next door, I believe you know them – the Somerfeld family.'

'Of course, everyone in Schalhagen knows them.'

'Have they been in touch with you recently?'

'Who are you?'

'My name is Jung.'

'Well, you probably want my son. He has always had more to do with the Somerfelds.'

'Your son – is that Friedrich Schmidt?'

The old man nodded slowly, warily. 'Aye, it is. But he's at sea right now, trawling for herring. Come back in a day or two if you want him.'

'Are you in radio contact with him?'

'Herr Jung, whatever it is you require of my son, it will wait. The last thing he needs while bringing in the herring is a conversation about our neighbours. Good day to you.'

Wilde kept one eye on the road and one on the fuel gauge. The tank had not been emptying as fast as he feared, but he still had doubts whether it would get them eighty kilometres or more to the coast. Nor had they seen a petrol station.

'I'm hungry,' Klara said.

'You had a huge breakfast,' Sunny said.

'But that was hours ago and I'm hungry again. Where are we going? You don't tell me anything,' she said grumpily.

'We are going to the seaside.'

'In December? We can't swim in December.'

'No, we're going on a boat – to get you safe.'

She was silent for a few moments, digesting this new information. The child sighed.

'You said I could have a puppy. When can I have it?'

'When we have you safe in your new home.'

'I want a baby lion, too,' she said, deciding she had the upper hand and now was the time to drive home her advantage. 'I loved Edda and Frau Göring's lion. He was so sweet.'

'Yes, he was,' Sunny said. 'But lion cubs turn into grown-up lions – and then they kill you and eat you.'

'I bet Frau Göring and Edda won't get eaten!'

'No, because the cub is just borrowed by them – and he will go back to the zoo when he gets too big.'

'Frau Göring said one baby lion they had could open all the doors in the house and he came into her room while she and her husband were asleep. It gave them such a shock! But they let the lion stay on their bed.'

Wilde laughed. 'Well, I think we can promise you a kitten or a puppy, Klara, but I'm really not sure about lions.'

'Our school principal said the German people were like lions, kings of the jungle – and that all the lesser races had to kneel before us or we would devour them.'

Sunny snorted with derision. 'I'm sorry to have to tell you this, Klara dear, but your school principal is a *Dummkopf*. There are no lesser races. Humans, whatever their race, are all one species, and no race has to kneel before another.'

'You're lying!'

'Have you ever heard the word Narzisse?'

'Of course – it is a spring flower. Why?'

'You remind me of one, that's all. I think you may be your father's daughter.'

'That's silly. Every girl is her father's daughter.'

An uneasy silence ensued.

Wilde had been listening as he drove, wondering uncomfortably where this conversation was going. Why was Sunny allowing herself to be taunted by this child? Nothing good could come of it.

'I'm sure there will be some food on the boat,' he said by way of changing the subject.

And then the car crested a rise and there, stretched out before them like a seascape by Caspar David Friedrich, was the vastness of the great Baltic.

'I do believe we must be almost there,' he said, noting with relief that there was still a little fuel in the tank.

'Your son's not fishing, Herr Schmidt.' Jung had removed a small jewel-handled pistol from his inside jacket pocket. 'Where is he? Or shall I blow a hole in your brains?'

The old boatman barely reacted to the threat.

'I thought there was something bad about you. I saw you earlier, going to their house. What are you, Gestapo? Himmler's damnable crew?'

The tightening, the throbbing, was beginning in Jung's head. A sensation he knew all too well, one that had been there since childhood when first he gave the cricket captain a beating for suggesting he might be better off further down the batting order. The boy's parents had wanted him expelled; the head had given him one last chance.

He was panting. He swung the butt of the pistol into Schmidt's temple, throwing him to the deck of the yacht.

Through the red mist, realisation was dawning on Jung. He was in the wrong place. They weren't coming here, were they? Far too dangerous with all this military activity. They'd be at a quieter stretch of coast. God, yes, it was clear enough now – all the checkpoints coming here, the endless lines of military vehicles, the air patrols overhead, the ever-present flak guns poking their dark noses into the sky as though this sparsely populated place was a great city. Usedom island across the water must be one vast naval and air force operation. And of course the Schmidts, living here, would know all about it. And so they had had to go elsewhere to pick up their passengers.

'Five seconds, Schmidt, where is he meeting them?'

The old man lifted himself from the deck. Blood was flowing from his ear. Still clutching his varnishing brush, he painfully pulled himself to his feet, using the railing to steady himself. He wiped blood from his head and gave Jung a withering look of disdain.

'Either shoot me or put your stupid little gun away, you pathetic excuse for a man.'

Jung was drooling. His teeth and gums were bared. No one spoke to him like that. He pushed the muzzle of the pistol into the old seafarer's eye and squeezed the trigger. The man jerked back over the edge of the boat and fell onto the concrete floor with a dull thud. Jung looked down at the body with a strange longing; he wanted to kill the man again, and again, and keep killing him.

An electric current surged through him.

He watched the body for a few moments, then jumped down from the deck of the boat and kicked Schmidt hard in the torso and then in the head, marvelling at the strangeness of the transformation of life to death. How a man could stand there deriding him one moment and, the next, lie powerless at his feet. After a few minutes, when no one came at the sound of the gunshot, Jung looked around and found the office at the back of the repair shop, up a metal staircase in a glass-walled room.

The desk was covered in charts, but it was the one on top that told him everything he needed to know. A cross was inked in on a promontory between Greifswald and Stralsund, thirty or forty kilometres west of here. And on a blackboard, in chalk, the name of a trawler: *Harald*, with dates and times of trips and the weight of herring taken.

He had to be sure, though, so he walked with speed and purpose around the boatyard, checking the names of those boats ashore for work to be carried out and those moored at the private quay. In all, there were twenty-two vessels of various sizes and functions. None were called *Harald*.

CHAPTER 20

Wilde parked the car on a rough track deep in a wood, and they remained there, waiting for darkness to fall. According to Sunny, Schmidt had arranged to come at six o'clock, two hours after sunset, and they would meet him on a small beach between two rocky outcrops, a walk of two kilometres from here.

In the meantime, all they could do was wait in this car, cold and dejected, while the rain pattered on the windows and roof. They had crawled here from Carinhall, using farm and forest roads as often as possible, too small to have checkpoints. Even so, they had been stopped often and had passed enough traffic to tauten their nerves – long columns of troops, both motorised and infantry, farm vehicles drawn by wood-gas generator tractors, horse-drawn drays, slave workers and guest workers (only the letters on their jackets told them apart), even a few cars.

The soldiers at the roadblocks had taken a keen interest in the car. Not many American vehicles in these parts, and the name of Göring on the papers only served to increase their interest but also, fortunately, their respect for the occupants.

'I have some food,' Sunny said as Wilde applied the handbrake. 'Emmy very kindly had sandwiches made for us. Sausage or cheese, Klara?'

'Is there jam?'

'No.'

'Then I want sausage *and* cheese. Both.' Her voice was petulant.

Wilde understood her ill-humour. After the dramatic events at her house and then on the road from Carinhall, the journey had been long and dreary. Any child would be fed up. But of course her tetchiness was nothing compared to the inner turmoil the girl must be struggling to contain. In the space of two days she had lost her loved ones, had her spirits lifted at Carinhall – and then the shattering experience of gunfire and death on a public highway.

Sunny took a brown paper parcel from her bag, and unwrapped it on her lap, revealing thick-cut sandwiches of brown bread. She handed one from each side of the pile to Karla.

'There you are. Now, Tom, would you like one?'

'Cheese for me, please.'

'She also gave me a little something to drink – lemonade for Klara, a small flask of whisky for you, Tom.'

Just what he needed at that moment.

'Suddenly I feel a lot happier.'

'And cake for when the sandwiches are gone.'

'This is like a picnic!' Klara said.

Wilde and Klara ate in silence for a few minutes, then he noticed that Sunny wasn't eating.

'You need food, too, you know.'

'I can't eat, Tom.'

He reached out and brushed a tear from her cheek with the back of his hand.

'Do you want to tell me about him?'

'I do, yes. I want to tell the world about him, because he was a hero. He was the sort of man Germany needs right now. I knew him from childhood. Our families were friends. But I spent so much time in America that we somehow lost touch and of course I married someone else. But then, after Werner's death, Anton came to the memorial service and, well, it was like old times. Some would condemn us for the speed with which we got together, but it was just so natural – and no insult to Werner. I loved Werner, too, but very differently.'

Tom nodded sympathetically. 'I'm not going to judge you. But tell me more about you and Anton, if you would. From outside

Germany it's not at all obvious that there is any kind of resistance to the regime. I am impressed by your courage, but rather despondent that the resistance seems so hopeless.'

'Oh, there are plenty of us, mostly in the foreign office, army or air force. But our organisation is woeful. Unless you have known someone a long time, you do not dare to speak out or try to recruit others. How can you reveal your true feelings about the Nazis when the Gestapo and SD have their spies everywhere and all our phones are tapped? Every servant could be reporting to Himmler. Some have been denounced by their oldest friends – even by members of their own families.'

Wilde shook his head. 'Bloody awful, Sunny.'

'That's the understatement of the year. You can be denounced for the most innocuous criticism of you-know-who – and then you'll end up in Sachsenhausen or Ravensbrück.' Her eyes indicated Klara, who was too busy with her food and lemonade to listen. 'So organising a resistance movement is almost impossible.'

'What about those Luftwaffe officers at Carinhall?'

'Great friends of Anton's. And like him, they are patriots. They will kill or die for Germany in this present war, but they are not Nazis. If a coup can ever be staged, they will be on our side.'

'They knew you were coming to Carinhall. It was all planned, wasn't it?'

'I suppose that's obvious now. I knew we could not afford to wait before going to Kossertheim – but I also knew we could not come straight here. Schmidt wouldn't have been ready for us. Of course the plan was to drive to Carinhall, not to trudge across country.'

'And Anton . . . I still don't understand his part in this. Or yours, for that matter.'

She shook her head. 'I'm not going into that now.'

For a few minutes they were silent, each lost in their own thoughts. He broke the spell by passing her the whisky flask.

'Have some of this, won't you? It'll do you good.'

She smiled and took a swig.

'Better?'

'Not really.'

'Well, if you won't tell me how this all came about, talk to me about something else. Tell me about your time in America – we may know the same places, the same people, even. What made you choose Germany as your home?'

'Do you really want to know?'

'Yes, I do.'

'Anything to pass the time, eh?'

'I don't believe you're as cynical as you like to make out, Sunny.' Her gut-wrenching desolation after the death of her lover had shown that clearly enough. 'Where did you live in the States? Jim Vanderberg mentioned Lexington.'

'I was born in Cincinnati, Ohio, among the large German community there, but my mother came from just outside Lexington, a little way south, in Kentucky. Her family had a very successful stud farm, but when my grandfather died my grandmother sold the farm and moved the family lock, stock and barrel to Cincinnati where they lived in suburban comfort. My father was over from Germany visiting relatives – neighbours of ours – when he met my mother. It was a quick courtship in the quiet days before the Great War. And I followed soon after.'

'When did you first come to Germany?'

'Oh, that would have been 1912, when I was two, and we stayed for the duration. I grew up mostly speaking German. In 1919 things were so bad in post-war Germany that we moved back to America. My father's an oil man, so it was the obvious place to be. But we travelled back and forth, and the strange thing was that much as I loved America, Germany always felt like home. You probably don't understand that, Tom.'

'Oh, I understand. I'm a mongrel, too. Half American, half Irish, largely raised in England.'

'The thing is, Germany began to feel less like home after the election of 1933, but by then I'd met Werner Somerfeld and, well, his home was my home.'

He wondered why she hadn't started a family of her own, but that was not something you could really ask. She read his mind.

'Three miscarriages in three years,' she said. 'The doctors said that was it, that I'd never bring a child to term. That was very hard for us. I suppose that's when Werner and I began to drift apart a little. He wasn't happy at the thought of not having an heir. The most important thing in the world for one of his class. And so he went his way, and I went mine, without ever separating or thinking of divorce. Still best of friends, I still loved him, I was still devastated when he died.'

This was all touching on intimate places where the pain was still too raw. They both recognised it.

'Ach, Gott in bloody Himmel, Tom – enough of this maudlin stuff. We have enough problems as it is.'

He smiled at her. She could be difficult, but she was brave and had principles.

'What are you going to do, Sunny? You haven't told me whether you are coming to England with us. I hope you are – because I'm hardly qualified to care for a ten-year-old girl on my own, even if the journey is relatively quick.'

'I'll come as far as Sweden, that's all. Schmidt will bring me home so that I can continue my work against these devils. After that, you're on your own. You'll be fine with the bloody Narzisse. She likes you better than me.'

*

At 5.30, they abandoned the Buick. Whether it would ever get back to its owner did not seem their concern right now, especially as Göring had probably stolen it in the first place. Wilde took the pistol from the glove compartment, and pushed it snugly into his waistband. The three of them walked at an even pace through dripping woodland paths down to a beach no more than six metres across by three metres deep, and protected by jagged walls of rock projecting into the sea.

Once they were out of the trees, the blast hit them. The rain was horizontal and icy, straight down the Baltic from Finland and the North Cape. The darkness was cut by columns of light moving slowly across the sky in search of enemy aircraft approaching across the sea.

'We're a little early,' Sunny said, crossing her arms and hunching her head down against the sleet and wind. 'So we wait again. Gott in bloody Himmel, but it's cold.'

Wilde looked at his watch. A couple of minutes before six. The sooner they were off this damned beach, the better.

'This coastline is constantly patrolled by land and sea. To the east, off Swinemünde, a flotilla of large warships, including destroyers, is at anchor,' Sunny continued. 'And here, though it is quieter, Friedrich Schmidt says the water is mined and the whole coast is fortified. But that's OK, because Schmidt knows the channels and is allowed to go about his business – fishing.'

Wilde was looking down the beach into the black emptiness of the Baltic. He was worried about Sunny. It couldn't make sense for her to come back to Germany, however many friends in high places she had here. Her enemy must know of her part in the events at Der Steinhof and Carinhall; the number plate on the burnt-out Horch was all they needed. Surely she would be better off waiting out the war in Sweden, or even coming to England?

She might affect not have a maternal bone in her body, but Wilde suspected that wasn't quite true. She had, after all, been pregnant three times. Anyway, someone would have to be a mother to Klara. His eyes narrowed and he wiped the icy rain from his face. Was it his imagination or was there a shadow moving out there?

'I think I see something.'

Within a minute the shape was very definitely a rowing boat with a single oarsman aboard.

'Is that Schmidt?' Wilde asked.

'I doubt it, one of his men more likely. But Tom, they are all trustworthy.'

How could she know that? He saw – or sensed – something else.

'Ssh,' he said urgently, lowering himself to his haunches. 'Get down, both of you.'

He had sensed movement to the west, beyond the rocks. A patrol, perhaps. His hand tightened on the butt of the pistol. He needed to warn the rower about the patrol, but there was no way of doing so without some sort of torch or lamp to send a signal. And they had nothing.

He heard a scuffling sound. Boots on sand and pebbles, perhaps – but no voices. Wilde crept along the rocks to try to get a view. An animal scuttled away back into the woods and he almost laughed. Scared by a fox; how the darkness and wind distorted our perceptions. There was no patrol.

The small rowing boat beached with a rush, tossed ashore by a crashing wave, and the oarsman jumped out, grabbing the prow to hold her steady. The man switched on an electric torch and allowed the beam to sweep across the three drenched people waiting for him, lingering on Wilde a little longer than the others. Then he gave a cursory nod by way of greeting. He didn't say anything, just gestured to the boat. The gist was obvious: *Get in, fast. This is going to be difficult.*

Sunny stepped forward and climbed in confidently, as though she had done this many times before. The boat rocked violently; even partially beached it was unstable.

Wilde picked up Klara.

'Come on, in you go.'

'I don't like this.'

'It's going to be fun. In a few minutes you'll be nice and warm in a big boat with a bed of your own.'

Without ceremony, he handed her over to Sunny, who accepted the child in her outstretched arms. Then Wilde climbed in himself.

Within seconds, the oarsman was pushing off into the swell, and they were at sea. The rower handed Wilde a pair of oars and indicated that he should sit on the bow bench, facing astern. With a huge effort, the two men pulled at their oars and drove the little boat through the crashing waves and back out into the Baltic. Soon they got a rhythm going, pulling hard against the incoming tide, stroke by stroke making headway into the darkness.

Wilde noted that Sunny was sitting with her arms around the child. Perhaps there was a spark of motherly instinct there after all.

The *Harald* was anchored a kilometre out to sea, all its lights extinguished. It took Wilde and the oarsman half an hour of back-breaking work to get there through surging waves and biting rain.

'Oh, Tom, I am losing my stomach,' Sunny said, and immediately turned aside and retched into the sea.

Klara put a hand to her mouth and did the same; they stayed that way the whole of the journey, unable to move away from their respective sides of the boat. Wilde was fine, perhaps because his mind was on the rowing or perhaps because of his many days of sailing with Jim Vanderberg. But he had never experienced a sea as rough as this. As they approached the trawler he was surprised by the size of the vessel, looming and swaying above them in the darkness. A rope ladder was slung over the bulwark. Then a mooring line was tossed down and the oarsman fought to tie her up against the ship.

Sunny lunged for the rope ladder and got a hold. Rung by rung, she was slapped into the side of the trawler, but she held on and, at the top, she was helped on to the deck by a sailor. Catching her breath, she waited at the railings. Wilde helped the child on to the rope ladder and ascended directly behind her, making sure she did not lose her grip and plunge into the icy waves. At the top Sunny reached forward, took hold of her arms and hauled her aboard with the assistance of one of the trawlermen.

At last they were all up, but they did not feel a great deal more comfortable; the trawler was heaving and straining against its anchor chain. A pair of seamen escorted them unsteadily to the wheelhouse where they were welcomed by skipper Schmidt. In the darkness, Wilde could not make out his features, but his voice, rough from cigarettes and salt spray, had a kindness behind the sense of command.

Schmidt shook hands with Wilde and Klara, and gave his old friend Sunny a triple cheek-kiss.

'And now you get down to the cabin. We have no time to lose. We must get far out to sea before we can use our lights. A coastal protection vessel will be here within ten minutes, and we must be gone by then. If they see us we will be stopped and searched.'

'Thank you,' Wilde said. 'Thank you for this.'

'Don't thank me yet,' Schmidt said. 'In these conditions we will not make the Falsterborev lightship for ten or twelve hours, maybe more. I would offer you food – bacon and eggs – but you would simply give it up to the sea, for you will all be sick the whole way unless you can get to sleep. One word of warning – if we look like being stopped, you will be moved at speed from the cabin into a concealed compartment within the bilges, which will not be pleasant. And you will have to be as silent as the grave.'

In the pitch darkness, they had to feel their way, guided by sailors, down a companionway to the cabin, which had two bunks. They were each handed a bucket and were then left to their own devices.

'Nothing to do now, but hope,' Wilde said.

He got no response. The woman and girl were busy bringing up the contents of their stomachs into their buckets. Wilde stretched out on one of the top bunks, closed his eyes and hoped for sleep to come. He heard the deep rumble and clank of the anchor chain being reeled in and then the throaty roar of the engines firing up. Had he really got this far? He was still in German territorial waters, but he was off the mainland. Strangely, he actually felt rather hungry.

And then he dared to think of Lydia and little Johnny again. She would be decorating the house for Christmas soon, buying a toy or two for the boy. Until this moment, he had almost given up hope of ever seeing them again.

CHAPTER 21

Otto Kalt could not believe the Dietrich woman was alive. He would kill Johanna for this. How had she let this happen? More importantly, where exactly *was* the midwife? Jung had told him he had seen a woman matching her description entering the American diplomat's apartment. But he didn't want her dead, he had said. Not yet. First he needed information about the American envoy and his contacts.

'You must talk to your friends, Kalt. You have friends in the SD and Gestapo, don't you?'

'Perhaps. Why?'

'Because I want you to use them.'

'How can they help?'

'Do I need to explain this to you like a child? They monitor the mail, Kalt. They listen in to telephone conversations. I want to know the names of those with whom this American has conversed or corresponded in the past few months. The conversations and letters will seem innocuous enough – nothing will be revealed. But I want to know the identities and locations of those he has dealt with. That is enough. Do you understand, Kalt? Your life depends on this, so don't let me down again.'

'I could lift this American. I am good at persuasion.'

'I know you are, Kalt. But that could cause a whole new set of problems, I'm afraid. Try the SD first. There is always a paper trail – you've just got to find it.'

Now Kalt was here in Berlin, alone. He guessed Brunner was dead; he had seen no sign of life in the body the Luftwaffe officers had carried away, before they removed the van.

Kalt did not like this new arrangement with Jung. He was used to taking orders directly from Bormann, which suited him fine; they went back many years and had prospered together. But this Charlie Jung was another matter – too weak to kill his own wife, what sort of a man was that? Did he even have a Party badge? Kalt had called Bormann to ensure he really was expected to do Jung's bidding. The explosion of anger down the line from the Wolfsschanze had made his body shake and had left him in no doubt that he had a new master.

As it happened, he did have a comrade in the Sicherheitsdienst. A cunning old Party hack, like him. If anyone could help him, then surely Horst Spahn was the man. One phone call was enough to fix a meeting.

Kalt didn't like this building at 8 Prinz-Albrecht-Strasse. Nobody did. It was the home of the SD and the Gestapo, the domain of Himmler and Heydrich and their dreaded legions. He found Horst Spahn in a spartan office on the first floor, surrounded by filing cabinets, his desk covered in papers. He immediately rose from his seat and they shook hands.

'Otto, old friend, how have you been?'

'A little overworked, Horst. Reichsleiter Bormann drives me like a slave.'

'Well, that's war, old chum. Same for all of us.' Spahn put a finger to his lips, then lowered his voice. 'You should consider yourself fortunate to be so close to Bormann. He is more powerful than ever. Some say he is the most powerful man in Germany, though I doubt my own masters, H1 and H2, would agree with that.' Spahn burst out laughing. 'Schnapps, Otto? Let me pour you a glass.'

Kalt knew his friend had influence, but was not at all sure quite how senior he was these days, nor even if he had a specific rank, for he wore civilian clothes. Having an office to himself suggested he had risen up the hierarchy, but perhaps it was not elegant enough for the very highest levels. The problem with dealing with Horst Spahn was that you never knew what lay behind the easy, helpful smile and the bonhomie. He would clap you on the back, laugh at your jokes, tell you he was on your side and then line you up against a wall in the yard and put a bullet in your neck. Or so Kalt had heard, and he had no reason to doubt it. For they were one of a kind.

'A Schnapps would be perfect, thank you.'

Spahn poured two large measures of plum liquor. They clinked glasses and knocked them back in one. The SD man wiped a finger across his little bristly moustache and licked his lips.

'Now then, old friend, what brings you from your farm up to Berlin? I thought you were a full-time pig man when not working for Herr Bormann.'

'Oh, the farm is where my heart lies, but I like to keep my hand in, Horst, and so I have a little work to do here in the big city.'

'Is there something I can help you with? You know I would always do anything in my power to assist an old Party comrade.'

Kalt adjusted his small round spectacles. 'It's true, I do have a favour to ask, Horst.'

'Let us get to the point, then. No beating about the bush between old Party chums, eh?'

'Very well. I want some information about an American diplomat named James Vanderberg. Do you know the name?'

'You know, it's possible I might have heard of him. What sort of information do you want – and why?'

'I want to know who he has contacted in the past few months – here in Germany and abroad.'

'And how would the SD come by information like that?'

'The usual way.'

'Ha! You are such a cynic, Otto. You think we spy on everyone, listen to their conversations, read their letters. Perhaps you think we listen to you?'

'If you did, you would fall asleep from boredom.'

Kalt held out his empty glass for a refill, and Spahn obliged.

'OK, maybe sometimes we listen in,' he said, taking a sip of his Schnapps. 'Maybe we even have ears in the American embassy. But you still haven't told me why you want this information. What interest can Reichsleiter Bormann have in a diplomat who will soon be declared an enemy alien and interned?'

'I don't know, Horst, that is the honest truth. I am merely a servant doing my master's bidding. I suppose he thinks Vanderberg is guilty of espionage against Germany.'

'A diplomat spying? Who could ever imagine such a thing?'

'Ah, you are having a joke at my expense. If I was able to tell you more about the reasons for Bormann's interest in Vanderberg, then I would do so. But my master never reveals more to me than he considers necessary.'

'And I am very happy to help you, Otto. But I need to know what I am getting in return. And I need to be sure that if I give you information it will not come back and bite me on the arse. So what are you offering me?'

'I have nothing to offer.'

'Then you will be in my debt, Otto. And you know what that means, yes? It means whatever I ask of you, you will provide.' He rose from his chair. 'Come on, old friend, let's go and look at the files, see what we can find.'

Kalt pored over a series of files stamped *Streng Geheim* – Top Secret. There was a great deal for him to examine, but one name quickly stood out simply because it was not that of a State Department professional, nor the subject's own family.

COMMUNICATION NOTED: June 20, 1940. June 4, 1940. by cable via Washington to Wilde, Thomas, Cambridge, England. TOM. JUST HEARD. CONGRATULATIONS ON THE ADDITION. I KNEW YOU HAD IT IN YOU. LOVE TO LYDIA AND JOHNNY. JIM

COMMUNICATION INTERCEPT: January 4, 1941. by letter via Washington to Wilde, Thomas (see separate file), professor of history, Cambridge, England. CONTENTS UNKNOWN.

And so it went on. The communications were all stamped and signed as read with the Sicherheitsdienst Berlin heading on each file. They were all either 'contents unknown' or the banal chatter of one friend to another. What made them different was, firstly, the intimacy of the subjects and, secondly, the discovery that there was a separate file held on Thomas Wilde.

He would like to see this file, but could only do so with Spahn's asistance. However, the very fact that there was a separate file on Professor Wilde told a story in itself; Kalt was sure that the SD did not, as a rule, keep tabs on innocent university professors in foreign lands.

An hour and a half later, Spahn returned with two coffees.

'Still working, old friend?'

'You have a lot of papers here.'

'Oh, you know, we have to be thorough. Have you found what you are looking for?'

'I believe I have, Horst.'

'Good. Well, I am most pleased to have been of assistance. Now then, how about another little Schnapps with our coffee, eh?'

'You know me too well, Horst.'

They sat drinking and chatting about old times back in the 1920s and the fun they'd had beating up Communists and Jews.

'Ah, those were the days, Otto. What times we had!'

'All washed down with foaming steins of wheat beer.'

'So give me a little clue, what exactly have you discovered in our valuable files?'

'A name. I can say no more.'

'An American?'

Kalt did not like this one bit. He was not dumb; he knew when he was being interrogated. He grimaced at Spahn.

'You will get me shot!'

'But an American man, yes? You owe me that little clue, surely.'

Kalt tapped his nose. 'Please, Horst, you know I can tell you nothing.'

'But Otto, we are on the same side!' Spahn told the lie with practised ease. No one was on Bormann's side. He shrugged. 'Oh well, old friend, I must admire you for your loyalty to your master.'

After Kalt had left, Spahn went through the file. He knew from Kalt's reaction that he was looking for an American, but of course there were many of those because James Vanderberg was in continuous contact with the State Department in Washington.

One name, however, stood out to him, just as it must have done to Kalt: a professor of history named Thomas Wilde, from Cambridge University in England. There had been letters and telegrams to America, before these avenues of communication had been shut down.

Thomas Wilde. Spahn cross-checked the name and discovered that Professor Wilde had crossed the path of the Abwehr and the

SD on more than one occasion. He was an enemy of the Party, there was no doubt about that. Typical academic. To hell with the shitty professors and all the other self-proclaimed intellectuals. The Party had been absolutely right to burn all those books. Treacherous bastards, the lot of them. But he wanted to discover why Kalt – and therefore Martin Bormann – was so interested in discovering the identity of this particular example of the breed.

He must have Kalt followed, but just as importantly, he needed to bring Vanderberg in for questioning – and diplomatic immunity be damned.

Kalt knew he had a tail as soon as he left 8 Prinz-Albrecht-Strasse. He would have done the same thing to Spahn. He knew, too, that Spahn would probably discover the identity of the man he was looking for. But this was unavoidable. Jung had told him to use his SD contacts, so he had. Now, he needed to stay one step ahead, get the information to Jung without delay. He called the number in Schalhagen.

CHAPTER 22

In the milling crowd at Berlin's busiest station, the Potsdamer terminus, under a vast arching roof of glass, Jim Vanderberg stood a few metres away from Romy Dietrich so that no one would imagine they had anything to do with each other. His colleagues at the embassy, along with press friends and others, had wanted to come to the station for the customary farewell drinks and a sing-song to wish him bon voyage, but he had dissuaded them. The last thing he needed was to draw attention to himself.

The huge train crept slowly along the long, central platform, clouds billowing from its stack, whistles blowing, all steam and coal smoke and iron power. It was already five hours late and he had started to fear it would never come. Now he could not wait to get aboard, well aware that this was likely to be his last chance of a train out of the country. Everyone knew that America would be at war with Nazi Germany within days, if not hours. The attack on Pearl Harbor had made that inevitable. And when that happened, everyone at the embassy was likely to become a permanent guest of Adolf Hitler. Vanderberg did not relish the prospect.

He was not really worried for himself, however. He would survive internment if it happened. And there was always the possibility of some sort of exchange with German diplomats in America. But if Romy Dietrich didn't get out, her hopes of survival were minimal. If a police check discovered that her exit papers were forged, she would – at the very least – end up in a concentration camp. That is, if her pursuers didn't kill her first.

He glanced across at her. The platform lighting was dim, but she caught his eye and smiled back fleetingly, then looked away. Her bandaged and gloved left hand was in the pocket of her maroon wool coat. Her right hand held the handle of a leather suitcase that had belonged to one of the junior clerks at the embassy, and had had its travel stickers removed with hot water.

Vanderberg could not imagine the pain and terror Romy had suffered at the hands of those brutes at the pig farm. She had told him, too, of her chance encounter with a Polish slave worker and the way he saved her, asking nothing in return. If such a man was willing to help her, Vanderberg decided, then surely he, too, must do all he could. Persuading the chargé d'affaires that the embassy should help her with new clothes and forged papers had not been easy in the first instance. But finally the boss had shrugged and said, 'What the hell, Jim, let's do it. Take my car around to your apartment and fetch her. We'll be banged up soon anyway. Might as well be hanged for a sheep.'

They had moved her, hidden in the back of an official embassy vehicle, from Vanderberg's apartment to the courtyard of the embassy, and from there she had been smuggled upstairs to be made over with a new hairdo to cover her bruised forehead, and dressed in silk stockings, skirt, cardigan, dark red coat and beret, all provided and fitted by a willing pair of female American secretaries. Finally, her hand was cleaned up and the fingers dressed with antiseptic ointment and individual plasters, so they could fit in a man's pair of gloves.

'We'll get you out of here close to departure time and leave you in a crowd,' Vanderberg told her. 'From there, you'll need to go straight to the Potsdamer railway station and keep your eyes peeled for me. We travel close to each other but not together. That way if one of us is hauled up, the other one might still get across to Switzerland. Until then we don't know each other, OK?'

'Thank you, Herr Vanderberg.'

'Oh hell, don't thank me. It's our duty to help the victims of this brutal regime.'

During the hours waiting for her to depart the embassy, they had sipped coffee together and Romy returned to her reminiscences of Geli Raubal, talking very quietly, aware the whole time of the possibility that the walls could be bugged. Vanderberg played jazz records on his gramophone to muffle her voice.

'Don't get the idea that Geli was perfect,' Romy said. 'She had moods and could be difficult like anyone else. But overall, she was a lovely girl.'

'I take it she had a sexual relationship with Hitler?'

'That is my assumption, yes. But decent people don't reveal the secrets of the bedroom, do they? But if that was not the case, why did Hitler ask her to live with him and give her a room in close proximity to his own? No, there is no doubt in my mind.'

Vanderberg agreed. 'Anyway, Frau Dietrich, you were going to tell me about the other men in Geli's life. And you still haven't explained to me how she came to be living with Hitler.'

'Well, first of all he put her in a furnished room in Königin-strasse, not far from his own place, then a small apartment nearby in Thierschstrasse belonging to one of his friends. Her studies had gone nowhere, of course, and she had broken them off during that first winter in Munich. There were other problems, too. Did I tell you about Emil Maurice, a disciple of Hitler? He was the one who played the guitar at the picnics. They had been friends since the end of the war and were in the Landsberg Prison together. Maurice even acted as his secretary. When they were freed he became his driver, and so he was there at all the picnics and frol-ics at Chiemsee. He was crazy about Geli – and she certainly had a soft spot for him. He was a lot more lively than Hitler and quite a bit younger.'

'Wasn't Hitler jealous?'

'At first he seemed to put up with their flirtation, but when it became a little more serious, he went into a rage. On one occasion Geli heard him screaming at Maurice and beating him with his riding crop. The result was that Maurice was ousted from Hitler's inner circle and Geli was no longer allowed to see him. Hitler then moved her into his new apartment in Prinzregentenplatz where he could keep her closely controlled. When he wasn't there, others usually were – his housekeeper Frau Winter, her husband Georg and their helper, Frau Reichert. Geli felt that their eyes were on her constantly.'

'Disapproving eyes?'

'They felt their first duty was to Hitler, but I think they probably liked Geli and sympathised with her. Most people did. Many men fell for her – even Goebbels had ideas of taking her as his mistress, until he understood the way things were. Hitler became more and more demanding, telling her what clothes to wear, what time she was to be home, forbidding her to dance, refusing to allow her to go away without him. He even threatened to beat her with his filthy hippo-hide crop. That thing – he always carried it, she said – it was like a talisman to him.'

'Not easy for a young woman.'

She smiled. 'She did not always obey him, of course. One point of contention was her desire to go to Vienna to take singing lessons from Sasha Heine, who had taught her before she moved to Munich. She came once in 1930, just for a weekend when Hitler was in the north electioneering, and she stayed with me. She saw Sasha then.'

'How did she manage to persuade Hitler?'

Romy's eyes clouded over as though a wonderful memory had suddenly been triggered and transported her to better days.

'It was my wedding. How could he have not let her come to her friend's wedding?'

'Did he know who you were?'

'Oh yes, we had met twice on my visits to Munich. As always, when meeting young women, he turned on the charm. He was always very gracious with me.'

'And the singing teacher, this Sasha Heine – was there something between him and Geli?'

'Oh, you know, youthful infatuation. Perhaps a spark was still there. But Hitler would have gone crazy if he found out – for Sasha was Jewish. It's a shame. He would have been good for her. At Prinzregentenplatz she was like a caged bird. I told you how popular she was, but she had enemies, too. Some Party members were madly jealous of her close association with Hitler.'

'Bormann?'

She nodded. 'The worst of the lot. He was vile to her – always creeping around her, touching her, brushing against her breasts, caressing her buttocks. She loathed him and went out of her way to avoid him, but that was not always possible. He thought he was God's gift and that if only he could seduce her, she could use her influence on his behalf to further his career. At that time he was running the SA's insurance office from the Brown House in Munich. No one had heard of him, but slowly and surely, he was finding ways to make himself useful and bringing in money for Hitler and the Party. He understood that the man who controls the purse strings holds the key to power. Strangely, though, Geli's mother *did* like Bormann. He charmed her and took her for meals and drinks whenever she managed to come to Munich from Obersalzberg – where she was still housekeeper at Hitler's rented house. Geli was horrified and told her to steer clear of the fat little greaseball, but Frau Raubal would have none of it. She had no other man in her life and here, for the first time in all her years of slaving in kitchens and living in hovels, someone was paying attention to her. Of course she was flattered.'

Vanderberg looked at his watch.

'Frau Dietrich, I think we have to go. Let's finish the story when we're safely ensconced in a hotel in Switzerland, shall we?'

'The rest of the story is very sad. I can hardly bear to think of it. My poor Geli . . .'

'I understand.'

At last, they were boarding the train. No hope of a sleeping berth or compartment to himself, but Vanderberg found the last seat in a carriage with a band of soldiers returning home on leave. It was a shabby compartment, the floor covered in ash and cigarette ends, the seats threadbare and the blacked-out windows filthy. He stuffed his single suitcase in the overhead rack and settled down with his book. Other men came in and found it was standing room only. At last Romy Dietrich appeared, too, the only woman. One of the soldiers immediately gave up his seat for her, and she thanked him decorously.

The train didn't move. It was after midnight.

The soldiers were beginning to become loud and unruly, laughing about their grisly experiences out east, talking of Kiev and a ravine and the overheating of guns. It made for unpleasant listening, but Vanderberg could say or do nothing. He could not even afford to catch Romy's eye. All he could hope was that their murderous stories were the braggadocio of young men showing off and trying to shock each other with invented tales of horror. He hauled down his suitcase and pulled out a bottle of rum, taking a swig before handing it around to the soldiers. Better to keep them on side than antagonise them. They gratefully accepted the drink and asked him where he was going. When he told them he was American on his way to

Switzerland, one of them, a sergeant, said with a grin, 'Before we start fighting you, yes?'

'Hell, I don't want to fight you guys. I love Germany.'

The sergeant shrugged. 'But anyway, we fight.'

And then the police arrived, demanding papers.

Exhausted by the previous day's drive through northern Germany and the gruelling trip out to the trawler, Wilde found sleep came easily. He awoke many hours later and the cabin was silent, which he hoped meant that Sunny and Klara had managed to doze off, too.

But the storm had not abated. If anything the vessel was pitching more violently as it carved a path through the steep waves. There was a light metallic rap at the door, which then opened. Yellow light came into the darkness from the companionway, silhouetting a man.

'*Mein Herr?*' the man said softly.

Wilde replied in German that he was indeed awake.

'*Komm mit mir, bitte.*'

Wilde slid from the bunk. He took a quick look at Klara and Sunny on their own beds and was pleased to see that they were still fast asleep. On the floor, their full buckets slid back and forth, slopping with the movement of the ship. He followed the trawler-man from the cabin, ducking as he exited, and soon found himself back in the wheelhouse with Captain Schmidt. There was now a little light, and he was able to see that Schmidt was bearded and almost bald on top. A cigarette protruded from the side of his mouth as he peered out into the blackness, keeping one eye on the compass.

'Ah,' Schmidt said, 'You are awake, Herr . . . what do I call you? It doesn't matter. I don't want to know your name. Have you slept well?'

'Yes.'

'And were you very sick?'

'No, but my friends were.'

'Then you must be hungry. Potato soup? Bacon and eggs? Bread and cheese?'

'I like the sound of bacon and eggs.'

'Then that is what you shall have. Coffee, too?'

'Black coffee, no sugar, please.'

'Good, good. A man after my own heart. Now then, we haven't yet discussed what I am to do with you. All Frau Somerfeld said was Sweden. My initial thought was to take you to Malmo because it is closest, but then I began to worry about the German navy. They defend the Öresund heavily to prevent British shipping entering the Baltic and we would most certainly have to undergo a search. So I have altered course and I am taking you further north along the eastern Swedish coast. The question is, how far do we go? Do you have any thoughts about this coastline – where you wish to be landed? Stockholm is a long way still.'

'I don't know Sweden, but I guess we have to get to Stockholm one way or another. Either by sea or land.'

'Perhaps that is best then, but the longer I am at sea the more concerned I become. For the moment, come to my cabin. I will have food and coffee brought to us.'

The food was swimming in grease, but Wilde ate it all with relish and mopped up the plate with a hunk of fresh bread. Schmidt offered him some nameless alcoholic spirit to go with his coffee, and Wilde gladly accepted. He was feeling a lot better about life, and for the first time since arriving at Tempelhof airport was finding himself at ease with the German language.

'I owe you a great debt for all you have done for us, skipper,' he said.

'Don't worry about that. It is all being taken care of by Frau Somerfeld.'

Did he mean money? Was Sunny having to pay for this journey?

'But you are taking a huge risk on our behalf.'

Schmidt laughed. 'Fishermen risk their lives every time they go to sea. Anyway, I am told you are an American, so you are not my enemy. Now if you were British or Russian it would be another matter, for then I would have you thrown into the raging sea,' he added with a grin.

'You're right, I am happy to confirm that I am American. Well, half-American, half-Irish.'

'Then you are a friend of Germany on both sides, and everything is in order.'

Wilde knew very well that it was a lie, that America and Germany were anything but friends and must soon be openly at war, but if Captain Schmidt needed to tell himself that he was engaging in nothing dishonourable or treasonable, then Wilde was more than happy to go along with the pretence.

Hurrying footsteps clanged on the deck above them, then the door burst open and one of the seamen entered the cabin.

'Skipper, a vessel is approaching, signalling to us that it intends to board, that we must cut our engines.'

'In this storm? He wants to board us in weather like this?'

'First mate says it is an E-boat, sir.'

'God damn it, this is madness.' He waved the seaman away, then rose from his seat and indicated that Wilde should move, too. 'I'm afraid this is going to get extremely uncomfortable. Get that drink down you.'

'E-boat?'

'Fast attack vessel armed with cannon and torpedoes. At home in rough seas, no chance of outrunning her. We have to get you and the ladies hidden. Come.'

Klara and Sunny were bleary eyed, their faces drawn and bloodless, their lips cracked and dry. Hours of vomiting had taken a heavy toll and they were dehydrated and aching. They followed Wilde and the trawlermen down through a hatch into the fo'c'sle, where the crew ate and relaxed, then took them further down into the blackness of the bilges. The sailor flashed his torch around but all they saw was slapping water, rusting iron and old ropes. The stench was terrible – engine oil, rotten fish, salt water. The cold was worse than anything Wilde had ever experienced, a bone-freezing chill that made him gasp.

Klara fell to her knees and retched, but there was nothing left to come up. Sunny knelt at her side, trying to comfort her with an arm about her shoulders, though she looked in no better condition than the child.

'Is this where we hide?' Wilde asked.

'Wait,' the sailor said. He handed the torch to Wilde, then went forward and prised a metal panel free at one side of the V-shaped bulwark of the bows, pulling it clear to reveal a space. 'In there.'

Wilde was horrified. He guessed they used this space for smuggling goods from Sweden into Germany, but it certainly wasn't suitable for concealing two adults and a child. Apart from the lethal cold, there was simply not enough space. An old English house party game came to mind – Sardines.

The sailor pushed Wilde forward.

'You first. Quick. We have little time.'

Wilde knew he had no option, so he crawled into the hole and sat with his back against the icy metal of the hull. The sailor helped

Sunny in after him and finally squeezed the child in. She was too exhausted to put up a fight, but her whimpering told Wilde everything he needed to know about the state she was in.

'Now you be quiet,' the sailor said. 'I leave you the torch, but if you hear footsteps you switch it off – and you put these on.' He handed them three gas masks.

'You mean they'll try to gas us out?'

'It has happened to others. There may be dogs, but we place meat and pepper to confuse and distract them. Good luck. No talking, no coughing, no smoking.'

And with that, he replaced the panel, and the three of them were enclosed in a space in which they could not avoid physical contact.

'We should all hug,' Sunny said, putting her arms around Wilde and Klara. 'For warmth.'

Charlie Jung was standing beside the captain on the bridge of the E-boat.

'We need to get aboard that trawler.'

'Impossible to get a boarding craft afloat in these seas,' the naval officer said. 'Or perhaps if I got a little closer you would like to take a chance and leap from deck to deck.'

Jung saw the mocking smile on Kapitänleutnant Flettner's face.

'Damn it, captain, don't take that tone with me. I have information that there are dangerous enemies of the Reich on that vessel. Cross me and you will lose your command – do you understand?'

The naval officer understood only too well.

'Well, we can shadow her if you like, until the storm eases.'

'How long will that be?'

'The shipping forecast says three more hours. Certainly two.'

'We turn back for the German coast, then. You tell them to do the same.'

'Are you sure? That will not be simple.'

'Do as I damned well say!'

Kapitänleutnant Flettner had never been spoken to in such a way, not since he had taken command of his own vessel. No one spoke to a ship's commander like that. But he bit his tongue; orders to help this civilian and to search for the *Harald* had come down from the Wolfsschanze itself, via the Oberkommando der Marine, without explanation.

'Very well,' he said. 'Tell me exactly what you would like me to say.' He offered Jung his loudhailer. 'Or perhaps you would like to give them the command yourself.'

'No, you do it. Tell them to turn about and make way to their home port, Schalhagen.'

'Heil Hitler!' the captain barked, clicking his heels. 'As you wish, Herr Jung.'

'And warn them that if they try anything, we will blow them out of the water.'

CHAPTER 23

The train ran on through the night, the rattle of its wheels soothing and constant. Jim Vanderberg and Romy Dietrich had both survived the first check of their papers and tickets and after a raucous hour or two the carriage had quietened down. Soldiers slept hunched up in corners or in the corridor, every space occupied. Vanderberg didn't sleep and nor did Romy. Occasionally they looked at each other and when he was sure no eyes were on them, he gave her a smile. Of all their fellow passengers only one really worried him: a man in a grey suit with a Party badge in his lapel, standing alone in the doorway. His eyes occasionally fixed on Romy, who did her best not to return his gaze.

Vanderberg tried to read a German translation of *Don Quixote*, but he couldn't concentrate and found himself going over the same paragraph time and again without taking in any of it. The heating wasn't working, or hadn't been turned on and the carriage was cold.

With the arrival of dawn, a guard appeared and pulled back the blackouts. Vanderberg looked out on the slow, lazy sweep of the Rhine and wondered when, if ever, he would see it again. The fields of southern Germany had been sprinkled with a thin scattering of snow and the world looked beautiful. A waiter came around and offered coffee, which they both gratefully accepted, even though they knew it would be ersatz. As the soldiers woke, they were less boisterous than before, but they all smoked a great deal and filled the carriage with the acrid smell of cheap cigarettes. At midday, they arrived at Freiburg and everyone disembarked, some to await the onward train to the border, others to go in other directions. Not far to go now. Forty miles or so, and they would be in Basel, Switzerland.

He found himself wondering about Tom Wilde. Perhaps he should never have got his old friend into this mission, but he was certain there was no better man for the job. And these were days when men had no choice but to steel themselves to hard tasks; the alternative was to hand the world over to the barbarians. God willing, Tom and the child were out of Germany by now.

Vanderberg wanted very much to talk to Romy Dietrich, but he didn't dare, not until they were safely over the border. He was all too aware that the hardest part would be the actual crossing; the border post was where the checks were most thorough, carried out under the lethal eye of the SS.

In the morning, Kalt put a call through to Bormann at the Wolfs-schanze. He had been unable to make contact with Jung.

'What is happening, Kalt?' Bormann's voice had a sharp edge to it.

'The man Jung, I have information for him but cannot make contact.'

'What sort of information?'

'I have the name he asked for. An American called Thomas Wilde. It appears he may be the man with Frau Somerfeld and the girl.'

'Well, that may be of interest. Who is he?'

'He lives in England. He is a university professor.'

'What in the name of the devil's dog turd is he doing in Germany, then?'

'I fear we have been victims of a plot.'

'A plot? You can say that again, with a few choice adjectives thrown in. And how, pray, did you discover this information?'

'I have a source, Herr Reichsleiter.'

'A source? A porter on the railways? A waiter in the Adlon? Your mother's pet cat? Don't beat about the bush, Kalt – *what* source?'

Kalt could hear the deep sucking of cigarettes and Bormann's growing anger, all the way down the line from the Führer's eastern headquarters. Prevarication was pointless.

'The SD, sir. An old Party friend from my Brownshirt days gave me access to their surveillance on the American embassy. It soon became clear that the diplomat James Vanderberg has a close relationship with Wilde. More than that, the SD has a separate file on this man, which made me wonder whether he has worked against the Reich before. This is all information that Herr Jung was seeking, but I can't find him – which is why I have brought it to you, sir. I didn't know what else to do.'

'This old friend of yours at the SD – give me his name.'

'Please, sir. He helped me in confidence. He would be in trouble if his name were to come out.'

'Indeed he would. So what is it?'

This was unavoidable. 'Spahn, sir.'

'Horst Spahn?'

'Yes, sir.'

'That grubby little pig. What did you tell him?'

'Nothing, sir.'

'Don't take me for a fool, Otto. You and I both know Horst Spahn. He wouldn't help his grandmother cross the road unless she paid him. What did you give him for this information?'

'Nothing – I swear it.'

'But you told him you were looking for someone close to Vanderberg. He'll work it all out soon enough.'

Kalt realised he was trapped, just as he knew that Spahn was having him followed and would very likely act against him sooner rather than later.

'He knows nothing about Frau Somerfeld or the girl. Nor did I mention you, Herr Reichsleiter.'

'He knows you work for me, *Dummkopf*!' Bormann sighed audibly, or was he simply lighting another cigarette? 'Well, I suppose I must at least commend you for your work in finding out the name of this American professor. Leave it with me – I'll make contact with Jung. But you know what you must do now, don't you, Otto?'

'I believe so, sir.'

'You need to kill Horst Spahn – and quickly.'

A rush of footsteps on metal and then the panel was ripped out without ceremony. The three of them had been huddled in the tiny space in the bilges for less than five minutes.

'You have to get out now,' Schmidt said. 'We have gone about – turned south – and are being escorted back to Germany where you will assuredly be found, because they will tear this ship apart. That would mean death for every one of us.' He reached in and took Klara in his arms. 'Come on, child, there's no time to lose.'

'What are we going to do?' Wilde asked.

'You have to make your own way to land in the open boat. From the chart, I would say we are probably close to, or even in, Swedish territorial waters. We have seen land to the east, which we take to be the Danish island Bornholm, so you need to head north and west. Unfortunately, I can tell you no more. Our visibility is too poor.'

'Well, if we're in Swedish territorial waters, surely a German naval vessel can't touch us.'

'Indeed, and if you believe that, you must also have trolls in your garden. Come on, we have to get you into the boat and pray that you are not seen.'

Getting into the rowing boat was no easier than it had been disembarking. And now there was an added problem; this time they were on their own without an oarsman/navigator to help them.

'The one thing you have on your side is that the rowing boat is presently on our starboard, as is the shoreline,' Schmidt said. 'The E-boat is to port, so we will eclipse you from their line of sight for a short while. When we untie you, don't row, don't speak, show no lights, just drift backwards with the wind and current. Within a few minutes, the *Harald* and the E-boat will be gone. Then you row – for your life. As soon as you see land, head for a flat stretch of coast and then when you are closer in, a sandy beach, not rocks. Good luck to you all. When the war is over we will meet in Stockholm, you can tell me your name and we will drink some beers.'

And with that he handed Wilde a small compass and put Klara in his arms, then urged him down the rope ladder.

They did precisely as Schmidt had said, crouching as low in the boat as possible without moving. The line was cut and within moments, they were swirling away, without direction or control, past the angry churning of the screw, into the grey fury of the storm. Wilde and Sunny both held on to the girl, but the truth was the three of them were utterly at the mercy of nature and of chance. If the boat capsized, they were lost. If they were seen by the E-boat, it would be no better.

From Freiburg, the train ran steadily until they reached the border post, where it stopped and everyone was ordered to disembark. The crossing did not amount to much. A few huts, wooden barriers and barbed wire. On one side, a handful of SS troops, police and customs officials; on the other side, a hundred metres away across no-man's-land, helmeted Swiss troopers and their own customs men.

'This is it, Frau Dietrich,' Vanderberg whispered in her ear as he passed. 'See you on the other side.'

His voice was jaunty, but he could not entirely conceal his misgivings. They lined up to have their papers and bags checked. Vanderberg was a few places ahead of her, his hand tightly gripping the handle of his bag, sweat soaking his shirt and brow. He had to trust that she had her story straight, for they would certainly ask her the purpose of her visit, and she must not hesitate in her reply: she had been given compassionate leave from her job at the hospital to visit her father in a village near Berne for Christmas; he had a cancer and was not expected to live more than a few weeks. Nothing more, quite simple. Something that might even touch the heart of the stoniest SS man, he hoped.

'Papers,' the plain-clothes officer demanded.

Vanderberg handed over his ID, his diplomatic accreditation and his exit visa. The official scrutinised the documents carefully, checking them against some sort of list, then he asked Wilde to wait a moment while he summoned a tall SS officer.

The SS man ambled over, flicking a riding crop against his thigh. He looked at Vanderberg's face, then his papers, glanced down at the list and said languidly, 'Herr Vanderberg, would you come with me, please. There seems to be some sort of problem.'

'But my exit visa is in order, surely.'

'It seems it was cancelled, first thing this morning. I will need to call Berlin to check on the present situation. Please, come into the customs hut with me.'

As he followed the big SS man into the building, Vanderberg saw that Romy was now just one place away from the checkpoint. He wanted to smile at her, to reassure her, but he couldn't communicate with her in any way without endangering them both. The hut was warmed by a pot stove, that steamed up the windows and made him sweat even more. Vanderberg knew the game was up, that he wouldn't be leaving Germany any time soon. If only he'd left a day or two earlier, everything might have been OK. He stood by the window as the SS man put a telephone call through, occasionally looking his way.

The call took several minutes. At last he put the phone down.

'I am sorry, Herr Vanderberg, but your exit visa is indeed cancelled. You are to be escorted back to Berlin. Did you leave any further luggage on the train?'

'No, just this bag. I travel light.'

'Please take a seat while an escort is found for you.'

'Are you serious? I've got to take that damned train all the way back to Berlin?'

'I'm afraid so – it's out of my hands.'

'Then so be it. Can I at least phone the chargé at the embassy? Let him know what's going on.'

'I'll take advice on that.'

Jim Vanderberg demisted the centre of the window with his hand, then glanced out at the long line of people hoping to succeed where he had failed. He almost gasped with pleasure. Romy was through. She was in Switzerland. She was free. He felt like crying with relief. He wanted to shout out loud. Instead he smiled and chuckled. The bemused SS man shook his head and shrugged.

'Gott in bloody Himmel, Tom, I'm sorry. I never intended to get anyone into a situation like this! I thought it would be all so easy.'

'We're still alive, Sunny.'

'I should take the other oars, but my stomach . . .'

She lurched towards the side and tried to puke again.

'Don't worry about the oars, Sunny. You look after yourself and Klara. I'm OK.'

He was about to say that he had had a good feed, but it was probably the last thing she wanted to hear in her current condition.

The trawler and the E-boat had long since disappeared into the lashing rain and sleet. Wilde had been rowing for an hour now, studying the compass, but without sight of land, he couldn't know for certain where they were heading. It was all very well being told in which direction to row, it was quite another actually holding a course amid the surging waves.

At least he felt the storm was easing a bit; it definitely wasn't getting any worse and he no longer feared they would capsize. The wind had dropped considerably and the rain wasn't whipping into his face quite so fiercely.

'I can't bear this,' Klara said quietly. 'I hate the sea. I'm so cold and my clothes are all soaked through.'

'I think the wind is dropping,' Wilde said. 'I really do.'

'I'm going to die.'

'No, you're not, Klara. We promised your father we would look after you, and we will.'

The child sobbed. Dry, retching, tearless sobs.

'Do you see land yet?' Sunny said, her voice little more than a whispered breath.

'No . . . Oh God . . .'

Hope had come too soon, only to be snatched away.

'What is it? Tom?'

'A ship – heading straight at us.'

The vessel had loomed out of the grey, heading on a steady course, hard at their stern. Wilde frantically switched all his energies to the starboard oar, trying to steer them to safety, but the ship was closing in, threatening to plough them into the depths. And then, like a miracle, it slowed as though its engines had suddenly cut out.

Wilde dropped the oars and waited.

After a minute, he heard the tinny sound of a loudhailer, then a voice in a language he didn't understand; he threw a questioning look at Sunny.

She nodded. 'Swedish.'

'Thank God.'

The loudhailer message was then repeated, this time in German.

'This is the maritime pilot. Do you need help?'

'Yes!' Wilde shouted, his voice thick with salt.

'You wish to go to Sweden?'

'Yes!'

'Then let us help you aboard.'

Wilde leant forward and hugged Sunny and Klara.

'Looks like you're going to Sweden after all, Sunny.'

They were free of Nazi Germany. And even as the realisation dawned, he found himself looking at Klara Rieger and wondering what her future held.

What he didn't know was that freedom came at a price.

And that their troubles were only just beginning.

CHAPTER 24

Charlie Jung knew something was wrong. They definitely had the right boat, the *Harald*, but the calmness with which they accepted the order to return to Germany – without any argument – worried him more and more.

What if they had already dropped their passengers in Sweden? Perhaps they had landed briefly a little further south and were now heading north to some more abundant herring grounds. That would explain their direction of travel at the time they were located.

He stood on the bridge of the little warship, watching the trawler pitching and rolling through the weakening storm. After ninety minutes, he decided they had to be sure. The storm had eased considerably, so he ordered the captain of the E-boat to board the *Harald*.

'Very well, Herr Jung. I think the wind has calmed enough.'

'Then let us do it. I want every centimetre of that boat examined and every member of the crew interrogated.'

'I'm sure they'll be very relieved.'

'Why do you say that?'

'Because once we're finished they'll be able to get back to catching herring to fill hungry German bellies. That is why they're out here.'

Horst Spahn was puzzled. The deeper he delved, the stranger this whole affair became. The Sicherheitsdienst had influence and informants in every police agency throughout the state, and so Spahn instigated a wide-net search, which quickly produced dramatic and surprising results.

Spahn discovered that Martin Bormann's office had made a car registration check on a Horch belonging to Frau Sigrun Somerfeld, the widow of Generalmajor Werner Somerfeld, the great Luftwaffe hero.

Now why, Horst Spahn wondered, would Bormann do that? Why was Bormann interested in Frau Somerfeld and that car?

Spahn made further checks and soon discovered that the Horch had been found burned out on a road outside a village called Kossertheim in Brandenburg, north of Berlin.

And then he unearthed something else from the local police. There had been two deaths in the vicinity of the car, and during the same hours as the fire. The victims were a husband and wife named Matthias and Maria Rieger. They had almost certainly been murdered. The man, a schoolteacher, had died of a gunshot wound to the head, deep in the woods near his home. The absence of a gun by his side ruled out suicide. His wife had fallen or been pushed down a flight of stairs in their house. And there was something else: their daughter, Klara, a gifted pupil at the local school where Herr Rieger also taught, was now missing.

So a child is missing, her parents are dead, and a burnt-out car is traced to the widow of a flying ace. What could any of this have to do with Martin Bormann, Hitler's closest aide?

And there was another thing: the matter of the American diplomat and his communications with a professor at Cambridge University in England, by the name of Thomas Wilde. Why did Bormann want to know about these people? The SD had a separate file on Wilde and it made interesting reading; he had first crossed the path of the German intelligence services at the end of 1936, and again in June and September 1939. In all three cases, he had worked against Germany's interests and was believed to have had links to Britain's secret intelligence services. On the first occasion he had suffered a glancing gunshot wound to the side of his head. Unfortunately, there was no photograph in the file.

Given the gravity of the information coming in, Spahn realised this was a very big affair. Handled correctly and with delicacy, these were matters that might win him great favour with his own masters, Himmler and Heydrich. But one never knew until one had the whole picture, and so he held back from sending any information further up the line. First he needed to understand Martin Bormann's role, for he was a dangerous man to cross.

A few years earlier Bormann had been a relatively minor cog in the Nazi machine, the sort of man Himmler looked down on and used for his own ends. But Bormann had moved on, had latched on to Rudolf Hess, then Hitler himself, leapfrogging almost all those who once despised him. Bormann was no longer the coming man. He was *the man*, the power behind the throne. Himmler, like every other potentate in the Party, now loathed and distrusted the oily Martin Bormann. But had to defer to him if he wished to get the Führer's ear.

Today, Spahn had to find out the truth. The American diplomat had been stopped at the border and was on his way back to Berlin, under escort. In a few hours' time, Spahn would make it his business to be at the railway station to welcome him personally – and escort him to the cellars of 8 Prinz-Albrecht-Strasse where he could sample the pleasures of enhanced interrogation. The embassy would never know. Vanderberg had embarked on the train for Switzerland but hadn't arrived. It would be a mystery. Many people disappeared in the night and fog of Germany at war. Few dared ask questions.

But first, there was Otto Kalt. He had had long enough at liberty. Time for him to come in and talk.

Horst Spahn pulled on his leather greatcoat and summoned his young assistant, whom he liked to call Babyface, after hearing the name in an American newsreel reporting the death of a gangster, Baby Face Nelson. It amused him to give his assistant a notorious gangster's name, because his skin was fresh and smooth and the boy had such bright blue eyes. He didn't even drink alcohol.

Baby-face entered the office, clicked his heels and saluted.

'Heil Hitler, Herr Spahn.'

'Ah, Baby-face, we have important work to do. Something to get us out of this accursed office.'

'Of course, sir.'

'Good boy. Order a car – and bring your weapon.'

After phoning Bormann from a telephone kiosk close to his guest house in a side street off Alexanderplatz, Otto Kalt hunched into his coat, pulled his hat down over his brow and headed out into the heart of Berlin. It was another working day, the roads full of trams, bicycles and military traffic.

Through the gusting sleet, he noted the SD agent sheltering in the cinema doorway across the road, where a Hans Stüwe film was advertised, but Kalt ignored his pursuer, dug his hands deeper into his pockets and hastened westwards, over the Spree on to the museums island, then to the broad stretch of Unter den Linden. He knew the SD man was still following him; he could feel his presence without looking. No one could pursue Otto Kalt undetected.

He was angry with himself, which was an unfamiliar sensation. Angry that he had somehow attracted Martin Bormann's displeasure. In all the years they had worked together, he had never once let his master down. How had it come to this? The fucking dog, of course, barking its warning in the night. It had been a pleasure to shoot the bastard animal, but the pleasure had been short-lived.

Kalt stopped outside a large, busy cafe on the corner of Friedrichstrasse. He hesitated, as though wondering what to do next, then pushed open the door, releasing a gust of warm, steamy air, and quickly found a small table by the window where his pursuer could easily see him. Kalt ordered a coffee, drank it slowly as he read a discarded copy of the Party newspaper, the *Völkischer Beobachter*, then summoned the waitress and paid her.

He headed for the front door, then stopped, called the waitress back and loudly asked her if they had a toilet. She pointed to a passageway at the rear of the large room. He nodded, thanked her and set off in the direction indicated. The toilet was down a short corridor at the back of the restaurant close to the kitchens, which he entered instead.

A chef with a large belly and a walrus moustache put up a hand to stop him.

'Whoa, where do you think you're going, little man?'

'Do you have a rear exit?'

'Yes, but not for you. Off you go. Out of here.'

Kalt removed his pistol from his pocket and stuck it in the chef's face.

'Want to taste this?'

The chef backed away, pointing nervously towards a door along another narrow passage at the rear of the kitchen.

Kalt thanked him and took the exit into a maze of backyards, with horses and carts and vans being unloaded, supplies for all the thriving commercial enterprises in this part of the city. Two Hitler Youth boys were scrubbing graffiti from a long high wall which had been smeared with the slogan of the Red Front – *Rotfront siegt!* Victory to the Reds! Kalt put the gun back in his pocket and broke into a loping run, threading his way through the back streets, always in a vaguely southerly direction. To a pursuer, his path would probably have seemed haphazard, but he knew where he was going. Apart from the building works around the new Chancellery, Berlin hadn't changed much in the years he had spent out of town on his beautiful farm.

Within five minutes, he arrived at Prinz-Albrecht-Strasse just as the black-coated figure of Horst Spahn and another, younger, officer were tripping down the two exit steps of the baleful headquarters of the SD and Gestapo. Well, well, that was convenient. He had expected a long wait, perhaps until the end of the day.

Horst Spahn stopped on the steps, looked right, then left. Damn, it was filthy weather. He wiped the sleet from his eyes. Ah, the car was approaching.

'Now then, Baby-face, we are going to lift a man who I know to be an enemy of the state. He has been watched since yesterday and is holed up in a guest house in Alex. When we find him, I don't mind roughing him up a bit, but we must take him alive, for there are questions for him to answer. All understood?'

'Yes, sir.'

'Good boy. If you have to shoot him, then go for the lower legs – calf or shin or knee. Always do that when you want to bring them in alive.'

'Yes, sir.'

Their car was just pulling up. Baby-face stepped forward to open the rear door for his master.

It was only at the last second that Spahn saw Kalt and felt a spark of irritation. Where was his fucking tail? He'd kill the bastard for letting his target give him the slip. Spahn gave Kalt a welcoming smile, his left hand rising in greeting, his right going into his pocket, feeling for the grip of his Luger pistol.

'Otto, old friend—'

They were the only words he got out. Kalt's first bullet drove through the exquisite leather of Spahn's greatcoat and into his narrow chest. The SD man's eyes opened in astonishment. His hand went to the wound, then he crumpled forward. Kalt's second bullet smacked into the nape of his neck, knocking his head forward into the pavement. A third bullet went through Spahn's hat, into the top of his skull, and deep into the brain.

Blood spattered Kalt's gun hand. He ignored it, fired a couple of shots in the general direction of Spahn's companion and the driver of the car, then turned on his heel to run.

He was too slow. Baby-face had his own pistol out and calmly shot the assassin in the back. Even as he did so, he was aware that he had disobeyed Herr Spahn's instruction that he was only supposed to shoot the man in the lower legs. As Kalt fell to the ground, Baby-face approached him, removed the pistol from the victim's hand and felt for a pulse in the neck. Was he alive or dead? Baby-face wasn't certain.

As an afterthought he shot him again, once in each calf.

The *Harald* had only one secret to reveal. The crew of the E-boat found the false bow and the empty space behind the panelling.

'What's it for, Schmidt?' Jung demanded. He was carrying a length of old rope that he had found in the bilges. 'Smuggling Jews out of Germany – or bringing in enemy spies?'

'Insulation, Herr Jung. In summer, the space keeps the ship cooler and helps keep the herring fresh. In winter, it keeps us a little warmer.'

'Bullshit, you fucker. You're as treacherous as your filthy father.'

'My father? What has my father got to do with this?'

Jung lunged at Schmidt, twisting the rope around his neck.

'I'll do the same to you.'

Schmidt was stronger and wrenched himself free. His eyes widened in horror and anger.

'What have you done to my father?'

Jung could feel it again, the beginning of the beguiling madness and blood lust. Not here, though, not with naval officers on hand.

'You'll find out – if you live long enough. But for that to happen, you had better start talking. Where did you drop them, the girl, the man, and the woman?'

Schmidt was grim-faced. 'Tell me about my father.'

Jung lashed out with the rope, catching the skipper's head with a savage blow.

'Talk, damn you! Where did you take them. I know you took them to Sweden – but where exactly? Talk or I throw your dirty crew overboard, one by one.' He looked around, saw an elderly deckhand and grabbed him by the arm. 'This one to begin with . . .'

Schmidt was still reeling from the blow to his head. But he managed to throw his arms around his friend and workmate.

'No, kill me, but don't harm Klaus. He has done nothing wrong – nor have any of us. You will not harm a single member of my crew.'

Jung hit Schmidt again, full in the face, breaking his nose and spraying blood. The skipper fell at his feet, still desperately clutching hold of his crewman's legs to protect him. But Jung had the edge now and dragged the hapless Klaus away from his skipper, prying him free from the frantic fingers – then pushed the elderly trawlerman to the side railing and heaved him over. He fell without a cry, plunging into the icy water with a dull splash.

Alerted by sounds of an altercation, Kapitänleutnant Flettner emerged from the trawler wheelhouse where he had been examining the *Harald*'s log. He saw the crewman go over and shook his finger at Jung.

'That's enough of that. We are the Kriegsmarine and we prize our honour dearly. We are not thugs.'

Jung glared at him. 'You make the bastard talk, then.'

The captain turned to the other members of the trawler crew.

'Fish your friend out of the sea if you would.' He picked up Schmidt from the deck. 'Are you all right, skipper?'

'I've had worse injuries.' He spat a tooth onto the deck with a mouthful of blood. 'This swine says he has hurt my father.'

'Well, he's not going to hurt you. Come, Herr Jung, put your gun away. We are going to allow these men to go about their business. You are a disgrace to my country. I will return you to Germany and it is my heartfelt desire that I never make your acquaintance again.'

'No,' Jung said. 'Not Germany. I have another idea.'

CHAPTER 25

The Swedish police didn't seem to know how to deal with Wilde and his companions. They were put up in a private house in the seaside town of Skillinge on the south-eastern coast. A series of telephone calls finally reached the American embassy, where Wilde was told he might be better off talking to the British.

'We're all a bit up in the air here, new ambassador arriving any day, Germany's declared war,' the envoy, a second secretary, said. 'Your best bet might be to talk to Harrison and say I suggested they might be able to help. He should be able to put in a word with BOAC, who still run some sort of service out of Bromma.'

Wilde got through to the British Legation in Stockholm and asked for Bertrand Harrison. He gave him a severely edited version of events, then said, 'We need to get to England.'

'Are any of you actually British?' the envoy asked in a slow, upper-class drawl.

'I'm an American citizen, but I live and work in Cambridge.'

'And the lady and child?'

'The lady is half-German, half-American. The girl is German.'

'Well, I don't really see how I can assist you then, Mr Wilde. I would like to help, of course, now that we seem to be allies in this war, but it would be highly irregular. Perhaps you should call the American mission for assistance.'

'They suggested you.'

'Indeed. Very tiresome for you.'

'Look, we have to make our way to England. You are the people to organise flights, are you not? I think it would probably be best if you called a man named Philip Eaton in London. He's MI6. Tell him I have the package.'

'MI6? What is that?'

'Oh, don't play that game!' Wilde couldn't disguise his exasperation. 'Everyone in the diplomatic service knows what MI6 is. You're probably a member yourself.' This ridiculous British conceit of pretending – even to their own people – that the Secret Intelligence Service didn't exist. Who did they think they were kidding, and why? He gave the man Eaton's number. 'You'll speak to a man named Carstairs, who will put you in touch with Eaton. I promise you, this will be a matter of priority for MI6. Just call him, OK.'

'I'll get back to you, Mr Wilde.'

And he hung up.

Gunther Freest sat at Spahn's desk and wondered exactly what had happened out on the street in front of 8 Prinz-Albrecht-Strasse.

'Otto, old friend,' his master had called out in the moment before he was shot. Otto Kalt, the man's papers said, and he was clearly an old Party member. But why had an 'old friend' shot Horst Spahn?

There was so much paperwork on Spahn's desk, and none of it seemed to refer to anyone called Otto Kalt. Everyone else was flummoxed, too. But Freest had been told he had to come up with answers, and quickly. Himmler himself was taking an interest and wanted to know why one of the SD's longest-serving men had been shot.

The only information Spahn had given Freest, however, was that they were going to Alexanderplatz to arrest an enemy of the state. Was the assassin, Otto Kalt, the man they were to have brought in?

He did find another possible clue on a notepad on Spahn's desk: a time – 20.30 – and a railway station, Potsdamerbahnhof. All in black ink. But no name of any passenger.

Eventually Freest was called to Himmler's office and explained his difficulty to the Reichsführer in person.

Himmler listened, then rose from his desk and shook the young man's hand.

'Well done, Freest. I will be recommending you for an award for the way you dealt with the assassin. But your duties do not end there. Spahn was one of my best men,' he said. 'We need to find out who was behind his death, and their motive.'

Freest had never met Himmler before, and he had been under-standably nervous. He saluted stiffly and promised that he would bring those behind the assassination to book.

But now, back in Spahn's office, he had his doubts. Who was to say the killer wasn't a lone wolf? Many people working in the SD had enemies and Spahn must have had more than most. The problem with finding out who they were, however, was that Spahn was one of those men who kept things to himself. Now that he was dead, all his knowledge was gone, too.

Well, he would go along to Potsdamerbahnhof at 8.30 p.m. and see what he could find, but he didn't hold out much hope. He didn't even know who – or what – he was looking for.

The only other things of note in the office were a couple of box files. One was for a man named Vanderberg, the other an American resident in England named Wilde. God alone knew what these two men had to do with any investigation involving Horst Spahn. And there was nothing to suggest either of them had anything to do with the assassin named Otto Kalt.

Freest put his feet up on his old master's desk and sipped a black coffee. With luck, this whole thing would blow over and Himmler, who had plenty more on his plate, would forget all about it. Still, one good thing had come out of the murder. No one would ever call him Baby-face again.

Two days later, Wilde, Klara and Sunny were on their way by train to Stockholm. It seemed as if there was colour in their life for the first time in days: the pretty houses; the green fir forests sprinkled with snow; the still dark lakes; a touch of blue peeping through the clouds. It was such a contrast to the harsh, regimental greyness of Germany, a monochrome world in which the only permitted colour was the red slashes of swastika pennants.

It was already turning to dusk when they arrived in Stockholm and were met at the station by the attaché, Bertrand Harrison.

'Welcome to civilisation,' Harrison said, sounding a great deal more accommodating than he had done when first they spoke; conversations with Philip Eaton of MI6 could have that effect, Wilde mused. 'And an auspicious day it is, too,' Harrison continued. 'You may well feel as though you have emerged from darkness, for today is the Feast of St Lucy, otherwise known as the Festival of Light, when all our Viking cousins light candles, eat saffron buns, drink mulled wine, and girls stick lighted candles in their hair.'

'Sounds dangerous,' Wilde said.

'It's all very pretty actually – all about looking forward to the days beginning to lengthen again, which you need when you only get five and a half hours of sunlight in the day. Hopefully, you three will also have more light in your lives from now on.'

'Thank you.'

Wilde accepted the man's good wishes in the spirit in which they were intended. But in the days and hours since being picked up by the pilot, his initial feeling of relief and optimism had evaporated. He wouldn't feel totally at ease until he was home with Lydia and Johnny.

'We have two rooms booked for you at the Excelsior,' Harrison continued. 'One for the young lady and Frau Somerfeld, and an adjoining suite for you, Mr Wilde. You'll be flown home as soon as feasible. These things can take quite a long time to arrange, but you do have priority – London's orders. I know you have also been in touch with the US Mission and they have agreed that we should deal with your needs on their behalf.'

Wilde smiled dutifully. 'Thank you, Mr Harrison. The hotel, then. I think we could all do with a bath, a meal and a good sleep.'

Harrison led them to a chauffeured car with CD plates and they made their way through the largely traffic-free streets to the tall, elegant Excelsior. Before they got out, Harrison turned from the front passenger seat. He smiled reassuringly in that way that only English envoys can, as though once the British diplomatic service was involved all was well with the world.

'You will, of course, be perfectly at liberty to come and go as you please, but I would advise caution. There are many German agents in Stockholm. If you are wanted for questioning in Germany and are believed to have left the country by covert means, it is highly likely that word has gone out to Abwehr station heads in other capitals, particularly here in Sweden. It is possible they already know you are here.'

Wilde had thought as much himself.

'Don't worry. We'll lie low.'

He *was* worried, though. Seen together, the three of them would be very conspicuous. Perhaps it might be better to take meals in their rooms when possible.

'Now then, is there anything you need before I clear off and leave you to your own devices? Some Swedish money, perhaps?'

'That would help. What I want most is a telephone to call home, though.'

'Of course, Mr Wilde. You might find it advisable to make the call from the legation rather than your hotel. More secure. If you wish I will have the car pick you up a little later, at a suitable time. And you, Frau Somerfeld, is there anything extra we can do for you and the girl?'

'I believe Klara would like some new clothes,' Sunny said. 'The family in Skillinge was very generous, but she would like to pick her own outfit, I think.' She turned to the girl. 'Would that be nice?'

Klara shrugged and looked at her feet.

'Klara, I asked you a question.'

'I suppose so.'

'I think that's a yes,' Wilde said.

Harrison gave Wilde and Sunny a knowing smile, as though to say he knew all about difficult children.

'Well, you're in the right area for shopping,' he said. 'Talk to the concierge. He'll point you in the best direction for the top stores. You might even find some Christmas presents to take home. But keep them small – every ounce counts when flying home through enemy airspace, as you will be doing. Oh, and Mr Eaton sends his kind regards, and compliments on the success of your mission.'

Success? Not yet. And, more than that, there was something else worrying him. Something he hardly cared to think about.

Wilde went to his room, kicked off his shoes and stretched out on the bed. He could hear Sunny and Klara moving about next door; he thought he heard raised voices. He wondered whether Sunny, having lost three babies through miscarriage, might now resent children in some way. Her relationship with Klara was certainly not proving easy, but on the other hand there had been incidents of warmth at sea, which had suggested that motherhood might not be completely unwelcome. Adoption? Was that a possibility?

That was the itch, wasn't it: the matter of Klara Rieger's future. Now, within a few hours of home, that was the question that had been nagging away at his unconscious and must be dealt with. He had been sent to Germany to save a child's life, but what was he taking her to?

Half an hour later, he heard their door bang shut and then silence. Good. With luck, that might mean they had gone out shopping with the money Harrison had given them, an expedition that could do them both some good. He shut his eyes for a moment and must have gone to sleep because he was brought to his senses by a knock at his own door. He rose from the bed, aware that he still had the pistol in his pocket. No one here in Sweden had seen fit to search him.

'Hello?' he said through the door.

'A car is waiting for you downstairs, sir.' A foreign-accented voice, speaking English. 'From the British embassy.'

Wilde opened the door. A liveried bellboy was standing there hopefully, so Wilde found a coin for him.

'Tell the driver I'll be down in a couple of minutes.'

He went to the bathroom and washed his face, then combed his hair and put on his shoes. Time to call home.

The embassy was only a short drive away, a broad-fronted red-brick building with a wealth of white-framed windows. Somewhere between Lutyens and Queen Anne, Wilde decided as the car drew up in front of the glazed front door.

He was directed to Bertrand Harrison's office.

'Ah, Wilde,' the envoy said. 'Hope you've managed to wind down a little. Been a damned stressful time for you, I'm sure, taking responsibility for the ladies.'

'It wasn't quite like that.'

'No? Oh well. Two bits of good news for you. Firstly, we have a telephone call booked to your good lady in Cambridge – ten minutes from now. And secondly we have a flight for you this evening. Midnight, in fact. Thick cloud cover forecast over Norway and Denmark, so you shouldn't be troubled by flak or Me109s.'

'Well, yes, that is good news.'

'Can I offer you a drink? Scotch, perhaps?'

'Thank you.'

The line was surprisingly good with only a short time-lapse.

'Lydia, darling, I'm coming home. Tomorrow with luck. Are you well? And our little boy?'

'We're fine, Tom. Oh, but how are you? How have you ended up in Stockholm?' Her cheery tone couldn't disguise her anxiety. 'No one's told me anything – only that you're safe.'

'Long story. I'll tell you all when I see you. Give Johnny a kiss.'

'Tom . . .' The line went scratchy for a few moments.

'Lydia, I didn't catch that.'

'I said there was a phone call for you earlier today. He asked if you were there, and when you were coming home.'

'Who? Who was it? Cashbone?'

'No, I didn't recognise his voice.'

'American or English?'

'Very definitely English. He was pretty insistent – rather over-keen to speak to you, if anything. He seemed on the verge of losing his temper. To tell the truth I was a little preoccupied. Tom, I don't like talking to you like this. I love you and I want to see you.'

'And I love you. Until tomorrow.'

'Goodbye, darling.'

Wilde replaced the handset.

'Everything all right, Wilde?' Harrison asked.

'I . . . I think so.'

'Another Scotch?'

Wilde nodded. Yes, more whisky might take the edge off the next few hours. And then a flight through Nazi-dominated air-space.

*

Back at the hotel, Wilde knocked at Sunny and Klara's door, but there was no reply. He needed to tell them about their flight plans and was surprised they hadn't returned from the shops yet. He went back down to reception and asked whether they had left a message.

'No, sir.'

'Have you seen them?'

'They returned with some bags but after that, nothing. If they are not in their room I must have missed them going out again. Unless they are in the lounge – have you looked there, Mr Wilde?' The receptionist pointed towards a side room.

Wilde was about to follow his directions when a gust of wintry air blew in from the front door and he turned to see Sunny and Klara, all rosy cheeks and brightly knitted mittens as they tumbled into the hotel lobby, laughing and smiling.

'Am I pleased to see you two!' he said. 'I didn't know what had become of you.'

'Santa Lucia became of us,' Sunny said. 'It's all such fun, Tom. You should have come with us. It's everywhere – carols and processions, everyone carrying candles and wearing white robes. Oh, it's all so beautiful, Tom.'

'Sounds wonderful – and I've got even better news. We're flying tonight.'

The BOAC Lockheed Lodestar took off from Bromma aerodrome right on the dot of midnight with a passenger list of twelve and a cargo of ball bearings. The twin-engined plane rose quickly to over twenty thousand feet, well above the cloud cover, and kept within Swedish airspace until it had reached its maximum cruising height of twenty-five-thousand feet.

The windows were blacked out, the exterior lights extinguished, and the pilot was flying on altimeter and compass, at least until they were well past enemy territory.

Wilde looked around at the other passengers; they were all men, five in British service uniforms, the others in smart civilian suits. Every one of them on business of some sort. The words 'intelligence gathering' came to mind. He was at the back of the plane with Sunny and Klara, who soon fell asleep, her head resting on Sunny's shoulder.

The captain informed them that once out of Swedish airspace they would be cutting south-west across the open waters of the Skagerrak between Norway and Denmark, and so long as they didn't meet any enemy interference there, it should be plain sailing across the North Sea.

Six hours later, they landed at RAF Leuchars on the east coast of Scotland, near the town of St Andrews. It was 6 a.m., still dark outside and Klara was groggy.

'We're here, Klara,' Wilde said. 'This is Scotland – have you heard of Scotland?'

'Yes, of course,' she said, waking up in a rush. 'I've told you, I'm not stupid. Am I going to live here, then?'

'That's still to be decided. First we need to take you down into England, and we can discuss your future. But you can be sure that everyone here is your friend.'

'The Führer says England is our enemy.'

'Well, perhaps the Führer is not right about everything,' Sunny continued. 'You're safe now – no one here wants to hurt you.'

Why, Wilde wondered, was that an assurance he was reluctant to give?

CHAPTER 26

From the outside, no one would have guessed that the Old Rectory was the most important of the Secret Intelligence Service's safe houses. The gardens were skeletal now, but in summer climbing roses blossomed in profusion across the whole of the front wall and the scent of lavender filled the air.

It sat at the entrance to a short lane which led to the thirteenth-century All Saints Church in the village of Harkham, halfway between Cambridge and Saffron Walden. Inside the house, there was nothing to set it apart from any other English country cottage.

The villagers, however, knew there was something unusual about the place. Too many comings and goings, too many men in pinstriped suits and military uniforms for them not to realise something out of the ordinary was going on there. 'Men from the ministry' was about as far as they would go in speculation, because the villagers knew when to keep their mouths shut. They might laugh and gossip about the place among themselves, referring to it as 'the funny farm', but they would never mention it to anyone outside Harkham, nor would they take kindly to questions from strangers.

At the end of a long and meandering train journey southward from Scotland, a local taxi was waiting for Tom, Sunny and Klara at Harkham railway station and they were driven, exhausted, to the front door of the cottage. For Wilde it was a return to the place where his German had been polished by the stern-faced Mrs Rosamund Kemp. Today, as she welcomed them on the doorstep, she was smiling.

'Ah, Professor Wilde, so good to see you back safe and sound. And it is my pleasure to be able to call you by your real name at last, and in English.'

'Good to see you, too, Mrs Kemp.'

'Come in and make yourselves at home,' she said. 'The beds have fresh linen, supper will be ready in an hour, the fires are lit for you and there's piping hot water if you want baths. I do hope you've had a pleasant journey. And before you ask, Mr Eaton and Mr Cashbone will be down from London first thing in the morning.'

When he had been here before, he had assumed Mrs Kemp had been sent here merely to act as his instructor, and he was surprised to find her still here.

'I had thought you would be long gone, Mrs Kemp.'

'I'm live-in and permanent, Professor Wilde. Didn't you know? Teaching German is perhaps the least of my duties.'

He recalled that he had slept downstairs and that her rooms were on the top floor, at the back overlooking the garden.

'I'm here to provide all of your requirements, sir, for as long as you're here,' she continued. 'Now then, coffee, tea – or something a little stronger?'

'Thank you.' Wilde took a second look at the woman. 'And yes to the last of those drink options as far as I'm concerned.'

'Very well, sir – I recall your tipple is Scotch whisky.'

'You remember correctly.'

'And how about you, Frau Somerfeld?'

'I think I'd like a coffee.'

'Klara?'

'Lemon or orange.' Her voice was flat, sullen.

'Well, that's easy – and you'll find plenty of books to read in various languages, including some lovely children's volumes which I have acquired especially for you. I'll just get your drinks, and then leave you to yourselves. Oh, and there is a telephone for emergencies, but Mr Eaton specifically asked that you do not call home just yet, professor. He'll explain why tomorrow. Your wife has been informed that you are home safe but that you will be out of contact for a little while during debriefing.'

They ate supper together virtually in silence, utterly wiped out by the gruelling journey, then Klara said she wanted to go to bed. Sunny took her up to her room and returned ten minutes later to the sitting room, where Wilde was reading the British and American newspapers from the past week. He looked up.

'What now? What are the plans?'

'I think we'd better wait until we meet your friends tomorrow, Tom.'

'I mean you – what will you do? Would you like to return to Germany, or go to your other homeland, America?'

'I need time to think about that.'

'You know you haven't really told me how you became involved in all this.'

He said the words casually, but it was a question that had been troubling him from the beginning.

'Jim Vanderberg asked me to help.'

'Just that? You weren't involved with Romy Dietrich before that?'

Did he sense a certain tenseness as he asked the question?

'No,' she said.

'And though you admit our visit to Carinhall was planned, you still haven't explained the Görings' role in all this. I suppose you were working on their behalf, but I'm still not sure what they wanted from you.'

'Tom, you're being ridiculous.'

Wilde shrugged. 'Really? In what way?'

'Am I being interrogated? This is like the Gestapo – a fine way to welcome me to England after what I have been through to get you and the girl out of Germany.'

Wilde felt her hostility, but ploughed on regardless.

'No, of course I'm not interrogating you – but I do have one question. Why would the Göerings have helped us if they weren't getting anything in return?'

'This is too much—'

'OK, let's go back a bit. Why now, ten years after the child was born and her mother, Geli Raubal, died, did Bormann suddenly bring all this back to the surface? He must have discovered something – but how?'

Sunny gave him a look bordering on loathing, something he had not seen from her before.

'That is something you will have to ask Martin Bormann, I'm afraid. You know, Tom, I thought we could relax together for the first time, enjoy a drink and get to know each other a little better. But instead all I get is this – Tom the policeman. So goodnight. I am going to bed.'

Charlie Jung parked outside a prim-looking house in a tree-lined street in Sevenoaks in the south-eastern county of Kent. By the standards of most people, the building was quite large and desirable, but for a man who had grown accustomed to great wealth, it was a little pokey and middle-class.

Once back in Germany, he would have to ask Martin Bormann if he would use his influence to have this quaint, self-satisfied little town bombed. Flatten it – reduce this suburban house and all those like it to rubble.

He climbed out of the Bentley and approached the front door. He knocked, then took a couple of paces back, fixing a smile on his face. A maid answered the door wearing a black dress and white lacy pinafore.

'Yes, sir?'

'Are Mr and Mrs Young at home?'

'May I ask who you are, sir?'

He smiled. 'I'm their long-lost son, Charles. They may or may not remember me.'

The maid looked flustered. 'Sir?'

'Don't worry.' He stepped inside the hall. 'I'll announce myself. I want to see their faces.'

Philip Eaton arrived at the Old Rectory at 10 a.m. His limp was no better, but Wilde's initial judgement that he was recovering seemed justified. Despite the loss of his left arm and difficult fractures to his left leg, the two and a half years since the road crash had worked in his favour. Perhaps the war helped; Eaton had always been one of those men who thrived in interesting times.

He smiled warmly as they shook hands.

'Well, old boy, you did it. Welcome home.'

They were in the sitting room. Wilde had got up early and had been fed an English breakfast by Mrs Kemp; Sunny and Klara were still enjoying a lie-in.

'Thank you.'

'Cashbone will be along presently. Just had an errand in Cambridge. So, tell me all about it.'

Wilde indicated an armchair.

'First you tell *me* a couple of things, Eaton. I want to know about Jim Vanderberg. What's happened to our boys and girls in Berlin now America's at war with Germany?'

'All the American diplomats and journalists have been rounded up. I'm told they're being shipped to a hotel in Bad Nauheim – a small town near Frankfurt – until such time as some sort of swap can be arranged for German officials presently in America. I'm afraid I don't have any specific information about Vanderberg.'

'I thought he had an exit visa.'

'I've heard nothing about that. Ask Cashbone – perhaps he'll know.'

'Which brings me to my second question. How much do you know about Bodie Cashbone?'

'I thought we went through this before you set off for Germany.'

'Come on, Eaton, there must be more to it than what you told me. He turns up from the State Department to join Bill Whitney's fledging COI outpost in London. Don't tell me MI6 don't know a hell of a lot more about him than that. I know you guys – you spy on your friends even more than your enemies.'

'You have a very cynical view of the Secret Intelligence Service.'

'With reason, Eaton. With *very good* reason. So?'

Eaton shrugged. 'Well, he's a sound man. Harvard educated, comes from Houston, Texas, if I remember correctly. Never served abroad before. Perhaps not right at the heart of things, but certainly acquired the education for the job.'

'Not right at the heart of things? You mean he's not quite Long Island. What are his politics?'

'God knows – Democrat or Republican, I imagine. Everyone's one or the other in America, I believe. Unless you are wondering whether he's a Bolshevik or a Nazi, in which case I can reassure you that he most definitely is not.'

'Married?'

'No, I'm pretty sure he's not, nor with any immediate plans.' Eaton looked bemused at this line of questioning. 'Does that help at all?'

Wilde felt as if there was something missing from this picture of the bear-like Bodie Cashbone. The only time he'd heard the name Cashbone before was in connection with the oil business. Wilde guessed it must be the same family, especially if he hailed from Texas. But that didn't help much, nor put his mind at ease; he still knew very little about the man. Sunny Somerfeld had told him half her life story within a few hours of meeting. Cashbone had revealed nothing.

'Not really,' he said, 'but we'll leave it for now. Let's get some coffee.'

He called Mrs Kemp and she took their order.

'Now let's get on to the girl. Keep your voice down, Eaton, because I don't want her to hear. We need to find Klara some sort of foster family. Someone very discreet. I did wonder whether Sunny might be interested in taking her on. She doesn't have children of her own and she seems to have developed something of a bond with the girl. And the language would help, obviously.'

'Plenty to talk about.'

Wilde frowned. Eaton seemed evasive.

'I suppose a temporary alternative would be a boarding school. She speaks very good English.'

'Our boarding schools can be pretty unforgiving places for foreigners, as you probably discovered yourself at Harrow, Wilde. A German accent probably would not go down well at present. But look, let's wait until Cashbone gets here, shall we? It's his operation. Anyway, I still want to hear the whole story from you – and he might as well hear it at the same time.'

Wilde knew Eaton too well. He might not always be able to read the MI6 man, but he could sense when he was holding back.

'Something else on your mind?'

Eaton ran his hand across his forehead. 'Actually, Wilde, there was something – might be nothing. An E-boat entered territorial waters off the east coast. It was engaged by one of our corvettes and was sunk. The thing is, she was actually heading back out to sea at the time. It's possible she dropped an agent off first.'

'An E-boat?'

'Yes, I made the connection, too. I had heard from Harrison in Stockholm about your to-do with an E-boat in the Baltic. Also, I checked with the police around Southwold, the closest town to the little naval battle. A car was stolen that night, and it has since turned up abandoned in London. Call me paranoid, Eaton – but it's my job to be paranoid.'

'Any survivors from the E-boat?'

'Most of the crew. But they're saying nothing.'

'Well, I'd certainly like to talk to them. Where are they?'

'The captain's at Camp 020, the crewmen are in transit to a PoW camp. But no, you can't talk to them. Look, Wilde, I'm worried that whoever was trying to get to the girl in Germany has followed you here. That's all you need to know. This is why I didn't want you to call Lydia just yet. It's not beyond the bounds of possibility that they have worked out who you are through your connection with Jim Vanderberg. I doubt they have the means to put a tap on your home telephone and I'm pretty sure they can't know about this place but . . . Well, better safe than sorry.'

Wilde thought about his conversation with Lydia and the stranger who had phoned her. Was that worth mentioning? Before he could say anything, Mrs Kemp arrived with the coffee, and then there was a knock at the door.

Bodie Cashbone had to duck under the door frame. Here, in the Old Rectory, with its low ceilings, he looked even more a bear of a man than he had when Wilde had first met him. A handsome bear, but a bear nonetheless.

He had someone else with him: a man with spectacles, a round lined face, thinning white hair and a large briefcase. Wilde estimated him to be at least seventy.

'Wilde, what a man!' Cashbone threw his arms wide. 'My God, Wilde, let me shake you by the hand. You're a miracle worker, buddy. We owe you a Medal of Honor for what you dared do.' He shook hands vigorously.

'You're very kind.' Wilde retrieved his hand from Cashbone's paw.

'Hell no, kindness has nothing to do with it. It's men with your sort of courage that are going to win this war for us. Now, let me introduce Professor Malcolm Bromley, also the holder of a chair at your esteemed university.'

Wilde shook hands with the new man, not someone he had ever seen around Cambridge.

'Pleased to meet you, Professor Bromley.'

'Actually, I'm emeritus professor.'

Wilde kept smiling, searching the man's eyes for some clue to who he was or why he was here.

'And before you ask, Wilde,' Eaton interjected, 'Professor Bromley is an anthropologist, and a leading expert in the field of facial recognition.'

Leading expert. They were words to dampen the spirits of any academic. Or indeed, anyone with half a brain.

'Well, I'm sure you're here for a good reason, Professor Bromley.'

'Bromley has helped the police in the past and has offered to assist my department as and when he might be needed,' Eaton said. 'We are harnessing the finest intellects in Britain to the cause and he's offered his expertise.'

'Now then,' Cashbone said, looking around. 'Where are the girls? In particular, where is our very special ten-year-old?'

Wilde frowned. Something in Cashbone's tone and choice of words unsettled him.

'They're not up yet. We had a long day yesterday. But tell me, Cashbone, would I be right in thinking that you *knew* what the "package" was before you despatched me to Germany?'

'Would you have gone if I'd told you? Hell of a difference smuggling out a live human being rather than an inanimate object, don't you agree?'

Wilde didn't like this one bit.

'That's not the point. I happen to dislike deceit – especially when it's used on me. What about you, Eaton?'

'No, I didn't know. Not until two days ago. I'm sorry if you feel you were deceived or misled.'

'That's not the half of it.'

'Wilde, buddy, stop this!' Cashbone boomed. 'All's well that ends well, for pete's sake. And you're a hero. Now how about some coffee and we'll tell you what's next on the agenda. Where's the scary Mrs Kemp?'

'Wait a minute,' Wilde said. 'I want to know why this guy's here.' He pointed at Bromley. 'And what's in the briefcase?'

Cashbone put his hands on Wilde's shoulders.

'Calm down, buddy, calm down. You're still wound up. We'll take it from here. You've done your bit – now you can relax and leave the rest to us.'

Wilde wrenched himself free. 'My bit? Are you talking about saving a girl's life – or something else?'

While they were talking, Bromley had put his briefcase on the table and was opening it up. Papers, photographs and a pair of steel calipers spilled out.

The door opened and Sunny Somerfeld appeared. Cashbone smiled broadly.

'Frau Somerfeld, I'm Bodie Cashbone – let me shake you by the hand.'

He moved towards her and for a moment Wilde thought the American was going to envelop her in one of his bear hugs. Instead he took her hand formally.

'Pleased to meet you, Mr Cashbone.'

'Likewise. Now where's our other girl?'

They all turned as Klara walked into the room. Her eyes were wide and questioning, flitting between the three newcomers before coming to rest on Wilde. She was shivering, though the room was warm, a fire burning nicely in the grate.

'Tom?'

He tried to smile reassuringly at her, but knew it would be false.

'Hello, Klara, these men are here to help us. We're just having a little chat.' He moved towards her and tried to shepherd her back towards the door. 'Why don't you wait in the kitchen for a few minutes? Ask Mrs Kemp for some breakfast.'

Klara hesitated, then nodded briskly, taking the hint, and closed the door behind her.

'I think I had better go with her,' Sunny said.

'So that's Hitler's daughter. Well, well, who'd have thought the greasy guy with the toothbrush moustache had it him. Pretty little thing, ain't she?'

Cashbone had parked himself on the sofa and was grinning.

Had he really said that? Wilde was aghast.

'Maybe she takes after her mother,' Cashbone added.

Wilde turned to Eaton. 'Is this really happening?'

Eaton looked more ill at ease than Wilde had ever seen him.

'This is an American operation, Wilde – I'm just here to observe and assist.'

Wilde had had enough. He stabbed a finger at Cashbone. 'Goddamn it, don't talk like that,' he said, his voice an urgent whisper. 'She might hear you. She speaks English. She doesn't have any idea about her real parents. Eaton, tell this moron to shut up.'

'I think Wilde might have a point, Cashbone. Far be it from me to tell the COI how to manage their affairs, but I would suggest this business requires a little subtlety.'

Cashbone remained unabashed. 'To hell with that. If she doesn't know already, she's gonna find out soon enough. Might as well break it to her now. We've got a war to fight – nothing subtle about Hitler's damned bombs falling on your cities or sinking our ships, is there?'

'No, she's not going to find out,' Wilde insisted. Again, he appealed to the MI6 man. 'Is she, Eaton?'

Eaton's lips remained firmly sealed.

Wilde turned towards the table. He picked up the calipers that had fallen out of Bromley's briefcase.

'And what are these designed to do, for pity's sake?'

He had a horrible idea that he knew exactly what they were for. He picked up the papers and flicked through photographs – all were of Adolf Hitler or Geli Raubal, from various different angles.

'I take cranial measurements,' Bromley said, with a certain amount of professional pride, 'and from them I will ascertain the child's parentage with ninety-nine per cent certainty.'

'And why exactly would you want to do that, *Professor* Bromley?'

He added a contemptuous stress to the word 'professor', telling the man exactly where he stood in his estimation.

'Wilde, you're not a fool,' Eaton said. 'You must have worked out what this was all about, surely?'

'Well, Eaton, I confess I *was* a fool. I had my doubts, but I never thought for a moment that England or America would stoop so low as to use a child in the front line of propaganda warfare. You know, Eaton, I was beginning to revise my first impression of you. But the truth's out, isn't it? You're planning to turn the child into a freak show exhibit!'

CHAPTER 27

Charlie Jung barely recognised his parents. He sat in a stiff-backed chair in their parlour, a room stuffed with the usual detritus of empire: the tiger-skin rug, its teeth bared, its eyes dead; the finely carved juggernaut panel; the faded photographs of men with solar topis sitting atop elephants; silver salvers and cigarette boxes donated at the end of a posting by colleagues at the club or regiment; ivory ornaments and gold trinkets bought for a song in Indian bazaars.

If his parents were looking at him with bemusement, he was looking at them with corresponding amusement. They hadn't seen each other since 1911, when he was seven years old. His father wore an ancient blazer with a soup-stained tie. He looked eighty and doddery, but Jung knew he could not be more than sixty-five and his mother fifty-nine. She was dumpy and frumpy with two strings of pearls and a tweed skirt, looking rather like Queen Victoria.

Jung sat smiling at them, enjoying the awkwardness, deliberately allowing the silence to stretch out between them. What was there to say? They could always ask each other how they had filled in the intervening thirty years, but that wasn't really going to happen.

'Would you like a cup of tea, Charles?' His mother's voice sounded rather regal.

'Is it time for tiffin? I say, how splendid.'

If his parents spotted the mockery in his choice of words and tone of voice, they didn't acknowledge it. His mother simply summoned the maid, while his father picked up a silver cigarette box from a side table and leant forward, opening the lid invitingly.

'Do you smoke, young man?'

'Don't mind if I do.'

He took a cigarette; his father took one, too, then looked around for a match.

Another long silence as they smoked their cigarettes.

'So tell me, Charles,' his father said eventually. 'What do you do these days?'

'Oh, this and that.'

His father nodded, as though Jung's answer explained everything.

'Married?'

'Actually I was, but the poor darling was murdered in her bed.'

'Dear me. Dear, dear me.'

'Frightful to-do.'

'How simply shocking,' his mother said.

'You can't imagine the laundry bills. Blood everywhere.'

His mother went even more rigid and the silence echoed until the maid returned with a tray full of tea things and poured out three cups, bobbed neatly and departed.

'How's Sevenoaks?' Jung asked. 'Not quite Simla? Rather deficient in the houseboy department, I imagine.'

'Indeed,' his father said.

'But Mavis is a treasure,' his mother said.

'She looks it. Do you think she'd like to go to the flicks with me? Should I ask her?'

'No,' his father said. 'No, I don't think that would do at all.'

'Does she not have an afternoon off? Pretty little thing and, well, you know, having lost my wife in such unfortunate circumstances, I'm keeping half an eye open for another one. Do you think Mavis might be the one for me?'

'Mavis has a young man,' Jung's mother said stiffly. 'We believe he is presently serving in North Africa. I trust you're doing *your* bit for the war, Charles.'

'Why yes, I am, mother. I'm spying for Germany.'

'Spying for Germany?' His father spluttered tea.

'Jolly good chaps, the Nazis, don't you think, Daddy? Herr Hitler's an awfully decent fellow. Deserves our support, what?'

His father rose from his chair.

'That's it, young man. You might think you're damned funny, but I don't. I won't listen to that sort of thing, not in my house.'

'But I haven't finished my tea. I was hoping for biscuits.'

'Out. I want you out.'

'Are you turning me away again, Daddy?'

'What are you talking about?'

'1911 – don't you remember? You sent me off on a boat so I could get thrashed and buggered at prep school. Don't you remember that, Daddy?'

'Damned pup! I won't have that sort of language. Get out.'

'I was rather hoping for some money, actually. Think of it as an advance on my inheritance. I'm a bit strapped for cash at the moment. Came over from Germany at a moment's notice, you see. Didn't have time to go to the bank.'

His mother was shaking. 'Give him some money, Henry. Anything. Please.'

'Thank you, Mummy. I'm so glad one of you still loves her little creature. You must have missed your creature all these years.'

'What are you talking about?'

'I'm *the creature*, am I not? Isn't that what you called me?'

'Ten pounds,' Henry Young said, his red face turning puce. 'I can give you ten pounds, but I want you out of this house – and I never wish to see you again.'

Jung stood up and walked to the fireplace. He drew his forearm along the mantelpiece, knocking a lifetime's collection of ornaments down onto the hearthstone, sending shards of glass and porcelain spraying onto the carpet. He walked over to his mother, who was struggling to get out of her chair, and slapped her cheek hard.

'Please don't get up, Mummy,' he hissed, baring his teeth.

His father was hobbling to her assistance. 'What do you think you're doing!'

In answer he grabbed his father by the balls and squeezed hard.

'Let's say five hundred, shall we? And then we'll call it quits. What do you say to that, Daddy? You don't want me to cause a scene, do you? Think of the laundry bills . . .'

Wilde was dismayed. He had been played for a fool.

'What do you hope to gain from this, Cashbone?'

'Peace, Wilde. That's what we all want, isn't it – peace for the children of the world. Peace for your own little boy.'

'What's that got to do with Klara?'

'Think it through. We now have the means to reveal the truth about Geli Raubal and her affair with Hitler, the truth about the birth of Klara and Geli's murder. None of this could have been done inside Germany with the Nazis in control of the press and wireless. But we can provide detailed evidence, with photographs and scientific comparisons of features, dates and locations of conception and birth. It'll be all over the world's newspapers and airwaves. There will be leaflet drops over Germany and the occupied territories. The German people will know the truth soon enough.'

'And then what?'

'The godlike Führer will be seen to have feet of clay. No more will he be able to hold himself above the common man without base needs and desires. He will be no better than the man in the Bierkeller with a stein of lager in one hand and a busty waitress in the other. He will be utterly discredited – and his henchman Martin Bormann will be seen as the filthy murderer he is.'

'And you think that will bring peace?'

'No, Wilde, we're not so naive to think we can bring down the Nazi regime in one fell swoop. But we can shift the balance of power to Reichsmarschall Göring. If he can displace Hitler – and we realise it's a big if – then we'll have a man in power with whom we can do business. We know Göring's a vile anti-Semite, the founder of the concentration camps and the Gestapo – a Nazi of the worst sort – but he's never wanted this war. He believes that it will lead to the destruction of Germany and the end of European civilisation. So if we can help him into power, we will be able to treat very favourably with him. We believe he will give up the occupied territories in the west in return for a cessation of hostilities.'

'And the east?'

'That will no longer be our concern. Few tears will be shed where we come from if Nazism and Bolshevism destroy each other.'

Wilde met Eaton's gaze. 'Do Churchill or Roosevelt know about all these fanciful plans of yours?'

'I can't discuss that.'

'But Göring, he knows, doesn't he? He has been involved from the start – probably organised the whole darn thing, paid for the trawler, everything? It was a power grab – but somehow Bormann got wind of it.'

'Hermann wants peace,' Sunny said. 'What you need to understand is the power that resides in the women of Germany. They are in a majority after the slaughter of so many millions of men in the Great War. They are the ones who urge men to take courage and fight to protect them.'

'So what?'

'The women of Germany love Hitler. He is untainted, a single man, unmarried, no children, no mistress. These are special attributes, and he knows it – which is why Eva Braun is a closely guarded secret and why Geli Raubal was hushed up. Women of all ages have adored him from the very beginning. They are a constituency he has played to all his political life – and one he daren't lose. For if he lost the affection of Germany's women, he would lose the country.'

Wilde had had enough.

'Measure the girl's face, then – just don't tell her why you're doing it. Tell her it's a health check or something. And don't tell her about her father, not yet. If it's all the same to you, I need some fresh air – so I'm going for a walk to clear my head.'

Wilde strode out into the brisk morning air. The sky was overcast again, threatening rain or even snow. When he reached the corner of the street, he glanced back to see if anyone was following him.

Well, the scales had fallen from his eyes all right. Klara was to be thrown to the wolves, and he, Wilde, was the only adult in her world who thought that might not be a good idea.

It was a working day, a Tuesday, and the village was coming to life. He wandered past the pub, the Cock Inn, and noticed a telephone kiosk. He looked around again, stepped inside, put coins in the box and called home.

'Lydia?'

'Tom, darling – where are you?'

'I'm nearby. Village of Harkham. I haven't got long – so listen to me. Pack small bags for you and Johnny – toothbrushes, nappies – along with a basket of food. Tell Doris to stay away until further notice – then lock up Cornflowers and drive over here, to Harkham. Park in the little road to the side of the pub. There's only one pub, the Cock Inn. Wait for me. I can't tell you how long I'll be. Make sure the tank's full, and don't breathe a word to anyone. Please, trust me on this.'

'That's a lot to take in.'

'My money's about to run out. Try to think of somewhere safe. Not relatives – too easily traced. Can you do that for me, Lydia?'

The coins ran out before she could reply. He replaced the phone and slipped out of the kiosk.

They were still there when Wilde returned. Bromley was measuring Klara's nose with the calipers. She looked close to tears. Eaton shifted uneasily as Wilde appeared.

Wilde gave Klara what he hoped was a reassuring smile and spoke to her in German.

'It will soon be over, Klara – we're just trying to make sure you're healthy and well after our difficult journey here.'

'I told them I was well. They wouldn't listen.'

'I'm sorry.' He turned to the American intelligence officer. 'And Cashbone, please forgive me. I sounded off a bit back there.'

'Forget it, buddy.'

'I was out of order – been under considerable stress these past few days and, like you all, I only have the child's best interests at heart. Having thought it through, I can see that your scheme actually has a lot to be said for it.'

Cashbone beamed. 'Glad to hear it. Nothing more to be said.'

'All I ask is a little sensitivity and a little patience.'

'Of course,' Eaton said. 'We understand that. The excitement of getting you home safe . . . Well, perhaps we weren't thinking clearly ourselves.'

'Are you nearly finished with her? I think I could do with another coffee and a quiet word or two about the best course of action – and, importantly, the timing – to bring your plan to fruition.'

'Certainly,' Eaton said. 'Let's retire to the kitchen and leave Professor Bromley to his deliberations.'

'You understand, don't you, Cashbone? Eaton? You've got a plan that might just work, but we've also got to do our best for the girl. I think it's possible to get your publicity out there without ever telling her what's going on. Ten-year-old girls can be steered clear of the wireless and newspapers. If necessary, she can be given a false identity so that she doesn't get bullied at school. It wouldn't look good for America or Britain if we paraded her like a prize catch.'

'Point taken,' Eaton said.

'But we need photographs,' Cashbone said. 'Our photographer will be here tomorrow. Astonishing what you can do with light, shade and the perfect angle. He'll bring out the similarities between our two subjects.'

'We'll make sure she has a good night's sleep, then. Fresh as a daisy so she looks her best. But she doesn't need to know what you're doing with the pictures, does she?'

'She'll find out one day, whatever happens. We can't protect her from the truth for ever,' Eaton cautioned.

'No,' Wilde agreed. 'But hopefully she'll be better able to deal with it in a year or two's time. And if the plan works as we hope, we might be able to present her to the public as something of a heroine – the girl who helped bring peace, tragic victim of the Nazis who slaughtered her mother. That sort of thing.'

'I like the way you're thinking, Wilde.' Cashbone grinned.

Eaton said nothing. He was looking at Wilde in that quiet way that he often used when analysing information.

'But in the meantime,' Cashbone continued, 'I want the three of you to stay here. Mr Eaton has told you the Germans have sent someone after the girl?'

Wilde nodded.

'Then this is the safest place for you for now. Mrs Kemp will see you have everything you need.'

'Thank you. And I think some decorations would be in order, don't you?' Wilde added. 'Nothing like a Christmas tree to bring some cheer to a house with a child in residence.'

Eaton, Cashbone and Bromley left before lunch. Cashbone said he would be in touch within the next twenty-four hours to keep Wilde updated.

'We'll have Professor Bromley's report by then. His initial findings are very promising, but he needs to double-check the figures. Must be seen to be scientific – it's the detail that matters. Can't allow Goebbels to lie his way out of this.'

Wilde nodded. *Scientific.* Bromley was about as scientific as a newspaper horoscope merchant.

Eaton looked uneasy and, once again, gave Wilde a thoughtful look as he said goodbye.

'If you need to contact me, talk to Mrs Kemp. She'll get a message through. And be careful, old boy.'

'I'm always careful, Eaton – learned everything I know from you.'

Wilde ate a lunch of bread and soup with Sunny and Klara, who still wasn't eating much. Sunny chivvied her along with little success.

'We need to talk, Tom,' Sunny said as the girl retired to her room to read and Mrs Kemp cleared away the plates. 'You say you understand why we're doing this, but I'm not convinced – and I don't think Mr Eaton is either.'

'Oh, you've got me all wrong, Sunny. I think it's a fine idea – just came as a surprise, that's all. I thought I was just saving a child, you see – now I know I was saving the world, too. Bit of a shock . . .'

'Don't be flippant, Tom. This isn't easy for anyone. I hated seeing that ghastly man with his calipers measuring the child's face.'

'Well, yes, that's what did for me. Look, I know you've been through a hell of a time, Sunny – and you still have a lot of grieving to do. This has been tough for you.'

Sunny shrugged. 'That's what happens in war. You lose people you love. As for Klara, don't you think she might actually be quite proud to discover the truth about her father? She seems pretty keen on the mad bastard.'

'Well, we don't know for sure that she *is* his daughter – and I doubt Bromley's calipers will make us any the wiser.'

'Oh, come on, Tom – you know she's his kid.'

'Then prove it. Tell me everything you know, Sunny. How did this all start? You can tell me now, can't you? Everything about Romy Dietrich. You knew her all along, didn't you? Did she come to you first – or did you hear the story and go to her?'

'OK, Tom, those are fair questions. Let's start at the top, shall we? You know Hitler has a sister called Angela, Geli Raubal's mother?'

'Yes.'

'Well, she is still alive and has remarried. She is now Frau Professor Hammitzsch, wife of a renowned architect. They live in Dresden.'

'Jim mentioned that to me.'

'Well, Hitler disapproves of the marriage – and Frau Hammitzsch, in turn, despises Eva Braun. She thinks Eva has taken her place in her brother's life. So they now have little to do with each other.'

'I see.'

'Emmy Göring is also jealous of Eva, though she has never been allowed to meet her. She feels her position as First Lady of the Reich has been usurped by this silly girl from the photographic shop.'

Wilde was intrigued; this was a story of intertwined domestic rivalries far removed from the thunder of war and international politics, but conceivably its influence would be felt around the globe.

'By chance, Hermann Göring ran into Hitler's sister and her new husband on a visit to Dresden. He invited them to Carinhall, and they accepted with enthusiasm. A few weeks ago – at the end of October – they duly arrived, and Angela enjoyed a few glasses of Schnapps. She drinks rarely, but when she does, she doesn't fare well – this has always been her curse.'

Wilde sipped his coffee.

'She told the Görings all about the events of ten years ago – her daughter's pregnancy, her own indiscretion in drink when she revealed too much to the up-and-coming Martin Bormann, her certainty that Bormann then killed Geli. From there, you can work it out for yourself, Tom.'

'But how did Bormann get wind of these recent events?'

'Who knows? A mole in the Göring camp, perhaps? A bug in the wall at Carinhall? They all spy on each other, these top Nazis. Or perhaps it was another indiscretion by Hitler's simpleton sister?'

'But in the meantime, Hermann Göring saw an opportunity?'

'Yes, for peace.'

Wilde wanted to laugh, but managed to restrain himself. The very thought of it! Hermann the great warrior desired peace, did he? No, Hermann Göring wanted nothing more than to do down his arch-enemy Martin Bormann. It was clear: Hermann Göring, fat and slippery as a whale, had used the British and American secret services for his own ends. And Sunny Somerfeld had been his conduit.

Wilde looked pensive, as if Sunny's story had finally convinced him.

'Well, that helps a great deal. I'm beginning to understand things. Look, I think I'll take Klara for a walk. She needs some fresh air – and it'll give me time to do some more thinking.'

She frowned. 'Is that wise?'

'Why not?'

'I think I should come, too.'

He managed a smile. 'Fine by me.'

But it wasn't. Somehow he needed to lose her.

And there was something else. Before Cashbone left the house, Wilde had seen something which sent an electric current racing through his body, though it lasted only a second. It was the way he took Sunny's hand and seemed to give it a little squeeze. Had Wilde been mistaken in what he saw? If not, then formality had turned to familiarity at a remarkable pace.

CHAPTER 28

Cambridge's colleges reminded Charlie Jung of his public school. They had the same ancient stone and sense of history. And yet Cambridge was also like a military town these days, full of soldiers of all stripes. More khaki and tin hat than gown and cap. Whole regiments marching through the streets, and camped in tents out on the green spaces. Charlie Jung eyed them warily, then parked in a side street and walked to the college.

Information about this place and about Professor Wilde had been transmitted to him on the E-boat, directly from Bormann at the Wolfsschanze. There had been no home address, perhaps because so many dons lived on the premises, but Jung was not worried; he knew Cambridge well. It had been the closest town to his bloody public school.

He entered the archway and pushed open the door to the porters' lodge.

'I am looking for Professor Wilde,' he said. 'Is he in his rooms?'

'Afraid not, sir,' the porter said.

'Do you know when he might be?'

'Couldn't say, sir. He's probably at home.'

'Then he doesn't live here in the college?'

'He has a set of rooms, but he lives out. Feel free to leave a message. I'll make sure he gets it.'

'Do you have an address for him? I need to see him urgently.'

'Might I ask your name, sir?'

'My name is Charles Young. He doesn't know me, but I have rather sad information about an old friend – a mutual friend.'

'Well, I could try and place a call for you, sir, but we don't give out personal details such as telephone numbers and addresses.'

'But this is not the sort of news that should be given over the phone. I need to speak to him in person.'

'Well, why don't I call him – and find out if he can make himself available to you?'

'Would you? That would be very kind.'

Scobie pulled the black book across the counter and flicked through to the letter W, then placed his left finger on the page while he dialled with his right finger. The phone rang and rang. No answer. The porter shook his head and put the phone down.

'Sorry, sir. Not at home.'

'Well, thank you for trying.' He handed the porter a coin.

He left with a spring in his step. Working in the Höffle auction rooms had given him a remarkable talent for reading the worst scrawls, even when they were upside down.

'Ready?' Wilde said. 'Go and get Klara from her room. Then all we need's a dog and we'll look like a proper family out for an afternoon stroll.'

'I'm not sure, Tom,' Sunny said. 'Is this really such a good idea?'

'The dog? That was a joke. But yes, a walk is a very good idea. Klara needs fresh air.'

'I'm worried we might stick out. You know – if anyone hears us talking. And if we have been followed—'

'I suppose you could be right. But I don't think it's healthy for Klara to be cooped up inside the whole time.'

'Ok, you go, Tom. I'll stay here.'

'Just a short stroll, and I'll make sure we don't do any talking in hearing distance of nosy locals. And you can have a bit of time to yourself.'

Sunny looked pensive, then nodded. 'I'll get her for you. But don't go far, please.'

Two minutes later, she returned with Klara, all wrapped up in her winter clothes from Stockholm.

'Come on,' he said with a smile, 'we'll walk as far as the pub.'

'That means nothing to me,' Klara replied.

'No matter.'

Wilde ushered her towards the door before Sunny could change her mind. Mrs Kemp was standing there.

'I'm unhappy about this, Mr Wilde. My instructions—'

'Oh, to hell with your instructions, Mrs Kemp. This is still a free country and I am a free man.'

He brushed past her with Klara in tow.

Lydia had been waiting for two hours and was beginning to wonder whether she had made a mistake about the location.

Johnny had had enough, however, and was becoming increasingly fractious. He was normally a placid child, but this was too much for him and he was crying and wriggling as she tried to settle him. Dear God, the boy was becoming as strong as his father.

And then she saw him, turning right into the street, fifty yards up the road. But he wasn't alone. There was a girl with him. A child. What was going on here? Lydia immediately opened the car door and got out.

'Tom?'

He was smiling, but she knew him well enough to see the tension beneath the easy-going surface. He gave her a perfunctory kiss, then said, 'Lydia, I want you to meet someone. This is Klara.'

'Hello, Klara.'

It was more a question than a greeting. Who was this girl?

'And Klara, this is my wife, Lydia.' His eyes flashed Lydia a warning not to correct his description of their marital status. 'And in the car, you will meet our little boy, Johnny. He's one and a half years old, so he doesn't really speak yet.'

'Hallo,' Klara said to Lydia, with a little click of the heels and a bow of the head.

For a brief moment Lydia wondered if the child was about to give a Hitler salute, but mercifully, she didn't. It was clear to Lydia that the girl was German. More than that, she was a very well-brought-up German girl, clear-voiced and confident in the presence of strange adults.

'Very pleased to meet you. Are you German?'

'Yes, Mrs Wilde.'

'Well, I speak a little German. So we can mix it up.'

Wilde held the door open. 'Klara came with me from a village near Berlin. We had to get her away, you see. But we're all safe now.'

His eyes told Lydia the opposite, as had his phone call. They were anything but safe.

'Now then, Klara,' Wilde continued, 'Lydia is going to take us for a little drive – show you some of the beautiful English countryside. Would you like that? We might even find some ice cream some-where. You can sit in the back with Johnny. He would love to play with you, I'm sure. Perhaps you'd look after him.'

Lydia took Wilde's arm, speaking close to his ear.

'Tom, are you sure about this? What's going on?'

'I'll tell you everything, but not just yet. And yes, I *am* sure about this.' He lowered his voice to a whisper. 'We have to get her away.'

'It feels like we're abducting her.'

'Lydia, it's felt like that all along – but we have no choice, I'm afraid. She's in grave peril.'

Lydia gave him one of her looks. 'You're going to have to have a very good explanation for this, Tom. Do you want to drive?'

'No, you drive. I'll watch.'

'Climb in, then. Where are we going precisely?'

'I wondered about London. Easy to get lost in London.'

'We'll never make it – no ration allowance left for petrol. We've less than a quarter of a tank left. But I did have an idea – Harry Taylor's house in Cambridge. Do you remember he left the key with me when he joined up? Asked me to look in on the place from time to time.'

'It's very close to the centre of town.'

'Is that a bad thing? No one but us knows about it. If that's no good, you'll have to give me a few more clues as to who we're trying to avoid, and why.'

'Well, just drive for the moment. Head out of the village back along the Cambridge road. You might just be right about Harry's place. Let me think it through as we go.'

They pulled out of the side road, and turned at the pub. Lydia put a hand on Wilde's arm, gripping hard.

'There's a woman in the rear-view mirror. Arms crossed, staring at us. She doesn't look happy.'

'Damn, that's Sunny. She's seen us.'

'Who's Sunny?'

'Sigrun Somerfeld – she came over from Germany with us. I'm no longer sure whose side she's on. Put your foot down, Lydia.'

Dr Harry Taylor's house, Trinity Villa, was a large building of soot-darkened brick in a narrow lane not far from Trinity College, in the very heart of Cambridge. On the way there, while Klara and Johnny seemed to be amusing each other in the back of the car, they had discussed the advantages and disadvantages of the house as a bolt-hole. One thing it had going for it was that it had that rarity in Cambridge, a garage, so that their car could be taken off the street. They had agreed that there were pros and cons to being so close to home. For the moment, they decided it would have to do; Wilde had no real plan beyond trying to prevent Klara from being used as a political pawn.

They arrived outside the house and Lydia handed Wilde the keys. Getting out of the car, he shuffled through them, found the one labelled 'Garage' and opened it up. Lydia drove straight in with the children still in the back.

'Let's get in the house quickly,' Wilde said. 'Then we can try to work things out.'

The house had been neglected, and even Harry's prized Viennese cold-painted bronze animals had a coating of dust. He had not spent much time here in the past two years. Sheets covered the furniture and the curtains were closed. It was cold, but there was coal and Wilde quickly got a fire going in the living room. The electricity was still on, as was the water, but the phone was dead. Lydia managed to get the wireless working and a classical concert came over the airwaves from the BBC Home Service. Warmth and music worked wonders.

While Klara and Johnny explored together, Wilde told Lydia everything that had happened in Germany and since.

'I promised her a lovely home, Lydia. Cashbone is offering a life-long stigma – a stain that will never wash out. The fact that she is innocent of any crime will never reduce her notoriety.'

She put her arms around him and held him close.

'You don't have to explain yourself to me, Tom. I would have done the same. The question is, what do we do now?'

Finally the children returned.

'Is this where you usually live?' Klara asked Lydia.

'Well, we live in this town, but not this house. It belongs to a friend of ours, but we can stay here a little while.'

'I like it, Mrs Wilde. It's nicer than the last house with those men. It was warm there and the food was good, but I didn't like it.'

'No, nor did Tom. That's why we've brought you here, Klara. Please, call me Lydia – I want to be your friend.' She smiled at the two children. 'Perhaps you'd help me look after Johnny while we're here.'

She was holding his hand. 'He's so sweet, isn't he.'

'I think he likes you, too.'

Klara gave Johnny an appraising look. 'He walks well. But he doesn't talk yet.'

'No. He tries to say Mummy and Daddy. But that's all. Perhaps he can learn to say Klara.'

'I'd like that.' She grinned sheepishly, then whispered, 'I think his nappy needs to be changed.'

Lydia set about the task while Wilde cleaned the coal dust off his hands, before having a rummage in Harry Taylor's wardrobes. The young Trinity don was about the same size as Wilde, perhaps half an inch taller, but of a similar build. He found a distinctive herringbone coat and a trilby. Perfect for Wilde to bury himself in, perhaps. He tried them on and found Lydia.

'How do I look?'

'You look like Thomas Wilde to me, but it might camouflage you a little. If you don't want anyone to recognise you, the best thing you can do is alter your gait and posture. Slump your shoulders and shuffle – you'll look twenty years older.'

'Good idea. Look, I'm going to leave you all here for a bit. Perhaps I'll find some ice cream or cakes, you never know. I may be a little while.'

'We'll need a few more basic groceries, Tom. I'll have to go out with my ration book and see what I can find.'

'Later, Lydia. Stay here with the children. I have to get the Rudge first. I need transport and we can't use the car.'

It was late afternoon and already dark. A cold mist was rising off the Cam. Wilde attempted to alter his stride as Lydia had suggested, but he wasn't convinced the result looked very natural. Finally he gave up and just walked at a brisk pace, the trilby wedged firmly down over his brow.

Apart from the military presence, the sandbagged buildings and the occasional evidence of bomb damage, the centre of town had a festive feel to it, with Christmas fare on show in the shops; perhaps not quite of pre-war proportions, but heartwarming nonetheless.

Twenty minutes later he arrived at the end of their street. He stopped and looked about carefully first. He knew that if Eaton was intent on finding him, this would be the first place he'd stake out. But it seemed to Wilde that Eaton had been ambivalent about the whole Klara plan. Perhaps he would not provide Cashbone with entirely wholehearted assistance. He needed to speak to the MI6 man soon, though, to be sure how things now stood.

Wilde was a little surprised to see a Bentley parked some way up the street on the far kerb. This was a reasonably well-to-do area, but the residents didn't tend to have such expensive motors. He shrugged it off. Neither MI6 nor America's COI would ever use such an ostentatious car in a surveillance operation; the idea was *not* to stand out.

Feeling more secure but still wary, he approached Cornflowers and opened the front gate. There was a figure in the dark grey gloom. He froze. Someone was ahead of him, at the front door.

The man was already turning and his face emerged in the dim light.

'Hello?' Wilde said.

'Ah, good day. Are you Professor Wilde? Thomas Wilde?'

He hesitated no more than a split second.

'No,' he said. 'But I'm looking for him, too.'

The man came closer.

'I see. Got some sad news to impart about a mutual friend. I'm Charles Young, by the way. Friends call me Charlie.'

Lydia was trying to get it out of her mind that the girl playing with her son was Hitler's daughter. She tried to focus on the thought that this was a child in need, a child in danger.

'Mrs Wilde?'

'Yes, Klara?'

Clearly the girl had no intention of calling her Lydia. Far too informal for a respectable German girl.

'Why do you wear that stuff on your face?'

Lydia laughed. 'The make-up, you mean? Well, it's just a little rouge and eyeliner. Otherwise I look horribly pallid at this time of year.'

'It is not correct to wear make-up,' Klara told her with a serious expression.

'Is that what you've been told? Well, you may very well be right, but it is a personal choice. And in England we women do not need someone else telling us how to live our lives or what to wear.'

'But in Germany—'

'Yes, I know, Klara. But we're not in Germany now.' Her eye caught a glint of silver from the necklace at her throat. 'Anyway, I see you like to wear nice things, too.'

Klara removed the locket and handed it to Lydia, who examined it carefully. The silver was quite thick, a good solid weight, and there was some intricate engraving of hearts and flowers on the front.

'It's lovely, Klara. Does it have pictures in it?'

'There was a band of my parents' hair, braided together. It's all I have left of them. But the man at the house – the one who was measuring my face – took it. He said he wanted to look at it under a microscope for some reason, but that he would return it. I didn't want him to take it. He might mess it up.'

'I'm sorry. I agree – he shouldn't have done that.'

Tom had told her about Bromley; the man sounded an absolute charlatan. What could he possibly learn from a few strands of hair? That it was the same colour as Hitler's? So was the hair of millions of people. And as for measuring Klara's face with calipers? Wasn't that the sort of thing the Nazi race department did? It sounded quite ghastly.

Lydia handed the locket back. The past of this vulnerable and rather nice child seemed lost in a fog of mystery. Tom was right; it was almost certainly better if it stayed that way. Sometimes secrets were best left secret.

'Fletcher,' Wilde said, shaking hands. He had just seen the name of Fletcher's the butcher's on the side of a van. 'Ken Fletcher.'

He was getting used to adopting false names.

'And what's your business with Professor Wilde, may I ask, Mr Fletcher?'

'I heard he had a car for sale. Thought I'd drop in and see if it's still on the market.'

'Well, we both seem to have missed him.'

'Indeed we do, Mr Young.'

Wilde was aware that this man was studying him closely, examining him like a lepidopterist might scrutinise a new butterfly, wondering whether it merited gassing and pinning. The suspicion was mutual. Charles Young was handsome, well dressed, with slicked-back, neatly barbered hair – but who was he? One of Eaton's agents? That had been his initial reaction and the reason he had given a false name, but on reflection there was something about him that suggested otherwise. Eaton, he was sure, would have opted for someone more anonymous.

'Your accent, Mr Fletcher. You're not American by any chance?'

'Lincolnshire born and bred, Mr Young.' He sighed. 'And you, sir – you say you had some sad news to impart?'

'The death of a mutual friend, an RAF hero shot down over France. His wife asked me to pass on the news in person, as I was travelling through Cambridge.'

'Ah.' Wilde, in the guise of a mere car buyer, could hardly ask who the unfortunate pilot was. 'Well, yes, sad news, Mr Young. Anyway, if the professor is not here, I shall have to be on my way. Perhaps I'll call again and hope for better luck. Good day to you, Mr Young.'

'And you, Mr Fletcher. I'll just write out a note for the professor and pop it through the letterbox, then I'll be on my way, too. Wasted journey for both of us, eh?'

Perhaps, Wilde thought. *Perhaps not.*

He turned and walked back along the road the way he had come, aware of Young's eyes on his back with every step. He trusted his instincts and his knowledge of humanity, and they told him that Young's urbane exterior concealed something deeply unpleasant.

CHAPTER 29

The Führer was in full, spittle-flecked flow and Martin Bormann was taking a thorough written note, as always. The subject of Hitler's dinner-table diatribe this evening was the perfidy and cowardice of the Italians in North Africa and the uselessness of his own generals in the east. No man was more diligent than Bormann, the ultimate administrator, and so he continued to take notes with his usual attention to detail, but this evening his mind was elsewhere, and he was worried. He had smoked a hundred cigarettes since breakfast.

Otto Kalt was dead, killed after shooting Horst Spahn. He knew that now, though the men at the SD were still not sure who Kalt was, only that he was registered as a pig farmer and Party member. The only good news was that Spahn was dead, too, which had effectively shut down the SD's interest in the case.

Charlie Jung was another matter. He was out of contact – possibly dead or in captivity.

Bormann could trace his movements only so far. A small naval vessel had conveyed him from the Baltic, across the North Sea to England. The second-to-last message from the E-boat had told Bormann that he had been taken ashore by ship's boat and had landed safely on the east coast late at night. After that, there was another, final, message in which the E-boat had reported coming under fire from a British naval vessel. Then nothing.

And so he must assume that the E-boat was destroyed, and that Jung was somewhere in England. It was the not knowing that shredded Bormann's nerves. Why had he not contacted Vickery and wired a message back?

The only other fresh information Bormann had received was from Stockholm, where Abwehr agents had plotted the movements of a man, a woman and a child, taken under the protection of the British Legation before being flown out from Bromma. Presumed destination: Leuchars air base in Scotland.

All Bormann could do now was wait. He had no fears that Jung would be turned by the British secret services. He might be English by birth, but his great wealth resided *inside* the Reich and they both knew that Germany would ultimately be victorious. Bormann trusted him; they were like two men bound together as they plunged into a cataract. Either both survived or both died.

They had too much on each other.

Martin Bormann had been secretary to deputy Party leader Rudolf Hess when he met Jung in 1936, at a Berlin drinks party to celebrate the opening of the Olympics. Jung was there to meet Bormann because he had recently persuaded his father-in-law that it would be wise to make a large donation to the Nazi Party. With the new Nuremberg laws, things were looking decidedly uncomfortable for Germany's Jews – and it would be best to keep in with Hitler's crew.

By all accounts, old man Höffle had been appalled by the suggestion of handing over any of his wealth to a bunch of anti-Semites but, at the urging of his fearful wife and daughter, he had gone along with Jung's suggestion. As a senior official, in control of much of the Party finances, Bormann had been the right man to approach with the offer. Even now, the thought of it made Bormann laugh; money had never been so easy to come by.

Jung and Bormann had both seen into the other's dark heart; they were like scorpions mating. Each had a lethal sting, but they both had much to gain from an alliance.

Hitler slammed his fist on the table so that the plates and cutlery jumped – jolting Bormann back to the present.

'Yes, Mein Führer,' he said, making a mental note to himself to have a large bouquet delivered to Eva at the Berghof.

Hitler's bloody women. When the Führer drove past them in the street, the young girls flaunted themselves like prostitutes, some tearing open their blouses to reveal their breasts. One would have thought he was a sports champion or a movie star. Women would be the undoing of him because the ones he liked were all crazy bitches in heat: the Berchtesgaden shop girl Mitzi Reiter, who'd tried to strangle herself with a cord attached to a door when he jilted her; the actress Müller who'd leapt to her death; the English hellcat Mitford; Eva Braun and her overdose . . . but worst of all, Geli stinking Raubal.

She had deserved to die. Not that Bormann had gone to Hitler's Munich apartment at Prinzregentenplatz in September 1931 with the intention of killing her. Anything but. He didn't want her dead – he wanted her secrets.

That filthy serving wench Angela Raubal, Geli's mother, had hinted at a secret child and Bormann wanted to know more. Of course he did. Secrets were his currency.

If Hitler had a child and only he, Bormann, knew about it, there would be endless possibilities for advancement. And so he needed to prise those secrets from Geli, as leverage for his own ambitions. He chose that particular day because he knew Hitler would be away on his electioneering tour to Nuremburg and then on to Hamburg, and that Frau Winter, the housekeeper, would be out at the cinema with her husband Georg and Frau Reichert, the landlady – though they would later deny this. That only left Frau Dachs, Reichert's mother, and she was profoundly deaf and kept to her own room.

Geli had been twenty-three, but she did not seem that mature. Everyone said she was a fun-loving girl, the only woman the Führer had ever loved. Fun-loving? If so, why had she been so frigid and difficult? He had walked in on her when she was writing a letter, pen in her right hand, phone clasped to her ear with the left. She instantly seemed angry to see him. All he had wanted from her was the truth about her child and a little *fun*, but she had flown off the handle, had sworn at him and told him to leave – had threatened to tell the Führer about his visit and his vile slurs against her.

When he slapped her, she went mad. She reached for the Führer's Walther 6.35mm pistol, the one he always kept in the apartment, loaded. Bormann had had to wrestle it from her. It was her damned fault that the thing went off, the bullet hitting her in the chest. The stupid cow. It had been an accident, for pity's sake! Suicide, maybe. No blame could be attached to anyone else; the police doctor, Müller, was clear about that in his report.

They had found her body inside her room, locked from the inside; and so it had to be suicide or an accident. No one else had been in the apartment, no one among the neighbours reported hearing a gunshot. How could it be anything but a self-inflicted wound when she was found in a locked room?

Well, perhaps not quite an accident. He could admit these things to himself, couldn't he? She was a juicy little slut, that Geli. *Why had she resisted me*, wondered Bormann? Other tarts associated with the Party bigwigs were quite amenable to a quick jig-jig with ever-ready Martin Bormann. Why not Geli? Why did she have to make a song and dance about his hand on her tit? Why did she have to react so irrationally when he pushed her on the bed, put his hand up her skirts and relieved her of her undergarment? When she slapped him, of course he slapped her back.

And then she squirmed away from him, ran out and returned with the Führer's pistol. She waved it about in his direction. He *had* to take it from her. And then the inevitable struggle and the bloody result. An accident.

What no one knew – or wanted to know – was that there was a second key to Geli Raubal's room, and that Martin Bormann had removed it and thrown it in the Isar. And that was it; the whole thing had been quietly put to rest because no one wanted any publicity about a young woman being found dead inside the apartment of the man who, within sixteen months, would be Chancellor of Germany.

Over the past ten years, Bormann had almost managed to put the incident out of mind. But every so often Hitler would be reminded of Geli when he gazed at the framed photographs he kept on the walls of his homes in Berlin and Munich, and a tear would come to his eye. On these occasions, Bormann would shrink at the very thought of what his penalty would be should the Führer ever discover his part in her death.

That fear was always there, in the background, like a venomous snake hiding beneath the bed. Threatening, malevolent, disturbing your sleep.

He feared it would slither out one day, and inevitably it did. The serpent came in the form of a typed envelope containing just one sheet of thin card – a photographic copy of the birth and baptism certificate of a girl named Klara Wolf . . .

'What is this?' Klara asked.

Lydia was boiling a pan of water so they could wash. No hot water was coming through the sink or basin, and the cold water had to be run forever to lose its rust colour. Johnny was asleep in an enormous bed and Lydia's thoughts were elsewhere. She turned around, smiling.

'Why, that looks like a menorah, Klara.'

'I found it by all those lovely model animals. It's funny. What's it for?'

'You put candles in each of the holes and light them at a certain time of year. It's a religious thing for Jewish people.'

'For Jews? Then why is it here?'

'Because this house belongs to a very good friend of mine called Harry Taylor, and he happens to be a Jew.'

'How can he be your friend if he's a Jew?'

'Because he's a very nice man, very clever, too.'

Klara said nothing while she digested this piece of information.

'Perhaps you've heard bad things about Jewish people, Klara?'

The girl nodded.

'Have you ever met any?'

She shook her head.

Lydia looked at her earnestly. 'You know, they are just people like you and me. Some are good and kind, some aren't. Some are clever, some are stupid. Some are rich, some are poor. Just like everyone else in the world. We're all humans – and humans are all the same species, wherever they come from or whatever they look like.'

'Our teacher told us Jews are subhumans. They are not as good as humans.'

Lydia frowned. 'Oh dear, that's not a very nice thing to say. I wish you could meet Harry Taylor – I'm sure you'd like him very much, because I think you'd find he's every bit as human as you and me.'

Klara looked dumbfounded, as though she had heard for the first time that the world wasn't flat.

'You don't look as though you believe me, Klara.'

'It's not what I have been told before.'

'Come on, give me a hug. You're such a lovely girl – I'm so pleased I've met you.'

Klara accepted the offer tentatively, but then relaxed and allowed herself to be folded into Lydia's embrace.

There was a knock at the door.

'That'll be Tom. He's been an awfully long time. Come on, let's go and see if he's found any ice cream!'

Wilde had turned away from Cornflowers and walked to the end of the street, then turned the corner. He had stopped and waited. Ten minutes later, when the man he had met on the doorstep didn't appear, either on foot or in a car, he returned to their home. There was no sign of Mr Young, nor the Bentley.

Wilde opened the front door of Cornflowers, turning the key as quietly as possible. There was no sound inside, only darkness. His finger was on the trigger of his pistol and the safety catch was off. Lydia had put up the blackouts before coming out to meet him at Harkham. There was an electric flashlight on the hall stand. He switched it on and proceeded through the house.

Someone had doubtless been here. A ground floor window at the rear had been broken and opened. But there was no evidence of him now. He hadn't stayed long, nor had he ransacked the house. All that Wilde could find to be missing was a photograph of him, Lydia and Johnny, which had stood on the mantelpiece in the sitting room.

Wilde checked again. No, that was it. But it was enough. An unnerving discovery to know that someone could now identify Lydia and Johnny. He went to the kitchen and filled a couple of shopping bags full of food and some spare clothes, then exited as discreetly as he had entered, uncovered his motorbike and placed the bags in the saddlebags.

The bike was a Rudge Special 500cc. He'd had her over five years now and loved her. As usual, she started easily and he was pleased to see that the fuel gauge showed that the petrol tank was full.

'Food!' he said as Lydia opened the door. 'And soap and more clothes.'

'No blankets, I suppose?'

'Sorry, I didn't think.'

'Don't worry, I'm sure Harry will have plenty of bedding.'

'But – and this is a very big but – I did find some chocolate.' He dug a bar of Cadbury's Dairy Milk from his pocket and handed it to Klara. 'English chocolate, Klara! What do you think of that?'

'I don't know – I've never had it.'

'There's a first time for everything. Now, where's Johnny? He'll want some, too.'

'He's asleep, darling. Needs his nap, you know.'

'Of course he does.' He kissed Lydia.

'I was saving that chocolate for Christmas, by the way,' Lydia said, wagging her finger. 'Very hard to come by these days.'

'Well, Christmas has come early.' He grinned. Then he looked at her with a serious expression. 'Now, I'm sorry, but I have to go.'

'What do you mean? Where?'

'I've got to go to London. There's something I have to do. We can't just let this situation ride. I have to sort things out.'

'Tom, what am I supposed to do?'

'You've got to stay indoors, all three of you. You'll be safe. In the unlikely event of anything happening, I noticed a telephone box across the road. Go no further than that – just call Doris and get her to do whatever needs to be done.'

He was sure their loyal cleaner would do anything for Lydia if called on.

'I take it you have some sort of plan?'

'The beginnings of one.'

Jung looked at the picture. So, that had indeed been Thomas Wilde at the door. If only he had seen the picture *before* his meeting with the man who called himself Fletcher. And the woman with him – letters he had seen on a table suggested her name was Lydia Morris. So they weren't married, but they had a child. He rather liked the look of Lydia Morris. Intelligent, warm eyes. Not really his type, but if the opportunity ever presented itself, why not?

He put the picture down on the front passenger seat and turned his attention to his other acquisition from Wilde's house. An address book from the hall stand by their telephone. Now that might produce some interesting results.

Wilde rode at a steady pace, trying to conserve petrol, but conditions were hard on the road south – light snow flurries misting his goggles, and ice on the road increasing the risk of skidding. Once he reached, London, the bomb-damaged streets, with heaps of rubble lying in the roads, proved equally treacherous. The journey took almost three hours and he was relieved when he arrived close to Philip Eaton's home in Chelsea. He parked in the next street, so that he could approach the house unobserved.

It took a full two minutes for Eaton to answer the door. He was in pyjamas and dressing gown, the sleeve of his missing left arm neatly tucked into the pocket.

For a few moments he simply looked at Wilde, standing there with his goggles perched on his head, then sighed.

'I was hoping I might hear from you, Wilde, but I wasn't expecting you to just turn up. What in God's name do you think you're doing?'

'Are you going to invite me in? It's bitter out here.'

He stepped back and held the door open.

'I suppose you'll want a whisky, too.'

'Thank you.'

He followed Eaton through into his large sitting room with its comfortable old furniture, its worn Morocco and picture-strewn walls. He had never been here before, but he had heard all about it from Lydia.

'You've taken leave of your senses, man,' Eaton said as he handed Wilde a Scotch. 'You've managed to make enemies of the Germans and the Americans. Takes a rare genius to do that.'

Wilde looked at him. 'What about you and the British – have I made enemies of you, too?'

Eaton poured himself a brandy. 'Me personally? Of course not. But the British, certainly. Nothing that happens on British soil must embarrass us with your countrymen, Wilde. Churchill knows about the package. If he has any reservations about using the girl, he's keeping them to himself. We want her back. You've abducted her – and you have to return her.'

'You know I can't do that, and you know why.'

Eaton picked up his brandy and they clinked glasses.

'Of course I do. Would it make you feel any better if I told you I had no part in Mr Cashbone's scheme? When he sent you off to Berlin, I had no idea what you were expected to bring back.'

'Strangely enough, I believe you. So now you can help me.'

Eaton looked grim. 'You don't understand the mess you're in, do you, Wilde? And you've made it all the worse by involving an innocent party, to wit, Miss Morris. What does she think about all this?'

'She's behind me, one hundred per cent.'

He smiled wryly. 'Of course she is. One of my favourite people in the world, Miss Morris. I even like her idealistic outlook and her rather bohemian left-wing passions, but she's a complete stranger to realpolitik. As you well know.'

'So you won't help me?'

'Did I say that? First tell me what you're planning.'

'That's just it, I don't have any plans. Lydia and the children are well hidden and safe, but I simply don't know what to do next.'

'Easy. Hand over the girl and I promise you'll face no charge. I'm sure I can keep the dogs at bay.'

Wilde shook his head. 'Not good enough, Eaton, and you know it. I think you feel the same way as I do.'

'No, just because I understand your actions and may be willing to help you, that doesn't mean I agree with what you've done. Because Cashbone is right. We need something. The war in the Far East is looking bloody disastrous, Western Europe is lost, Russia could fall at any moment and Rommel's hitting us hard in North Africa. So we need a victory over the Nazis, however small – and producing Hitler's daughter would be a propaganda coup to put the flight of Hess into the shade.'

'It would make us look like heartless opportunists.'

'You're wrong. It will raise a cheer in every bar from Boston, Lincs to Boston, Mass. Songs will be written. Everyone in Germany will know that their godlike dictator is no better than the rest of us. And, more seriously, there will be difficult questions about the death of the girl's mother ten years ago. It will tear a gaping hole in the upper echelons of the Nazi Party – and in Germany as a whole. This is gold dust.'

Wilde finished his whisky. It was a delightfully peaty single malt from Islay.

'Another?'

'I'll get it, if it's OK with you.'

'Help yourself.'

'Tell me, Eaton. Have you had a man outside Cornflowers? Has it been under surveillance today?'

'Do you think I'd tell you if I had?'

'Please don't play games. There was a man there when I went to get the Rudge. He broke in and stole a picture.'

'I can assure you that wasn't my man.'

'Is Cashbone running a separate operation to you?'

'If he is, I know nothing about it. But I seriously doubt he has the manpower. The COI is barely up and running. Look, Wilde, you still haven't told me – why exactly have you come here? There's nothing I can do for you – except give you advice which you're going to ignore anyway. Other than that, all I could do is place you under arrest.'

'I want you to take me to see the E-boat captain. I want to know what he knows. Where are you holding him?'

'Come on, Wilde. He's a prisoner of war.'

'Bullshit. He was sunk on an espionage operation. We've got him and we can give him a hard time.'

'We don't do torture,' Eaton said firmly.

'Of course we don't – but we can explain to him that the penalty for espionage is a great deal more severe than just being incarcerated in a PoW camp on the Isle of Man.'

Eaton thought for a moment, then held out his brandy glass.

'Fill mine, too, would you? I'm going to get dressed. Our E-boat skipper, Kapitänleutnant Gustav Flettner, is not a million miles from here. Let's go and say hello to the fellow.'

Wilde sat on the Morocco, nursing his whisky, and waited. There was a newspaper on the coffee table. A very thin copy of the *Evening Standard*. He picked it up and looked at the front page. It was all bad news: Japanese advances in the Philippines; Bulgaria and Hungary entering the war on the Axis side; shipping lost. But then he turned the page and a story closer to home caught his eye. Murder and rape in the home counties.

The details were chilling enough, but it was the names of the victims that got Wilde's attention.

Henry Young, MBE, and his wife Elizabeth had been slaughtered in their own home, while their maidservant Mavis Triston was near to death after a brutal sexual assault and an attempt to throttle her.

Young. That was a common enough name, and yet he had heard it once before today, outside his own home, Cornflowers. Charlie Young, he had called himself. Was it just coincidence, or would the name mean something to Kapitänleutnant Flettner?

Eaton returned. 'Now then, we'll save a lot of time if you do up my shoes, cufflinks and tie. And then we're going in my adapted car – because I'm damned if I'm clinging on to you on your pillion with only one arm.'

CHAPTER 30

Despite his limp and the loss of his left arm, Eaton had become adept at driving. Hand signals were impossible, but the gear shift could now be operated with a flick of the thumb, without removing his right hand from the steering wheel.

Latchmere House, known to the Secret Intelligence Service as Camp 020, was a rather forbidding Victorian building of thirty rooms, now converted into cells and interview rooms at Ham Common, Richmond, ten miles from Eaton's Chelsea house.

Surrounded by barbed wire and heavily guarded, its purpose was not known to the public. This was where suspected enemy agents were brought by MI5 for questioning by a team of hardened interrogators led by the austere figure of Lieutenant-Colonel Robin Stephens, known as 'Tin-Eye' because of the metal-rimmed monocle that had taken up permanent residence in his right eye.

On the way, Wilde and Eaton discussed the *Evening Standard* story about the murders in Sevenoaks.

'I know it's a long shot, but if the killer is the man I met, it means our would-be assassin is English,' Wilde said. 'How do you find one Englishman among millions?'

'We'll get a good description off you, and the car you saw – and put out an alert to all police forces and home guards.'

'I can't provide a proper description of him. It was dark, no street lights or house lights. I got a sense of him, that's all. But he knows what I look like because he has my picture. Worse, he has a photo of Lydia.'

'But she's safe.'

Yes, she was safe – so long as she stayed indoors – at least until his return.

'Perhaps we should talk to the Youngs' maidservant?' Wilde suggested.

'Let's see what our Kapitänleutnant says first.'

'By the way, what are you going to do with Sunny? For all that I profoundly disagree with her motivation, she *did* risk her life helping us get Klara out of Germany.'

'After what you did, I'm afraid that Frau Somerfeld's present whereabouts and ultimate destination are considered none of your business, Wilde. Anyway, enough of that. We're here.'

An armed guard stopped the car at the gate of the compound and looked at Eaton's papers before waving him through. He parked on the tarmac at the side of the mansion, along with various other civilian and military vehicles.

At the main door, an army sergeant told Wilde that Lieutenant-Colonel Stephens was not on the premises, but that he could be reached by telephone. Eaton called him.

'What have you got from the E-boat captain, Stephens?'

'Flettner? Nothing as yet. He's in solitary and hasn't been interrogated. Not sure why he was brought to us, but if he's got anything to say, solitary will soften him up. Normally our next stop would be to put him in with one or two others and listen in through bugs. After a while in solitary, they sometimes can't stop talking when they meet up with a countryman. In his case, if nothing comes of it, we'll just ship him off to a PoW camp. No real cause for the gallows as far as I can see.'

'Can I talk to him?'

'Feel free, Eaton. House rules, though. No Gestapo stuff. But barking at them is not only permissible but de rigueur. Only thing they seem to understand for some reason. Probably used to being shouted at by Hitler's chaps.'

'Thanks, old boy.'

'Leave a note to let me know how you get on.'

Eaton and Wilde were directed to a cell on the second floor and a guard unlocked the door.

Flettner looked remarkably relaxed considering he had lost his ship and was now in solitary confinement. He was sitting on the edge of his bed, but instantly rose and clicked his heels with a respectful bow of his head as Wilde and Eaton entered the room. No Hitler salute, Wilde noted.

Eaton waded straight in without introducing himself, addressing the man in German, his normally refined voice louder and rougher than Wilde had ever heard it. Not quite a parade ground drill-sergeant, but heading in that direction.

'You brought a plain-clothes agent into Britain by stealth. You have been engaged in espionage, Herr Kapitänleutnant.'

'I was obeying orders, sir.'

'That's no defence in British law.'

'But I was on active service. If there was a plan to bring ashore a spy, a U-boat would have been used, would it not?'

'Clearly not in this case. As for you being on naval duty, that doesn't look like a Kriegsmarine captain's uniform to me.'

He nodded at Flettner's casual clothes. Flettner, unshaven and tousled, looked down at his thick blue pullover and civilian trousers and boots.

'That's because I was soaking and coated in oil. When I was brought to land I was given these clothes, for which I was grateful.'

'I don't believe you. You're part of a spy ring.'

'I deny that, sir.'

'Denial will not save your neck.'

'Can I ask who you are, sir? And where I am? I have been here two days and no one has said a word to me.'

Eaton waved a hand dismissively. 'We will answer your questions when you start to answer ours. The man you brought ashore, we know his name. We know he is engaged on a mission of assassination.'

'I know nothing of that, sir.'

'His name is Young – Charles Young.'

Wilde saw that this information had an effect. Flettner was a disciplined officer, but he rocked back on his feet.

'I know nothing of this, sir.'

'God damn you, Flettner. There is a firing squad waiting for you if we don't find this man. He's already killed two people and now he has plans to kill a child. What do you know about this?'

Flettner looked troubled.

'Did you say he intends to kill a child?'

'We have certain knowledge that he has a mission to kill a ten-year-old girl. How does the heroic Kriegsmarine officer feel about that? Perhaps you knew all along?'

Eaton's aggressive questioning seemed to be having an effect. Wilde decided to let him get on with it for the time being.

'Well?' Eaton almost shouted the word.

'I know nothing of this. I was merely commanding my vessel. You would expect the same of your own naval officers.'

'No, Herr Kapitänleutnant, I would not expect the Royal Navy to land a man in Germany with orders to kill a child.'

'But I swear I know nothing of this.'

'Not true. We have established that you were responsible for landing Charles Young on British territory. Now I need more. What weapons does he have? Who is his contact in Britain? He must have at least one. He must also have access to a wireless for sending messages to Berlin. And an escape route must have been planned for when he has finished his foul task. Was that also your job – to pick him up? I need details, Flettner – and I need them fast. An innocent child's life is at stake.'

Flettner was silent for a few moments. Wilde could see him weighing up his options. At last he stiffened.

'I think I have said more than enough, gentlemen. I am a German officer. You can have my name and rank and nothing more. If you wish to shoot me, so be it, but I will not dishonour my service.'

He clicked his heels again and pulled his shoulders back.

Eaton took a step forward. 'You're a damned fool, Flettner. You're working for a bunch of slimy, child-murdering criminals and you're talking about honour! There is no honour in the Nazis or their methods – and I suspect you know it.'

The German's genial expression had long since disappeared. His mouth was gripped so tightly shut that Wilde wondered whether it were possible for the man to crack his teeth. Wilde was tempted to hit him, but Eaton saw the look in the American's eyes and shook his head.

'Leave him, Wilde. Let Tin-Eye's boys have a go at him. Come on, we're going to get nothing more here without cutting his balls off.' He knocked twice at the door and it was opened by the guard. He threw one last look at Flettner. 'You're brave enough, Herr Kapitän-leutnant. I'll give you that much.'

'I will pray for the child,' he said.

Eaton snorted in derision. 'And a fat lot of good that will do. I'll send you a picture of her murdered body when your man has done his worst.'

Lydia entered the children's room.

'Come on, Klara, put your book down. It's bedtime. Johnny's asleep.'

'Where is Tom? Is he coming back?'

'Oh yes, he's coming back. He just has a few things to sort out. I expect you'll see him in the morning.' Lydia handed the girl a toothbrush and a tin of tooth powder and directed her towards the bathroom. 'I know it's cold in there, but you'll soon warm up in bed.' She held up a hot water bottle. 'And look what I found for you.'

'Oh, I love those. Thank you.'

Lydia almost felt like weeping. The child looked worn out and listless.

'Come on, little *liebling*, give me another hug.'

They held each other for a long time as Klara sobbed against Lydia's shoulder. She had wanted to ask Klara more about her parents, how much she knew, but perhaps that would be better left to another day. If there was another day.

'I don't feel very well, Frau Wilde,' Klara said, looking up, her eyes red.

Lydia stroked her brow. 'You've had a lot to put up with. Come on, bed. Sleep is the best thing.'

'What do you think, Wilde?' Eaton asked.

They were sitting in his car outside Latchmere House with the engine switched off.

'I think he told us everything he knows. From his reaction to the name, I think we can safely say Mr Young was on that boat. But Bormann wouldn't have wanted anyone but Young to know the details of the mission.'

'I agree. I almost felt sorry for Herr Kapitänleutnant Flettner. He was shocked rigid when he heard what his passenger is up to. I could see he believed us and he feels disgraced.'

'Do you really think Young has a contact here in England? And access to a wireless?'

'Almost certainly.'

'What will happen to Flettner?'

'PoW camp, Isle of Man. Probably better food than our boys are getting over in Germany. Certainly better than the poor damned Russians are getting.'

Wilde grinned. 'You always did have a soft spot for the Reds, didn't you?'

'Give it a rest, Wilde. Do you want to go to see this unfortunate young woman in Sevenoaks?'

Wilde wanted to get back to Lydia and the children, but he was still interested in the events at Sevenoaks.

'It is damned odd that he should take the time to go to Kent to kill his family. Why the hell would he do that?'

'They say most murders are family affairs.'

'You'll get Special Branch on to the case?'

'Indeed.'

'Then I'll leave it to them.'

In his heart he doubted there was much to be learned from the maid. He was more worried about Cashbone and Sunny. He couldn't believe they were just sitting on their hands waiting for something to happen. There was something else, too.

'Eaton,' he said, 'could I put a name to you? Anton Offenbach? He was my shadow in Germany, also involved with Sunny Somerfeld. Dead now, as Sunny may have told you. I couldn't work out for the life of me who he really was.'

'Offenbach? I'll look into it,' Eaton replied casually.

Wilde knew Eaton well enough to realise that the name definitely did mean something to him.

'Meanwhile, I think you should come back with me and finish off that bottle, old boy. Have a kip in my spare room and weigh up your options. Come morning, you might see my point of view.'

Wilde nodded slowly. The offer sounded a fair option, for he needed sleep, badly. But it wouldn't change his mind. He had to get back to Cambridge.

Eaton had thoughts of his own.

'Look, Wilde, I know you're not going to tell me where Lydia's hiding with the German girl, but answer me this – was there anything in your own house to connect you to the hideout?'

Was there? It was a worrying notion, but for the life of him he couldn't think what it might be. But then he was also aware that he was too tired to be thinking as lucidly as he might.

Soon they were back in Chelsea, a couple of streets from Eaton's home.

'Drop me off here,' Wilde said.

'I thought you were coming in.'

'No. For all I know you have a welcoming party.'

'Oh, to hell with you, Wilde.' He braked hard. 'It's quite bloody obvious that you're holed up in Cambridge itself. We will find you, you know.'

Wilde opened the door and stepped out.

'Good night, Eaton.'

CHAPTER 31

Jung sat in the passenger seat of his newly acquired car. He had ditched the Bentley in the station car park and hot-wired an anonymous black Austin 10. Now, as he gazed at the blacked-out windows of the house, he weighed up his choices. He had to know who was in there and whether they were armed. He looked at his wristwatch. Almost 10 p.m. It would be better to wait until the early hours. If there was an armed guard in there, they might not be so alert at 3 a.m.

'OK, drive on,' he said.

The woman at the wheel depressed the clutch, engaged first and pulled away from the kerb. She was not a good driver, but she had other, more important, uses.

Her name was Felicity Vickery. He had met her a few hours earlier in her pretty cottage on the outskirts of the small market town of Spixton, south-east of Cambridge. She was at least sixty-five, perhaps seventy, with a sweet, kindly face and blue-rinsed hair.

The encoded message to the E-boat from Bormann had contained few details, save her name and address, that she was to be trusted and that she had access to a wireless transmitter.

She lived down a short private lane, so the house was not overlooked. He had approached her with caution, one hand in his pocket resting on the butt of his jewel-handled pistol. There was such a thing as a double agent. And when he saw a smiling little old lady at the door of her picture postcard English cottage, he hesitated. Had he got the wrong address? Surely, this couldn't be Bormann's English contact? But she was looking at him as though she were expecting him.

'Mr Young?'

'Mrs Vickery?'

'The very same, dear. But everyone calls me Mrs V. Do come in. And wipe your feet on the mat, if you would.'

'Is there a Mr V?'

'No, dear. My husband fell from a cruise liner in the Mediterranean. Very sad. So now I'm a widow.'

Indoors, her house was spotless. She offered him tea, explaining that Herr Bormann had been in touch and was worried about him and his progress.

As the kettle boiled, he told her about the people he was seeking. He also handed her the address book from Wilde's house.

'Look through there, if you would. See if any names or addresses jump out at you. Something out of place . . . not quite right.'

'I'd be happy to, dear, but if they're in the hands of MI5 and they're in this area, the most likely place they'll be is a village not too far from here called Harkham. In fact the secret service seems to bring people there from all over the country. It's what they call a safe house. But safe or not, I'm sure a man of your courage and resourcefulness will find a way in.'

She spooned tea into the pot, arranged milk and sugar and two cups on a tray, then carried it through to the parlour.

'And shall I fetch some biscuits, too, Mr Young? I have rich tea or digestives.'

'Ah, digestives, yes please! Haven't had them in years, Mrs V. Tell me more about this safe house.'

'Oh, everyone in Harkham knows about the place, Mr Young. I have a very old friend in the village, and she couldn't resist telling me about it when we met up for the carol service last year. It's by the church and it's called the Old Rectory – you can't possibly miss it. The secret service boys are in and out all the time and they're convinced no one knows, but of course they do. Everyone in the village does. And people do tend to tell me things, you see. They say I have a kindly, trustworthy face.'

'Indeed you do, Mrs V.'

'Appearances can be deceptive, can't they. Do I surprise you, dear?'

She was pouring the tea, but looked up at him with a quizzical smile.

That was when he saw through her. That sly smile. It told him everything he needed to know about Felicity Vickery. This little old lady was the same as him. Exactly the same. She would kill her dearest pet or her best friend with that kindly smile fixed to her face.

'Yes, I *was* a little surprised.'

'Good. And that's just the way it should be if I am to go about my important work on behalf of the Führer. I am English through and through, but I have been a disciple for more than ten years now and have spent many happy holidays in Germany. Those Nuremberg rallies! That's where I met Herr Bormann. Such a lovely man – even back then I knew he was going places. The Führer is very lucky to have him. Just a shame we had such second-raters in our own Blackshirts. As for Mosley, what an absolute disaster.'

Jung nodded. 'I've heard of him – vaguely.'

'Silly, posturing ass – a pale imitation of a strong leader. Anyway, Mr Young, we'll have the real thing soon. Look.' She went to the sideboard and opened a drawer. 'Herr Bormann gave me this – a Party badge. I've never shown it to anyone in this country until now. But I felt so proud, so honoured when I received it.'

'It is a fine thing.'

Jung had never bothered with such baubles. He had joined the Party as a necessity, to ensure the continuation of his trade and make life in general easier. And because Bormann told him it was a good idea.

'I believe you have a radio transmitter.'

She nodded. 'I use it as infrequently as possible, and I try to keep moving it around the area, or I'll be discovered rather quickly. I think a little message to Herr Bormann might be in order. Just to say you're here.'

'Of course.'

'But first I want to help you. I have heard this name Wilde before. Cambridge professor of history, yes? There was a story in the *Cambridge News* two years ago, just after the start of the war. He was named in it, I remember that much, as was one of his undergraduates, a young man who had gone off to the Spanish War. There were some strange elements to the story and I got a feeling it wasn't fully reported, that something was being covered up by the intelligence services.'

'What happened?'

'All I can tell you is that there were two – no, three – murders, which is a very unusual thing in this part of the world. A house burned down and there was a court case. What I'll do is look through the address book with great care – it's quite possible that a name will ring a bell.'

'Thank you.'

'I want to help you in any way I can. I may have a little arthritis nowadays, but I'm quite robust, you know.'

'I'm sure you are.'

'But just wait until you see what I have for you. Have you heard of a Sten gun? It's a British weapon. I'm told it's very reliable. It's in the garden shed.'

When they had finished their tea, they strolled down to the end of the garden. In a box on the floor of her preternaturally tidy shed was the gun, wrapped in oily rags, along with several boxes of ammunition.

'How did you acquire this, Mrs V?'

'The same way I got the transmitter. Our masters in Berlin make sure we're properly equipped. You don't need to know more.'

He weighed the weapon in his arms. It had a nice feel to it.

'There's a disused quarry a few hundred yards beyond my garden. Why don't you go and fire off a few rounds there? Get a feel for it. No one will hear you.'

She reminded him of his great aunt, Mab as she had been known. Mab was the one relative he had had time for out of the crew of reluctant aunts and uncles, cousins, grandparents and casual acquaintances who had taken him in during school holidays. Of the whole unpleasant bunch, Mab was the only one who had seemed at all pleased to see him when he turned up with his trunk and tuck box.

One day he overheard Mab talking to a friend.

'She never could stand him, you know. Loathed the sight of him from the day he was born. She never even used his name when talking about him. Called him *The Creature*.'

Even at the age of nine, Charlie knew that Mab was talking about his mother, and that *he* was *The Creature*. That was why Mummy and Daddy had been so keen to ship him off to school in England and never set eyes on him again. That was why they had deserved to die. But he didn't want to think about such things now. There were other people who needed dealing with.

'Show me the quarry, Mrs V. And then perhaps we'll go for a little drive.'

Lydia did not need a thermometer to know that Klara had a fever. She put a hand to her forehead. The girl was burning up. This was more than just exhaustion. In her mind, she went through the possible childhood illnesses: scarlet fever, measles, chicken pox, German measles, polio, influenza, diphtheria. Now, which one of those started with a fever, and which might have taken a few days to incubate? She should know all this as the daughter of a doctor and a mother herself.

She found a clean facecloth in an airing cupboard and soaked it in cold water, then knelt by the side of Klara's bed and gently patted her brow. She moaned quietly in her sleep. Lydia felt hopelessly inadequate. This wasn't something that required hospital treatment, but in normal circumstances your GP would come out to check on the child, something that she couldn't risk with Klara.

Lydia put her hand to Klara's neck; she was pretty sure the glands were inflamed. Childhood fever . . . the very words struck terror into her heart.

Leaving Mrs Vickery in the car, Jung approached the house. Wrapping his jacket round his arm, he punched out a downstairs casement window at the front, then reached in and eased it open. Without hesitating, he climbed in, pushing the blackout aside. The sound would have woken the occupants, but he had the Sten gun and the element of surprise on his side.

Back against the wall, gun held across his chest, he stood by the door into the next room, which he took to be a hallway, and listened. No sound. Had he really not woken anyone? Perhaps the blackout curtain had muffled the sound of the shattering glass.

He waited a full minute. Still nothing. He turned the handle and pulled the door towards him, then flicked a switch and a low wattage bulb lit the room. It was some sort of study, with shelves full of books and a radiogram. It was difficult to gauge the layout of this house. Where were the bedrooms? Most crucially, where was the girl? Jung opened another door and switched on another light. Now he was in the hallway. To his right the front door and a telephone, to his left a carpeted staircase. Slowly, step by careful step, he ascended the stairs to the landing. The light from the hallway gave a faint glow. He had a choice of doors.

In the first weeks of the war, soon after she had joined MI5, Rosamund Kemp had done a stint of weapons training at an army range in Surrey. She had been quite proficient, particularly with a rifle.

But weapons training in the controlled environment of a firing range was very different from the real thing. And since coming to the Old Rectory at Harkham in the summer of 1940, there had been no further instruction or practice.

Now her hands were shaking so much she could hardly hold the revolver. It was a .38 Enfield, very heavy at one and a half pounds, with a difficult trigger requiring a full double-action pull for every shot.

She was well aware that an enemy agent was on the loose looking for the German girl. The fact that Tom Wilde had removed her did not necessarily mean the house was secure.

Rosamund sometimes heard more than her masters thought she did.

In this way, she had got the gist of the disagreement between Tom Wilde and Bodie Cashbone. The latter had a loud voice, and she wasn't deaf. Rosamund wasn't at all sure that she disagreed with Wilde's action in removing the child.

An emergency telephone sat on her bedside table. But she did not want to risk making a sound, not with the intruder already in the house. Not even the soft sound of dialling or the whisper of a plea for help.

The footfalls had ascended the staircase and were now on the landing, not quite deadened by the carpet. She could hear her own breathing and feared that the intruder could, too.

She was not usually here alone. Most of the time there were agents here – highly trained agents who would know how to deal with a deadly situation like this. She tried to think. What would the intruder do when he turned her handle and found the door locked?

She heard the footsteps come closer, and the sound of the door handle turning. The door was locked and bolted, but the proximity of the intruder, just feet away from her on the other side, was terrifying. The door was made of of pine and not especially sturdy. She edged closer, held the pistol out at chest height, jerked the trigger hard and fired. The recoil jolted her backwards, but she kept pulling the trigger, again and again – three shots: left, centre, then right. She heard a groan and a dull thud.

A body falling to the floor.

Mrs Kemp waited, not sure what she was most afraid of: that she had killed him, or that she hadn't. She had always known that MI5 would send potentially dangerous men here, but no one had told her she would have to use the gun she had been given.

Her arm was shaking. Her whole upper body ached.

She waited one minute, two. Still not switching on the light, she unbolted and unlocked the door, then turned the handle. She opened the door, still holding the pistol out in front of her.

A shapeless figure lay on the floor by the railings. She reached out and flicked the light switch and found herself looking down at a man on his haunches pointing a sub-machine gun up at her. He nodded at the pistol.

'Put it down,' he said.

In her shock and confusion, instinct took over. But before her finger could fully depress the trigger, she was being cut down by a vicious burst from the Sten, slumping to the floor like a broken marionette.

CHAPTER 32

Lydia was becoming increasingly concerned. She had no medicines, not even an aspirin to help the child, and her attempts to reduce Klara's fever were failing. She had to get help – and that meant leaving this house, whatever Tom had said.

With the lights switched off, she pulled back the blackout and looked out into the narrow alley. Tom had said there was a phone box across the road, but she couldn't see it. Without street lights, she couldn't see anything at all. If anyone was out there, she would never know.

At least Johnny was asleep, which was something. She had moved him to another room; with no notion of how infectious Klara might be, it was the only sensible option. Childhood illnesses were episodes that had to be endured, but not for Johnny just at the moment, thank you.

She went to look at him, kissed his forehead, which was gratifyingly cool, and tiptoed from the room. Her purse was on the kitchen table, and she removed some coins and a cigarette lighter.

Leaving the front door unlocked, she looked both ways into the gloom. Her eyes soon began to adjust and she was confident no one was about. Darting across the road, she ducked into the kiosk, picked up the receiver and dialled a number she knew by heart. When it was answered, she quickly fed some coins into the slot.

'Hello, Edie?'

'Is that you, Lydia?'

'I'm so sorry to wake you.'

'Don't worry, darling – I'm used to it. Curse of the GP's wife. Is something the matter?'

'Is Rupert there? I have a sick child – I'm very worried.'

'Better to get him to Addenbrooke's – that might be quicker.'

'I can't – honestly, Edie, I can't – and I can't explain. I'm not at home. If Rupert could come here. We're in Harry Taylor's house, but please don't tell anyone. Not a word, we're in grave danger.'

Lydia felt terrible that she was communicating her panic down the wires to her friend, but what else could she do?

'Ok, Lydia, I'm not going to ask what this is about, but I'm afraid Rupert's out on a call, so I tell you what I'll do – *I'll* come over. Would that help? To be frank, I probably know as much as him about childhood illnesses. Or do you want to put Johnny in your car and bring him over here?'

'I can't use the car. Truly, I can't. You come here, Edie – and please hurry. She's burning up with fever. I'm terrified.'

'She?'

'It's not Johnny. I'll explain when you get here.'

'This name catches the eye.' Felicity Vickery pointed to the entry in the address book. 'Rupert Weir. He's the police surgeon in Cambridge. There's something in the back of my mind about him being involved in an incident with the professor.'

Jung wasn't convinced, but perhaps it was better than nothing. The house at Harkham had revealed no clues.

'Is he far from here, this doctor?'

'Girton. That won't take us very long.'

Edith Weir parked her much-loved Wolseley in front of Trinity Villa and eased her considerable girth out of the car. She and her husband Rupert enjoyed the fine things of life – food, wine and laughter. They were also faithful friends to Lydia and Tom.

'Now then,' she said, bustling upstairs from the hall, carrying a small leather valise. 'Where is the poor little wretch?'

'Listen, Edie, you have to know one or two things. The girl's name is Klara. She is ten. She is German and she has only just arrived here by means of which I am not at liberty to tell you. But she is entrusted to my care.'

'My German's not very good, I'm afraid.'

'Her father taught her English. If you speak clearly, she will understand you. But at the moment she's not at all responsive.'

'And where are her parents ?'

'Both dead. And there are people who wish Klara dead, too. Which is why I am hiding out here rather than home.'

'Gosh, Lydia, you have got yourself into a pickle. Does this put me in danger? Oh well, never mind if it does. Let's just see what we can do for the child.'

Klara seemed agitated, but unaware of their presence. Her face was coated in perspiration and her breathing was troubled. Edie Weir took her pulse, placed the back of her hand on her brow, checked her lymph nodes for swelling, then turned to Lydia.

'Has she been coughing?'

'No, but her breathing has been fast.'

'Convulsions?'

'I don't think so.'

'Have you given her any water?'

'Just a few sips. That's all she'll take.'

'What's her appetite been like?'

'I couldn't really say, Edie – the child has only been in my care today.'

'But you think these symptoms have developed while she's been with you?'

'Yes, she was quite chatty this afternoon. Playing with Johnny.'

'And Johnny's OK?'

Lydia nodded. 'It all happened rather suddenly, I think. She became listless and tired and wanted to go to bed. I just thought she was exhausted, which would be no surprise. She's had quite a time of it, I'm afraid. Anyway, I found her like this an hour ago and tried to get her fever down with a cool flannel.'

'Is Harry Taylor home on leave – is that why you're here?'

'No, I keep an eye on the place. It seemed like a perfect hideout for a day or two.'

'I see.' Edie bent close to the girl. 'Klara, dear, can you hear me?'

Klara reacted to the voice. '*Zu heiss, zu heiss,*' she said, her head nodding from side to side, her chest heaving as she struggled for breath.

'She's saying she's too hot.'

Edie stood up. 'Well, at least she's not unconscious, but nor is she properly aware of what's going on. I'd say her temperature is at least a hundred and three. She really isn't a well girl. Darling Lydia, I think to be on the safe side I'd like to get this child to hospital. It's probably measles, but we won't be sure for a day or two. If she's come straight from Germany, we can't have any idea what's going around in her home town, but measles is my big worry. If a rash comes in a day or two, then we'll find out. To be honest there's not much you can do in the way of treating the virus. But Addenbrooke's will keep an eye on her.'

'I'm scared, Edie. I know no one takes a child to hospital for measles, but if we can't be sure . . .'

'Well, *I* could take her if you trust me.'

'Of course I trust you. But I have to stay with her.'

'Let's all go then – in my car. I'll carry Klara down and you fetch Johnny.' She smiled broadly. 'This is all something to do with Tom's absence, I suppose. You two do get in some scrapes, don't you!'

'Won't Rupert be home yet? Couldn't we go there?'

'I don't know. It was a police call. They can last a few minutes for an inebriated driver or hours for something more serious.'

'But we could wait for him at your house?'

She could see Lydia was not happy about the idea of taking Klara to a hospital.

'Oh, all right – we'll go home and wait for Rupert.'

The door was unlocked when Wilde arrived back at Trinity Villa. Just inside, there was a note on the mat. Wilde picked it up with trepidation. *'Klara sick – maybe measles. Called Edie W. She came here and is taking me to her place.'*

Wilde uttered a low curse. This was all they needed. He consulted his watch. The journey back had been frustratingly slow and now it was close to dawn. When his tank got close to empty, he had to find a motorbike and siphon fuel from it, leaving a pound note in the saddlebag with a scrawled note of apology for the theft. This stealing business – clothes from a washing line in Germany and now this – really had to stop.

He couldn't help being angry with Lydia. The Weirs' house in Girton was the last place she should have gone. Far too obvious. Despite her note, he checked the garage to reassure himself that the car was still there. His first instinct was to ride straight out to Girton, but sense told him to call first. He crossed the road and dialled from the kiosk. The phone rang and rang. He was about to replace the receiver when he heard a click at the other end.

'Hello?'

Silence. But there was someone there. He was sure he could hear breathing.

'Hello, Edie? Rupert?'

Nothing. The line went dead and Wilde was left looking at the phone, his heart pounding.

Within moments, he was back on the Rudge, heading north through the dark, deserted streets. A route he knew well. He saw a beat constable crossing the road, but didn't slow down, merely swerved round him, leaving a shaking fist in his rear-view.

Edie and Rupert Weir lived in a large detached house in a wide, pleasant street not far from Girton College. It had a short driveway leading to a gravel forecourt. Wilde ditched the motorcycle at the kerb between a couple of cars, neither of which he recognised, and approached on foot. In his pocket, he gripped his pistol – the same one Sunny had given him in Germany.

He stopped. In the shadows he saw two figures watching the house from a concealed position to the right of the house, next to the garage and shed. Even in the gloom it was clear he was looking at Bodie Cashbone and Sunny Somerfeld.

But why here? Eaton, of course. It had to be Eaton putting two and two together and coming up with Rupert Weir. The larger, plusher of the cars parked on the road must be theirs. But what were they doing standing there in the shadows? Waiting for him, he supposed. Had they been in the house, looking for Lydia and Klara? Had that been Cashbone's sinister breathing on the phone?

No, some instinct told him that they were not the ones who had picked up the phone. In which case, someone else was in the house. Or had been. Someone even more dangerous. So where were Lydia, Klara and Edie?

These thoughts flashed through his mind in a split second. Cashbone and Sunny were his main concern right now. Nothing for it. He moved slowly in their direction. If Charles Young was in the house, then Wilde and Sunny and Cashbone had to work together. He was no more than fifteen yards away when Sunny turned, recognising him in the grey predawn light. She put up a hand urgently, palm towards him, and he froze.

At that moment, the front door of the Weirs' house was opening and a man was emerging. No more than a dark shape in this light. But one thing was clearly visible – the stark outline of a sub-machine gun, its barrel scanning the spaces between the trees.

CHAPTER 33

The moment he saw Wilde, Jung sprayed the forecourt and the trees. Wilde instantly dropped to one knee, pistol out, firing back as fragments of wood and stone cut through the air around him. Cashbone was firing, too. While Sunny seemed to be throwing herself towards Wilde.

Wilde only had a few rounds left. He tried to get the man with the sub-machine gun in his sights as he backed away from the porch, and fired again, but trying to hit a moving target from this distance with a handgun was virtually impossible.

Jung was retreating to his right, firing sporadically. At five hundred rounds per minute, the Sten's 32-bullet box magazine was quickly spent. Slinging the Sten over his shoulder, he pulled his pistol from his waistband and held it at arm's length. He fired at two-second intervals. First at Wilde, then Cashbone, then back again. The shots were wide or high, but they covered his retreat. Within moments, he was gone, into the undergrowth at the far side of the house.

The noisy havoc of gunfire was replaced by an eerie silence punctuated by a single sound. Sunny lay prostrate at Wilde's feet, and was moaning softly.

He knelt at her side, realising with horror that she had been hit. As he touched her, he felt blood seeping through his fingers.

'Cashbone!'

But Cashbone ignored his call; he was going after the shooter.

'Cashbone – she's been shot! Help me! We have to get her to hospital.'

The big American stopped in his tracks and edged back, all the while keeping his eyes and pistol trained on Jung's escape route.

Wilde had his fingers pressed to her neck. There was still a faint pulse, but her eyes were closed and her breath was coming in short gasps. Blood was bubbling at her lips. Wilde gently rolled her on to her side to prevent her drowning in her own blood. He opened her coat and saw the entry wound on her back, close to the spine.

Please, God, let it have missed her heart.

He pulled out his shirt tails and ripped off a large piece of cotton, then bunched it in his fist and pressed it against the wound to try to stem the bleeding.

'Is your car out there, Cashbone?'

'Yes.'

'I'll carry her. Then you take her to hospital – I've got to get into that house.'

'Which hospital?' Cashbone growled. 'I don't know any hospital. I sure don't know where I am in this town.'

'God damn it, stay here with Sunny.'

Wilde ran to the house. The front door was open. He ran from room to room, calling out.

'Lydia . . . Edie . . .'

No response. All the doors to wardrobes and cabinets had been flung open by the intruder. It was a large house. He checked everything at great speed. There was no sign of a struggle. No one was there. Where had Lydia, Edie and the children got to?

He tried the garden, the garage, the outhouses. Finally, he was back on the forecourt. He was relieved that he hadn't found them – and yet he was desperately worried, too, for Lydia had said they were coming here.

Cashbone was carrying Sunny up towards the road. Wilde followed them and pulled open the rear door of the car. Together, the two men eased her into the back seat, then Cashbone slid into the front and took the wheel.

Sunny was limp, but there were signs of life. What had she been doing, flinging herself in his direction when the firing started? It was a crazy thing to do. And then it struck him – she had seen the man in the porch lining his weapon up at Wilde and, without thinking, had tried to shield him. Why would she do that? Why would she risk her life to save him? He was suddenly filled with shame for having doubted her. And yet . . .

'Sunny, hold on – we'll have you at the hospital before you know it. Please, Sunny – we need you. Klara needs you.'

Cashbone drove hard, with Wilde calling out instructions from the back. He held Sunny in his arms. Blood continued to trickle from the side of her mouth. The cotton wad he had ripped from his shirt was soaked with gore.

Dawn was breaking properly now, but the sky remained grey and cold. Flecks of snow danced in the air.

'Sunny, stay awake. Talk to me.'

Her breathing was so faint. Her pulse was vanishing.

'Sunny. Do this for me. Do this for Klara. Stay with us.'

His hand caressed her forehead.

'Sunny, please . . .'

'You were right,' she said, her voice barely audible, blood bubbling at her mouth. 'Look after her, Tom.'

'That's it, Sunny. Keep talking.'

'I'm dying, Tom.'

'No – you're staying with us.'

He mopped her brow with the back of his hand and whispered in her ear, soothing words about Klara and Anton Offenbach and courage. All he could do was try to make her listen to whatever nonsense he could think to say, anything to stop her from slipping into unconsciousness.

He reminded her of the long, arduous journey that had brought them here. She had to stay with him to make it all worthwhile, what they had done together, the three of them, crossing northern Germany, braving the Baltic, flying through hostile skies to Scotland.

Within a few minutes, Cashbone was braking outside Addenbrooke's Hospital.

But Wilde knew they were too late. There was no pulse, no breathing. Sunny was dead in his arms.

Wilde and Cashbone stood in the lobby of the hospital as the body of Sigrun Somerfeld was wheeled away on a trolley. Outside, the day would be lightening, but it felt to Wilde as though a pall of darkness had fallen on the world. He had no idea where his family had gone, and a woman with whom he had been through a kind of hell had lost her life. What had happened to this beautiful university town and its comfortable certainties?

The lobby was busy at this time of day, with shifts changing and day patients appearing for their appointments. Had Lydia come here instead – or had she gone back to Harry Taylor's house? Surely one of those alternatives had to be the answer.

'OK, buddy?' Cashbone put a big hand on Wilde's shoulder.

'No.'

'Me neither. She was a brave young woman.'

'What now, Cashbone? What in God's name do we do now?'

'Nothing's changed.'

He threw him an exasperated look. 'You do talk some shit. Everything's changed. You and your damned intrigues.'

He wanted to say, *your conspiring has resulted in the death of a decent woman and has turned an innocent child into a fugitive.* Would that have been too harsh?

You were right, Sunny had said at the end. Right about what exactly? Had she seen through Bodie Cashbone?

Through the melee his eyes suddenly fell on the imposing figure of Dr Rupert Weir, striding purposefully in his direction. As always, his large body was encased in tweed with a bulging waistcoat and watch-chain.

'Rupert?'

'Tom, thank God you're here. I was hoping you'd turn up. We need to talk.'

'What's going on?'

'Edie was here with Lydia and Johnny and another child named Klara, who had rather a high temperature. I think she's a German refugee. Anyway, perhaps understandably, Lydia had a bit of an overreaction to the little girl's fever. I suppose she felt responsible for the girl's well-being. As it turned out, there was nothing to concern anyone, so they were all reassured and sent home—'

Wilde didn't like hearing this in front of Cashbone, but the information had tumbled out in a rush.

'Rupert,' he broke in before Weir could give anything else away, 'there are things I have to tell you – but first, let me introduce you to Mr Bodie Cashbone of the US diplomatic service.'

Cashbone extended his hand. 'Pleased to make your acquaintance, doctor.'

Weir turned towards the American as though he hadn't noticed him standing there and shook hands absent-mindedly.

'And you, Mr Cashbone.' Then the realisation seemed to dawn that Wilde had deliberately broken into his diatribe to introduce the man. 'What brings you to Cambridge?'

'I'm working with the professor here.'

'Ah . . . secret stuff eh, Wilde? Well, I've had a devil of a night with the secret stuff. Been out at a village called Harkham looking at the corpse of a woman. Riddled with bullets. She's now on the table in the mortuary.'

'My God – the Old Rectory?'

'Does the place mean something to you, Tom?'

Wilde nodded, his heart hammering. *Please, God . . . not after Sunny.*

'Tom? You don't look well.'

Wilde steeled himself. 'Rupert, tell me everything.'

'Looks as though she had a whole magazine from a sub-machine gun unloaded into her. Must have been pretty well instant, if that's any comfort. A couple of MI5 lads turned up while I was there. Shut everything down. Threatened me with the Official Secrets Act and God knows what. I don't actually react well to threats.'

'The woman – did you get her name?' Wilde asked, though, of course, he already knew it.

'Mrs Kemp. Rosamund Kemp.' Weir winced. 'I can see from your face, Tom, that you knew the poor woman.'

'We both did. Rupert, listen. We've just come from *your* house at Girton. Another woman, a woman we also know well, was shot and killed. We brought her here – she died just before we arrived.'

'Dear God – Edie . . . Tell me she wasn't there!'

'No one else was there. But the killer broke into your house. He is trying to find Klara – the German girl – to kill her. I can't explain everything at the moment.'

'Damn it, Tom, I'm sorry, I have to go. I have to be with Edie.'

Wilde had never seen his friend look so distressed. But nor had he ever seen him when he felt his family and home were endangered in any way.

'Go – we'll talk later.'

'This is too much to take in. Maybe she's still at Harry's place, do you think? Should I call in first at Trin—'

Wilde cut in. 'Don't say any more, Rupert.'

'Sorry, old man. Still trying to get my head around all this.'

He looked abashed, nodded awkwardly to Cashbone, then turned and started walking briskly away.

Wilde watched him disappearing through the hospital doors, out on to Trumpington Street. What he didn't notice was the kindly looking old lady with the blue-grey hair, standing between him and the reception desk, pretending not to listen to their conversation.

'We still have a problem, Cashbone. We need to work together – but you need to stop pursuing the girl, you understand?'

Cashbone was unyielding. 'Not that simple, buddy. I need her. The COI needs her. Sunny Somerfeld died to bring this project to fruition and I'm going to see it through. We owe Sunny that.'

This was outrageous, to use Sunny's name in such a manner. Wilde couldn't stomach Cashbone a moment longer.

'I'm going now, on foot – if you want to try to follow me, feel free.'

Wilde strode out of the broad-fronted hospital and turned right down Trumpington Street. He didn't bother to look around to see whether Cashbone was pursuing him. Nor did he see the elderly woman with the blue rinse climb into the passenger seat of an Austin 10, which then did a U-turn and began to grind its way down the road at a discreet distance behind him. In the race here from Girton, he hadn't seen the little car trailing in their wake.

After a few hundred yards, Wilde ducked into the ancient gateway of his college and sought out the head porter, Scobie.

'Keep a weather eye out for strangers today, Scobie. If you don't know someone, don't give them admittance. OK?'

'Of course, sir – and welcome back from wherever you've been.'

'If anyone asks for me, tell them I'm uncontactable.'

'I understand, sir.'

'The only calls I will accept are from Miss Morris, Dr Weir or Mr Eaton.'

'I shall make a note of it, professor.'

For a brief moment, Wilde wondered whether he could be endangering the porters. But he had confidence in them; they might look like ledger clerks in their bowlers and office suits, but these men were solid in defence of their colleges and all those in them. Anyway, the chance of Charles Young trying to force his way into a Cambridge college was vanishingly small.

Wilde crossed the courts and ascended the staircase to his room. Bobby, his college servant, greeted him, but Wilde wasn't in the mood and merely grunted back.

'Coffee, professor?'

'No, I'll be no more than two minutes. I want you to go out into the new court and keep an eye on the gateway. See if anyone is loitering, then come back and report to me.'

'Certainly, sir.'

His rooms were cold and unlived-in. Everything was where it should be, but there was ice inside the windows and his books and papers all looked like things from another life. Two minutes later, Bobby returned.

'All clear, professor. No one about except Mr Scobie.'

'Right, now we're going back. You'll be twenty or thirty yards ahead of me. If you carry on walking, it means there's no one about. If you stop, it means you've seen a stranger – someone not associated with the college. Is that clear?'

'Yes, sir.'

'And I'll be going out the back way, past the chapel.'

*

The Austin 10 came to a halt fifty yards past the college's front gate. Mrs Vickery turned and smiled at Charlie Jung. Then she pulled the address book from her handbag and began to flick through it.

'What are you looking for, Mrs V?'

'Someone called Harry or Henry. Could be Trinity College or Trinity Hall – or Trinity Street, perhaps. Not far from here, I feel, Mr Young. Soon have it, I'm sure.'

CHAPTER 34

'I'm so sorry, Edie. I can't believe I've put you through all this.'

'Darling Lydia, it's always better to overreact than do nothing. Truly, I was delighted to help.'

They were back at Trinity Villa. Lydia had changed her mind yet again on the way to Girton and begged Edie to go to Addenbrooke's after all. But once there, the hospital visit had been little short of embarrassing. The doctor had examined Klara thoroughly but had been a little bemused.

'Well,' he had said eventually, 'she is a little feverish. But I'm not sure why you've brought her here. Take her home, put her to bed and give her as much water as she'll take. It may be measles, we don't know. But even if it is, there's very little we can do here that can't be done by you at home. Call your GP and he'll keep an eye on her.'

And then, to make matters worse, they had run into Rupert, and Lydia had had to admit her ridiculous loss of nerve. He had had a hard night on a police case and seemed distracted, so they had left him to his work.

Edie could see that the night's events had taken their toll on Lydia, so after putting Klara and Johnny back to bed, she made a pot of tea and they sat drinking and chatting until she felt Lydia had calmed down enough to sleep.

'Right, dear, I think it's time for me to go home.'

Lydia clutched her hand. 'You won't mention this place to anyone, Edie? Not a word . . .'

'Of course I won't, darling.'

'I feel so hunted.'

Edie sighed deeply. 'Whatever it is, Lydia, it's clearly absolutely bloody.'

'I feel ashamed about complaining, though. Just think how those poor Jews in Berlin must feel. Hunted, hiding in lofts and cellars so they don't get transported to the east. Juliet Vanderberg told me about them in a letter from America last month – all the terrible tales Jim tells her. You remember Jim and Juliet, don't you, Edie?'

'Of course I do, Lydia. Look, it's about patience and fortitude. That's all we have to fall back on in circumstances like this. Do you want to give me some clue as to what this is all about?'

'I can't, Edie. I would if I could – but I can't.'

'Well, you know where I am if you need me.'

Edie was about to put on her coat when she stopped and held out her hand to Lydia. Something on her palm shone in the dim light.

'I took this from Klara when we arrived at the hospital, for safe-keeping. I know how easy it is for things to go AWOL in hospitals.'

'Thank you.' Lydia took the locket and chain. 'Apparently it's the only thing she has from her parents, so it's very dear to her.'

'I've seen one like it before, actually,' Edie said. 'Sweet little things. You think you've opened it up and you see the little photo or lock of hair or some other little memento, but then there's this other tiny secret compartment.'

'Really? Where?'

Edie took the locket back. 'Here, this hairline, barely visible. Do you want me to see if I can prise it open? We might need a razor blade or a very finely honed knife.'

Lydia went into the kitchen. She opened a couple of drawers and came up with a slim little fruit knife. She handed it to Edie.

'Here you are, try this.'

Edie removed her glasses and held the locket up to her eyes. In a few seconds she was holding the locket on the palm of her hand with a wide smile.

'There we are. Open sesame!'

Lydia took the locket and peered at the new compartment. Something was etched there, but the letters were so tiny she couldn't work it out. Edie dug into her handbag and produced a magnifying glass.

'I always carry this thing for small print. My eyes aren't what they were.'

'Thank you. Now then, let's have a look.'

Lydia moved the glass back and forth until she had it precisely focused. Finally, she could see it clearly: two sets of initials in a finely wrought Gothic script. On one side, *GR*, on the other *AH*.

Wilde slipped out of the back of the college and made his way up to St Andrew's Street. The snow was swirling but not quite settling. In his rooms he had an officer's greatcoat from the First World War, a thing he had picked up at Christmas 1939 after so much of his clothing and property was lost in the fire that destroyed his house. The coat was old and tattered, but warm – a handy thing to keep in college for bitter days such as these. Now he was wrapped up in it, his hands deep in the pockets, the gun firmly gripped in one of them. He had checked the chamber; there were two rounds left.

He stopped close to the police station and sheltered briefly in a doorway, head down but watchful. He was pretty sure Cashbone would not have been able to follow him through the college grounds and that he wouldn't know about the rear exit, but you couldn't be too careful. When he felt as certain as he could be that all was well, he entered the phone box and called Philip Eaton's office. He was put through at once.

'Wilde, is that you?'

'I take it you've heard what's going on up here.'

'Fragmented reports. Two women dead – our own dear Mrs Kemp and Frau Somerfeld?'

'That's the headline, but there's a lot more. We're still very vulnerable to the killer – and bloody Cashbone won't let up on his insane quest. He wants Klara – and he's still insisting on using her for his own ends. You've got to call him off, Eaton.'

'I can't.'

'Then how do I protect her?'

'I think you'll just have to admit defeat, Wilde. This all goes much higher than you and me. This is international politics – way above our rank.'

'You need to get up here, Eaton.'

'I'm just arranging it. I'll be at the Bull.'

'No, I'll find you rooms in college. I'll get Scobie to help you out.'

'Good man. What are you doing now?'

'Hiding.'

'You've got a bloody gun, haven't you? A souvenir from Germany.'

'What makes you think that?'

'Sunny told me after you disappeared with Klara. Just be careful what you do with it. Do for Charles Young by all means – but if you shoot Cashbone, you'll be hanged.'

He went back to Trinity Villa by a circuitous route. The lane was empty. No sign of Edie's car, so she must have gone home. The door was locked but Lydia quickly let him in. She was bleary-eyed and he realised that, like himself, she must have gone the whole night without sleep.

'Johnny? Klara?'

'Asleep.'

'The fever?'

'I'm trying to give her sips of water, as instructed. God, I feel such a bloody fool, Tom. What must that doctor have thought of me? Probably telling all his colleagues about the hysterical little woman bringing a child in because she's got a little temperature. Meanwhile, there's a murderer on the loose – and I expose Klara to the world's prying eyes!'

'You did what you thought was right. Come on, we need to get a few hours' sleep. You sleep in the room with Klara, I'll go with Johnny. When we're refreshed hopefully we'll be able to think straight and plan our next move. But we can't keep moving Klara, not until she's better.'

'First I have something to show you.' She led him by the hand to the sitting room where she had left Klara's locket, with the hidden compartment open. 'Edie found this. I don't know if you can see that clearly, Tom, but it shows two sets of initials – GR and AH.'

'Good God. Geli Raubal and—'

'Precisely. Don't say it.'

'Did Edie understand the significance?'

'I don't know. She said nothing. But then she is very discreet.'

Wilde closed the locket carefully.

'Whatever happens, we must make sure Bodie Cashbone never sees this.'

Wilde awoke in the dark. Johnny was crawling on top of him, crying. He looked at his watch and saw that it was five o'clock in the afternoon, then hugged his son and rubbed his back until the crying subsided.

He put Johnny back to bed and went in search of Lydia. She was carrying a fresh glass of water from the kitchen to Klara.

'How is she?'

'The same.'

'Did you get any sleep?'

'I'm ashamed to say I slept like a top. Some nurse I am. Would have slept through like you, but Johnny woke me demanding food.'

'Thank you. I'm sorry to do this to you again, but I've got to go out.'

'And leave me in this madhouse isolation ward? Thanks, buster.'

'I need to see Eaton. He's the only one who can help us.'

The snow flurries had gone and the sky was clear but the cold was biting. In Trumpington Street, outside the college, he scanned the road for Cashbone, but there was no sign of him. Scobie told him that Mr Philip Eaton had arrived and was presently taking tea with the master.

'Put a call through to him, Scobie. Tell him I'll be in my rooms if he'd like to join me there.'

Fifteen minutes later, Wilde heard the uneven steps of Eaton on the staircase. He carried a stick and paused at every step before moving on upwards. Wilde met him halfway and offered his arm to help him.

'No, damn it, I can do it on my own.'

Wilde shrugged and left him to it.

'Whisky?' Wilde said when Eaton had made it to the top.

'Bit early for me, but what the hell . . . ?'

'You've got to help me, Eaton. Two women dead, murdered in cold blood, and Cashbone won't move an inch from his entrenched position on the girl.'

'Nor will you by the sound of it.'

'That's because I'm in the right – and you know it.'

'This has all become a great deal larger since the two murders. My friends in Five are crawling all over the house at Harkham – you realise it was theirs, not Six's, I imagine?'

'I gathered as much.'

'Analysis suggests the bullets used to kill both Mrs Kemp and Frau Somerfeld came from a British-made Sten gun. What does that suggest to you?'

'Our killer, Mr Young, has a contact in England.'

'Indeed. Guy Liddell, director of B Division, has taken on the investigation personally. His boys and Special Branch are combing their files for likely fifth columnists. Perhaps in this area. Certainly BP has produced a couple of decrypts from radio messages intercepted near here. There must be an agent, but he keeps a very low profile, communication infrequent.'

'BP?'

'Bletchley Park.'

'Ah, of course. The code and cipher place. What do the decrypts say?'

'Nothing to do with you, Wilde. Nothing so far, anyway. But we do have more on our killer. Mavis Triston, the maid he molested in Sevenoaks, said he introduced himself as the Youngs' son. Mavis had worked for the Youngs for eight years and had no idea they had a son. There had never been any mention of him, nor were there any pictures in the house. But the police did find an old bundle of letters in a trunk in the attic, from a boy named Charles at prep school, then public school, addressed to his mother in Bangalore. In some ways they were typical letters – please send money; when will I see you? – but they became gradually angrier. The last one was dated Hamburg 1920. It bore only one word. *Goodbye.*'

'That's rather chilling.'

'After that the trail dies. One must suppose he made a life for himself in Germany with a new identity. An English-speaking public-school boy ... not a bad cover for a Nazi agent. He took the opportunity of getting even with the parents he hated, I suppose.'

Wilde topped up their glasses.

'Not sure how much it helps us, though. I'm more interested in the possibility of finding his contact. This doesn't go away until we've dealt with the man, so we have to find him. It would be a damned sight easier if you could get Cashbone off my back, though, Eaton. Then we could protect Klara properly and concentrate all our resources on Bormann's man.'

'You seem to have done a good job so far.'

'But how did Young get the idea of Rupert and Edie Weir – how did he find their address?'

Even before he finished the question, a horrible possibility arose in his mind. Young had been at Cornflowers, and had stolen a photograph of Wilde and Lydia and Johnny. What if he had taken something else? The address book on the telephone stand in the hall? Wilde hadn't noticed it missing, but nor did he remember it being there.

'Oh my God, Eaton – I think the bastard has my address book. Anyone in it is now in danger.'

Harry Taylor's address must surely be in the book.

CHAPTER 35

'Oh, you look like a very strong young man, won't you help me, dear?'

'What?' Wilde's thoughts were elsewhere. In the darkness, he hadn't seen the little old lady approaching him and now he looked at her with puzzled irritation. 'I'm sorry, I'm in a terrible hurry.'

'It really won't take you a moment, dear – I just need to lift a box out of the back seat of my car and I can't quite manage it. I'll be all right after that.'

It wasn't worth arguing about.

'OK,' he said. 'But then I have to dash.'

'Oh, you are a dear,' she said. 'The car's just there at the side of the road. Once I've got the box out I'm sure I'll be fine. If not, some-one else will help me.'

Wilde followed the woman to the car. She was small and bent, could barely have weighed more than a child. She opened the rear door for him, then stood back.

'There it is, dear. If you could just lift it out for me . . .'

He stepped past her and peered in. There was nothing there. He was turning back towards her, confused, when the blow hit him on the side of the head, knocking him almost senseless.

He was a boxer. In his mind, he was in the ring, but he was on the floor, scrabbling for purchase, and the referee was counting. He felt himself flailing as he was bundled into the back of the car, then pushed down onto the floor head first.

Someone was getting in beside him and he felt a weight on his back, rendering him immobile in the cramped space.

'There's a gun at your head, Mr Wilde. Don't try to move.'

He *couldn't* move. A man's foot was pressing on his spine and cold metal was pushed into his skull. Through the mist he recognised the voice. Charles Young.

Charlie Jung had never been trained in the dark art of torture, yet how difficult could it be to make a man talk? Professor Wilde was stretched out on a bare metal bedstead. His naked back rested on cold bed springs and his wrists and ankles were tied to the iron bedposts with thick cord.

It was a cosy little room with dainty floral curtains. The mattress had been removed from the bed and placed against the pretty papered walls, close to a Victorian watercolour of a rose garden.

Jung's face was inches from Wilde's. His right hand gripped his captive by the throat.

'You know what we want, Wilde, and we will get it from you. So tell us where we can find Klara Rieger, and save yourself a great deal of pain.'

Wilde said nothing. His head was still pounding from the blow delivered by Jung. He had been brought to this cottage twenty minutes or half an hour from Cambridge. He had no idea where they were or even which direction they had gone, because he had been kept face down in the footwell the whole journey.

Once here, he had been marched down a footpath to this lonely little house and had been forced to take off his coat, jacket, tie, shirt, shoes and socks. He supposed it was a small mercy that he had not been made to go naked; perhaps that was in deference to an old woman's sensibilities.

What would come next, he had no idea.

Jung released Wilde's throat and took Mrs Vickery by the arm.

'Leave him to stew awhile.' He marched the old woman downstairs. 'We need results fast,' he said.

'Well, Mr Young, I would say that heat and fire are where pain and panic lies. And eyes – anything to do with the eyes must inspire fear.' She shivered. 'The very thought of someone sticking a pin in your eye, dear – bursting it like a balloon. Gives me the heebie-jeebies. But I do have a good selection of needles and pins in my darning box, should you consider that to be the way to go.'

Charlie Jung nodded. This woman . . . how had Bormann found her? God, he had a talent for the dark side.

'Fire and needles?'

'And shall I bring you a cup of tea?'

'Bring the address book. Wherever they are, it must be in there.'

'Well, if it is, it's not very obvious, dear.'

No. They were looking for someone called Harry, but almost all the surnames came with initials, and at least twenty initials were H. Nor was there any sign of an address with the word Trin or Trinity in it. Except one – Professor Taylor (no initial or first name), then just the one word, Trinity V, and a telephone number. Was that Staircase V in the college? Was there such a thing? They tried calling the number in the book, but it was dead. If Klara was somehow hidden within rooms at Trinity College or Trinity Hall, she would be difficult to find.

They needed information, but time was short. The police and intelligence services would be all over the houses at Harkham and Girton by now. And what if Mrs Vickery was under surveillance? Transmitters could be traced.

Jung felt the net closing in.

Wilde's eyes were open, observing his captors closely. He tried to recall all he had learned during his intensive few days of training before going to Germany:

Talk to your captors. Become a human being to them. Delay them. Unsettle them.

'We know all about you, Young,' he said. 'You went to Hamburg after the last war and acquired German citizenship. And now you're back, murdering your parents and trying to kill a child. You also thought you'd killed your parents' maid – but you didn't, so she will be a vital witness at your trial. We know, too, that you were aboard that E-boat. Kapitänleutnant Flettner told us all about you. He didn't like you one little bit.'

Jung stabbed his cigarette into Wilde's exposed throat, and held it there. Wilde screamed in pain, his back arching against the bare metal springs. Jung held the cigarette there until it had been extinguished. The smell of burning flesh and tobacco smoke filled the room.

'Now talk.'

Wilde opened his eyes. The old woman was holding a lighted candle. She knelt beside Wilde, her movement slightly strained as though she might have a touch of arthritis, then she eased herself underneath the bed and held the flame up to his spine, playing it back and forth. He roared out as the fire began to sear his flesh, his body bucking vainly against his bonds.

After ten agonising seconds she pulled the candle away and he slumped back against the metal of the bed.

Jung stood and watched. 'This will get worse, Wilde. Where is she?'

He was fighting for breath. His heart was thundering in his chest. He knew he couldn't put up with this for long. No one could.

'Just a few simple words, then this is over.'

'You're not going to get out of this, Young – you know that.'

'Perhaps not. But nor are you, Wilde – and unlike me, you will suffer untold horrors. I wonder how painful a red-hot needle through your eye would be.'

The room was cold but Wilde was bathed in sweat. Even without the flame to his back, the pain was still raw and unbearable, and he knew it was only the beginning.

'Fuck you both!' he spat.

The flame rose again beneath his back and once more he emitted a howl from the depths of his soul. The smell of burning meat filled the room. This time she held the flame for longer and closer, extending the line. Perhaps a quarter of a minute, the hot wax dripping over her fingers. Through the agony and the raging Wilde wondered whether he would lose consciousness. He wished for it.

Wilde's screams had subsided to a low groaning. In the sudden quiet, Jung pricked up his ears.

'*Scheisse* . . . Is that a car?'

Mrs Vickery stopped what she was doing and listened.

Jung frowned. 'I'm sure I heard something.'

She slid out from under the bed. 'Would you like me to go and have a look?'

'Take the pistol.'

'Mr Young, look at me.' She smiled sweetly. 'Don't worry. I'm just an old lady. If anyone's there, I'll soon send them on their way. In the meantime, perhaps you should put some sort of gag on our guest.'

Mrs Vickery skipped down the stairs more lightly than she had done in decades. Finally she was doing something worthwhile. How she envied those lucky young things in the League of German

Girls and the Strength Through Joy movements. How she wished she could have been one of them. In Germany she had heard the Führer speak, and had stood rapt among the vast crowds, beguiled by the raw power of his rhetoric. He spoke to her very soul.

Herr Bormann had introduced her to several among the Party faithful, including deputy leader Rudolf Hess. She had not thought a great deal of him, and her judgement had been proved correct when he showed his true treacherous colours with his insane flight to Scotland.

Ah, but how the movement had inspired her. Now, at last, she had a way of doing her bit.

The blackouts were all in place, of course. It wouldn't do to attract attention from the air raid warden. She turned off the light, pulled back a little corner of the blackout and peeked into the darkness. Oh dear, Mr Young had been correct. There was the dim outline of a car. No, there were two cars. Her hearing might be going, but there was nothing wrong with her eyesight, even in semi-darkness.

The car had its lights off and she couldn't make out the occupants. She thought she saw a movement but couldn't be sure. Quickly she took a butcher's knife from the kitchen and went back upstairs.

'There are two cars out there,' she said. 'I think we have visitors.'

Jung looked flustered. 'We need to get out.'

She looked at the prostrate figure twitching and moaning on the bed.

'What about him?'

She held up the knife and raised her eyebrows questioningly.

Jung shook his head. 'No, he's coming with us. We need him alive. Cut him loose.'

The gag, torn from his own ripped shirt, was almost choking him. He had wanted to lose consciousness, nature's anaesthetic. Now he knew he needed to stay conscious and alert. Jung and the old woman had been panicked. If they weren't going to kill him, then there would be an opportunity, and he had to be in a fit state to grab it.

She was slashing at the cords that bound him, then Jung hauled him upright, quickly bound his hands and ordered him – at the point of the sub-machine gun – to the staircase.

The sharp jab of the weapon's muzzle against the burns on his back – in an arc from the top left shoulder blade, down across his spine to his lower back – brought fresh torment. There was no escaping the agony. He had dealt with physical pain many times in his life. It was the first lesson of boxing: take the pain, accept it – and hit back. But this pain was of a different magnitude. Raw and constant.

'Down the stairs.'

Jung prodded him again. Wilde stumbled on the carpet, nearly lost his footing, then steadied himself.

In the kitchen the back door was open, cold wind gusting in from the garden. The sky was cloudless and speckled with stars and a sliver of moon. Wilde was pushed again. This time he tripped over the doorstep and fell forwards onto the flagstones.

Then the bloodshed began.

CHAPTER 36

Bodie Cashbone had no staff to call on, so he had been keeping Philip Eaton under surveillance with a private detective funded out of his own deep pockets. He hadn't trusted the one-armed limey from the beginning of this operation. He wasn't sure why he had even been required to work with the British intelligence man, but the order had come from Bill Whitney that there must be co-operation with the host nation.

So if he was right that Eaton was not to be trusted, he knew it would be only a matter of time before Wilde came to see him – or vice versa. And Cashbone didn't have to wait long to be proved correct. Eaton soon arrived at the college, followed by Wilde.

The professor had stayed awhile and left. As a precaution, Cashbone had the back gate covered by the PI, name of Penrose, and watched the main gateway himself. Penrose was under strict orders to follow Wilde along whatever winding route he took, but in the event it wasn't necessary; the professor emerged from the front gate, close to where Cashbone was parked. He slid his large body low into the seat of the car and peered through the driver's side window. The dark came early without street lights, but he could see Wilde well enough. He was leaning into a car, while an old lady stood at his side.

Cashbone was still trying to work out what Wilde was doing, when a figure emerged from the darkness and swung what looked like a wrench hard against the side of Wilde's head, then pushed him into the back of the car while the old lady – suddenly looking anything but frail – climbed into the front, and the car set off. Cashbone's engine was already running. He put it into gear and followed.

He kept a discreet distance and was pretty sure he hadn't been spotted as the car led him eastwards out of Cambridge, into an area of scattered houses, allotments and open countryside.

When they stopped, he braked too, and watched from a distance as they removed Wilde from their car and marched him to a small house a short way down an unmade track. When they were safely inside, Cashbone turned his car and drove into the village in search of a phone kiosk.

Now, an hour later, here he was again, with backup. Four armed Special Branch and MI5 men from Harkham.

Wilde's fall started it. His loud grunt of pain ... the sudden movement. Torchlights instantly illuminated the wintry back garden, three powerful beams directed at the back door. Jung was raising the Sten gun towards the lights but Wilde, whose wrists had been hastily bound in front, pushed himself to his feet and swung a double-fisted blow into Jung's belly before he could pull the trigger.

Winded, Jung staggered backwards, gasping for breath. A bullet from the far end of the lawn smacked into the door frame six inches from his head.

Jung turned the Sten on his assailant, but Wilde was already throwing himself at him like a rugby player making a last-ditch tackle, driving into him with his shoulder. Jung almost fell, then righted himself enough to raise the Sten and bring it down hard on the crown of Wilde's head. Stunned, Wilde buckled and reeled sideways, dimly aware of more shots coming from behind him.

Behind them, the old woman was firing wildly into the garden with Jung's little jewel-handled pistol. She crumpled, then slumped to the ground. Regaining his senses, Wilde could tell that she had been hit. He heard the rattle of the Sten and flinched away.

He saw two of the lights spin away into the darkness, their owners clearly hit. Jung fired until the magazine expired, then flung the Sten down, clattering on to the paving, and hurtled into the darkness.

The hastily-tied bindings on Wilde's wrists had loosened in the struggle. He managed to undo them, then bent down and picked up the Sten before racing after Jung, holding the weapon like a club.

Bodie Cashbone was at the front of the house when the shooting started. He edged around the side of the property to the sound of dozens of rounds, and found the rear garden eerily lit by swaying torches and the flash of gunfire. As the torches fell away in a cascade of bullets, he knew he had lost men.

He saw an old woman falling and guessed she was the one who had lured Wilde to the car. Then Cashbone saw Wilde stumbling after a fleeing figure and shouted to his men to stop firing.

Wilde didn't feel the cold. All he felt was the searing pain of the deep wounds burnt into his back and a desperate need to bring down his tormentor. He could hear more than he could see. They were in a small open meadow between woods, then suddenly at the lip of a quarry.

He was like a hound with a scent, unafraid, using primal senses to follow the sounds of panicked breathing and running feet, focused only on following his prey until he had it cornered. He was getting closer. Wilde was fit and strong. Despite his ordeal, his body pulsed with energy, fuelled by his visceral hunger for retribution.

He followed Jung to the edge of the quarry and looked down. It was deep. One false step could see him plunging into its unforgiving maw of loose rocks and sheer sides.

To his left, he heard a grunt. Young had slipped and fallen in the wet grass. Wilde threw himself at the shadowy mass, hammering at him with the metal stock of the Sten gun – but Young was already rolling away, towards the edge of the quarry. Then the glint of a blade in Young's right hand caught the thin moonlight, thrusting upwards at Wilde's face. Wilde evaded the strike, dropped the gun and caught Young's wrist in one seamless movement. Using both hands, he held the wrist ratchet-tight.

Young lashed out with his left hand, driving his fist twice in quick succession into the side of Wilde's head. The blows stunned him momentarily and he almost lost his grip on Jung's wrist, the blade stabbing at his throat.

Wilde scrabbled back, still not releasing his grip on Young's knife hand. He redoubled his grip and something snapped in one of Jung's wrists. The assassin roared with terrifying pain and the knife fell away from his grasp.

For the first time, Wilde was on top. His fist smashed into Jung's nose, sending blood spraying from his nostrils. Then he delivered two sharp blows to his abdomen. He grasped Young's hair and pummelled his head into the ground.

Jung lay unmoving and Wilde rolled away from him. He experienced a moment of exhilaration, then his shoulders slumped with utter exhaustion and all he could feel was the awful touch of the flame on his back once more. He fought off a wave of dizziness and hoisted himself up to his feet. For a few moments, he considered picking Jung up and slinging him over the precipice. But he couldn't do it – not in cold blood.

Instead, he grabbed Young by the arm and dragged him up.

'Walk,' he said, pushing him forward.

Young stumbled, falling back to his knees. Wilde pulled him up again and got him in an armlock, his mouth close to his ear, his breath hot and urgent.

'You walk now, Young. You try anything and I swear I will either throw you over the edge or break your fucking neck.'

'This isn't over, Wilde.' He was panting as he spoke, his voice edged with something like desperation.

'I think it is.'

'It'll never be over. Not while the child's alive.'

Wilde pushed him forward again. In the near distance, the house lights were all blazing, a beacon summoning them from the darkness.

'Who is she, Young? Do you even know?'

'I never needed to know. And I wasn't going to waste time on speculation. I have been paying a debt.'

'You owed something to Bormann?'

Young snorted. 'You think this ends here? You don't know who you're dealing with.'

They were at the end of the garden. A flashlight lit them and Bodie Cashbone's voice boomed out.

'You got him, Wilde! You got the bastard!'

'You're welcome to him,' Wilde said wearily.

'I should kill him here and now. We got two men down. One dead, one critical.'

Wilde saw the body of the old woman a few yards away. Vaguely he wondered about her. What was her story? From her accent she sounded English enough. A crypto-Nazi, he guessed. One of those who had made their minds up that Britain was on the wrong side in the war, just waiting for her time to come. Well, it had come all right, and it had ended in miserable failure and death.

'Here.' He handed his captive to Cashbone. 'He had a knife, but that's out by the quarry. You'd better search him for other weapons.'

Cashbone signalled to one of the officers to come and help him. More assistance had arrived, and suddenly the place was crawling with men and lights. Wilde's eyes drifted involuntarily back to the figure of the old woman on the ground, illuminated rather gruesomely by lights from her own back door. She was moving. Not dead, then. An armed officer was standing close to her, his revolver holstered. He seemed to be looking elsewhere. Well, the struggle was over for the old woman. She had been savage and merciless while he was in her power; now she was a pathetic bag of bones and skin, little more than a carcass.

Wilde shook his head in incredulity. She was looking at him, her watery blue eyes malign and radiating hatred. She was turning on her side, and she still had the gun with the jewelled handle in her own small, wrinkled hand. She was deliberately showing the gun to Wilde. Then she aimed it at Young.

A shot split the air and Young let out a cry. His legs gave way.

The old woman seemed to laugh, her lips drawn back from her yellowing teeth.

'Now he won't talk.'

They were her final words. The guard at her side belatedly removed his revolver from its holster and put two bullets into her chest, and she lay still.

'I don't think I've thanked you yet, Cashbone. How did you find me?'

'Guess.'

'You were watching the college?'

He grinned.

'I was careless.'

'Lucky, you mean.'

They were in the back of a police car. Wilde was sitting sideways with his shoulder against the seat so as not to put any pressure on his wounded back. He had retrieved his address book from the house and had it clasped tight in his hands; Cashbone wasn't going to get a look at it.

'We'd better get you to hospital. Want to tell me where your lady and the girl are? They'll be worried about you.'

'Hospital yes, the other part no.'

'God damn it, Wilde, I saved your life – you owe me!' There was barely controlled rage in his voice.

'You're right, Cashbone, I do – but Klara doesn't.'

'You're a sanctimonious prig, you know that? How the hell are we going to win the war if you're worried about hurting the enemy's feelings?'

'She's not the enemy, Cashbone.'

Cashbone shook his head in exasperation. 'There's no way out of this for you, Wilde. Your Brit friends have made it clear – they won't cross us. You're all alone, and we'll find you.'

CHAPTER 37

Christmas Day at Trinity Villa was a strange affair. Klara's temperature had come down and she had not developed a rash, so measles
was crossed off the list. But she was still lethargic. Wilde's back was
in a bad way. The burns had turned to suppurating blisters and he
could not lie on his back. His dressings had to be changed frequently
so that the lint did not become embedded in the wound. Even in
this wintry cold he spent much of the time wandering around the
house with his shirt off. The hospital said he had been lucky, the
flame being played up and down his back had meant most of
the injuries were second-degree burns, but there were small patches
where the wounds went deeper into the flesh. He would be left with
a long, jagged ridge of scars.

Fortunately Harry Taylor had left half a wardrobe full of billowing
Sea Island cotton shirts, and Wilde made good use of them. One
day they would have to pay Harry well for the use of his house and
possessions. They hoped he would understand.

Lydia had decided that come what may, they were going to have
some sort of celebration and would sing 'Silent Night' in English
and German. She had managed to secure a chicken on her ration
card, and roasted it with potatoes and sprouts, which all went down
very well. And she had found presents for them all. A bobble hat
and a bag of oranges for Klara, a wooden toy car for Johnny and a
bottle of whisky for Wilde.

Wilde was mortified. 'Lydia, I've got nothing for you.'

'I'll have half the whisky, then.'

He laughed. 'I'll make it up to you.'

'I'll make sure you do.'

They tried to make the house happy, but there *were* worries. He had spent two hours at the police station after his visit to hospital. Eaton had been there and so were Special Branch officers. He told them all he knew, and Eaton confirmed his story.

The local detectives were not really digging too deeply and Special Branch were less worried now that the threat from Charlie Young had been neutralised.

And yet he was still wary of the local constabulary. A beat constable had seen him on the lane twice and Wilde wasn't sure whether he had been recognised. He had had to avoid going into the house, simply carrying on along the road until he was sure the danger had passed and then tracking back. It wasn't that he thought the police would be looking for him – why would they? He had committed no crime – but because they knew that Harry Taylor lived in Trinity Villa and was away on military duty.

Fortunately, it was a large house and so it was easy for them to keep away from the front windows where they might be seen or heard. It wasn't quite so easy to keep an excitable nineteen-month-old boy's noise down, but fortunately the walls were thick.

On Boxing Day, Klara had perked up considerably and she and Johnny were happily pushing the toy car across the floor to each other. Wilde left them to it, and made his way by a long and circuitous route to college. Eaton wasn't there, but Wilde was able to call him at his home in Chelsea.

'Actually, Wilde, I was hoping you'd call. I very badly want to see you.'

'Bad news, I suppose?'

'I hope not, old boy. You know this impasse can't go on – not healthy for anyone. So we need to talk. I also have a present for young Klara.'

'I'm intrigued.'

'Well, she deserves something nice. I could get up today. Shall we say your rooms at four?'

'Will Cashbone be watching you?'

'I will use my best tradecraft to avoid him.'

'Unlike me, you mean.'

'Nonsense, Wilde. You always were a natural at this business.'

Wilde was still in his rooms when Eaton arrived four hours later. He had stayed at college because he couldn't face another laborious journey back to Trinity Villa at the moment. Twice in a day was simply too much. Overdo it and he'd become sloppy, as he had done before when he had been abducted.

When he got home, he would make sure that Lydia got some time out of the house. The sitting around at Trinity Villa, waiting, was bad for all of them. Waiting for what? For the end of the war? The invasion? Capitulation from Cashbone?

Waiting without any end in sight.

Lydia had returned to poetry and was scratching away in all her spare moments when the children weren't making demands. Wilde had spent some time thinking through a vague idea for a new book on the lives of the Roman Catholic priests in the late sixteenth century. How they survived on the run, hiding in the houses and estates of the faithful. The inspiration behind the idea was obvious, of course. As Lydia herself had said, 'Sometimes it feels as if we're stuck in a bloody priest hole, Tom.'

Wilde was at his desk in his rooms jotting down a rough synopsis when he heard Eaton making his way up the stairs. The clicking of his walking stick on stone was unmistakable. Wilde held the door open for him.

'Welcome – and a very merry Christmas, Eaton.'

'And you, Wilde. How's the back?'

'Pretty bloody awful if I'm honest.'

'Well, be sure to get it seen to if there's any sign of infection.'

'Don't worry. I'm well looked after.'

'Of course you are. Now then, let's talk. First of all, there's the question of Young – or Jung, as he prefers to be called.'

'Are you telling me he's still alive?'

'Very much so. In better condition than you probably. Flesh wound to the upper arm from Mrs Vickery's bullet. Cuts and some very nasty bruises from your manhandling.'

'Plenty of pain, I trust.'

'Not as much as you endured. Anyway, he's in Five's tender care and so far he seems to be co-operating, which could be to Klara Rieger's advantage – and yours.'

Bobby, his college servant, was away for Christmas, so Wilde had made a pot of tea. He poured two cups and proffered one to Eaton.

'Thanks.'

'Sugar?'

'No, just like this.'

'How so then? How could Young's co-operation help us?'

'Well, first off he's well aware that if he doesn't help us, he's for the long drop. Whatever else he may be, he's not thick. He's been charged with high treason, the murders of his parents in Sevenoaks, Rosamund Kemp at the safe house, Sigrun Somerfeld at Girton, an officer at the home of Mrs Felicity Vickery, who is also now deceased, woundings, kidnapping, possession of a banned weapon, car theft, grievous bodily harm and false imprisonment of yourself. Oh, and entering the country as the agent of a hostile power. I've probably missed out a couple there. Ah yes, sexual molestation was another. The maidservant in Sevenoaks.'

'So the future doesn't look too bright for Charlie Young.'

'Indeed not. He's never going to be let out of clink. But he could just save his miserable skin by working on our behalf.'

'Explain.'

'Well, in the first instance I want him to communicate to his master in Germany that Klara Rieger is dead and her body disposed of. We won't have him anywhere near a radio until we're absolutely sure of him, of course. The chances of him sending a coded warning are too high. But once we've done that, Klara will be a whole lot safer.'

Wilde laughed. 'You've forgotten something, Eaton – the rather large matter of Mr Bodie Cashbone. As soon as he gets the chance, he'll be splashing Klara's name and picture all over the newspapers and organising leaflet drops to the Fatherland.'

'Which is what I want to talk to you about. Now then, I've had a change of heart about the girl. I have an idea – but if it's to work you must trust me and tell me where you're hiding her.'

'You know I'm not going to do that.'

'First listen.'

'Shoot.'

'Over the years, Wilde, you and I have worked together pretty well. We haven't always seen eye to eye, but it's fair to say we have been of assistance to each other. If I do something for you now, however, I will have to go way beyond anything I have done before and you will be in my eternal debt. Do you understand?'

Wilde took a sip of his tea. 'Carry on.'

'I think I have a solution, but it will mean betraying my country and, more to the point, disobeying orders that come from the very top of the Secret Intelligence Service. If word of this gets out, my career will be dead and I may very well end up in the Tower. The slightest suspicion would be enough.'

Wilde was definitely intrigued now.

'You had better tell me more, then.'

'Will you take me to her?'

'Look, Eaton. Just asking me to trust you isn't enough. I'm pretty damned sure, for instance, that it was you who put Cashbone on to Rupert Weir's house in Girton.'

'I confess that was me. But things are different now.'

'Of course, I want to trust you. We all want this to be over. But you must give me some clue what you are planning.'

'Fair enough. I believe I have a way of spiriting Klara to safety. No one will know she has gone, or that she ever existed. I'm not going to explain more until you allow me into your hideaway.'

'It's flimsy as hell, Eaton. I need to talk to Lydia about this.'

'No, I want your answer now. I've already spent too much time on this whole affair. I have operatives to look after all over the world, and they need me as much as you do. Just coming up here today is taking me away from important work. I am offering you the best chance you will get. Give me your address and within two or three days I will come to you.'

'What's Cashbone's role in all this?'

'He's not part of it. He'd probably kill me if he found out what I'm doing. This is just me.'

'But Cashbone's still here. I can't see him, but I feel his presence.'

'Oh, come off it, Wilde. Cashbone is on to other stuff. He can't hang around Cambridge for the rest of his life any more than I can.'

Wilde's back was alive with pain, his mind flooding with doubts. He let out a long sigh, then nodded. Trust. It was a word the priests in Elizabethan England must have considered every day of their fugitive lives. Who to trust?

'No,' he said. 'I'm sorry, Eaton, the answer's still No.'

CHAPTER 38

The return journey was the most dangerous. It was easy to slip out of Trinity Villa unseen, because no one was observing his departure. But once at college, he could not be sure that the gates weren't watched by Cashbone again, or someone employed by him.

And so he took great pains about the return journey. He still had not retrieved his motorbike from Girton, so he walked to the far corners of Cambridge to find empty spaces where he could be certain he was not watched; only then would he double back.

After the shoot-out, he had been taken to hospital, where he had stayed for twenty-four hours. From there he had been taken to Girton, to the home of Rupert and Edie Weir. In the early hours, when the roads were deserted and they could be certain they were not spied on, Rupert had driven him to Trinity Villa. Since then, he had been to the telephone kiosk and shops close by, but this was only the second time since then that he had been to college.

He went south and strolled along the Cam all the way to Grantchester, before cutting east and northwards again towards the railway station. He felt uneasy without being sure why. Grantchester Meadow had been almost empty. A couple of dog walkers, no one else. At the station, he bought a platform ticket and went through the barrier, then halfway along as though waiting for the London train to arrive. The platform filled up with passengers. Just before the train began to pull in, he left the platform and waited to see if anyone else came back through the barrier. No one did. He was in the clear.

He felt easier now and carried on north, well away from the town centre. It was dark and he considered going home to Cornflowers to see if it was being watched, then thought better of the idea. Not worth the risk. Instead he zigzagged through empty back streets westward and found himself once again outside Trinity Villa. The lane was empty and cold, as though no one lived there.

One last look around, then he turned the door handle.

A neighbour's door opened and an elderly man stepped out with a dog, some sort of mongrel, on a leash. Wilde froze, the hairs prickling on the nape of his neck.

The old man grasped Wilde's arm with a rather feeble grip.

'Are you a burglar, young man?'

Wilde smiled. 'No, sir, I'm a good friend of Mr Taylor's.'

'Ah. Is he home, then? Haven't seen him for over a year.'

'No, still away at the war. But he said my family and I could stay here for a few days. We're old friends. The water tank in our loft burst and flooded the house. We won't be here much longer, hopefully.'

'You sound foreign. What are you?'

'Canadian. The name's Lycett. Peter Lycett. I'm a manager at the Pye factory.'

The old man nodded, then released his grip.

'Never liked that Taylor fellow. Something very strange about him. I think he's a bit foreign. Too many of you, if you ask me.'

Wilde bit back a stinging reply. 'Not much I can do about that, I'm afraid.'

'I'll be watching you, young man. You better mind your step.'

'And a merry Christmas to you, too,' Wilde replied, opening the door and closing it behind him. The last thing he needed right now was a suspicious and ill-disposed neighbour.

Indoors, Lydia didn't look happy.

'You took your time.'

'I'm sorry. I wanted to make sure I covered my tracks. And I just met our rather odd neighbour. I told him my name was Peter

Lycett. I'm Canadian and I'm a manager at Pye. He doesn't like foreigners.'

Lydia ignored the news. 'How long is this going on for, Tom? We have lives to get on with, you know.'

'I've been thinking on my long walk. Perhaps we should leave Cambridge. Maybe the highlands of Scotland or north Wales? Some wilderness. What do you think?'

She shrugged. 'You're the bloody secret agent, Tom. You decide. But for pity's sake, do *something*.'

He didn't like her being like this, but he understood her frustration. She had held it in pretty well until now. The thing was, he agreed with her; something had to give. And if they went to Scotland or Wales, what then? How would that help Klara? She'd seem more out of place there than in Cambridge which, by comparison, was pretty darned cosmopolitan. Anyway, running further away, living a furtive life looking over their shoulders in a far corner of the country, simply was not an appetising long-term prospect for any of them, least of all Klara. It was no more a true solution than this sojourn in Trinity Villa.

'You know, every time I sneak out to the shops I think I'm going to get shot or stabbed,' Lydia said.

'No one's going to do that. The killer is locked up.'

'Well, that's how I feel. And I'm scared for Johnny. And for you, come to that. I'm worried about your burns. They need proper attention. You should have stayed in hospital.'

Klara appeared at the door with Johnny on her shoulders. Wilde stared, wide-eyed, for a moment, then laughed.

'He thinks I'm a horse, Tom,' Klara said, laughing.

'Well, don't let him exhaust you. You've had quite a fever.'

'Come on, Johnny, down you get.'

Klara swung him from her shoulders and deposited him gently on the floor but he immediately started stamping and whining and holding out his arms, indicating he wanted to get back in the saddle, so she sighed and picked him up again.

Wilde looked at Klara, wishing Sunny could have seen her like this, rather than as a 'bloody Narzisse'. And what was it Eaton had said on the phone about having some sort of present for her? A shame he hadn't handed it over – she deserved something nice. He glanced at Lydia. She, too, was smiling. Perhaps the crisis was over for the moment. Somehow or other they would get through this.

'Well,' Wilde said, 'I suppose it's my turn to make some supper as you cooked Christmas dinner. Anyone for leftover chicken sandwiches?'

'Perfect,' Lydia said. 'If they come with a good shot of whisky. My need is great.'

For the next two days they didn't leave the house at all. It was the weekend, which somehow seemed less safe than anonymous weekdays. They had found a pack of cards and Klara taught them *Skat*, an entertaining German game that occupied them for hours. They also listened to the wireless, mostly classical music punctuated by the occasional news bulletin. The war in the Pacific was looking dire for both America and Britain. Allied shipping continued to take a hammering and, in Eastern Europe, the Leningrad siege intensified. At least Hitler's troops hadn't made the promised breakthrough to Moscow. Wilde didn't envy the soldiers on either side; it would be a cold and bloody winter for all concerned, hunkered down in icy trenches far from home. This place might be their prison, but it was decidedly cosy by comparison.

On Sunday evening, after Johnny had gone to bed, there was a knock at the door. Wilde was about to deal a card and his hand stopped in mid-air. Lydia and Klara didn't move.

'Someone knows we're here,' Lydia whispered.

'Wrong house, perhaps. Or kids messing about. Maybe that ghastly old man next door. Just stay still and keep quiet. Whoever it is, they'll go away.'

'I think I might have heard a car. Maybe it's Harry Taylor, home on leave.'

'He wouldn't knock.'

Then they heard a voice, calling through the letterbox.

'Wilde, it's me, Eaton. Open the door, old boy – I know you're there.'

Wilde and Lydia exchanged glances.

'He doesn't really know we're here,' Wilde whispered. 'He couldn't do.'

'Well, if it's a guess, it's a bloody good one. Go on, Tom, answer the damned door.'

Eaton was leaning heavily on his walking stick, the hint of a sly smile on his face. Behind him there was a dark, official-looking car with a driver. And there was someone else, standing at Eaton's side.

'Are you just going to stand there gawping, Wilde? Or are you going to invite us in?'

'Us?'

'Ah, you haven't met, have you? I'd like to introduce you to Frau Romy Dietrich.'

Klara had come into the hallway with Lydia. For a moment, she went rigid as though she had seen a ghost, then her eyes opened wide and she cried out.

'*Tante Romy! Tante Romy!*'

Wilde stepped aside. The girl and the woman threw themselves into each other's arms, hugging, laughing and crying all at once.

'I really think we all ought to come inside or we'll have the ARP or worse on our case,' Eaton said at last, gently urging Romy and Klara into the hallway. They seemed unable to break away from each other's arms. Romy was holding Klara's face in her hands, kissing away the tears, then hugging her again.

'Do come in,' Lydia said.

Wilde let them pass and Lydia guided Romy and Klara towards the sitting room, leaving the men in their wake.

'So, this is your Christmas present for Klara,' Wilde said, pushing the front door closed.

'Rather a good one, it seems.'

'How did you get her here? I'm astonished that she's even alive – Jim Vanderberg was pretty sure she had been murdered in Berlin.'

'That's a very long story – she can tell you herself, assuming your German's up to it. She doesn't have much English, I'm afraid.'

'No problem for me these days. And Lydia knows enough. But tell me, Eaton, how the hell did you find us?'

'Well, I had you followed, of course. Couple of Special Branch men. They're experts at tailing a mark when the mark is doing everything in his power not to be tailed. They said you were good – very good, actually – but not good enough.'

'What about Cashbone?'

'We've got to be very careful. If he finds out about any of this, we're all in deep manure. He has been making trouble at a high level, telling the State Department the goddamned limeys are refusing to help, calling us unreliable allies. It's not a good start to our joint endeavour.'

'I don't suppose it helps to point out to him that I'm an American like him?'

'He thinks you've gone native. Maybe he's right.'

'Could he have followed you here?'

'No. He doesn't have the manpower and Bill Whitney is keeping him busy elsewhere. But he won't forget you, Wilde. These next few days are critical.'

'I suppose you have a plan other than simply bringing Frau Dietrich here?'

'I do. But it's difficult to organise, so please give me a little time. It involves Frau Dietrich adopting Klara.'

Wilde couldn't help grinning. 'Well, that alone is wonderful news.'

The warmth between the German woman and the girl who called her Auntie Romy was evident.

'Fingers crossed, eh? Now, I'm leaving Frau Dietrich here with you. I'll be back in a day or two. You need to be ready at all times.'

'Consider it done.'

'Before I go, there's a little something in the boot of the car for you. Hamper of decent food and a case of claret. Care to help me unload it?'

'I don't know what to say, Eaton. I should have trusted you when you asked me to.'

'No. You were right not to. You're a bloody good agent, Tom. Sooner you get a full-time role with the COI the better. And there's something else. I do have a plan. Don't tell Frau Dietrich or the girl yet in case it doesn't come off . . .'

'Go on.'

'I took a bit of a liberty, I'm afraid, and made contact with Jim Vanderberg's wife in America.'

'You spoke to Juliet?'

Eaton nodded, that same enigmatic smile playing around the corner of his eyes.

'My plan is to get Klara and Frau Dietrich to America with new names and ID papers. They'll be concealed among a shipload of refugees. Juliet Vanderberg will be their American sponsor and will meet them in New York.'

'You're a bloody marvel, Eaton.'

'From you, that is high praise indeed, Wilde. Oh, and by the way, it's confirmed – Jim Vanderberg is safe. He's with the rest of the American diplomatic corps in a swanky hotel at Bad Nauheim. I'm sure they'll be exchanged in a few weeks. These things are difficult to arrange between hostile powers, but they'll get there eventually.'

Klara wouldn't go to bed. She curled up on the sofa beside Romy as though she would never let her go. Her eyes were drooping, but she was in a kind of heaven.

Romy was telling Wilde and Lydia about her escape. They had finished one of the claret bottles and were halfway through a second.

'Before we left Berlin, James Vanderberg said I should go to the British Legation in Switzerland, that they would have the best opportunity to get me to Britain. He and the chargé despatched messages to David Kelly, the British ambassador. Once in Switzerland, the legation was, indeed, prepared for my arrival. He is a wonderful man, your friend Vanderberg. Without him I would be dead.'

'We think he's rather wonderful, too,' Lydia said in her faltering German.

Romy continued with her story. 'But you know, I think Mr Kelly and the others at the embassy were rather cautious at first. Perhaps a little suspicious that I might be some sort of Nazi undercover agent. Only after they had made contact with Mr Eaton in London was I totally accepted. And soon it was all arranged. I was to be the first woman to use their underground route from Switzerland across France to Spain. I wondered at the time, and I wonder still, whether anyone really expected it to work, but it did.'

'It must have been terrifying.'

'For me, no – but for those who helped me? I was a stranger and yet they hazarded their lives for me. Once across the border into Vichy France, I was in the hands of the Resistance and was passed from one to another, accompanied all the way, either by road or train. In all, dozens of people – both men and women, even children – helped me and fed me. It would require a book to tell every detail, but I think it helped that I speak a little French. In the event, everything went as planned. I suppose I was not the sort of person the Gestapo were looking for – they wanted escaped RAF pilots and spies.'

Wilde and Lydia listened with astonishment to her tale, narrated so casually. In Spain she was once again taken under the wing of British agents to protect her from the numerous German spies roaming the country, and was escorted to Lisbon, from where she was flown to London.

Romy's hands were shaking. Lydia could not take her eyes off her damaged left hand. It was healing well, but the injury clearly still bothered her. Romy caught her eyes and held up her fingers.

'This?'

'I'm sorry, I was staring.'

'Bormann's men did this to me.' Her other hand, a little less shaky, was delving into her jacket pocket and she produced a pack of du Maurier cigarettes. 'Do you mind if I smoke? Mr Eaton gave these to me – so much better than the ersatz German ones.'

'Please do,' Wilde said. 'Lydia would probably like one, too – but I'm sure you're not going to, are you, darling?'

'You know, Tom, I rather think I deserve one after all you've bloody well put me through.'

'Go ahead then. Your funeral.'

'That from the man who drinks whisky like water!'

Romy handed a cigarette to Lydia and Wilde gave them both a light. He saw that Klara's eyes were closed and the lightness of her breathing suggested she was asleep.

'You haven't really told us about you and Klara. Are you actually her aunt?'

'I am her godmother. No blood relation – but we couldn't be closer. I am a midwife, you see, and I brought her into the world. Her mother couldn't keep her, but she was my friend. Although I would love to have adopted her as a baby, I couldn't because my husband wouldn't allow it. So she was given into the care of two very good friends of mine – Matthias and Maria Rieger. After my divorce, I stayed with them often. Klara and I have always had a special bond. I was the only person with whom the Riegers could always be totally at ease, because I knew the truth, you see.'

There was a little silence as though Romy was considering how much to tell.

'You don't have to say any more, you know.'

Romy drew deep on her cigarette.

'Oh, I know that, but I think I would like to tell you some things. I have already told so much of the story to Jim Vanderberg, and I was going to tell him the last part when we were safely in Switzerland together. But that wasn't to be, so I would like to tell you, if I may. First, though, I think we should put Klara to bed, don't you? Little ears . . .'

She placed her cigarette in the ashtray and gently eased Klara into her arms. Klara was so at peace that she flopped like a three-year-old. Lydia showed Romy to the room she had made up for the two of them.

'You and Klara will be in here. Tom and I will be with Johnny in the other room. He may come and see you at some dreadful hour, I'm afraid.'

'I don't mind.'

'I'll leave you to get Klara settled, then.'

CHAPTER 39

A few minutes later, Romy returned to the sitting room. She took a gulp of her wine.

'And so I begin my story. It was in a little village in Upper Austria called Braundorf. My very good friend Geli was six and a half months pregnant and it was showing. She had managed to get away from Munich where she lived in Hitler's apartment.

'Hitler thought she was overweight and depressed and had reluctantly agreed to let her go away for a few weeks to get some mountain air. He even offered to pay for her to go to the spa at Bad Gastein to take the waters, but instead she and I agreed that she would go to Braundorf where my old friends the Riegers lived. Matthias was the village schoolmaster.

'Geli had confided her plight to me – and pleaded with me to join her. I was recently married, but my husband was away with his work, so he did not notice my absence from Vienna. In Braundorf, Geli and I lodged with the Riegers, who fed us and looked after us. Together we all lived through the last weeks of Geli's confinement, knowing that it was a great secret that must never be told.'

'Hadn't anyone in Munich noticed anything?' Lydia asked.

'You mean Hitler? No, he was very preoccupied at that time. He could feel power nearing his grasp. Geli was never skinny, so at first it was easy to dismiss her weight gain as a few too many strudels and schnitzels, and she wore loose-fitting clothes. In the end it was her mother who noticed, of course. Mothers always do, don't they? She was desperate for Geli to get away, for she knew this could all be ruinous for her brother's political ambitions – and for herself.

'Once or twice I travelled to Gastein to send Hitler postcards written by Geli, as though she was there. If he ever wrote back

I have no knowledge of his letters. He was certainly not a man to keep in touch by telephone. But those were good days for Geli and me. We laughed a lot at her situation, but at the same time we knew the happiness couldn't last and that great sadness awaited us.

'It was not a difficult birth. The baby weighed almost four kilos and was very healthy. I wasn't sure about calling her Klara, because I thought it was provoking trouble. You know that was the name of Hitler's mother? But Geli was amused by the idea and insisted on it. "Anyway," she said, "I like the name and it will annoy my own mother!" Of course Geli's mother is a half-sister to Hitler and they have different mothers. Geli's grandmother was actually called Franziska Hitler.'

Romy was chain-smoking as the story unfolded.

'There was a priest in the village, Father Huber, a kind but foolish man. He was the only one included in our secret, sworn to secrecy in the confessional. But like all priests and nuns, he thought he knew better than the rest of us about all questions of life and morality. He didn't know the whole truth, but he knew enough to be scared. Reluctantly, he agreed to baptise the child and, again, Geli was indiscreet and insisted the baby be named Klara Wolf and the father be marked down as "soldier, absent".

'The thing about Father Huber was that he had great influence with Maria Rieger, our host, who was extremely religious. It was he who persuaded the Riegers that they should adopt Klara. He also told Geli she could not possibly bring up a child as a single unwed mother, hiding away in some city or village. She would be cast out and scorned wherever she went. Huber said the child would be tainted as illegitimate. Damned Catholic Church! How I loathe it. But Geli listened to him – the Riegers were good, respectable people, he said. They would give Klara a much better start in life. And perhaps he was right. After weeks of constant pressure, Geli agreed.

'I can't tell you how heartbreaking it was for Geli to give up her baby. She handed Klara to me and we were both crying. She turned her face away and I walked out of the room and put the baby into the arms of Maria Rieger. And that was the last Geli ever saw of Klara.'

Wilde and Lydia were listening in silence. He already knew some of the story from Vanderberg, but this intimate account of such a remarkable personal drama was something else. He felt he should say something.

'Did Geli think she was in danger?'

'Not then. This was March of 1931. She felt she had to go back to Uncle Alf – that's what she called Hitler.'

'Why? Why would she go back to him?'

Romy laughed without any trace of humour. 'Have you not noticed the hypnotic power he wields, Mr Wilde? Geli was in thrall to him.'

'Did she talk to you about their relationship?'

'Of course – but not the sexual side. I always assumed he was Klara's father, but she never spoke a word about such things. For all her love of mischief, she could be very discreet when she wanted. Anyway, she thought everything would be all right when she returned to their apartment in Munich.'

'But it wasn't?'

'In the summer of that year something happened – something by the name of Martin Bormann, the devil himself. Geli called me in Vienna. I had never heard her in such a state. She told me she was in mortal danger. Bormann had found out something and was blackmailing her, threatening to tell Hitler about the baby. He wanted to know more. Where was the baby? Who was looking after it?

'He kept pestering her – threatening her and intimidating her. And he was trying to get her into bed. Whenever Hitler was away, she had to steer clear of Bormann. But still he would appear at her door, cajoling and demanding, trying it on.

'Geli knew she was in grave danger but her greatest fears were for the baby. She told me that the child had to be moved to safety – she was terrified someone would tell Bormann about Braundorf. And so I contacted the Riegers and told them they were no longer safe and that they would have to leave Austria. Maria wasn't happy. As a good Catholic, she did not like the idea of living in Lutheran northern Germany. But in the end, she had no choice, and they moved to Kossertheim in Brandenburg. It was easy enough for Matthias to find work as a lowly-paid teacher and they quickly settled in.

'I had also moved to northern Germany at that time. I visited them often – but I knew that we were never really secure as long as Bormann was alive.

'I was desperately worried for Geli – and tried to get her away from Munich. I even begged her to leave the country – go to England or America. But she would not listen. Not at first. Finally I persuaded her and she said that yes, she would come to me in Berlin. Her plan was to leave Munich while Uncle Alf was away on one of his electioneering tours. On September 18, 1931, she called me and told me she was packing a small bag and would be leaving that evening. Hitler had gone away and the housekeeper, Frau Winter, would be out at the cinema. It was the perfect time. She said she would get the train – and that she was longing to see me. Those were her last words to me. Bormann stopped her with a bullet.'

'You are certain it was him, not suicide?'

Romy smiled. 'No one who knew Geli could ever imagine her taking her own life. She was sunlight. It was him – Bormann. The phone was off the hook, you see. I heard it all – his demands, her cries and pleas, his vicious insults. He said "Die, bitch" and then I heard it – the shot.

'For a few minutes I heard the sound of him moving around the room, perhaps arranging things. I heard his pig-like breathing. Then finally the phone went dead.'

'Then you are a witness,' Wilde said.

'A witness without evidence. Anyway, what use are witnesses and evidence in Nazi Germany? If you are a Nazi you are innocent – if not, then you are guilty. But I think Geli's mother also knew the truth about Geli's death. Someone told me that she left Obersalzberg to get away from Eva Braun. But I think she was getting away from Bormann.

'After that I watched his rise with increasing alarm, because I knew that Geli and her baby would always haunt him. And I knew that one day he would come after us. But what I don't understand is how he found Father Huber when he did. That was the day everything fell apart.'

'The day Huber called you and you went to Jim Vanderberg?'

She nodded. 'But how? How did Bormann find Huber? Who told him about Braundorf?'

Wilde grimaced. 'I think I may have an answer to that question for you. Bormann was tipped off by someone in the Göring camp.'

Romy looked confused. 'What has Fat Hermann got to do with this?'

'He chanced upon Geli's mother in Dresden and invited her to Carinhall a few weeks ago.'

'Don't tell me. They plied her with drink and she gave up Geli's secret.'

'And Bormann's part in her death.'

'Ah, that woman! Two glasses of Schnapps and half a litre of beer – that's all it takes to loosen her stupid tongue. Geli used to laugh about her, but she is a danger to all around her, like a Panzer without brakes or a steering wheel. But what is the link between Göring and Bormann, apart from the fact that they are both big Nazis?'

'They are engaged in a bitter power struggle. Göring wanted to let Hitler know what Bormann had done to his beloved Geli – for that would most certainly have done for Bormann.'

'Yes, of course – I see it.'

Romy fished in the cigarette box, but it was empty. She looked beseechingly at Lydia, who shook her head; she had no cigarettes either.

'And then,' Wilde continued, 'Bormann was tipped off – and the race was on. Bormann had to kill Klara, Göring needed her out of the country so she could be used as Allied propaganda. Poor Klara was caught between two warring factions, neither of whom had her interests at heart.'

'It was you that brought Klara out of Germany, Mr Wilde? That was a very courageous thing to do.'

'Well, I had a little help – from both Jim Vanderberg, of course, and Sunny Somerfeld.'

'Sunny? She was involved?'

'Of course. Are you saying you knew her?'

'We were old friends. It was Sunny who suggested I go to seek help from Mr Vanderberg.'

CHAPTER 40

The office was on the first floor of the US embassy in Grosvenor Square. A coolly efficient secretary immediately alerted her boss on the intercom.

'Professor Wilde is here, sir.' She put the phone down. 'He says to go straight through, professor.'

Bill Whitney was sitting behind his desk in one of the more cramped offices in the embassy, a building Wilde knew well from his many visits when Jim Vanderberg had been posted here. Whitney stood up with a shiny American smile of welcome, and they shook hands.

'Professor Wilde, I've heard a heck of a lot about you. You've been running poor Bodie Cashbone ragged from what I hear.'

'Pleased to meet you, too, Mr Whitney. As for Mr Cashbone, I'd have to say the reverse is true.'

'Well, he's on his way up, so I can hear both sides of the story. Take a seat, won't you. Sorry there's not a great deal of room but we'll find better quarters soon. Coffee?'

'Coffee would be good.'

'Shirley'll bring it through in a couple of minutes.'

The door opened and Bodie Cashbone made another of his grand entrances. He nodded to his boss, the head of the COI in London, then turned his attention to Wilde.

'So, do you have her with you?'

Wilde didn't bother to answer the question.

'Mr Whitney, I haven't come here to be interrogated. I have questions of my own to put. First off, how closely have you been involved in Cashbone's plans for Klara Rieger?'

Whitney sat back and regarded Wilde coolly. 'Are you suggesting I don't know what's going on in my own outfit?'

'I'm suggesting nothing. I'm merely posing a question. Has Cashbone gone rogue or is he operating on your orders?'

Whitney had a glass paperweight in his right hand and slammed it down on the desk.

'What in God's name is this? Bodie told me you were a piece of work – and it looks like he was right.'

Wilde pressed on. 'He pushed you into this, didn't he? The information somehow came directly to him from Germany and he wanted an operation to have the girl extricated, which is where I came in. I was the useful idiot. Is that how it was?'

'No, not at all. The State Department heard from your friend Jim Vanderberg that Bormann was about to kill the girl – and Bill Donovan got on to me. Seems like the president had made a special request for your services.'

'Are you saying that Cashbone didn't tell you anything before that?'

Whitney was silent, his jaw tight and grim.

'Bodie, help me out here,' he said. 'You did mention something about the girl before Donovan ordered us to act, didn't you?.'

Cashbone shrugged, but he didn't look comfortable.

'Sure, come to think of it, I did mention it to you in passing that there was a rumour from our boys in the Berlin embassy that Hitler had a secret daughter.' He tilted his double chin at Wilde. 'So what, professor? What are you trying to suggest? And I've got a question for you – where is she, goddamn it?'

Wilde had a briefcase with him. He clicked it open.

'I've been doing a bit of research on you, Cashbone. Actually, some friends in America have been doing the work for me. Easier that way.' Juliet Vanderberg, to be precise. But he wasn't going to tell Cashbone that. He had called her from Philip Eaton's office. Oh, she had been more than happy to delve. The daughter of a celebrated lawyer and the granddaughter of a senior judge, Juliet Vanderberg knew where to dig for bodies.

'Here, let me read you a couple of things, Mr Whitney. You know who Sunny Somerfeld is?'

Whitney scowled. 'Of course I do, Wilde. She helped you get the girl out of Germany. Now she's dead.'

'And you knew she was American by birth?'

'I did. You're not telling me anything.'

'Did you know her father was a man called Berthold Falken?'

Whitney seemed momentarily taken aback. 'No, and the name means nothing to me.'

Wilde turned to Cashbone. 'But it means something to you, doesn't it, Cashbone?'

Cashbone looked uneasy. 'Not that I can recall, no.'

'Well, it should do. He ran your family's oil business for the best part of a quarter century. Look here . . .' He tossed a paper on the desk. 'Berthold Falken, chief executive officer Cashbone Oil International.'

Cashbone feigned ignorance. 'You mean Berthold was Sunny's father? Hell, I never knew that.'

'Bullshit, Cashbone. You've known her all your life. I saw the closeness between you at the house in Harkham. That little squeeze of the hand? You weren't strangers.'

'You know nothing, Wilde.'

'Well, I certainly know that your family firm has been trading heavily in Germany for years, particularly since 1933 when the Nazis came to power.' Wilde flung another sheet of paper on the desk. 'That's from the Internal Revenue Service. Details of payments made to various organisations in Germany and written off as expenses. You see that one? *Carinhall Gesellschaft*, two hundred thousand dollars for services rendered. There's plenty more like that. Germany under Hitler was making up more than sixty-five per cent of all your trade, and Berthold Falken was doing the deals. And who, in Germany, had oversight and control of the ministry of economics and the Reichsbank for most of these years? Hermann Göring. He authorised the cheques and he accepted the kickbacks.'

Cashbone was speechless.

'But then,' Wilde continued, 'it all ground to a halt with the war. Cashbone Oil profits went through the floor.'

Whitney had half-risen from his chair and was leaning forward across his desk.

'Is this all true, Bodie?'

Cashbone growled like a cornered animal. A grizzly at bay.

'You don't know what you're talking about – there are other markets.'

'But not as lucrative, maybe.'

'God damn you, Wilde.'

'This whole plan involving Klara was nothing to do with ending the war, Cashbone,' Wilde said. 'You're just Hermann Göring's lapdog. As was poor Anton Offenbach, I'm sorry to say. Mr Eaton's reliable sources have revealed to me that he was not only attached to the Abwehr but was, primarily, a senior officer in the *Forschungsamt*, the intelligence department of the Reich Air Ministry. But whereas Offenbach served out of loyalty to Göring, you helped him out in his internecine power struggle with Bormann, hoping there might be some scraps for Cashbone Oil when Germany had conquered the world. And Göring the peacemaker? More horseshit. He was always just in it for himself, and Bormann needed to be got out of the way. Getting Hitler's daughter across the sea to you – to use in your filthy propaganda campaign – was his way to achieve his ends. As for you, Cashbone – you were just a money-grubbing mercenary.'

The big American swung at Wilde, but Wilde saw it coming and ducked the blow with ease, pushing himself up from his chair. His own punch connected with Cashbone's paunch, instantly stopping him in his tracks. Cashbone stumbled back, regained his footing and lunged again. This time Wilde expertly tripped him and the giant American sprawled forwards to the floor.

Wilde looked down on him contemptuously.

'Anyway, Cashbone, you're too damned late. Klara is free of you now – beyond your reach. You'll never see her again. And if I ever hear that you're so much as looking for her, I swear I'll come after you.' He brushed himself down and picked up his briefcase. 'I'll leave him to you, Mr Whitney.'

Martin Bormann was out of cigarettes. He yelled through the open door.

'Heidi, get me cigarettes. Now!'

'Yes, Herr Reichsleiter.'

'And I want to know as soon as a message comes through from Jung.'

'Yes, Herr Reichsleiter.'

'Run, Heidi!'

He ran his hand lightly over his head, smoothing down his oiled-back hair.

Everything in his life was perfect. The Führer relied on him more than ever. Even here at the Wolfsschanze, he could order the chiefs of staff to do his bidding, and none dared countermand him. Even Keitel, chief of the Wehrmacht high command, took orders. When Bormann needed a fast navy boat for his man Jung, it was made available. Without question and without explanation.

The enemy, he now knew – the *real* enemy – was Göring. Well, he would get his comeuppance in time. However long it took, Bormann did not allow such things to go unavenged. But first, he had to be sure the child had been disposed of; that the last trace of evidence had been destroyed. And he wasn't sure.

Everything in his life *would be* perfect if it were not for this doubt that crawled like a worm through his brain at night and stopped him sleeping. Was the girl dead? Why had Jung not made contact since that first transmission from England?

Heidi was back, out of breath, in under two minutes. She slammed the pack of Swiss cigarettes down on the table.

'No more Luckies?'

'I'm told they are no longer allowed, sir. Perhaps because we are at war with America?'

He tore at the wrapping, ignoring her impertinence; several cig-arettes tumbled out. He fumbled for the gold swastika-embossed lighter that he prized so highly and cursed as it failed to make a flame.

'Matches, Heidi, matches – then fill this lighter. And *keep* it filled!'

'Sir,' she said, catching her breath. 'A message has started coming through. Just this very moment . . .'

Wilde stood beside Eaton and an MI5 officer whose name he hadn't caught – perhaps because the man hadn't offered it – keeping his eyes firmly fixed on Charlie Jung, as he had learned to call him. He was sitting at a table in a spacious loft. They had driven here to the former home of Mrs Felicity Vickery, deceased, from Kensington Palace Gardens where Jung was being held and interrogated.

Jung's fingers were working slowly on the neat little German transmitter, which had been found hidden in a second property belonging to Mrs Vickery. The man was not well trained in Morse code, but that didn't matter – because it was what Bormann would expect.

'Don't forget to tell him Vickery is dead or he'll wonder why she isn't sending the message,' Wilde said.

Jung looked up with a frown. 'I'm doing it just as we agreed.'

'Two bluffs, yes? Misspell the girl's name. Insert the word *beer*. That's all? Because if you try any tricks,' Eaton said, 'your days are numbered. Your miserable life is already hanging by a very slender thread. One false move and you're for the gallows.'

'Believe me, I understand.'

'Then carry on, Mr Young, and you might just live.'

'What does it say, Heidi?'

'This takes time, Herr Reichsleiter. Jung is like a tortoise, he makes mistakes.'

He ripped the fresh decrypt from her hand and read it at speed.

KARLA DEAD, BURIED IN LAKE. VICKERY DEAD. TIME FOR BEER. ADVISE METHOD OF RETURN.

Bormann read it, then read it again. Then he burst out laughing, struck a match and burned the message to a cinder. He was in the clear. Nothing could stop him now. Not Goebbels, not Göring, not Himmler. He was untouchable.

'My locket, my locket!'

Klara clutched at her throat, just visible above the collar of her new coat.

Lydia and Romy looked at each other. Romy put her arm around Klara's shoulder and whispered in her ear.

'Not too loud, Klara darling. Now then, where did you leave it.'

'It was taken off at the hospital. I was told it would be brought back to me.'

'Don't worry,' Lydia said. 'I'll send it on to you as soon as I can. I'm sure it will be fine.' She unclasped a fine gold necklace and heart pendant from around her own neck and handed it to Klara. 'Here, this is for you in the meantime – from Tom, Johnny and me. A little token of our love for you.'

Klara took the pendant. There was still a tear in her eye, but she brushed it away.

'Thank you, Frau—'

'Lydia. I must always be Lydia to you. And be sure that you will find a lovely puppy as soon as you arrive in your new home.'

'Like Bismarck?'

'The prettiest one you can find. And you must know that our home will always be your home if you can ever get back to England.'

She gave her a huge hug, and then Johnny demanded one too.

They were on the dockside at Liverpool. Boarding had begun and everyone was excited – but nervous too. No ship was safe from the U-boat wolf packs in the Atlantic these days. Lydia and Romy had discussed the locket before they left Cambridge.

'She must never see it,' Romy had said. 'She must never have the slightest inkling of her true parentage.'

'No,' Lydia said.

'But what if . . . ?'

'Romy?'

'I'm just thinking, what if AH stands for someone other than Hitler?'

'But who else could it be?'

'Of course, I haven't told you about Sasha Heine – Geli's Jewish singing teacher in Vienna. They were very close.'

'Sasha?'

'A diminutive of Alexander. I told Jim Vanderberg all about Sasha Heine. There was a time in 1930 when he and Geli spent a little time together. The dates are just possible. But we will never know, will we?'

Lydia smiled. 'No, we will never know – but I think I know which father I would prefer for her.'

'It doesn't matter. Klara is who she is – and I love her as though she were my own daughter.'

An hour later, as the moorings were loosened and the tugs began to pull the liner away from the pier, Klara and Romy leant over the railings, smiling and waving to Lydia and Johnny, who were waving back even more vigorously.

Johnny and his mother watched until the figures of the two Germans became indistinguishable from the crowd of passengers at the rail. Then Lydia walked to the edge of the dock, removed the silver locket from her handbag and let it slide through her fingers into the dark, oily depths.

ACKNOWLEDGEMENTS

I am indebted to the fabulous team at Zaffre for their superb professionalism, particularly my publisher Kate Parkin, whose encouragement and kindness always sustains me when the going gets tough. It also gives me pleasure to pay tribute to my agent Teresa Chris; her steadfast support and advice – and sometimes just a chat about the weather, tennis and the state of the world – keeps me vaguely sane. My thanks, too, go to a very fine friend named Jon Zackon, who is a treasure chest of knowledge – and who has helped me in more ways than he probably realises.

None of what I do would be possible without the practical help and dedication of my brilliant wife Naomi – as well as all the other members of my family and friends.

Dear Reader,

To research *Hitler's Secret*, I walked the broad avenues of Berlin and Potsdam in Germany and explored the lakes and rivers that divide the two towns. I drove northwards via Oranienburg, then on to the forest of Schorfheide and finally made my way to Greifswald and the Baltic coast.

It was a pleasant journey through some lovely towns and gorgeous countryside. But it was not without reminders of the way things were in the Nazi years between 1933 and 1945.

At Oranienburg, I took a small detour to visit the Sachsenhausen concentration camp, one of the first to be established (in fact it was under construction at the same time as Germany was hosting the 1936 Berlin Olympics). Experiments were carried out there to determine the most efficient ways of murdering people, including gas. Over one hundred thousand died within its grey stone walls.

Fittingly, perhaps, it was damp and overcast when I visited. At the gate was the grimly ironic sign beloved of the criminals who designed these hideous camps: *Arbeit macht frei* – work sets you free.

Nowadays, Sachsenhausen is a memorial and a museum. Most of the buildings have been torn down. The stench of decay, disease, burning bodies and raw sewage is long gone. And yet the malevolence of the place is still there, hanging like a pall, seeping into your soul.

As I drove on through northern Germany, I found myself imagining life under the Nazis wherever I went.

At the entrance to each village I saw in my head a sign saying, *'Jews not welcome'*.

At each town hall and important building, I had a vision of the fluttering pennants in red and white with a black hooked cross at the centre.

Sachsenhausen Gate

In every park I seemed to see massive anti-aircraft guns poking their noses into the sky.

At every factory gate and in every field I visualised streams of slave workers being marched in and out.

At every corner, I saw Gestapo men watching me intently. And in the baleful buildings behind them, there were surely dungeons where torture was all in a day's work.

At every bridge I half-expected to be stopped by a military checkpoint with machine-gun trained on the car.

And behind walls and high fences I saw barracks full of black-clad young men with death's head insignia, in training for the onslaught in the east.

This was the world of late 1941, as I imagined it. This was the deadly world into which I placed my protagonist, the Cambridge history professor Tom Wilde, an avowed enemy of the Nazis and all they stood for.

On the Baltic shore in northern Germany

The very thought of it makes me shudder. Just to live under such a regime is ghastly enough; to be a hunted foreigner in the middle of a war, unarmed and with no prospect of any help from outside is simply terrifying.

I hope that I have properly depicted the truth of that dreadful time in *Hitler's Secret*. I hope, too, that I have got somewhere close to portraying the true characters of Martin Bormann, the Görings, Adolf Hitler, Geli Raubal and her mother. Historical fiction – like history itself – is always a matter of deep research, weighing up the evidence and doing one's best to interpret it for a modern audience.

As always, I thank you for your interest in Tom Wilde and Lydia Morris and the world of Cambridge and Europe in the 1930s and 1940s. To find out more, please visit my website *www.roryclements. co.uk*. You can also join the Rory Clements Readers' Club at *www. bit.ly/RoryClementsClub*. It only takes a moment, there is no catch and new members will automatically receive exclusive extras. Your data is private and confidential and will never be passed on to a third party, and I promise that I will only be in touch now and then with book news. If you want to unsubscribe, you can do that at any time.

Of course, I would be delighted, too, if you could spread the word about my books. Online reviews are particularly welcome, and I always read them!

I sincerely hope that my books give you as much pleasure as I take from researching and writing them. Even the scary bits . . .

With my best wishes,

Rory

Want to read
NEW BOOKS
before anyone else?

Like getting
FREE BOOKS?

Enjoy sharing your
OPINIONS?

Discover
READERS FIRST
Read. Love. Share.

Sign up today to win your first free book:
readersfirst.co.uk